TIME'S DIVIDE

ALSO BY RYSA WALKER

Rysa Walker

TIME'S DIVIDE

BOOK 3
IN THE CHRONOS FILES

SKYSCAPE

SKYSCAPE

Published by Skyscape, New York

www.apub.com

Amazon, the Amazon logo, and Skyscape are trademarks of Amazon.com Inc., or its affiliates.

ISBN-13: 9781503946583
ISBN-10: 1503946584

Cover design by Cyanotype Book Architects
Printed in the United States of America

*This book is dedicated to
Pete—my Constant in any timeline.*

∞ 1 ∞

BETHESDA, MARYLAND
September 8, 9:37 p.m.

Julia Morrell Waters is not a patient woman. Less than five minutes after I open her note welcoming me to the Fifth Column, some guy holding a pizza box starts banging on Katherine's door. A message on the same stationery as her welcome note is taped to the top of the box: *Max will bring you to me. Go out the back. Climb the fence and he will pick you up one street over. Come alone. JMW.*

The pizza box is empty—yes, Connor checked before he handed it to me—but the car out front has a Valenzia's sign slapped on the top, so the Fifth Column has done their homework. It's certainly not the first time Valenzia's Pizza has pulled up to the house at this hour. But the guy they sent—Max, I guess—seems closer to a linebacker or a bouncer than a pizza guy.

"She's not going alone," Connor tells him.

Max's eyes look like they're going to pop out of his head. He jerks the box from Connor, pulls a pen out of his pocket, and scrawls the word *bugged!!!* on the back of the note. He shoves it toward me, then points to the kitchen and the patio door beyond, as though the matter is settled.

It's not. I snatch his pen and write: *Still not coming alone.*

Trey looks at Katherine, who is still on the sofa, and then at Connor. They both nod. Then he taps his chest and points to me.

Max takes two menacing steps toward me, and judging from his expression, I'm pretty sure he'd have tried to sling me over his shoulder if not for the fact that Connor and Trey both move toward him at the same time. I kind of wish they hadn't. This guy needs an attitude adjustment, and being flipped onto his back by a girl half his size would be a step in the right direction.

And he's obviously not thinking things through. Julia's instructions say for me to go out the back. If anyone is watching the house, they'd find it very suspicious if the pizza guy returned to his car with a passenger, especially one fighting him every step of the way.

Daphne has clearly picked up on the vibe in the room. She barks again, and as soon as Katherine lets go of her collar, she takes up position next to me, growling softly.

Max shakes his head like we're being totally unreasonable, then reaches for something in his pocket. Daphne growls again. "Hold back your dog, okay? I need to call the office and see what happened with your order."

I kneel down and put one arm around Daphne. She relaxes slightly but keeps her eyes on him.

We wait. Finally he says into the phone, "They say they ordered *two.* Not just the one."

Max listens for a moment, then looks at the four of us—five, counting Daphne—and says, "No, I don't think that's gonna work . . . Okay . . . yeah."

He stashes the phone back in his pocket. "Two it is. I'll be back with the other pizza shortly."

Connor says, "Sure. No problem. But we get a freebie, right? Since you messed up the order?"

Max rolls his eyes. "I'll ask my boss." He gives me a long stare, looks toward the kitchen door again, and then he's gone.

Trey and I follow the directions on the note and sneak out the back. We hop the fence and squeeze through the neighbor's cypress hedge, and we see the Valenzia's car waiting at the curb. Max is on the phone again, keeping an eye out for us through the open driver's side window.

The car is an old red junker. I think it used to be a cab because it's got one of those partitions between the front and rear seats. After we get in, Max turns around and looks through the opening. "Okay, here's how it's gonna go. You can ride with her, but you're gonna have to wait in the car when she goes in. Security reasons."

"Nope." Trey opens the car door, and we start to get out.

"Wait, wait," Max says, raising his hand. "Hold on a minute."

Eventually we reach a compromise. Max confiscates our phones and my backpack. Trey can come in the building, but not inside the office when I meet with Ms. Waters. I don't especially like either of those provisions, but as long as I have my CHRONOS key, I can go for help if we run into trouble.

The car's windows are tinted so dark that we can barely see outside. When Trey says he doesn't think that much tint is legal, Max just grunts. I'm pretty sure we crossed the Beltway a few minutes back, but that doesn't really help to pin down our location. A twenty-minute drive means we could be in DC, Northern Virginia, or still somewhere in Maryland.

We pull up in front of a row of ordinary-looking townhouses and walk up an ordinary-looking sidewalk toward an ordinary-looking door. The numbers by the door are missing.

The living room is clearly lived in. The coffee table is heaped with papers, envelopes, a computer manual, and several detective novels. Trey parks on the couch with something by Janet Evanovich. And then Max ushers me into a tiny office to meet the head of the Fifth Column, a resistance group within the Cyrist ranks that might, just might, give us a fighting chance at stopping the global disaster my grandfather is planning.

∞

"No offense," I begin, instantly wishing I hadn't. In my experience, that phrase almost always sets someone up to take offense. "But I don't know you. This could be a trap Saul has set up. There's no way I'm handing over the keys or anything else until I'm convinced it isn't."

Julia Morrell Waters tilts her head back slightly and levels me with a stare. Physically, she reminds me of her mother. Her skin is a few shades darker, and she's a little plumper, but she has the same deep blue eyes. The smile seems the same, too, although I only got a brief glimpse of it, at the beginning, when she thanked me for helping to get her parents out of Georgia alive. And while she's a good forty years older than Delia was when I last saw her in Georgia, it's obvious that Julia was just as stunning as her mother back in the day.

Her tone of voice and her attitude, however, are 100 percent Abel Waters, at least right at this moment. Because I've just questioned her orders. Again. Directly, explicitly, and this time, to her face.

I'm not trying to be combative. I'm just exhausted and not at all clear why this meeting couldn't have waited until morning. It's been less than three hours since I watched Abel, Delia, and Kiernan climb out of Martha's root cellar and into the back of Simon's car in 1938 Georgia, each still in possession of the CHRONOS keys I was there to collect.

A few hours of sleep doesn't seem like too much to request before being forced into a shouting match with their daughter. And while I feel bad about yelling at an old lady, she's not being reasonable.

"You do realize we could simply take what we want, right?" Julia says. "That would be even more true if I *was* working with Brother Cyr—"

"Saul," I say through clenched teeth. She's said *Brother Cyrus* half a dozen times in the past fifteen minutes, and it's beginning to grate. "The man's name is Saul Rand. There's no Brother Cyrus."

Julia closes her eyes and sighs. "Yes. But when you work on the inside trying to overturn an organization as massive and paranoid as Cyrist International, you learn to play things carefully. It's a good idea to cultivate the habit of calling the maniac at the top by the name that won't get you killed. They do that, you know. They kill people, especially people who have things they want and refuse to hand them over. They don't ask nicely."

I wouldn't say Julia *asked nicely* either. It was more of a directive to turn everything over to the Fifth Column. The keys that we've collected, all of the information we have, the sample from Six Bridges. Everything.

"Fine," I say. "Call him by whatever name makes you happy. And yes, just like Saul's people, I'm sure you could storm in and take anything you wanted. But keep in mind that we'd fight you, and if you harmed any of us, that would end the possibility of me working with you."

I watch Julia carefully as I speak, because all of this is a bit of a bluff. This Fifth Column could have its own little army of time travelers, just like Saul. Maybe the only things they need from me to stop the Culling are the keys and the information we've collected thus far.

But something in Julia's eyes tells me that's not true. And given their general attitude so far, I think they'd have done exactly what she said before. They'd have stormed in to take what they wanted, if they didn't need my help. And the only thing I can think of that I have to offer is my ability with the key.

Julia's first two fingers have been tapping out a quiet but steady rhythm almost every time I speak. She seems to be waiting for me to go on, so I add, "Unless you have everything under control already? Kiernan—"

She makes an odd face when I say his name, but she doesn't interrupt me.

"Kiernan," I say, "was pretty certain that the keys the Cyrists carry are the ones from your parents' time, from the future. The ones that belonged to the historians who weren't in the field that day. Is that still our working assumption?"

She nods, her fingers still tapping. There's a roll of tape on the desk, and I fight the urge to get up and tape them to the arm of the chair.

I settle for staring pointedly at her fingers until she stops. Then I ask, "And you need my help in retrieving those keys?"

"It would make things . . . easier," she admits.

"Okay, then. If you want my cooperation, it'll be on my terms."

"And what exactly are those terms?"

I haven't really had time to think this far ahead, so I decide to keep things vague. "First, I decide who's on my team. I need to pull in people I know, people I trust."

"We've already done that. Your file mentioned Harvey Tilson and the Singleton girl."

"What file? Who gave you that information?"

"My parents. Mostly my mother, once I realized we'd need your help to end this."

I think back to the night at Martha's, when Abel first said that we'd need allies. I don't remember mentioning Tilson, although I guess it's possible. But Charlayne? Why would I have said anything about her?

"I'm still not clear what value the Singleton girl brings to the team," Julia says, almost as though she's reading my mind, "but Tilson and the young man have been definite assets."

Okay . . . now it makes sense. By *young man*, she must mean Kiernan, and he knew about both Tilson and Charlayne.

"So who else?" Julia asks. "Who else do we need to pull in to make you feel all safe and cozy?"

Her tone pisses me off, but I let it slide. "Katherine, Connor, and Trey. My parents . . ."

"Why? Your mother doesn't even know about all of this."

"You're right. She doesn't. But I'll be changing that shortly."

"No, Kate," she says, leaning back in her chair. "I understand and appreciate that you're concerned for your mother's safety. But we have a full security detail attached to Prudence and Deborah. Your mother is safe, and the plan that we've developed is contingent upon secrecy. It's far too risky for us to allow you to deviate from the timetable for this kind of personal matter."

I shake my head firmly. "No. Mom needs to know what's going on, and I need to be the one to tell her. It's not that I don't trust your security personnel." That part isn't entirely truthful because I'm not sure that I *do* trust her security personnel. "It's just that I won't be able to focus on anything else until she's home. I'm leaving in the morning. Katherine agrees—"

"Katherine's opinion doesn't factor into this!" Julia stops and takes a deep breath. Her voice is still firm, but a little less unkind when she continues. "From what I've been told, she's much too ill to make logical decisions. To be honest, given her relationship with Brother Cyrus in the past, I'm not sure good decisions were ever her forte. But leaving that aside, it's hardly surprising that she'd put her daughter's welfare ahead of the cause."

Julia may not be surprised, but I was. As soon as Connor told me they had a tentative location where Mom and Prudence would be on Thursday, I began pulling up stable points in London, ready to go in immediately. Katherine talked me down, reminding me that I needed to get some rest first to be sure I arrived with a clear head. But she also helped me find the closest stable point to the hotel where Mom will be staying and the best time to jump in. We'd just begun discussing specifics for the jump when Max came pounding on the door.

I know Katherine is sick, and yes, her decisions are a little suspect right now. I'll even admit that I've had some of the very same reservations Julia voiced in regard to Katherine's relationship with Saul. But it bugs the hell out of me to hear this woman—this stranger—dismiss Katherine so casually.

"That brings me to condition number two," I say. "*You* don't get to decide whose opinions matter. Katherine sacrificed most of her life trying to fix the disaster that Saul created."

"As have I."

"That may be the case," I acknowledge. "But Katherine has an advantage here that you don't when it comes to any decisions that concern me. Katherine *knows* me. She knows that I won't be able to focus on what you need me to do if I'm worrying about Mom. So when we're done here, I'm going home to sleep. I've only had a few hours in the past several days. Then I'm going to London. Prudence and Mom—"

"Yes, yes," Julia says, waving a hand. "I know. They'll check into the County Hall Marriott day after tomorrow. Adjoining rooms, fourth floor. As I told you, we're monitoring their every step, even their private communication. In fact, I can already tell you they stay three days and then—"

"Why are we arguing about this?" I say, my voice rising. "Why is it an issue? I can just use the key. If time is short, once I've seen that my mother is safe, I'll jump back to this precise hour, this precise minute, if you insist."

"That's not the problem, Kate. We're concerned that something you do or say in London will tip off Cyrus's people. They're watching Prudence, too. In fact, one of their men often travels with Prudence to keep an eye on her and report back to Simon and Cyrus on her activities. She's . . ." Julia looks down and shuffles the papers in front of her. "Let's just say that Prudence is too far gone to realize she's being played."

I'm about to ask who the man is, but then it hits me. "Kiernan? No. He isn't on Saul's side. Or Prudence's. You're right on that part, at least. Kiernan is on *our* side. He's just getting information from her. From Saul as well."

Julia gives me a condescending smile. "My father told me you might think that. But you're wrong. There was some question for a while as to *which* faction he was with, but we've known for some time now that he's with Cyrus. He's been in on this from the beginning, Kate."

My mouth is suddenly very dry, and it's hard to pull in a breath. It's as though a giant fist is squeezing my lungs. For several seconds I can't even respond. Eventually I croak out, "I don't believe you."

"I'm sorry, but it's true. Prudence's faction is pretty much finished. Almost everyone who was allied with her is now either part of the Fifth Column or they've shifted back to the main branch of Cyrist International. Some of them never left the fold to begin with. They remained loyal to Br—" She huffs. "To *Saul*—all along. And I'm quite certain Kiernan Dunne is in the latter group."

"You're wrong. I know Kiernan. I know where his loyalties lie."

Julia Morrell Waters gives me a tight little smile. "Things change, Kate. That may well be the only *un*changing fact in the universe—everything changes."

∞

Twenty minutes later, I'm once again in Max's car with Trey, headed back to Katherine's house. I'm holding a password-secured and encrypted tablet that I was cautioned to operate only when I'm under a CHRONOS field. Which is totally not a problem, since I'm never outside of a CHRONOS field.

I'm supposed to meet Julia again on Friday morning at a location Max entered into my key. Julia assured me there's more than enough content on this tablet to keep me busy until then.

She also assured me—several times, in fact—that Mom will be fine and that it would be a very, very bad idea for me to go to London. And before I left the office, I promised her that I would wait to contact Mom.

That promise was, of course, a complete and total lie.

My only goal by that point was to get as much information from Julia as possible and then get the hell out of there. I don't believe what she told me about Kiernan, and that makes me question everything else she said.

I can't really talk about anything substantive in front of this Max guy, so I just give Trey a noncommittal nonanswer when he asks how the meeting went and lean my head against his shoulder for the ride back to Bethesda. I apparently drift off, because it seems like only seconds pass before I feel Trey gently shaking my arm.

Max stops at the spot where he picked us up. We're halfway back to the hedge when he rolls down his window. "Hey, Kate. You left this in the backseat."

He's holding a book. It looks like a CHRONOS diary.

"Sorry," I say. "Must belong to someone else."

"No. It's *yours*." His eyes lock onto mine, and then he looks over his shoulder at a dark blue van parked near the curb. "Here," he insists, pushing the book toward me. "Would you just take it?"

I do, and he peels off.

"What was that all about?" Trey asks.

"Not sure." I look over at the van, which is usually parked on the street in front of Katherine's. The van Kiernan says he hired to watch the house so he could funnel false information on our activities to Prudence.

Assuming he was telling you the truth.

The voice I hear is Julia's. I hate that she's planted that seed of doubt in my head.

If I'm totally honest with myself, however, what Julia told me simply nurtured a seed that was already planted. The doubt has been in my mind since I saw Prudence with Kiernan in his cabin. It grew when he lied to me about Simon being in Georgia.

But Kiernan explained all that. I believed him.

I really, really want to keep believing.

I give the van one last glare and follow Trey. We scale the fence into Katherine's backyard, and the most trustworthy of our home security systems—Daphne—sounds the alarm a moment later.

Katherine and Connor are in the kitchen. One look at Katherine's face tells me she shouldn't have waited up. I wish Connor had slipped some of her sleeping medication into her tea. She looks drained. I doubt she's had any more sleep than I have the past few days, but since I'm five decades younger and not terminally ill, I handle exhaustion a little better.

We move into the living room, and I try to calculate how much I can say when I'm certain we're being monitored. If not by Julia's people, then by Prudence's. Or Saul's. Or whoever the hell Kiernan is working for.

Connor starts asking questions before I've figured out what to say, so I make a little kill gesture with my forefinger. I glance around the room before looking back at him. He raises his eyebrows, then gives me a faint nod and slumps back into the couch.

I opt for the same lie I told Julia. There's nothing they can do to help me if I run into trouble and nothing they can do to stop me from going, so . . .

"I've decided to wait on London. It's too risky right now. Julia assured me that Mom will be okay."

Trey and Connor both look baffled—not surprising given how adamant I was on this point before I met with Julia.

Katherine doesn't even blink, just tilts her head to the side and watches me. Her eyes flick down to the tablet Julia gave me and the diary that Max insisted I take, both in my lap, and then she looks back up at my face. "And you're sure that they can keep her safe?"

"I think so. They're monitoring her movements, not just with traditional methods but also through the key. Mom and Prudence arrive in London day after tomorrow. Julia says they stay through the weekend, and then they go to a villa Prudence owns off the coast of Italy. So we have a bit of time."

Katherine considers that for a few seconds and then nods. "I suppose we do." She stands up, rubbing her eyes. "Let's call it a night. You need to get some rest, Kate. We all do."

"So I guess I should cancel the—ow!" Connor stops in midsentence, staring down at the floor where Katherine's slippered foot is pressing very firmly on his pinky toe. "Um. Cancel . . . the . . . welcome home party."

I'm not sure what that is all about, but I can't really ask them when the whole Cyrist world is listening. I get the feeling Katherine knows I'm lying anyway, so I stand and tug on Trey's arm.

"Come on. I'll walk you to the door. You could use some sleep, too—and your dad and Estella are probably worried."

When we reach the door, he leans down for a good-night kiss.

"Thank you," I say.

"For the kiss? My pleasure."

"No. For being here. For going with me."

He gives me a troubled look. "Kate, are you sure about canceling the trip? You seemed so certain earlier, and—"

"I'm certain," I say, placing a finger over his lips. "Things change."

∞2∞

The sun, peeking insolently through the tiniest gap in the drawn curtains, finally drags me awake. My alarm clock may have played a supporting role, but it would've been a very minor one, since it's been ringing for more than fifteen minutes. I resist the temptation to hit the snooze button and the even greater temptation to use the CHRONOS key to jump back five or six hours and crawl into bed again. It's a really big bed. As soundly as I was sleeping, I'd probably never notice a duplicate me. I could just curl up on the other side, and . . .

No. Get your lazy self out of bed.

And even though my body insists it could use more rest, my mind is buzzing. So I get up, shower, and pull on some clothes. Although part of me wants to do the jump to London right this second, I need breakfast, and I should at least glance through the files from Julia and the diary Max gave me.

I'm troubled by Julia's warning that going to London might derail the Fifth Column agenda, but I'm equally troubled by Julia herself. I don't know her. And although I don't believe, or at least I *mostly* don't believe, what Julia said about Kiernan, I didn't get the sense that she was actually lying to me. She really seems to think Kiernan is allied with Saul, so the question is *why* she believes that.

It would help to talk things through with someone else. If we're under surveillance, however, then I have to assume that extends to our phone and text messages. I called Dad before I went to sleep last night, both to check on Grandpa, who is recovering pretty well from his stroke, and to give Dad the same false cover story about London. He asked me twice if I was sure, and I could tell from his voice that he knows something is up. I have a hard time remembering another occasion I've outright lied to my dad. In retrospect, that was smart, because I don't seem to be very good at it.

I'm sure the tablet contains files I should read, but I grab the diary instead. Max is pretty obviously a by-the-rule-book sort of guy. If Julia knew about this diary, he'd have given it to me before we left, when he was programming the destination for our next meeting into my key. Whatever's in there must be fairly important for Max to risk going behind her back.

I put on a pot of coffee and pour myself a Connor-sized bowl of Cheerios, then head out to the patio to catch some of the rays that woke me up. When I open the diary, a folded scrap of paper flutters out, landing in my cereal bowl. I fish it out and open it. It's a handwritten note, two sentences. *Don't watch this in the house. Delete when finished and return diary to me only.* The last two words are underlined, and it's signed with the letter M.

I wad up the note and focus on the diary. It looks like the others—a computer disguised as a book, although it wouldn't be likely to fool anyone, even from an earlier century, if closely inspected. The spot inside the cover where the historian's name usually appears has been marked through with blue ink.

Thumbing through, I see that all of the pages are blank except the first, where there's just one link with the standard CHRONOS format for dates: <u>09192009</u>.

That's odd. I expected to see pages of text entries or a list of links like the ones at the back of Other-Kate's diary. I spent days clicking those links and watching entries recorded by the me from the other timeline. Kiernan's Kate, the alter-me who was erased by one of the time shifts that propelled the Cyrists from a sick idea in my grandfather's head into the largest, most powerful religion in the world.

I'm outside the house, so I've met the requirements in Max's note. I doubt surveillance equipment would pick up a CHRONOS video entry anyway. People without the gene can't operate the diaries at all, and even *with* the gene, I still need the tiny clear disk behind my ear to pull up video entries. But I decide to put a little more distance between myself and Big Brother. I carry my cereal and the diary out to the swinging bench in the backyard.

After I click the link, a holographic display of an elderly woman in a wheelchair appears in front of me. There are trees all around and heavy ground cover, which strikes me as strange. The terrain doesn't look like it would be accessible to someone in a wheelchair.

Also, there's something different about this video compared to the others I've seen, although I can't quite put my finger on what it is, at first. Then the woman adjusts her hands in her lap, and it hits me. All of Other-Kate's entries, and all of those I watched in Katherine's diaries, began with a close-up view of the hand or the body of the person recording the entry, until they moved away from the device. This time, however, there's just a glimpse of fingertip and then I see the woman, seated a few yards away from the camera.

Whoever's recording the video takes several steps toward the wheelchair, and I recognize the woman as Delia. Her eyes are still the same deep blue, but they're now set in a face that's lost the distinct lines of youth. The jaw is softer, and her hair is white and much thinner than before. I do the math quickly—if she was in her early thirties when they were stranded in 1938, then Delia is over a hundred years old here. She looks very good for a centenarian, and that has me wondering if she's still alive. Unlikely, I guess, but what's the average life expectancy for someone born at the end of the twenty-third century, with who knows how many genetic alterations?

A voice says, "It's recording." Then Delia clears her throat and begins speaking.

> Hello, Kate. If Max here does as I've asked, you'll be the first and only person to see this. I hoped I might still be around to talk to you in person. Doctor June says I might have made it if I'd eaten more broccoli and drank less bourbon, but as you may recall, I never was a fan of doctors or their advice. Anyway, I tire quickly these past few months and I decided I couldn't risk putting this off any longer. So I had Max bring me out here to the middle of nowhere so I can talk to you without people listening in.
>
> Julia means well and her heart is in the right place, but you've probably realized that she's most definitely her father's daughter. I loved Abel with all my heart and soul, but he had his share of faults, and one of the worst was that you were either his friend or his enemy. No shades of gray for my Abel, and I'm afraid Julia is much the same.

Delia laughs softly and then continues, her eyes focused a bit to the left.

And Max here inherited more than a touch of that attitude himself. If you're watching this, it's not because Max agrees with anything I'm saying. It's because he's a good boy who loves his Nana Dee enough to honor her last wishes and keep this one little secret from his Grandma Julia.

She turns back to look directly at the camera.

Keeping this secret shouldn't trouble him too much, because what I'm about to say isn't all that earth shattering. Just two things.

First, thanks to you and Kiernan, Abel and I had fifty-four more years together. They weren't without their problems, and I doubt it'll surprise you to learn Simon painted a rosier picture of life with Cyrists than we saw. But he was right that they accepted an interracial marriage without prejudice, which is more than we'd have gotten elsewhere in 1938—hell, in 1978, for that matter.

Any issues we faced were due more to Simon's fear that our being within the Cyrist fold might upset the apple cart and affect some of the historical changes they'd made. We kept a low profile, although Abel made some contacts on the outside that helped get the external branch of the Fifth Column started. I know you had some doubts about the three of us leaving with Simon, but I really do think it was for the best.

We weren't supposed to have children because Simon said Saul was worried that any offspring might be able to use the keys. Julia was an accident as far as they knew. I waited until the last minute to let anyone know I was expecting, and I did it in the most public way possible—right in the middle of Sunday services. Julia was born two months later, and they watched her like a hawk, but I made sure she never let anyone know she could activate the equipment. She's never been able to jump anyway—Julia can see the light and even pulled up a stable point a few times, or so she claimed, but she was never able to lock it in. Still, being able to activate it would probably have been enough for Saul to have her taken out.

That's what happened to Max's dad. Anthony always had more ambition than common sense, and I think the Cyrist message resonated with him. He thought Saul might allow him into his inner circle if he was a jumper, but he turned up dead a few days later. Accidents seem to happen pretty frequently to those who hang around Saul.

Max here has never let anyone at the Farm see even the slightest sign that he can use that key, and he never, ever will. Isn't that right, Max?

I hear a mumbled "Yes, Nana Dee," and Delia continues.

The second thing is just a bit of advice. Follow your instincts. Last time I saw you, you were beating yourself up thinking you'd mishandled Abel's escape. Abel wasn't making the situation any easier, but my point is that you went with your intuition, and I think it served you well. I'm pretty sure Abel would have died in that cell if you hadn't intervened.

Julia is going to tell you Kiernan is with Saul. And he may be. Julia may even think he had something to do with Anthony's death—I know Abel thought that.

Max says something I can't make out, and Delia sniffs disapprovingly.

Apparently Max believes it, too, but since he wasn't even two years old when it happened, he's going entirely off rumors. And he should know better. Abel and I saw Kiernan a sum total of three times after we left the root cellar at Martha's house. Truth be told, we don't know what happened. But I think Abel needed someone to blame when Anthony died, and Julia probably did, too.

She starts to say something else, and then she shakes her head. After a moment, she goes on:

Whether Kiernan was involved in Anthony's death isn't something that makes much difference to me, Kate, although I'd like to believe better of him. The bottom line is this—Anthony embraced the wrong set of ideals and trusted the wrong people, and he paid dearly for that mistake. But I suspect the issue of Kiernan's loyalty will matter to you, so . . . again, trust your instincts, because Julia—well, she might be thinking more with heart than with head. And while I'm sure she thinks she has everything under control, you'll need all the allies you can find, especially if one happens to be right smack in the middle of the enemy camp.

Just remember Julia needs you—partly because you can use that key. The Fifth Column has a lot of people who can be support staff, but they're short on keys. Simon took mine and Abel's after we left you in Georgia. No need to go into details, but Abel got his hands on one back in the early eighties. Unless something has changed between now and the time you get this, the key Max is wearing is the only one they have. Second, they lack jumpers. Max can use it once a day, maybe twice, and it may take him a few tries.

Max mutters something off camera. The only words I catch are ". . . be telling everybody my business." Delia just waves her hand dismissively and says:

Hush, Max. Stop acting like it's something to be ashamed of when it's just the God's honest truth.

Anyway, Kate, even if Julia had a full roster of jumpers and every key CHRONOS ever created, she'd still need you, because you're the only one who's a dead ringer for Sister Prudence.

So don't let her bully you. As her mother, I haven't the slightest doubt she'll do precisely that if you let her.

And that's really all I have to say, except good luck. You can cut it off now, Max—

The display sputters for a moment, and Delia is gone. I rewind, and about halfway through the second watching, Daphne joins me, carrying her ratty old green Frisbee. She drops it by my feet, then settles down on the grass with a huff when she sees I'm not in the mood to play.

When the clip finishes, Daphne nudges the Frisbee against my bare feet. Hint, hint.

"Sorry, Daph. I'm kinda busy."

She rests one auburn paw on top of my toes and looks up at me with big brown eyes. In Daphne's world, it's inconceivable that anything could be more important than Frisbee.

"All right, all right," I laugh. "One time, but then I really have to go inside."

Three tosses later, Daphne is momentarily distracted by one of her squirrel frenemies dashing behind the garage. She takes off barking, and I retreat to the kitchen.

Katherine is buttering a slice of toast, cinnamon raisin judging from the aroma. She gives me a smile over her shoulder. "Good morning, Kate! Lovely day, isn't it?"

She's unusually chipper, but her voice has a false ring. Katherine's moods can be mercurial, what with the tumor pressing against her brain and the medications she takes to control its growth. There's an edge to her voice right now that often comes just before she explodes, and I instinctively brace for a storm. But . . . maybe she's just putting on a show for whoever might be listening in?

"Mm-hmm," I say, pulling a coffee mug from the cabinet. "I was just outside, looking over . . . some files. I'm going to get some coffee and then go upstairs and . . . and read some more. I guess."

I feel like I'm reading lines in a play—a horribly lame, badly written play no one would ever want to see. Still, we have to say something, and I don't want to venture near any topic that might give information to the Watchers.

"By the way," Katherine says, "the scarf we talked about finally came in. You never can tell when you order online, but the fabric is just as beautiful as it was on the website. I left it on your bed."

We've never looked at scarves online. Biohazard gear, yes. Scarves, not so much.

"Oh, good. Thanks."

"You talked to Harry, right? How is your grandfather doing?"

"Better. Grandpa's back home. Physical therapy starts tomorrow. Dad's going to try to come back after that, at least briefly."

Katherine talked to Dad yesterday, so she knows all of this. She's just stuck in the same conversational dead zone that I am. I grab my coffee and hurry upstairs, sparing both of us the need to invent more inane chitchat.

When I open the door to my room, a shopping bag is on the bed, next to Julia's tablet. Inside the bag is a long silk scarf in a pretty shade of burgundy. I pick it up, and a sheet of paper tumbles out of the folds of fabric.

It hits the floor a bit too hard to be just a sheet of paper. After unfolding it, I see four pins attached, roughly the same shade as the fabric. The paper itself is instructions on wrapping the scarf to form a hijab.

Good call, Katherine. I'll have to change into clothes that are more modest than my current shorts and T-shirt to pull it off, but covering my hair will make it less likely that anyone Julia or the Cyrists have in London watching Mom will recognize me.

I pack a few things in my backpack and have now run out of excuses for avoiding Julia's homework. So I pick up the tablet she gave me and type in the password she made me repeat five times before I left the office.

This time there's no video, just a mostly blank screen with four documents, all labeled with a single digit. The document entitled 1 is a note instructing me to open the other files, verify the information, and add any other data I might have. The final sentence, in bold print, reads *Do not disable track changes in any document!* Someone clearly has control issues.

File 2 looks like an employment application. Everything has been filled in already, including private information like my social security number. There's a small yellow flag at the bottom with a red X, pointing to a bit of legalese releasing Julia Morrell Waters, individually, and Cyrist International, collectively, from any liability if I am injured, "unless said injury occurs during an action specifically ordered by a superior." There's a line for my signature and one for "Parent or Guardian."

Why would Julia be acting to protect Cyrist International? Last time I checked, that's the group we're trying to destroy.

File 3 is a graphic of a timeline, with colored boxes. The only key is a list of numbers assigned to the historians, so I can't tell if the colors mean anything or if they're just added for visual effect. Most boxes contain one or two numbers and a location, sometimes with a full or partial date. Maybe half of the boxes are crossed through. Some places and dates in the x'd-out boxes are familiar—the one labeled *Dallas, TX 11201963*, for example. It has two numbers inside, 15 and 16, assigned in their list to my dad's biological parents, Timothy and Evelyn Winslow.

08091938 is assigned to 2, 3, 4—Abel, Delia, and Grant, the trainee who disappeared just before all hell broke loose at Martha's farm. That box is shaded gray, with the 4 circled, which makes me wonder if they found out what happened to Grant. Katherine's 1969 jump is there, but the trip she was supposed to make to 1853 is missing. *Port Darwin 1942* is there, minus the date, and a quick glance at the section for the 1950s shows only a light blue box with the number 19, which they've assigned to Wallace Moehler. Thinking back, I'm pretty sure that I mentioned getting the Port Darwin key to Abel and Delia when we were at Martha's last night . . . well, last night for me. I don't think Kiernan or I said anything about getting Moehler's key in Copenhagen, however.

They're also missing all of the keys Katherine collected before she brought me into the picture, so updating this is going to take a bit of time. My first thought is *ugh, homework*. Then I remember this doesn't have to be *my* homework. Filling in these blanks is one chore I can assign Katherine and Connor.

The boxes grow increasingly scarce toward the right end of the timeline. One reads *????2024, Cyrus, Miami, FL*. Another box is even more cryptic—only the word *Deadline* with no specific year. The box just kind of floats below the 2030s.

Then there's a long blank space before the final box, labeled *04272305, Washington DC, 25–48+.* I'm not sure what the numbers at the end signify. The list below only goes through number 24, and there were only thirty-six historians counting the dozen who weren't scheduled to jump that day. Why would it say 48+?

The date, however, is easy. April 27, 2305, is when Saul destroyed CHRONOS headquarters—or will destroy it, depending on your perspective. I'm guessing he took really detailed notes at team meetings those last few months and knew exactly where and when each of his colleagues would land. That way he could zip back and kill all twenty-three of them, making sure that none of them interfered with his plans for starting the Cyrists. Or maybe he only planned to kill some of them, if he had an ally or two among his colleagues. His one mistake was assuming that he'd be able to travel freely through time and space once HQ was gone and there was nothing to anchor him back to his point of origin. He was stranded, too, and powerless to change anything.

Until Prudence decided to play around with one of the keys, that is.

The logical thing would be for me to go back, slap that key out of Pru's fourteen-year-old hands, and destroy it. Saul and the other twenty-three historians would be stuck wherever they landed. Mom would have her sister back. Prudence wouldn't be a nutcase—well, probably wouldn't be a nutcase. Kiernan's family might never have left Ireland. Connor's two children would still exist. Dad would probably have found the Emily woman from that alternate timeline, and they'd have two cute little curly-haired boys.

But that also means I'd never exist. While contemplating that doesn't exactly make me happy, I'd make the sacrifice given that all of our evidence points to Saul taking out billions of people in a massive Culling if we don't stop him. But Katherine's convinced that plan is too risky. Saul might have had an accomplice. We might still end up with the same situation, and I wouldn't be around to stop it. Everyone else—Trey, Dad, Kiernan, and Connor—agrees with Katherine on that point. I can't help but wonder, however, whether some of them might be a bit biased toward finding a solution that includes me being alive at the end.

My eye strays back to the unattached *Deadline* box hanging out near the 2030s. There are four bullet points in the square:

- 04272024
- 12252025
- 04272034
- ????

The first entry is the day and month Saul sabotaged CHRONOS headquarters, combined with the year he landed. The next is Christmas of the year after he arrived, and the third would be the tenth anniversary of his arrival.

Whoever wrote this list of dates seems to be choosing events relevant to Saul—although I'm not sure why Christmas is in the mix—and the label *Deadline* suggests that these are the best guesses as to the date of the Culling. The 2024 date seems unlikely to me at first, given the time and effort they've put into setting up the Cyrist religion and establishing a power base, but I could easily imagine Saul deciding it was worth a few years of dueling memories to have himself hailed as a messiah the second he arrived in the past.

Even thinking about that starts my head throbbing. And the fact that all three actual dates are crossed out, leaving only question marks, sends a cold shiver up my spine.

I close the chart and move to the last file, by far the most detailed. It's a collection of information about CHRONOS and the early twenty-fourth century, structured as a wiki, with hyperlinks to the various subsections. There's enough to fill a book—and a fairly long book at that. Judging from the occasional note highlighting an unsupported or questionable assertion, it appears to have been written by several authors. In addition to lengthy sections on CHRONOS, there's one labeled *History*, an odd word choice for a period nearly three hundred years in the future. It's broken down into subsections: *2100–2199*, *2200–2249*, *2250–2299*, and *2300–2305*. After that, there are links to sections on *Government*, *Economy*, *Demographics*, *Fashion*, and *Culture*.

This file stirs up some very mixed emotions. Katherine maintains a strict "need-to-know" basis for any information about the future and has generally held that I don't need to know much of anything. When it comes to the *near* future, events that I might actually live to see, I tend to agree with her. I steer clear of those locations in the *Log of Stable Points*, and I'm glad to see this file doesn't go too far beyond what the people of the 2300s would have considered modern history.

But Katherine also tends to be cryptic on eras that couldn't be considered spoilers for me, unless she's worried I'm going to leave messages for my great-great-great-grandchildren. It's nice that the Fifth Column is willing to give me a bit more latitude, and I'll definitely be reading this file closely once Mom is back in DC and I can focus.

On the other hand, the very existence of this document suggests the Fifth Column believes Kiernan was right—the keys in the Cyrists' possession were nabbed from CHRONOS headquarters.

That makes me very nervous. A black void, with short bursts of static, is all any of us sees when we pull up that stable point. It doesn't look very inviting to me.

As I think more on that, this file, which seemed massive a moment ago, strikes me as rather paltry. Although I researched every jump, I also went into those trips with a pretty solid background about those eras from books, movies, and TV—historical tidbits I learned long before Katherine arrived with the medallion. My background knowledge may have been spotty and even completely wrong on occasion, but it gave me a bit of confidence going in. The past is, at least to some extent, a known quantity.

But everything I read or saw as a kid about the distant future is pure speculation. For a future jump, I'll be going in with nothing except the information in this file and Katherine's scattered recollections about the world she knew as a young woman.

That seems like a very thin cushion to land on if I have to jump into that black void.

∞ 3 ∞

COUNTY HALL, LONDON
September 10, 3:16 p.m.

Tourists swarm from the red double-decker bus onto the already crowded sidewalk. It's a warm, sunny day, so I'm not surprised that the area is packed with sightseers. My original plan was to avoid the crowd by jumping in during the early morning when the streets were empty. I've never been to London, and even though I'm probably too nervous to thoroughly enjoy it, a few hours to walk along the Thames, see Big Ben, and collect my thoughts over tea and crumpets would be nice. While I'm not entirely sure what a crumpet is, the idea has a certain appeal.

But my plans for an early arrival were nixed. The stable point Katherine showed me last night, just before we were so rudely interrupted by Max, sits right inside the narrow stone entrance to the building. It's fully cloaked by shadows. Katherine used this location to jump in for a Women's Liberation Movement march in 1971, and unless someone is actually standing directly beside me in the tunnel, she swears I won't be seen.

I adjust the pins holding the burgundy scarf in place and pull my backpack over one shoulder. It still feels weird to arrive in public, in broad daylight. It seems that Katherine was right, however. None of the people walking past spare me a second glance as I step out of the alcove. I wish I wasn't surprised when Katherine actually gives me helpful information, but at this stage of her illness, the odds are against it.

Turning toward the river, I see the massive white lion that stands guard over the southern entrance to Westminster Bridge. I "walked" this street several times on Google Maps before I left Katherine's, and even though some of the signs have changed since those images were captured, I still have the comfortable sense of having been here before.

Several of the tour bus passengers are now reading a directory near the lion, trying to get their bearings, while others head to the walkway along the Thames without pausing. I guess they're familiar with the area, or maybe they caught a glimpse of their attraction-of-choice while riding across the bridge—the London Eye would be pretty hard to miss.

A young guy with dark-rimmed glasses leans against the base of the lion statue. I don't even realize it's Trey until he smiles. He hasn't shaved, and he's wearing a straw hat—not one of those boater things, but more like a fedora.

I stand there for a moment, stunned, and then run to greet him. Well, I *try* to run, but I have to dodge pedestrians every few steps. When I finally reach him, he scoops me into a hug, followed by a long kiss.

"How . . . and *why* . . . are you in London? And what's with the hipster look?"

Trey grins. "Well, your way is obviously quicker, but planes do fly from DC to London, you know. Several times a day, in fact, and since you jumped forward a day, I had time to catch you. I took a red-eye flight and slept on the plane. As for the hat and glasses, consider them the male version of your scarf disguise. Katherine's idea—she thinks we need to fly under the radar while here. But I kind of like it."

"You look like your dad. Just younger and scruffier. And you didn't answer the why question."

"That should be obvious. I'm here because you're here."

"But . . . you shouldn't be." I step away, shaking my head slowly.

"You're not happy to see me?" The question is entirely rhetorical. His eyes are smiling, and I'm sure the answer was written all over my face when I saw him.

But he must also know that his being here worries me, because he quickly adds, "Listen, I know everything you're about to say. My parents know I'm here. They're . . . well, I won't say they were overjoyed, but they didn't try to stop me."

"Katherine—"

"Katherine paid for the ticket, Kate. Connor was planning to come instead, but he was glad I volunteered. He'd rather be with Katherine, in case . . . well, in case she needs him. Your dad's busy in Delaware, and you need backup. Kiernan hasn't contacted you, so you'll have to settle for me."

"Don't. You're never someone I *settle for*. You know that. I just . . . I don't know what we may be walking into. Mom isn't going to be happy to learn I've been hiding things from her."

Even though I know I have to be the one to do it, telling Mom the secret I've been keeping for the past several months—the secret her own mother has been keeping for her entire life, the secret that has eaten away a good portion of her long-lost sister's mind—isn't something I'm really looking forward to. I still don't know how I'm going to explain it, although I suspect it will involve a good bit of show-and-tell, just like when I told Dad.

"And even Mom can tell that Prudence isn't stable. She just doesn't know why yet."

Trey turns up his palms in a so-what gesture. "Prudence's instability is all the more reason someone should be with you."

"I'm not going to be here for long, Trey. It's not like we'll have time for sightseeing or anything."

"I'm not here for sightseeing. I did the tourist thing with Mom a few years ago. I'm here as backup. A second set of eyes. Moral support."

I relent and give him a tentative smile. I won't deny that I can use the moral support, and he's just flown across the Atlantic to be with me. And he's said more than once that he wishes he could do something to help me, that he feels useless. This is something he *can* do, so I'm not surprised he jumped at the chance.

But I'd be better off doing this alone. Katherine should have understood that. I think she *would* have understood that if she was still thinking straight. While she may not know about the gun in my backpack, she does know about the CHRONOS key. If trouble arises, that medallion is my exit strategy, and it's not a strategy that can include Trey. Or Mom. So even though I really am happy to see him, I'm also worried he could end up being one more weapon for Prudence to use against me.

Still, Trey is considerably bigger than I am. Bigger than Mom, too. That could come in handy if I need someone to help me drag her to Heathrow. I'm not sure how airport security would feel about him boarding with an unconscious woman, but we'll cross that bridge when we come to it.

"They probably know you're here," I say. I'm not even sure who I mean by *they*. Saul's people? Prudence's? Julia's?

"Maybe. Connor said he was careful when he ordered the ticket. And unlike you, I never promised anyone I wouldn't go to

London. So . . . what's next? Do we give your mom a warning or just show up at her hotel door?"

"If I knew the room number, maybe. It seemed kind of an odd question to ask when she was in London and I was in Bethesda. I'll call her again once we're in the lobby. All I know now is that she's in a balcony suite on the fourth floor. And it must be at the far end of the hotel—she said she can nearly reach out and touch the Eye."

The Eye in question is the London Eye, also known as the Millennium Wheel. When Mom mentioned it, the image in my mind was of a tall tower with a needle's eye window at the top, so I was picturing her on the eighty-seventh floor of some skyscraper hotel. Then I googled it and was hit with an eerie sense of déjà vu as the image of an enormous Ferris wheel, larger even than the one I rode at the 1893 World's Fair, came onto the screen.

The size difference is even more apparent in person. This wheel sweeps high above County Hall, dipping down nearly to the river at its lowest point.

The early afternoon sky is mostly blue, although the clouds in the distance as we walk toward the Eye suggest rain could be coming. We stroll past a few storefronts, including a small café selling sweets and coffee. A banner outside the London Aquarium invites us to snorkel with sharks. That's what I feel like I've been doing for the past few months anyway, so I'm happy to pass.

We eventually turn into the main entrance of the hotel and, a few yards of stone tunnel later, enter the lobby. It's a large room, partially lit by the bluish glow of the glass-domed ceiling. While it's not exactly crowded, I feel conspicuous in the scarf, like everyone is watching me. And they may be, but I'm guessing their minds are registering *girl in head scarf* rather than anything else about my appearance.

I sit on one of the padded benches in the center of the lobby and pull out my phone, double-checking the time. It's 3:25, which means I'm just past the point where I had my last conversation with Mom. "Cross your fingers that Prudence isn't in the room with her. I'm hoping she'll meet us down here. Alone. It'll be hard enough explaining this to her without Prudence twisting everything I say."

"Yeah. I'm fine with avoiding Pru."

I can't blame him. The last time Trey saw my aunt, she was wearing a lacy white next-to-nothing, trying to pass herself off as me in his bedroom, in the dark of night. While nothing actually happened, she managed to deliver her message to me very clearly: she can get to the people I love, so I'd better not cross her. I can only assume this latest stunt, contacting Mom after disappearing for three decades, is her way of hammering that message home.

"Kate?" Mom's voice is surprised when she answers the phone and also a little amused. I jumped forward a day and phoned her before I left Katherine's, mostly to make sure she and Pru actually arrived on schedule. From Mom's perspective, we just hung up less than three minutes ago.

"Did you forget to tell me something?" she asks.

"Not exactly. Listen, Mom—are you alone?"

"Yes." She draws the word out, like she's humoring me. "Why?"

"Because I need to talk to you. Alone."

"Okay," she says, lowering her voice a little. "Go ahead. Prudence isn't here—we have adjoining rooms, but I knocked just now, and she didn't answer. I guess she's stepped out for a moment."

I glance around the lobby for Prudence, even though I suspect that she's "stepped out" with her CHRONOS key rather than in the more conventional fashion. She's probably many miles and many years away from this hotel.

"No, Mom. I need to talk to you face-to-face. Could you come down to the lobby?"

"Oh, really funny, Kate."

"Mom, please. I'm downstairs. I swear. There's this big glass dome in the lobby ceiling that looks like a sundial." Yes, I could have gotten that from the hotel website, but I'm hoping that doesn't occur to her. "I'll explain everything when I see you, but I need you to come down alone. Without Prudence. Please. I'm wearing a burgundy scarf, and we're sitting on one of these square benches—"

"We? Is Mother with you?"

"No."

There's a pause, and then she huffs, "Well, of course not. Why would I even assume that she'd want to see her daughter who's been miss—" She breaks off suddenly, and when she continues a few seconds later, her voice is more subdued. "Oh. That's why you're here. She's dead, isn't she?"

My throat catches as I remember standing in Katherine's living room last night, asking the very same thing about Mom. "No! No, Mom. Katherine's not dead. Please. Could you just meet me in the lobby?"

"Okay, okay. I'll be right down. *Alone*, since you insist. This had better not be some sort of cross-Atlantic practical joke."

But she's not alone. I can tell as soon as the elevator doors begin to open, because the cube is filled with a familiar blue light. Mom gives me an apologetic look as she walks toward us. Prudence is close on her heels, the CHRONOS key hanging openly from a long silver chain. The blue light of the medallion stands in stark contrast to the black, long-sleeved turtleneck Pru is wearing. It seems a rather odd fashion choice in this warm weather.

Two men follow them out of the elevator, and I think at first that the men are with them. One is tall, the other a bit below average height, and both look like they spend a lot of time at the gym. The tall one catches my eye briefly and looks confused for a moment, then they both walk toward the concierge desk, their heads huddled in conversation.

"Sorry," Mom whispers into my ear as she hugs me. While I suspect she couldn't help Pru tagging along, it's going to complicate things.

"Oh my God, Deborah!" Prudence says with a little squeal before she steps forward, pulling me into a hug. I stiffen, half expecting to feel the blade of a knife slip between my ribs, but she just raises her hands to my shoulders and then holds me out at arm's length. "You didn't tell me Kate was coming! And you didn't tell me she was so *gorgeous*."

That's not even remotely true. Still, I have to admit I'm a little annoyed to hear Mom laugh. I mean, moms are supposed to think their daughters are gorgeous, right?

The laugh, however, is at Pru's expense. "Why am I not surprised to hear you say that? I've had the strangest feeling for the past seventeen years that I somehow gave birth to *your* daughter. Your face, your curls—" She gives me a long, puzzled look and shakes her head. "Although you can't see those right now, under that . . . why on earth are you wearing hijab, Kate? And she has Harry's green eyes, so I'm not sure there's much of me in the mix."

Mom glances back at Prudence. "Not that I'm complaining. Kate looking like you always made me happy with you . . . gone . . ."

Her voice trails off as she watches Prudence, who's still gripping my shoulders. I feel a quick tug, and the scarf puddles around my shoulder.

"I never really understood the point in those things," Pru says. "It's just hair."

"Better than a lotus tattoo," I hiss loud enough that Prudence can hear but soft enough that Mom can't make it out.

As I shrug my shoulders to pull away from her, I catch a glimpse of the two men who followed them out of the elevator. Both look like they are on full alert, and they're staring straight at me. They're clearly security of some sort. The question, of course, is *whose* security. The shorter of the two has something clipped to his ear. The taller one might be wearing an earpiece as well, but his hair is a bit on the long side, so I can't really see it. What I can see is the arm angled across his waist in an awkward fashion, with his hand just inside his suit jacket. Which means they're *armed* security.

"And who is this handsome young man?" Pru asks.

I reluctantly look away from the security guys and glance at Trey, who is standing a few feet to my left, looking awkward and out of place.

He moves a step toward Mom, pointedly ignoring Prudence. "Trey Coleman, Ms. Pierce. I'm pleased to finally meet you."

Mom takes the hand he offers, giving it a momentary squeeze. "You can call me Deborah," she says, and then she turns to Pru. "As happy as I am to see Kate, I had no idea she was joining us. I certainly didn't know she was traveling with her . . . boyfriend. They've only been dating a few weeks, and—"

"Really, Deborah," Pru says, rolling her eyes dramatically. "You're so old-fashioned. Can't you see they're in love? I'm sure neither of them has eyes for *anyone* else."

The last sentence fairly drips with sarcasm, although I'm not sure whether Pru is digging at me about the time I've spent lately with Kiernan or at both of us about her own little adventure in Trey's bedroom.

Mom seems to pick up on the tone as well, because she gives Prudence a confused look before turning back to us. "Well, it's a pleasure to meet you, Trey, even if I'm baffled at the circumstances. Does Harry know you're here, Kate—and that you're traveling together?"

I debate my answer for a moment. Dad has enough stress right now without landing on my mom's dreaded List. Finally, I just nod.

"But why, Kate? It's such a huge expense, and I told you Prudence and I would be traveling back to DC soon. I'm taking the rest of the month off—my supervisor at the university in Genoa was very understanding when I explained the situation."

So Prudence hasn't admitted that she was behind the research grant. Great. It may pale in comparison to everything else she's about to hear, but that's one more bit of unpleasantness I'll have to break to Mom.

"It should be obvious, Deb. She couldn't wait to meet her Auntie Prudence after all this time!"

The smile on Pru's face is too big and too bright to seem at all sincere, at least to my eyes. Mom seems uncertain, too, but she returns the smile, nervously at first, and then her lower lip starts to tremble. She reaches out and puts one arm around Prudence and one around me, squeezing us both into a hug.

"I'm sorry, Kate," she says, her eyes a little teary. "Of course you wanted to come. This is just so unbelievable, to find her after all this time. Are you staying here, or . . ." She glances over at Trey again, a little embarrassed.

"I have a room," Trey says. "Not here—they were booked solid. I'm at the Park Plaza a few blocks over. I think Kate was planning to stay with you?"

I nod and smile, even though I have no intention of sleeping in London tonight. If things go as planned, Mom will be on a plane to DC and I'll be sleeping in my bed at Katherine's.

Prudence claps her hands, as though she feels compelled to pull everyone's attention back to her. When her arms move, a faint sliver of vivid blue light peeks through the thick cabled fabric of her left sleeve, just below the elbow. It seems like a weird spot to strap a spare CHRONOS key, but I guess it explains her out-of-season sweater.

"Enough with the logistics!" she says. "We should celebrate! They have the most divine afternoon tea in the Library, with champagne and these little sandwiches and—"

Mom holds up a hand. "Remember, Pru?" she says in the slightly patronizing voice I recall all too well from when I was a kid and she was trying to put the brakes on my suggestion that we go to Disney World, or get a puppy, or whatever. "You asked when we checked in. We'd need reservations weeks in advance."

Pru's shoulders slump like a kid who's just missed the ice cream truck. Then her eyes widen and the smile returns. She grabs the CHRONOS key on her silver chain and blinks out.

I expect Mom to be stunned, but she looks annoyed more than anything else. "Damn it! She did it again! You saw it, too, didn't you, Kate? Trey?"

We both nod, and she continues, her voice too loud, like it always is when she's stressed. "Well, thank God. I thought I was going crazy. It's the third time in the past few days. Last night, before we left Italy, I was looking straight at her and . . . poof. Just poof. It's not . . . possible!"

People are staring at us now, and not just the security guys, who are still on alert near the concierge desk. I'm not sure if anyone else saw Prudence disappear or if it's just because Mom is freaking out, but we're drawing far too much attention. I make a shushing noise and lead Mom back to the bench.

"That's why I'm here, Mom. Could we go up to your room now? There's a logical explanation for what you saw—"

"No," she insists. "There's not. She touches that . . . *thing* . . . and vanishes. How can there possibly be a logical explanation for that?"

"That *thing*," I hiss in a low voice, "is called a CHRONOS key, and it's the reason Prudence disappeared just now. Also when she was fourteen. It allows her to jump backward—or forward—in time."

Mom's eyes narrow, and she gives me her *yeah, right* look, but it's not convincing. She knows something really bizarre is going on, and she must know it's connected to the medallion. She just doesn't *want* to believe it.

The quickest way to convince her would be a demonstration. Unlike Prudence, however, I'm not inclined to jump out in a crowded lobby, especially with the security guys watching us.

"Let's go back to your room, okay?"

"No. We need to wait here. Pru will be back. At least, she came back the other times. But . . ." She starts looking around the lobby again. "It didn't take this long before. She came right back."

I tug on her arm. "Pru will go to your room if we're not here, right?"

Trey, who has kept silent so far, leans in and adds, "You probably don't want everyone looking on when Kate tells you what she knows about all of this."

Mom starts to object again, then notices a middle-aged couple two benches away watching us. They look more annoyed than anything else, so I'm guessing they're reacting to the noise rather than Prudence's unconventional exit. The man quickly shifts his gaze to a large planter a few feet to our left when I stare back. The woman next to him watches a moment longer before deciding that same planter is fascinating.

Mom's mouth tightens. "Let's go."

I watch the security guys from the corner of my eye as we head to the elevators. They seem confused. After a moment, the shorter man nods toward us, and the tall one hurries across the room. Fortunately the lobby is wide and we're a good distance ahead of him. When the door closes in front of us, he's still about ten paces away.

Once we're in Mom's room, she heads straight for the minibar. I've rarely seen her drink anything stronger than wine, but she tips back a tiny bottle of vodka, straight, her eyes tightly closed. A small shudder runs through her, and then she sits on the edge of one of the double beds.

After a moment, she opens her eyes. "Okay. Start explaining."

I pull out the CHRONOS key and am about to start when I notice the window. Although Mom may have been kidding about being able to reach out and touch the Eye from her balcony, she wasn't kidding by much. I don't know how well the passengers can see into the rooms from the clear observation capsules that are moving slowly back toward the ground, but there's no point in risking it.

Trey follows my gaze and pulls the curtains together. Without the bright sunlight streaming in, the medallion bathes everything in blue light. Mom and Trey can't see it, though, so I flick on the lamp by the bed.

Sitting back down next to Mom, I hold the key out. "I know you hate this thing, and I get it. Believe me, I *totally* get it. I might be able to explain without using it, but it would take much, much longer for you to believe me."

I run my fingers over the key to set a stable point and then roll the time back to 3:25, just after I called Mom from the lobby. "This is going to be a little uncomforta—"

"No." Mom grabs my hand. Her fingers brush the side of the key, and she pulls them back, almost like she's been burnt. "I don't want you using that thing, Kate. Take it off. Put it away."

"Sorry, Mom. I wish I could, but . . ." I pull up the stable point again, moving more quickly this time, so that I can blink out before she reacts.

Mom is standing at the window, staring out at the Thames, when I pop in. I clear my throat softly to get her attention.

She looks toward the bed where I'm sitting and says, "Oh, there you are—" before realizing it's her daughter and not her sister in the room. Her jaw hangs open for a moment and she stands there, speechless.

"Sorry, Mom," I repeat. "This will make more sense in about twenty minutes." And then I jump back to 2:46, about ten seconds after I left.

Mom is sitting on the bed now instead of standing next to the window, but the stunned expression on her face is almost identical to the one she wore when I blinked in. Except she also looks like she might hurl on the rug.

"You were here . . . earlier. Why do I remember that now, when I didn't before? What's going on, Kate?"

"That queasy feeling would go away much faster if you'd just hold your hand against—"

"No! I'm not touching that thing. I want you to take it off. Right now. I mean it, Kate."

"I can't. I really, really wish I could, but things are complicated beyond belief right now, and I have to keep this on. In fact, I've brought a spare for you."

"No," she says again, scooting toward the nightstand. "Keep that thing away from me. And take it off. Please, Kate. I don't know what kind of magic makes it work, but it's cursed."

"It's not magic." I'm about to add that it's not cursed, either, but given the trouble the thing has brought me in the past few months, she may have a point.

"It's from the future, early twenty-fourth century. Katherine brought it back with her to 1969. That's the year she was stranded in. She was with a group called CHRONOS that studies history by sending people back to view events as they happened. There was . . . well, it wasn't an accident, more of a sabotage. Since Katherine was pregnant at the time, you and Prudence were stranded, too. Pru inherited the gene that enables her to use the key. That's why she disappeared all those years ago. The gene isn't . . ." I pause for a moment, trying to remember the correct word. "It's not expressed in your DNA, but you passed the trait along to me. That's why I can see the light—remember how I called it 'Blue Light' when I was little? Anyway, when the gene is active, like it is for me and Prudence, the person can use the key to travel between stable points to different times and places. It's how I got to London."

She looks over at Trey, and he shakes his head. "No. I can't see the light or use the key. I took the normal route—eight hours, British Airways."

"The key is also how I went back and changed your memory. I set a stable point for this room, which means I could adjust the time on the coordinates and go back to when you were here before, just after we spoke on the phone."

I stop for a moment, expecting her to chime in with questions. The glazed look in her eyes worries me, and I decide to give her the rest of it in small, bite-sized pieces. The part about her biological father being a megalomaniac hell-bent on destroying a sizable chunk of humanity has to be discussed, preferably before Prudence gets back. Learning that Katherine arranged her failed marriage to Dad on the off chance that they'd produce me? I'm thinking that can probably wait, along with many of the other elements that make my head spin each time I try to sort them out.

"Mom," I begin as I pull the spare medallion from my bag. "I really *do* need you to wear this. Because what happened just now, me going back and talking to you? That was a tiny little ripple, a small time change. You remember it—and kind of don't remember it—only because you saw it happen. You were here when I changed it. But if a major time shift happened, if someone changes the entire timeline again and you aren't under a key, you won't know there've been changes. It's happened before. This all started back when we were in Iowa—remember my so-called panic attacks?"

That catches her attention, for some reason. She gets up suddenly from the bed, startling slightly when she notices Trey in the chair near the window, like she'd forgotten he was there. Then she gives me another odd look and goes into the bathroom, closing the door behind her.

After a few seconds, I hear water running in the sink. I wait about a minute, then get up and tap on the door. No answer.

"Mom?" The water goes off, so I knock again, louder.

Trey comes up and wraps his arms around me. "Maybe you should give her a minute. This is a pretty major sensory overload the first time."

I lean my head back against his chest. "I know, I know. But Prudence could show up any second and—"

"Want me to go into the hallway and keep watch?"

"I doubt it would give us much of a heads-up. Pru probably set a stable point in the hallway or in her room. Maybe even in here."

"True," he says, moving around so that he's facing me. "Still, it might be better than nothing. Your mom seems on edge with me here. Maybe she'll listen better if I'm not in the room. I don't think Katherine really thought that part through. Although to be fair, I guess I didn't, either."

I don't entirely like the idea of Trey hanging out in the hallway on his own. Unfortunately, there's no good way of saying that without it sounding like I think he can't take care of himself, and he's probably right about Mom. So I nod. He gives me a quick kiss and steps outside.

I go back and sit on the bed, trying to wait patiently.

I'm not good at that. Maybe twenty seconds later, I say, "Mom? Trey stepped out so we can talk alone. And we really do need to talk before Prudence comes back. That could be any minute now, so could you *please*? I need your help."

Mom comes out and leans back against the wall near the bed. She looks tired. I don't usually think of her as middle-aged, but the lines around her eyes seem deeper than a few weeks ago.

"So, all this stuff Prudence has been telling me is true? I mean, I was able to check some of what she said. I'd never really paid much attention to the whole Cyrist mythology. To be honest, I kind of avoided it. The fact that these Cyrists used her name—well, it was painful every time I heard it."

I'm so close to saying it didn't stop her from giving me the awful name, but I bite my tongue and let her finish.

"When Pru told me about Cyrist International, all I had to do was type in *Sister Prudence* to confirm that part of it. Her picture popped up all over the place, some with actual photos. But . . . you're saying she's really using that thing to travel through time? Nobody is crazy?"

"Well, *you're* not crazy." I pat the spot beside me on the bed because she still doesn't look very steady. When she doesn't join me, I go on. "Yes, Prudence is using the key to time travel."

"What about the rest of it? She said our father—not Dad, but some other, biological father I didn't even know we had—is alive. He's stuck a few years in the future, and she's trying to help him avoid some sort of global catastrophe. That's true as well?"

"No. I mean, yes, Saul is alive, but he and Prudence are *causing* the catastrophe, not preventing it." Her eyes narrow. "I don't know how much Pru understands about that, though."

I hate making excuses for Prudence. I can still hear her at the World's Fair, telling me that I could either join the Cyrists or line up with the rest of the sheep to be fleeced and slaughtered. The notion that she's an innocent victim doesn't sit well with me. But I also know Mom won't find it easy to accept my suspicion that the sister she loves is an evil, murdering bitch.

I take a deep breath, choosing my words carefully. "I think Saul lied to her about what he was planning, at least at first. And I *know* that she's been using the key a lot. Too much, even going back to alter things in her own timeline. Changing her own memories. That's not good. Katherine says—"

I immediately wish I could yank those last words back, because Mom's eyes flash at Katherine's name. "And how do you know Mother isn't the one who's lying? She's been lying to *me* my entire life! Maybe this Saul really is trying to—"

"No!" I say, packing every bit of certainty I can muster into the word. "No, Mom. Saul did a test run on a village in Georgia, back in 1912. I saw rows of bodies—kids, babies even—who died because Saul dropped something into their well."

Just thinking about the scene in God's Hollow brings tears to my eyes, and I have to blink them away.

Mom's expression softens a bit as she watches me, but she's still uncertain. "What about Prudence?"

I don't follow her question at first, and then I shake my head when I realize she's asking if her sister was involved in the massacre. "No. I don't think she knows that part. But I can't be sure."

"How can you be sure of *anything* that happened in 1912, Kate? How can you know that Saul was responsible?"

Because I was there. I heard him laughing, I watched him spin around with his face raised to the sky like the corpses before him in that chapel were a gift from the heavens.

Emphasizing the fact that I've been up close and personal with a homicidal maniac recently—several of them, actually—would only amp up Mom's current level of freak-out. I opt instead for a watered-down version of the truth.

"I was able to view it through the key, Mom. Saul was happy about it. Blissfully happy. I think we have a shot at stopping him now—some things have changed in the past few days. I have allies now, people who may be able to help me."

At least I hope I do. I still can't shake the feeling that I might be just as alone, maybe even more so if what Julia believes about Kiernan is true.

"I have to get back to DC as soon as possible," I say. "I just needed to see that you were safe first. I know she's your sister, but you can't trust her. I'm not sure she's even sane."

I can tell from Mom's expression that she's wondering about that last part, too. As she opens her mouth to say something, there's a knock, followed by Prudence's voice just outside the door.

"Deborah? Are you in here?"

So much for Trey being able to give us a warning.

Mom moves toward the door. I grab her arm and slip the spare CHRONOS key into her hand. "Please, Mom," I whisper. "You have to keep this on you. And we have to go back to DC. *Please*."

She takes the key and sighs, putting it in her pocket. "For *now*." She wipes the hand that held the medallion on her jeans like she's touched something nasty. "We'll finish this discussion later. And I won't leave Prudence here alone. I can't."

Pru steps in as soon as Mom opens the door. Trey stands behind her against the corridor wall with his eyes fixed on something to his left.

"Why didn't you wait in the lobby?" Prudence flashes an angry glare in my direction before looking back at Mom. "You knew I'd be right back!"

"Did I?" Mom sniffs. "Your track record isn't exactly spotless there. The first time you blinked out you were gone more than thirty years."

Pru's expression is so wounded that I almost—*almost*—feel sorry for her.

"Deb, I explained about that. It wasn't my fault. You said you believed me! And this time . . . I went back to make reservations. For *tea*."

Prudence's sad puppy act seems to work, although I'm pretty sure that Mom would never have bought it from me, even when I was a little kid.

She gives Pru an apologetic smile. "I'm sorry. I didn't mean it to come out like that. It's just . . . this is all so strange. I don't know what to believe anymore."

Prudence gives me a smug glance and takes Mom by the arm, pulling her into the corridor. "I know," she says sympathetically. "It's a lot to take in. Why don't we go downstairs and discuss everything over tea and cakes?"

Pru steers Mom to the left. She's still prattling on about tea, but her voice fades as they turn at the intersection just down the corridor and head toward the elevators.

My gaze has been locked on the two of them, so it takes a moment to realize Trey is still staring at that same spot, just to the right of the doorway. He must feel me watching, because he flicks his eyes toward me and then back. That's when I notice the shadow on the carpet. It's a man. He seems unnaturally tall, although I'm guessing that's an illusion from the lighting in the hallway.

Whoever he is, the bright blue light coming from that direction tells me he's carrying a CHRONOS key. And while the lines of the shadow on the floor are too blurry for me to be certain, I think he's holding a gun.

∞4∞

Snatching my backpack from the bed, I unzip the front pocket and grab the Colt. Trey is still rooted to the same spot.

Unfortunately, if Shadow-Man is holding a gun, there's no good way for me to approach. In the movies, the wall near the door is always free of obstructions so the heroine can press against it and pivot around the doorway, gun extended. Clearly this hotel wasn't planned with gun battles in mind, because a luggage stand is right smack in the way. I also suspect I'm at least partially visible from the man's vantage point, thanks to mirrored closet doors.

I advance cautiously, but before I reach the door, the shadow moves toward the entrance. My gun is raised. Trey is too close, however—and now Trey is also moving. I catch a fleeting glimpse of a very familiar face as Trey tackles him from behind, shoving him through the door and onto the floor.

"Bloody hell, are you both crazy?"

Kiernan's voice is muffled by the carpet. He starts to get up, but Trey pushes him back down with his knee.

"Are you coming, Kate?" Mom yells. "We can't keep holding the elevator."

"Go ahead! We'll meet you downstairs."

I motion for Trey to step away. He gives the gun in my hand an uneasy look, then takes his knee off Kiernan's back and moves toward the door, closing it behind him.

Kiernan props himself up, rubbing his head where it hit the carpet. He casts a wary eye at my gun, now pointed at the floor. "You can put that thing away, Kate."

"You first," I say, nodding at the Colt in his hand, identical to mine aside from the pearl grips on my handle.

He shrugs, sticking the gun into his pocket as he stands. It's only then that I get a clear look at his face, and all of the breath is sucked out of me.

He's . . . different. Older. He hasn't gone gray and there are no wrinkles, but I can tell he's aged. Five years, at least. His jawline is more defined, and his eyes . . . I can't quite place exactly how they're different, but they're the most telling sign of all.

Kiernan holds my gaze for a few seconds, then sticks out his hand toward Trey. "Kiernan Dunne. Who are you?"

A wide scar zigzags about four inches along the inside of Kiernan's arm, midway between wrist and elbow. It wasn't there when I left him in Georgia last night, but it's not fresh. It's faded—a silvery, knotted line against his skin.

Trey takes the hand Kiernan offers and gives it a brief shake, still eying him cautiously. "Trey Coleman."

As soon as he releases Kiernan's hand, Trey looks back at me and says, a bit defensively, "He came in with Prudence. They both just . . . apparated . . . or whatever, right there in the hallway. I didn't have time to knock, and he had the gun out, so . . ."

"It's okay." I give him a smile, then turn back to Kiernan. "Why are you here? Why are you standing outside my mother's hotel room with a gun? How long has it been for you, since last night . . . since Georgia? And what happened to your arm?"

Kiernan shakes his head. His expression is odd—I can't tell if he's amused at the barrage of questions or annoyed. "As usual, I'll take them in order. Pru said come for tea. I'm her bodyguard, so I did as I was told." He nods toward Trey. "There was a strange man lurking in the hallway when she pulled up the location on her key, which should explain the gun. Georgia was a little over six years ago for me. The scar . . ." He shakes his head dismissively. "An accident. Looks worse than it was."

I doubt that. The scar is jagged and wicked looking, wider than my thumb in some spots. It's really two scars, because there's a smaller, curved line, about an inch long, running nearly parallel. Both cuts clearly needed stitches.

I'm about to push him for more information when Trey asks, "So Prudence didn't tell you we were here?"

"No," Kiernan responds with a wry quirk of his lips. "I'm sure she thought it more amusing to have us all meet in the hallway. One side effect of working for a madwoman is dealing with her sense of humor. And she doesn't know about Kate's little toy there." His eyes rest on the gun, which I'm still holding.

"Neither did I," Trey says, giving me a worried look.

"I told you about the gun." I shove it into the backpack.

"I didn't know you were actually carrying it."

My own views on carrying it have changed pretty drastically in the past few days. A week ago, I'd have been terrified of the thing, but the fact that I was armed saved Kiernan's life and quite possibly my own at God's Hollow.

"I'm here to rescue my mom. From a madwoman, as Kiernan just noted. I thought it might come in handy. Why are you working for Pru in the first place, Kiernan?"

He shrugs. "We have common enemies. And a few common goals. But we're late for tea, so the details will have to wait." He motions with his head toward the door. "Shall we?"

As much as I'd like to tell him we shall *not*, at least not until I have more answers, I don't like leaving Mom alone with Prudence. I still don't think she'd actually hurt Mom, although I have to admit that Pru's current level of instability has made me less certain on that point. Either way, she's clearly on a mission to convince Mom to accept her version of reality. And in a battle for heart and mind, every second I leave them alone is risky.

There are two other passengers in the elevator, so we don't talk on the ride down. The three of us just stand against the back wall, awkwardly silent, with Trey casting occasional angry glances at Kiernan over the top of my head. I grab Trey's hand and lace his fingers between mine, hoping to signal that he has no reason to feel threatened.

If I'd had to guess which of the two would be acting jealous and territorial, I'd have picked Kiernan. But the vibe I'm getting from him is very different from when we were in Georgia. The change in his eyes I noticed earlier is one thing—he looks tired. Resigned, maybe. That spark that's always present when he looks at me is gone. Well, maybe not gone, but definitely muted. Distant.

His transformation is disconcerting. I almost feel like I'm standing next to a stranger. People can change a lot in six years.

Maybe he's moved on?

Maybe he's moved on with Prudence?

Ick. I inch closer to Trey because even if it's not rational, and totally unfair, that idea bothers me on so many different levels.

Trey and I step into the lobby and Kiernan follows, grabbing my arm to hold me back. "Give me your key," he says, yanking his own from his pocket.

"Why?"

He rolls his eyes and reaches over, pulling at the black cord around my neck that he knows holds my CHRONOS medallion. His fingers brush against my collarbone for only a moment, but it's still enough to trigger the shiver I feel when he's too close for comfort. And as awkward as that is at any time, it's a million times more uncomfortable with Trey watching.

Kiernan activates his key and slides mine out of the leather pouch that shields the light if you come into contact with someone carrying the CHRONOS gene. He holds the two together, transferring a set of personal coordinates from his medallion to mine. Some stable points, apparently the most popular destinations, are standard to all keys. Less frequently used locations are in the *Log of Stable Points* that Katherine has back home. With a local point, however, this is the quickest way to share it, otherwise you have to manually enter a string of coordinates pinpointing the exact geographical location and then another set pinpointing the exact time.

Trey is still a few feet away, eying us warily. I motion for him to join us. He glares at Kiernan for a second, then comes over.

"How did he get to London?" Kiernan asks.

"British Airways."

Kiernan's brow creases. "Why's he carrying a key? I can see it through his pocket. Before, you said Katherine wouldn't allow it. That it could hurt him."

Trey answers for me. "It was unavoidable. I was under the CHRONOS field when a time shift happened. And . . . I told Katherine I wasn't leaving. That I *volunteer*. I can't be much help to Kate if my memory keeps getting wiped."

Kiernan still looks troubled, but he hands me back my key and walks over to the registration desk. The woman points to the left, and he heads off in that direction, waving for us to follow.

A few minutes later, we're in the County Hall Library, which stretches along the front of the building. Floor-to-ceiling bookshelves separate the room into semiprivate dining nooks—small round tables covered with white linen, encircled by comfy-looking chairs.

Trey spots Mom and Prudence three tables back, in an alcove with a nice view of the Thames and Big Ben. A flustered-looking waiter stands behind them. I'm not sure why he's flustered until I realize there are now five of us and the table is set for four.

Pru waves her hand dismissively. "Don't bother. The dark-haired one is just my bodyguard. He can stand."

Kiernan seems entirely unfazed by the comment, but her tone pisses me off.

I'm about to press the point when I find an unexpected ally in the waiter. His mouth tightens. "I'm afraid the gentleman will have to be seated if he's to remain with you, miss. I'd be happy to pull up an extra chair if you ladies would be so kind as to move a bit toward the window."

Mom complies immediately. Pru, on the other hand, gives the waiter a stare that makes me hope for his sake that this is one of those places where the tip is added to the check automatically.

"Fine," she snarls, squeezing her chair a few inches to the right. I sit next to Mom, facing the entrance. Trey quickly drops into the chair the waiter placed beside me, leaving Kiernan to round out the circle.

The waiter sets another place for Trey and pours tea into the empty cups. Then he gives us a rundown of the items on the tiered tray near the center of the table—assorted pastries that look much too elaborate to eat, along with a variety of scones and delicate finger sandwiches.

When he finishes, Prudence clears her throat and purposefully taps the rim of her empty champagne flute. The waiter assures her he'll be back with champagne momentarily and hurries off.

Mom takes a sandwich from the tray and asks me, "What took you so long?"

"Well, the elevator was slow. And then we had to find the Library, since you didn't wait for us in the lobby."

Pru shrugs. "I wasn't sure how long they'd hold our reservation." A sly grin spreads over her face. "I thought maybe you and Kiernan were just catching up on old times. Although I guess that might have been *awkward* with your new guy around."

Mom chokes on her tea and gives me a questioning look. I start to respond, but Trey beats me to it.

"Perhaps," he says in a level voice, staring directly at Pru. "But no more awkward than sitting across the table from the aunt who sneaked into her boyfriend's bedroom."

Pru's eyebrows rise gradually, and she does a slow clap, her grin widening.

"Ooh, touché! After your rather . . . stoic . . . behavior that night, I'd pegged you as cute-but-boring. But it looks like Kate's little pet has claws." She catches Mom's expression out of the corner of her eye as she reaches the end of the sentence. I think maybe she'd forgotten her sister was there, because some of the color drains from her face. She pastes on her too-wide smile again. "Oh, excellent. The bubbles have finally arrived."

The fact that Pru calls champagne "bubbles" makes me want to vomit.

The waiter fills each glass in turn. Prudence's is nearly empty before he makes his way around the table. Over his shoulder, I see the two security guards near the entrance. Tall Guy is talking to the hostess, while Short Guy watches our table, his eyes on Pru.

When they shift to me, he realizes I'm staring back and quickly looks away.

I'm pretty sure I'm over the legal drinking age in Great Britain, but either Mom doesn't know that or it doesn't impress her.

"Could you bring her a bottle of water instead?" she asks the waiter. I shoot her a peeved look, although it's more for show than anything else. Skipping the "bubbles" is fine with me. I need to keep a clear head.

"Hmph," Pru says. "She'd be better off drinking the tap than bottled. You never know what's in that stuff. No need for this to go to waste, however." She scoops up my glass, then looks over at Mom. "Don't get me wrong, Deb. I'm the last person who'd ever complain about extra champagne, but your puritan streak is showing again. Since when did you become so much like Mother?"

Given Mom's opinion of Katherine, I expect her to take offense. And there *is* a tiny hint of offense in her expression, but she just says, "Possibly when I actually became someone's mother." She shoots me a quick glance from the corner of her eye and then looks back at Prudence. "Kate's mother. Whom you already seem to know pretty well. Maybe you'd like to explain how and why you wound up in her boyfriend's room?"

"I was teaching your daughter a lesson, Deborah. A little reminder to stop playing around in things she doesn't understand. Cyrist International isn't a game. We have a serious mission, and we mean to carry it out."

Pru's voice rises a bit with each sentence. Kiernan reaches over and squeezes her arm gently, looking pointedly around the room and then back at her. His meaning is clear to me—people are watching, lower your voice—but either Prudence doesn't catch it or she doesn't care, because she yanks her hand away and says, even louder, "I was trying to protect her. I thought you'd want that!"

"Of course I'd want that," my mother says. "What I don't understand is why you didn't contact me first, Pru. She's *my* daughter. It's my job to protect her, not yours, and I can't do that when everyone is keeping me in the dark."

A quick glance in my direction makes it clear that I'm included in that criticism. I give her an apologetic smile and pretend I'm absorbed in deciding which of the pastries to grab from the top tier.

I hate that Mom feels excluded, but to be honest, I'd make the same decision about informing her if I had to do it again. Except . . . I'd probably try to talk her out of accepting the research grant, now that I know whose money was funding it. It's not that I like lying to Mom. I just don't think she's capable of staying out of this. She won't be able to stand on the sidelines and watch me take risks. She'll go into crazed mother tiger mode and lash out at anyone—Katherine, Dad, even me—if she believes they're responsible for putting her cub in danger.

But I also see a touch of that same emotion in her eyes when she looks at her sister.

Prudence takes a deep breath. "I was trying to protect you as well, Deborah. Saul can't be trusted. He's—" She suddenly gets a deer-in-the-headlights look. Then she scoops up her medallion and blinks out.

There's a moment of silence before Mom says, "I must be getting used to her abrupt exits. That's not nearly as tough the fourth time around."

"The key's in your pocket, Mom. You're under a CHRONOS field."

"Hmph," Kiernan says, his face surprised and a bit amused. "Don't think Pru was counting on that."

I give him a confused look.

"She made a mistake, right?" he continues. "Pru didn't plan to let that bit about not trusting Saul slip out. So she's going to go back and fix it."

"Fix it how?" Mom asks.

"Tell herself not to say what she just said. That's a guess on my part, but I've seen her do it often enough in the past that it's a fairly educated guess."

"Why would she think that would work?" Trey asks. "She knows Kate has a CHRONOS key."

"Yeah, but it's Kate's *mum* she's trying to convince. She's not worried about Kate, or about us." He turns and looks at Mom. "I don't know if you've noticed, but your sister is a few cards short of a full deck. No. Strike that. She's an entire suit short of a full deck. To be frank, it's like minding a toddler. Sometimes Pru's all there, razor sharp. But she can't hold focus. If something else catches her attention, she's off like a hound after a rabbit. And she's not one bit hesitant about changing things she finds inconvenient."

"Then why haven't you taken the damned key away from her?" Mom snaps. "If you're her bodyguard, you should protect her. Even if it's from herself."

It's a valid point, but Kiernan shakes his head. "She'd just use the spare."

"Then we'll take that one, too!" I counter. "There are four of us."

"Yeah, well, unless one of you is a surgeon, it won't make a damned bit of difference. The bloody thing is embedded in her arm."

"*In* her arm?" Trey asks. "How?"

"An upgrade she got a while back. And those two guys you keep sneaking looks at, Kate? You're right. They're temple security—London branch. I think they're a little confu . . . sed—"

Kiernan goes silent because Pru has returned to her seat. Except . . . one side of my brain insists she never left, that she's been right there in her chair for the past minute. She never said Saul can't be trusted. Instead, she gave us this line about how he can't be troubled with handling all of the details, so she's going to take Mom back to her place in Paris. Or maybe they'll go to Greece. Or to Rome for a few weeks. Right now, she's saying something about the Colosseum and how they'll go back to when it wasn't in ruins, maybe catch one of those gladiator shows.

Even though part of me swears she's been sitting there, spouting this nonsense the entire time, I also remember sitting here at the table with Pru's chair empty. Just me, Mom, Trey, and Kiernan. The dueling memories are unpleasant, kind of like there's a mouse inside my head, near the front, chewing away at the synapses or something. It hurts—not a loud, roaring pain, but just that small, nibbling sensation.

I press the heels of my hands against my eyes for a moment, rubbing my temples with my thumbs. As I look around the table, everyone else—everyone except Prudence, that is—seems to be dealing with the same dual memory. Mom looks like the tiny roast beef sandwich she ate a minute ago is going to make a hasty exit. Trey just stares down at the napkin in his lap, his face pale.

Kiernan looks a bit rattled, too, but he catches my eye and gives me a see-what-I-mean look.

I turn toward Pru, even though every word I say is aimed at Mom. "I'm sorry, Aunt Prudence, but I need Mom to come home. Back to DC. My grandfather is ill, and I don't know how long Dad will need to be in Delaware. Katherine's dying. I need one of my parents—"

"Oh, boohoo. Cut the I-need-my-mommy crap, Kate." Prudence pauses to drain the rest of her champagne and pours herself some more. "You've been perfectly happy keeping Deborah in the dark until now. If you're old enough to butt into everyone else's business, you're old enough to be on your own, sweetie."

Prudence's eyes are clear and sharp now, blue-gray daggers aiming straight at me. The venom in her voice reminds me of the chat we shared at the Expo. She gives me a saccharine little smile before continuing. "You didn't want your mom in the way, interrupting your little trysts at the townhouse, or wondering what trouble you're getting into with Grandma. Otherwise you'd have warned Deborah about the research trip from the beginning."

My hands grip the edge of my chair, and I lean toward Pru, my voice angry. "If I'd known *you* were behind the trip—"

Prudence cuts me off with a loud laugh. "You didn't *guess*? And here I was worrying I was being much too ob . . . vi . . . ous . . ." She's staring at the top tier of the tea tray now, eyes fixed on a small layered cake with red jam on top.

Her face transforms to childlike joy as she picks up the dessert and sniffs it. "I think it's raspberry. I *love* raspberry!"

Pru sinks her teeth into the little cake and gives a sigh of pleasure. "*Definitely* raspberry! Here, Deb, take the other one. You'll love it."

Mom's hand slides down to cover my own, which is still clutching the edge of my chair. She leaves it there for a few seconds as she tells her sister that the cake does indeed look delicious. One last squeeze, then she reaches over to take the pastry from Prudence.

It was a tiny gesture. I don't think either Kiernan or Trey noticed, even though they're both looking at me oddly now. They probably think the tears in my eyes are from something Prudence said, or because I'm worried Mom is angry. No, they're tears of relief. I don't believe for a second we're done talking about all of this, and I'm pretty sure some of that talking will be of the yelling-at-me variety, but that one little squeeze telegraphed a message that couldn't have been clearer if she'd said the words out loud.

We're in this together.

∞

Prudence keeps her friendly face on for the next twenty minutes or so, happily sampling the various items on the tray and downing several more glasses of champagne. Kiernan pushes a little blue pill toward her when she starts on the fourth glass, but she just laughs and sweeps the pill to the floor.

Is she on an antipsychotic of some sort? She needs to be.

Pru keeps adding things to Mom's plate. She doesn't seem to notice whether the rest of us are eating. We aren't, for the most part. Even though it's all delicious, I think everyone is too on edge to be hungry.

The waiters, who are almost overattentive to the surrounding tables, give our group a wide berth. Did one of them see Prudence pop out earlier? Or maybe they've just noticed that everyone else at the table is acting like Pru is a bomb about to go off?

I feel like I'm the one who's going to explode, however. It's hard to sit here sipping tea when there are other things I need to be doing. I don't have time for Prudence's version of the Mad Tea Party.

My anxiety must show on my face, because when I look up again, Prudence is watching me. Her mind has apparently returned, at least for the moment.

"What's up, little niece of mine? You're mighty twitchy. Somewhere you need to be?" She glances around the table, a sour look on her face. "None of you seem to be in a very festive mood. I sprang for the unlimited bubbles, and that's still your first glass, Deb. This is *supposed* to be a party."

Mom tips back the rest of her champagne, but doesn't reach for the bottle to refill it. "It's all delicious, Pru. I'm just a bit tired. Travel always wears me out. Maybe we should go back to the room—"

"So that you can pack up your things and head back home with your darling daughter." It's a statement, not a question, and Pru gives Mom a bitter smile as she reaches for her CHRONOS key.

"So that I can get some *rest*, Pru. I still want to see a few things in London before we head off to Greece, or Rome, or wherever it is you've decided to go next. I'm coming with you, as long as you agree to stick to the present time so that I can actually follow."

"Mom! No!" I turn toward her, stunned. "Please. We need to talk about this."

Mom's eyes stay on Prudence, but her hand reaches under the table to squeeze my knee.

My first instinct is to brush her hand away and start arguing, until she digs her fingers in a bit harder and I freeze. Old habits die hard. I remember the knee squeeze from the time I was a little kid squirming next to Mom at a fancy restaurant. At a colleague's funeral when she couldn't get a sitter. In the car, in Iowa, when she was trying to talk the cop out of a speeding ticket.

I know this signal. It means sit still and stay quiet.

And I remember Mom's hand on mine earlier. She has a plan. I'm not sure I'm going to like it or agree with it, but she's up to something.

"I think you're right, Prudence. Kate's old enough to handle things on her own. I'd just be in the way at home. And," she continues in a drier tone, "since I apparently don't have an actual *job* to return to . . . well, a vacation would be nice. A sister trip."

Mom turns back to me, smiling regretfully. "I'm sorry the two of you traveled all this way if your goal was to bring me back. You need to get back to school, young lady. I didn't authorize this rescue mission, and I'm very happy here with Prudence—we have several decades of catching up to do. And as I told you on the phone, we'll be back in the States in a few weeks. Pru says she has business in DC and down in Florida."

"Is that a good idea?" Kiernan asks, his voice surprised.

Prudence turns on him, eyes flashing. "You're not here to question my decisions, Kiernan. I'm a far better judge of what's a good idea than you are. Maybe you should run along home."

Kiernan shrugs, but the look he gives her answers my earlier question. If he's moved on, it's not with Pru.

"Fine with me." He pushes his chair back, nodding first at Mom and then at Trey. "It was a pleasure meeting you both." He taps one finger very distinctly against the pocket of his jeans, where the light of his CHRONOS key shines through the denim. "Kate, you take care, okay?"

Prudence watches him walk off, then says, "I'm going to run check on a few things back home. Let's do the Eye at nine, okay? With more bubbles."

"That sounds like fun," Mom says. "I'll wait for you upstairs."

Pru has the medallion in her hand and is clearly about to jump away when her expression shifts again and she looks confused. "Where . . . was I going somewhere, Deb? I can't remember."

"You said you needed to go home and check on some things, but . . ." Mom glances around at the other people in the restaurant. "Let's go back to the room first, okay?"

"Oh, no, no, no. I remember now. Tickets for the Eye. Should I reserve seats for Trey and Kate? Oh, and maybe one for Kiernan. You haven't met him yet, have you?" Pru looks at the seat next to her, like she's trying to remember something. "Or . . . have you?"

"Yes, but only briefly. And don't bother with tickets for Kate and Trey. They're not staying."

∞ 5 ∞

COUNTY HALL, LONDON
September 10, 5:24 p.m.

Once we're back in Mom's room, she spends the first several minutes chewing me out for not telling her everything from the beginning. At first she seems reluctant to really let me have it in front of Trey, but that fades quickly. When she has completely and rather embarrassingly vented, she demands the full story. Then she cross-examines me, and I have to tell it again. I feel like I'm back in Georgia, being grilled by Deputy Beebe.

The clouds above the river are streaks of pink and purple by the time the interrogation is over. I don't know if Mom ran out of things to ask or is just exhausted, like me. Even Trey looks tired, and he's been on the periphery of the storm.

Mom leans back against the headboard of the bed nearest to the wall and closes her eyes. I'm lying across the other bed, facing her. Trey sits next to me, holding the soda we've been sharing.

After a few minutes of silence, I say, "You can't stay here, Mom. Prudence is dangerous. I know you're worried about her. I understand. Katherine's worried about her as well. So's Kiernan."

"And you?" Mom asks.

I start to say that I'm worried about her, too. It seems like the polite thing to say, but I don't want to lie. I've done so much of that lately, and Mom's bullshit detector is probably on full alert right now.

"I never knew her when she was different, Mom. Prudence has caused a lot of trouble for me. I don't wish her ill—" I stop, thinking back to a few nights ago when I learned she'd been in Trey's house, and amend the statement. "Well, most of the time I don't wish her ill. But I *am* worried that she's part of a plan that could kill many, many millions of people. And on a personal level, I'm worried she'll hurt the people I love. Including you, Mom. I can't just leave you here."

"She won't hurt me." Mom's voice is flat and she sounds tired, but there's no hint of doubt.

"You can't know that for certain."

"Yes. I can. She won't hurt me. And I might be able to help her." She leans forward and hugs her arms around her knees, resting her chin on top so that her eyes are at my level. "More importantly, Kate, I might be able to help *you*. From what you've said, there's nothing I can do back in DC. I'll worry every time you're taking a risk of any sort. If I have to sit there and watch and do nothing, I'll end up crazier than Prudence. If I'm with her, I can keep tabs on her. I can let you know where we are. Well, except for when she jumps away, but even then I may be able to get her to talk about where—when?—she's going."

"Not if she knows you're in contact with me."

"Kate, she told me the same thing three times yesterday, in the same exact words. Within a ten-minute period. I think I can handle her."

"Maybe. But can you handle her security detail?"

"What security detail?" Trey asks.

"The goons in the suits," Mom says. "The ones who got out of the elevator with us earlier. There were two different guys when we were in Florence, and I'm pretty sure two others were following me in Genoa a few days before she contacted me. Cyrist security of some sort. They all have that blue flower on the back of their hands. And here's the odd part—I don't think Pru even realizes they're following her. Or maybe they've followed her for so long that she doesn't see them."

I guess I look a bit surprised, because Mom laughs. "I'm not totally blind, Kate. I don't think those guys are professionals. They're kind of obvious, don't you think?"

I make a mental note to ask Kiernan exactly who "those guys" really work for, assuming he even knows. Saying they're local Cyrist security doesn't tell me where their loyalties lie. Are they here to protect Prudence or to watch her? Did she hire them? Or do they belong to Saul? Or Julia?

"Speaking of security guys," Mom says, "I'm not sure I trust this Kiernan. He seems much too old to have been . . . involved . . . with any version of you in any timeline."

"I agree," Trey chimes in, and I nudge him gently with my elbow.

Mom gives Trey a little smile, the first one I've seen on her face since we came back to her room. "How old is he, anyway?"

"When I saw him last night in Georgia, he was twenty. Maybe close to twenty-one."

"So if it's been six years for him, that makes him twenty-seven," Trey says. "Practically ancient."

Mom laughs. "Normally I'd take offense at that, but in this case, I have to agree. I don't like the way he looks at you, Kate."

If she's bothered by the way he looked at me today, I'm really glad she didn't see Kiernan with me before. "You don't have to worry. He's seeing *his* Kate, Mom. Not me."

"You're sure he knows the difference?" she asks.

"Yes. He knows."

I'm not sure I'd have answered with quite as much certainty last night. Given that Trey is sitting here beside me I'd probably still have said yes, even though I'm not sure it would have been the entire truth.

But now?

"What was he doing to your key?" Trey asks. "Outside the elevator?"

"Setting a local stable point. He must have information he couldn't give me here."

"And you're sure you can trust him?" Mom asks. "That he wouldn't . . . I don't know . . . sell you out?"

I debate telling the two of them about Julia's suspicions, but it seems disloyal to do that when I don't believe them myself. Trey and Mom are worried enough about Kiernan as it is.

"He saved my life at the Expo, Mom. He's put his life on the line for me and this cause over and over. You're sure Prudence won't hurt you. I'm equally sure about Kiernan." And on this point, at least, I don't have to fake it. Kiernan won't hurt me. He can't have changed that much.

"She's right," Trey says, grudgingly. "He won't hurt her. He's in love with her. I can see it in his eyes."

Again, I can't help thinking it's a very good thing that the two of them saw this Kiernan instead of when he was six years younger.

"Which," Trey goes on, "I kind of hate, but on the bright side, I know he'll have her back. I think she's right, Ms. Pierce. We can trust him."

"Deborah," Mom says absently. She's quiet for a moment and then bangs her fists into the pillow next to her, giving a little scream of frustration. "I don't want you using that damned key! I want you back home and in school and *safe*. I'm fighting a very strong urge to fly back home and ground you until you're eighty."

She takes a few deep breaths and then gives me a shaky smile. "And that's why I have to stay here. I'm guessing that's why you didn't tell me all of this sooner, and while I'm still not cool with being kept in the dark, I get why you . . . and your dad," she adds darkly, "decided it was best to put this off."

"Dad begged me to tell you before you left for Italy," I say, keeping the promise I made to him weeks ago. "Really, he did."

"R-i-i-ght." Mom smiles and tosses the pillow in my direction. I duck out of the way just before it hits me. "A valiant attempt at keeping your father's chops out of the fire, but I'm not buying it."

∞

It's almost nine when Trey and I leave Mom's hotel. The Thames looks like a black velvet canvas scattered with carnival lights reflecting from the Eye and the buildings along the boardwalk. It's beautiful, magical even. It would be the perfect setting for a long, romantic stroll along the river if not for the damp, chilly wind whipping around County Hall.

I shiver, pulling down the burgundy scarf still hanging around my neck so that it covers more of my shoulders. The whisper-thin fabric is almost as useless for blocking the wind as it was for disguise. I wish I'd worn something warmer than this lightweight blouse.

We take a right turn, walking past a park that's nearly as brightly lit as the Eye. Trey pulls me toward him, rubbing his hand along my arm as we walk. "Better?"

"Yes. Prudence's sweater doesn't seem quite so out of season now."

"Do you think she really has a CHRONOS key *inside* her arm?"

"They can alter people so they can time travel. Embedding the medallion would be easy compared to that, so I don't see any reason not to take Kiernan's word on it."

That thought, of course, brings to mind Julia's comments last night. I just hope I'm right about Kiernan's trustworthiness on a more general level.

I don't want to think about any of that right now, however, so I switch subjects. "When are you flying back?"

"My ticket is for day after tomorrow, but I'll see if they can get me out earlier."

"I hate you came all this way only to have me fail miserably."

"How exactly did you fail? You came to let your mom know what's going on, and now she knows."

"No. She was supposed to come back with me—well, technically, with you—and she's staying."

"But her decision to stay is based on full information now, something she didn't have before. And she's wearing a key. I saw the way she reacted at first, so the fact that you have her under a CHRONOS field is a major victory."

I shrug, but I guess he's right. Mom promised to wear the key at all times and keep it hidden from Pru. We worked out a plan for communicating through her university email, and Trey reinitiated the geo-location app on her phone, allowing me to track her if I need to get to her quickly. Assuming, of course, that they stay near cities historically significant enough to have a stable point.

I still feel bad about Trey having come all this way. "You should stay tomorrow. See a few of the sights."

"Not unless you're staying, too."

"I can't, Trey. I mean, I *could*, but I'll be lousy company. I need to go back and get the screaming out of the way." He gives me a quizzical look. "Julia. If she has people watching Mom, I'm pretty sure she'll know I've been here."

"Then I leave on the earliest flight back. I'm no use to you here."

We cross the street behind County Hall, and I spot the green-and-white angel of mercy icon a few shops down. Trey steers us inside the Starbucks without even pausing to ask. If I needed another reason to love him, I just found it.

There are only a few customers, probably because 9 p.m. is a bit late to be hitting the heavy stuff. We grab two large coffees to go. Trey is doctoring his with milk and sugar, and I'm teasing him about his hipster look fitting in nicely here, when I notice two familiar profiles outside. One tall, one short, both built like bulldogs. Even without seeing their faces, I know they're the guys Kiernan and Mom tagged as Cyrist security.

The shorter one comes in the front door, while the taller guy heads around the building to the side door.

"Let's go!" I tug on Trey's arm, abandoning my coffee on the counter.

The only reason we make it to the side door first is that the tall guy is blocked by a couple pushing a stroller toward the paved square between this building and the next. I kick the rim of the door hard, catching him by surprise when it crashes into his shoulder, and Trey and I take off across the square.

There's no cover, no alley to duck into, so either we outrun them or we fight. Of course, if they decide to use guns, we're doomed either way. I'm not pulling out a pistol with a family in the middle of the square.

Short Guy yells something and runs after us. His buddy follows a few yards behind. Trey gallantly rescued my coffee and is running with both hands full. The little green stoppers aren't quite up to this degree of sloshing, and coffee spews out in two thin streams behind him as we run.

The short one is closer now, and I can hear what he's yelling. "Sister! Stop! We're with the temple!"

No kidding. That's why we're running.

Wait. Sister? He thinks I'm Prudence.

I stop. Trey pauses a few steps later, throwing me a puzzled look, just as Short Guy reaches me. I tense up, ready to fight if necessary, but the guy bends over, hands on his knees, huffing to catch his breath.

"Sorry, Sister. Didn't mean to frighten you. We're with the Lambeth temple, assigned to keep an eye out. Make sure nobody bothers you here in London. They said you wouldn't be leavin' the hotel tonight—except for goin' up on the Eye with a guest. Tomorrow was the day they said we'd need to be on our toes, 'cause you'll be shoppin' and hangin' about town."

I'd love to find out which group assigned these guys to watch Prudence, but I can't think how to get that information without raising suspicion. They may not even know themselves.

Tall Guy says, "We got confused with the older woman blinking in and out. We even thought she was you until Eddie here got a closer look."

Eddie, a.k.a. Short Guy, nods. "I seen your face in the temple windows every Sunday since I was a lad. We both have." He glances over at Trey, his eyes wary. "Then we saw you leave, and I told Sean we should follow and make sure everythin' was okay. That he wasn't botherin' you or nothin'."

The wheels in my head start spinning. Which lie will make it less likely they'll report back to whoever assigned them?

"Um . . . you've actually followed the wrong person," Trey says. "Although we're kind of here for the same reason you are. Kelly looks so much like the images of Sister Pru in our chapel that someone suggested she might be a good body double—you know, for security."

I'm momentarily taken aback because he used the same fake name for me as when we visited the Sixteenth Street Temple—a misadventure that left me with a nasty scar on my thigh, thanks to one of the temple Dobermans. But that was in the other timeline, which means Trey doesn't remember any of it.

I push that mystery out of my mind for the moment and add, "Everyone is *always* telling me I look like Sister Prudence. Our Acolyte instructor said maybe that's my path along The Way, you know, to help keep her safe by being a decoy or whatever. So, anyway, he told Brother Conwell, and they sent Sister Prudence my picture. And she asked me to meet her here in London."

Trey moves a step closer and puts his arm around me. "We noticed you guys in the lobby and again when we were at tea. And when Kelly recognized you back there, it spooked her."

He's still holding my coffee, so I take it from him. As I do, Short Guy glances toward my hand, where a lotus tattoo should be, based on our hastily created cover story. I quickly slide my other hand on top and shiver, like I'm using the coffee to warm them, then look over their shoulders, where the Eye is spinning above the tops of the buildings.

"If you're here, who's watching Sister Prudence? She said they were going to ride the Eye at nine, right?"

The two guys exchange a nervous look.

"You got a point," Tall Guy says. "Maybe we oughta head back."

"Sorry for the mix-up," the other one yells over his shoulder as they hurry across the square toward the boardwalk.

We catch our breath for a moment and then continue at a more leisurely pace, sipping what's left of our coffee. Trey's hotel is across the next street and one block over—a tall, curved structure that looks more like a giant sculpture than a hotel.

"Quick thinking back there. But who is Kelly?"

Trey's eyes widen slightly. "Just a cover. I thought I should avoid your real name, you know, just in case . . ."

"Good idea. It's just . . . you used that same fake name when we went to the Cyrist temple before . . . in the other timeline. It seems odd that you'd come up with the same name."

It's hard to tell under the dim streetlights, but I think he's blushing. He's quiet for a moment, then shakes his head and smiles.

"Kelly was a colleague of my mom's who used to come for dinner when I was twelve or thirteen. She was just out of college, dark hair, pretty. Let's just say she made a vivid impression."

"What sort of *impression*?"

"Major crush. I was depressed for weeks when she was assigned out of the country. It was so bad that I called her one Saturday pretending to be a pollster, just to hear her speak. My voice cracked halfway through, so I'm pretty sure she knew it was me."

"So *that* was the big secret. The one you mentioned on the video you left for yourself, that you said you never told anyone?"

Trey pushes the door open. The lobby of the Park Plaza is similar to the exterior—sleek and modern, with lots of black and splashes of vivid colors. Now that we're inside under the lights, I can definitely tell he's blushing, and I feel a bit guilty for teasing him.

"Yes. She was cool about it, though—never told my mom."

"Or maybe she did tell, and your mom is the cool one?"

Trey laughs. "Oh, no. After you meet Mom, you'll know that's totally out of character. She'd have found dozens of ways to tease me about it, maybe not directly, but . . . if she knew, I'd have *known* she knew."

"You're all grown up now. What if this Kelly comes back and decides she likes younger men?"

"Uh . . . I'm pretty sure she's married with kids." He smiles. "What? Are you jealous?"

"Certainly not," I say primly and then give him a grin. "Okay. Maybe a teensy bit jealous."

I guess the word pulls Trey's mind back to the source of his own jealousy, because as we're about to get into the elevator, he says, "What do you suppose Kiernan wanted to tell you?"

"I don't know. I'll check with him once I'm back at Katherine's."

"Why wait? I mean, unless you're too tired? It would make our equal-time arrangement much simpler."

Overall, Trey's been pretty cool about me working with Kiernan. His one request is that any time I have a jump with Kiernan, I see him immediately after. And knowing Trey is back home waiting has generally worked very well as a counter-Kiernan charm.

"You could go now, see what he wants, and be back before room service arrives with dinner."

I don't know if it's the fact that we just got out of an elevator or the words *room service*, or both, but I'm suddenly reminded of our last disastrous experience with a hotel room. Trey must be thinking the same thing, because he gives me a rueful smile as he opens the door.

Fortunately, this room has just the double bed rather than a king-sized monstrosity like the room back in DC. There's also a living area beyond the bathroom, with a couch, a table, and a partial view of the Eye. The wheel spins slowly upward. Are Mom and Prudence in one of those neon-colored cars, sipping more *bubbles*?

"I'm afraid there are no chocolate-dipped strawberries this time," Trey says, then pulls me into a hug when he sees my expression. "I'm joking! Estella was very happy with those strawberries, by the way."

"Good. I'm glad somebody got something out of that nightmare. Trey, I am so, so—"

He presses a finger to my lips. "Hey. I got something out of it, too, Kate. It took you walking out—well, *blinking* out, I guess—to make me realize I can't sit on the fence. I'm in or I'm out, and if you're in, I'm in."

"But your parents—" I begin. He puts his finger back on my lips, grinning when I give it an annoyed little nip with my teeth.

"My parents will adjust. Like I told Dad, I'm eighteen. This is a war, with stakes higher than any other. If I'd walked in and told my parents that I was enlisting in the Marines, they'd have been angry, but they'd have acknowledged that it's my choice."

"Would your mom be angry if you went in the military? She's with the government, right?"

He laughs. "My mom would be ten times as angry as my dad about the military. The State Department is closer to Peace Corps than Marine Corps. But . . . she's worked with this Julia Waters. Not closely, but I remember Mom mentioning the name a few years ago. It's one of the few things that caused a duplicate memory for me. That and the whole Carrington Day barbecue—it makes my head hurt a little to think about those things. Like the deal with Prudence today at tea."

"You should have stayed away, Trey. Katherine and Connor should never have let you in the house. You don't have the CHRONOS gene, and we don't have any way of knowing what this could do—"

"Shh. Don't blame Katherine or Connor. They didn't even let me in the first time I knocked. Connor came to the door and said I needed to respect your decision. I sat there in the porch swing for a good half hour, hoping you'd come out, and then I got this . . . gut-churning feeling. I guess it was the time shift? After it passed, I went home, thinking I'd just call you in the morning. I was in the car when it occurred to me that Tilson might know someone who could analyze the sample you brought back from Georgia."

He stops, shaking his head. "He didn't remember ever meeting me. No memory at all of the retirement party. Said he retired from Briar Hill twelve years ago. But—here's the weird thing, Kate. He remembers meeting *you*, back in the 1990s. He wouldn't say anything else about it, though. Then I got right back in the car and drove to Katherine's. I banged on the door until Connor answered and practically pushed my way in so they'd listen."

He stops like he's waiting for me to say something, but I just stare down at the carpet. No matter how much he tries to shoulder the blame, he wouldn't have been in any sort of danger if I hadn't pulled him back into this mess. If I'd never tracked him down, never handed him that envelope, he'd be safe.

After a moment, he tips my chin up so that I have to look at him. "And don't blame yourself either, Kate. I made my choice, and you have to accept that. Just like my parents. My life, my choices. The only downside is that Mom and Dad may view you in the same light as a military recruiter, at least at first. They'll come around, though."

"You seem pretty sure about that, but—"

"I am. I think there's even a mathematical proof for it. Ask your dad. They love me, and I love you, so, ipso facto, they'll love you, too."

"I don't think it works that way. Otherwise the whole Romeo and Juliet story would have worked out different . . . ly."

When I realize what he just said, I reach up to take off his hat and the fake glasses. Then I pull his lips down to mine.

He just said *I love you*, and unlike the moment on the rooftop, there was no doubt in his voice, no hesitation. Just a simple statement.

And, ipso facto, my doubts are gone, too.

∞6∞

SOMEWHERE NEAR A BEACH
April 26, 1905, 7:00 p.m.

Given the date on the coordinates, I expect to see the cabin in Georgia or maybe the storeroom at Jess's tobacco shop when I blink in. But it's a hotel room, and instead of his usual jeans, Kiernan is in dark pants and a dress shirt, with a vest cut low in the front. There's a suit jacket over the back of the chair, a folded newspaper in his hand, and a cloth bag at his feet. He sits near the open window, staring out over a slate-colored sea. The sun hangs low on the horizon, giving the boardwalk and the small stretch of beach just beyond a grayish-orange glow.

The fact that he's looking out the window is almost as unexpected as the location. Before, if Kiernan was expecting me, his eyes were locked on the stable point. Even if he was angry, he still faced forward, almost like he had a physical need to see me the second I appeared.

I clear my throat softly, and he turns toward me.

He's grown a mustache and long sideburns. They don't suit him.

He gives me a perfunctory smile—not the wide, crazy grin I'm used to, but still better than a scowl.

"Where are we?" I ask.

"Eastbourne. Maybe fifty miles south of London."

"And why are we in Eastbourne?"

"Because Houdini's here," he says brusquely. "We should wrap up this one key from the past before dealing with present and future. And tonight's our best shot."

Kiernan hands me the newspaper, folded to reveal an advertisement:

The first appearance in Eastbourne of the world famous and Original HOUDINI. Winner of the great Handcuff Contest, as challenged by the London Illustrated Daily Mirror. *March 17, 1904. The Original. Not a Copy. The Original.*

Kiernan taps a heading about halfway down:

CHALLENGE!

HARRY HOUDINI, Hippodrome, Eastbourne

Dear Sir—You will pardon us, but we have figured it out that the Trunk Trick you are doing IS NOT GENUINE but is prepared, and we can prove it by challenging you to allow us to make an ordinary Packing Case of One Inch Deal into which we guarantee TO HAVE YOU NAILED AND ROPED up so that you CANNOT GET OUT without DEMOLISHING THE BOX. If you do not care to try it publicly, will you try it privately; if so let us know when to send the case and our men will be at your disposal.—Messrs. Cornwell & Son, Builders and Contractors, Grove-road and Ashford-road, Eastbourne.

Houdini Accepts the above Challenge For WEDNESDAY NIGHT, April 26, at the Hippodrome, Eastbourne. Everyone allowed to bring Hammer and Nails.

When I look up, Kiernan is dumping a hammer, nails, and a folded piece of notepaper from the cloth bag onto the bed.

"I've been snooping around his shows for the past few weeks here and in Scotland. Tried to arrange a meeting by handing one of his assistants the Boudini flyer several weeks back, which may explain the emphasis on originality in the ad you're holding. So I can't do this. You, however, might have a shot. The stage manager will be amused if a five-foot slip of a girl volunteers to drive a nail."

"Five foot three. And I can drive a nail. I built a treehouse once." I don't add that it tilted to one side and wouldn't have supported an overweight squirrel before Dad took over and brought it up to code. I might have confessed that to the younger Kiernan, but . . .

"Doesn't matter. These guys understand show business. They'll put you up front with a half dozen burly guys, just for visual effect."

"On stage?" Just saying those two words makes my heart pound.

"No," he says, giving me a look like I'm crazy. "Out back in the alley. Of course, *on stage.* Once you're up there, just get close enough to drop this note into Houdini's crate. And be sure your medallion is visible."

I unfold the note. A request for a private meeting at the bar inside the Queen's Hotel immediately after the show, above a rough sketch of the medallion. Below that is the question: *What color is the light for you?*

"Get this to him," Kiernan says, "and he'll meet with you."

"I don't think this is a good idea, Kiernan."

In fact, I think it's a horrible idea. I'm two steps away from a total freak-out merely contemplating stepping onto a stage. I've gradually reached a point where I can improvise fairly well on time jumps, but that type of performance has never petrified me like being onstage. I've only been on twice before—well, three times if you count the piano recital disaster when I was nine, but that wasn't actually a stage. The first time was in fifth grade. I was forced into a speaking role in the school play when some kid came down with the flu. Three years later, at middle school graduation, I tripped on the principal's microphone cord and fell face-first onto the stage, squashing the rolled-up diploma he'd just handed me.

I'm not inclined to admit this to Kiernan in his current mood, however. It probably wouldn't matter anyway since he's ignoring me. He walks to the closet and pulls out a dress. "It's a bit large, so I doubt you'll need a corset, but there's one in the dresser if you do. Shoes, bonnet, and so forth, in the closet. Hairpins and a brush are over there."

Kiernan turns to go, and I grab his arm. Julia's warning is blinking in my head like a big neon sign, and the change in his overall attitude isn't really helping to put me at ease.

"Wait. Could we talk first? I'd like some background going into this. I know Houdini was an escape artist and magician, but—"

"We need to get to the Hippodrome early so you're near the front," he says, pulling my hand away from his arm. "Get dressed. We can talk after the show."

I glance back at the showtime listed in the article—it reads 8 p.m. "Is the theater nearby?"

"A short walk."

Having experienced his idea of a short walk before, I know this can mean anything from three blocks to three miles. But before I can ask for clarification, he's gone.

I sigh and examine the dress. It's more elaborate than the 1905 outfit I wore in Boston, with yards of pale-green silk and an odd lace cape. Judging from the way it's arranged on the hanger, the cape drapes over the shoulders and rests just above my waist in the front, dipping down into a deep V in the back. With the low-cut bodice, I kind of like the idea of the lace in front, even if it does look sort of strange.

I soon discover this dress isn't equipped with Velcro down the back, so despite several minutes of twisting my body into a pretzel, some buttons remain unfastened.

I'm sitting on the bed trying to pull my hair back into something orderly when Kiernan walks in, not even bothering to knock. He curses softly when he sees I'm not ready and crosses over, quickly fastening the open buttons. Then he takes the brush and shifts the knot of hair to the side of my head before pinning the hat in place and tugging a few curls loose around my face.

All of this takes less than two minutes. Kiernan's expression is flat, businesslike, as he turns me around to check my appearance. His behavior is a seismic shift from a few weeks back—well, at least for me it was a few weeks back—when he helped me into the 1905 outfit he kept at Jess's store. Then, his fingers lingered on my skin, like he was looking for any excuse to make physical contact.

Now, it's like he's dressing a child who's late for the school bus—a child he doesn't especially like. I know I can't have it both ways. I should be relieved, and in one sense, I am. But this shift in his personality is too abrupt, too extreme, for me just to accept without question, especially after Julia raised doubts about his loyalty. I don't know what changed him, what turned him into someone I barely recognize, but we need to talk.

I grab his hand as he stashes the brush in the drawer. Again, he shakes me off and drops a black velvet ribbon in my lap. "Put your key on this. It looks stupid on the cord."

The shorter ribbon definitely works better with the dress and will make it harder for Houdini to miss, but again the words and his tone aren't in character. I attach the key to the ribbon and tie it behind my neck.

"Better?" I ask with a tentative smile.

"You'll do." He holds the evening bag out in my direction. "Now could we get moving?"

The smile freezes on my face. "Who peed in your coffee, Kiernan? Why are you acting this way?"

He lets out an annoyed huff and replies with mock patience. "Kate, we need to go or we'll be late. Do me a favor and at least *try* to act professional."

Both his tone of voice and the words are clearly intended as a slap in the face. I feel tears spring to my eyes and look away to hide them. There's a brief glimmer of something that looks like remorse in his expression when I glance back, but he gets it under control quickly.

"Fine." I snatch the purse from his hand. "But as soon as we're done, you *will* tell me what the hell is going on with you."

∞

Kiernan wasn't exaggerating. The Hippodrome is less than three minutes from the Queen's Hotel. For the first two blocks we use the boardwalk. Flocks of seagulls swoop along the beach, and they have the place pretty much to themselves. One lone couple huddles together on a driftwood log a yard or so beyond the reach of the tide. It's cold—cold enough that I wish Kiernan had added a coat to my costume rather than this useless cape.

The theater is a block in from the shore. It's general admission, and there are already people milling about, so perhaps Kiernan was right to suggest arriving early. Of course, he could easily have set the coordinates so that I jumped in an hour or two before the show and avoided a last-minute rush.

We push our way through to the front of the theater so that I'll be in position once they start asking for volunteers. Kiernan put the hammer and nails into the little evening bag I'm holding, and the handle sticks out in plain view. It looks stupid, and I wonder if Kiernan's preparations aren't overplaying my assigned role as the helpless little woman.

There are maybe three hundred seats in front of us as we enter the plush red auditorium, so my first impression is that it's much smaller than the one at Norumbega where Kiernan performed his Boudini act. Then I glance up and see that there are two seating levels above us. Most of those seats are already filled, so I'm guessing they're the less expensive option.

I locate two vacant chairs in the second row, just to the left of center. Kiernan puts his program on the seat next to me and says he'll be back later. "Keep an eye out for a stage manager." He nods at a door to the side of the stage that's slightly ajar. "Then announce loudly that you have hammer and nails. And don't get all pissy if they laugh at you."

"Why should I take it personally? I didn't pick this costume, so they'll be laughing at you, not me."

A faint ghost of his old grin surfaces, but disappears almost immediately. He heads toward the back of the theater. The seats around me start to fill over the next few minutes, with a good quarter of the spectators holding hammers and nails.

Eventually, a harried-looking man pushes the door open. He looks around and disappears again. A minute or so later, he comes back out holding a small pad of paper.

"I see a lot more hammers than we expected. Mr. Houdini would be delighted to have each and ever' one of you pound in a nail or two, but I think the local fire brigade might advise against a mob on the stage. So we'll take an even dozen."

Hands fly up. Some of the volunteers, all of them men, stand. Several look like they might be professional wrestlers, if they even have those in 1905. I wave my hand fervently, but the stage manager doesn't see me. He hands a little slip of paper to six or seven men, clearly going for the biggest and brawniest.

The fact that I'm a head or two shorter than everyone around me isn't helping. Although the chair doesn't look especially sturdy, it should hold my weight, so I yank the seat down and climb up. Once I catch my balance, I wave the handbag. "Pick me!"

Several people around me start to laugh. A few jeers are mixed in as well.

"You've picked only men." I'm suddenly conscious of my American accent in the sea of Brits and the fact that everyone is staring. "I think they're in on the game—you're paying them. Why not give a girl a chance?"

The manager rolls his eyes. "Sorry, miss, already picked my dozen—"

"So make it a baker's dozen," someone yells from the back.

"Bet she can't hit the bloody nail anyway. Give us somethin' to laugh at." That voice is clearly Kiernan's, and most of the men chuckle.

A woman near the front throws a dirty look in Kiernan's direction. "Twelve men and no women hardly seems fair."

Another man calls out, "I say give 'em the hammer and maybe they'll quit yappin' about wantin' the vote."

I'm thinking that *give 'em the hammer* could be taken two ways. Apparently the woman who asked for a bit of gender equity agrees, because her mouth tightens.

The stage manager shrugs. "Fine, we'll make it unlucky thirteen. If anything happens to Mr. Houdini, it'll be on your conscience, lady." He rips off another scrap of paper and hands it to me. "Now get down offa the chair an' behave."

He glances around at the others he selected. "The challenge comes at the end of the show. When they bring out the crate, you'll come onstage. Houdini'll most likely joke around a bit, then he'll climb in, and we'll close the lid. Each of you steps forward in turn. Two nails each—we ain't got all night."

He slips back through the stage door, and I sink down into my chair.

Kiernan comes back about ten minutes later and takes his seat. "Good work."

I snort. "Don't give me that. I heard you back there."

"Just seeding the crowd. A time-honored practice among showmen and politicians alike. When you get up there, make sure you're at the front of the line, before they close the crate. I slipped a few bob to the guy at the back and told him to yell out 'Ladies first,' so I'm guessing it won't be a problem." He runs his eyes over me quickly and then pauses to give my breasts a longer look. There's no lechery involved, however—it's like he's debating their effect. "Take off the cape thing and leave it here."

I give him a scathing look and then reach behind me to unclasp the lace bolero. Once it's off, I fling it into his lap. "Happy now?" I ask.

His mouth tweaks upward slightly, and I can't help but think that this new Kiernan would give Charlayne's friend Bensen some competition as the master of understated facial expressions. In Bensen's case, I had the sense that it was just his nature. Kiernan, on the other hand, has rarely tried to hide his feelings from me— good or bad, mutual or not. Or if he's tried, he's never been successful. Now, it's as though everything he does and says is an act.

Then the curtain goes up, and I turn my attention to the act on the stage.

∞

Houdini's two female assistants—one of whom is his wife, Bess—shackled and chained him well over ten minutes ago. Then they pulled a curtain around him so he could contort in private and retreated to the side of the stage.

A twenty-first-century audience would have yawned and walked out long ago, but the people in the Hippodrome stare intently at the curtain that hides Houdini. A few read the theater program while others chat softly with their companions. The rest have their eyes glued to the stage, waiting. The piano player's selection of music seems designed to build anticipation. Every now and then there's a collective intake of breath as Houdini's elbow or some other body part bumps against the fabric. Mostly, however, they just watch and wait.

A bright blue light is visible above the curtain and through a few areas along the bottom, but I'm pretty sure that no one besides Kiernan, Houdini, and I can see it. I'm not really sure where Kiernan is, in fact. He mumbled some excuse and left before Houdini first came onstage.

This is Houdini's fourth trick of the evening, with each clearly designed to build momentum for the main event. The first act was a card trick, followed by something called Metamorphosis. Houdini's hands were tied, then he was placed in a large bag and locked inside a trunk. Bess pulled a curtain in front of herself and the box. Next, we heard three quick claps, and when the curtain opened, Houdini was out of the box and Bess was inside, tied in the bag.

The third bit was an escape from a milk can filled with water, a trick that Houdini began performing a few years back. I remember seeing that one on some TV show I saw a long time ago, *Inside the*

Magic or something like that, so I know the secret. The top of the can isn't welded on. He just pushes upward and climbs out.

Suddenly the red curtain flies open, and Houdini struts toward the audience holding the chains and shackles triumphantly above his head. He started out in a tuxedo, gradually stripping down during the various acts to the black tank suit he's now wearing, much like the one Kiernan wore at Norumbega.

Houdini's eyes are dark and piercing, easily his most distinctive feature. Although he's not tall, his frame is muscular. Dark hair is parted in the middle, and some attempt was made to slick it down in deference to current fashion, but it doesn't seem to appreciate the efforts to tame it.

Before this trick began, Houdini had a few volunteers inspect the gear, making sure the chains were real and he wasn't hiding a key somewhere. One of them looked inside his mouth, and another examined the medallion around his neck. It's attached to a leather strap and tucked into the top of his swimsuit. Of course, to everyone else in the audience, the key looks like a plain bronze disk, wafer thin, of no possible use in an escape.

What puzzles me is that I've yet to see the blue light from his key disappear. In the first two escapes, it was cloaked by the box and the milk can, but this time, I could see the light above and below the curtain. Houdini never blinked out, even for a second.

The crowd applauds, complete with whistles and cheers. Houdini bows a few times, then nods toward his assistants, extending the applause to them. They curtsy, and once the noise dies down, Houdini hands the chains to Bess. Then he walks toward the audience, standing perfectly still until everyone is silent.

"Ladies . . . and . . . gentlemen," he begins, his voice loud and clear, with a hint of an accent I can't place. "I take great pleasure in having you here tonight to witness this next escape. Some have claimed that my talents are supernatural, but I assure you they are based on skill and athleticism alone, with no help from the great beyond. Other claims, however, are even more troubling than those of supernatural assistance. As many of you may be aware, a certain . . . party . . . here in Eastbourne has stated that I am a fraud."

He pauses as a mix of boos and laughter ripples through the room. "These individuals apparently do not accept the word of your police who publicly attested that I escaped from their jail this past Monday. These men insist that the escapes you have witnessed tonight are stage trickery and sleight of hand. And they believe they have devised a container that can contain . . . the great Houdini."

His eyes travel across the first few rows as he continues. "They have issued their chal—" He startles when his eyes reach my seat. What's confusing is that he's looking directly at my face. He doesn't seem to even notice the medallion, despite the fact that it's front and center on my now mostly exposed chest. He stares at me for several seconds, his eyes never once veering down toward the CHRONOS key.

When Houdini recovers, he raises his arms, looking out over the audience. "They have issued their challenge, and I will meet it this very evening."

The lighting changes, and two men wheel a large box to the center of the stage. The younger guy has a coil of rope flung over his shoulder. Houdini introduces them as Cornwell and Son, the builders who issued the challenge in the paper, and then says, "I don't suppose anyone happens, just by chance, to have a hammer and nails?"

Everyone laughs. About a third of the audience raises a hammer.

"Excellent! The people of Eastbourne come prepared."

I take that as my cue to move to the side of the stage. None of the other volunteers have begun to line up, but they start moving when I do. The twelve men follow, forming an orderly line behind me. It seems that Kiernan was right to assume that his bribe was unnecessary.

Houdini gives me a nervous glance and then looks back out at the crowd. "This young lady seems very eager. Are you certain you can strike a nail, miss?"

The audience snickers, but I just nod and climb the four stairs up to the stage before I lose my nerve.

On a strictly logical level, I know most of the people in the theater aren't actually staring at me. Almost all of them are watching Cornwell and Son as they tie up Houdini.

But my mind doesn't operate on a logical level when I'm onstage, and my body seems to go on strike. I have to remind my lungs to pull in a breath, but my nerves are on full alert. I feel every single eye in the auditorium physically touching me, crawling all over me like ants on a candy bar.

As the men tie the final knots in the ropes, Houdini nods toward the left side of the stage where we're standing. "I want to thank these members of the audience who have agreed to assist me in this challenge. Your actions tonight will help clear my good name. For these two gentlemen are mistaken. I am not a fraud, not a charlatan, not a fake. I am the one, the only, the *original* Houdini."

Just as I'm wondering how he'll get into the crate with his legs bound, the younger man grabs Houdini's shoulders and the older one grabs his feet. They hoist Houdini up and begin to lower him into the crate. As soon as he's inside, they reach behind the box for the lid.

"Wait!" My mouth is dry and it comes out as a croak, so I try again. "Wait!"

The men pause, holding the lid a few feet above the crate. Now everyone in the theater really *is* looking at me.

I gulp and rush forward, dropping the hammer and nails. "A kiss! I want to give Houdini a kiss for luck."

The audience is howling now. Houdini sits up in the crate, his dark hair and widow's peak making him resemble Count Dracula. He glances into the auditorium, where a bulky guy who is probably a bodyguard is hurrying down the outside aisle toward the stage.

But the audience is clearly eating this up—it's probably the Edwardian equivalent of a girl throwing her panties on the stage at a rock concert—and Houdini's inner showman wins out over his sense of caution. He shakes his head once, very distinctly, and the bodyguard pulls to a halt three rows from the stage, still watching me but not advancing.

Then Houdini smiles at the crowd. "What do you think?"

Someone yells, "Kiss her!"

"It would be very ungallant of me to refuse," he says, and then continues in a stage whisper, "but only on the cheek, dear. My wife is watching."

He's definitely correct on that point. Bess is standing in the wings looking straight at me. But her eyes aren't fixed on my face. She's staring at the CHRONOS key.

Leaning forward slightly, I brush Houdini's cheek with my lips. I make sure he sees the folded note before I tuck it inside the front of his suit.

And then I run from the stage, down the steps, and straight up the aisle to the exit. As much as I'd love to stay and do my part for women's rights, if I swing that hammer right now, I'll miss the nail and smash my thumb.

The street is empty now, probably because most of the residents and tourists are inside the Hippodrome watching Houdini. I head back the way we came, toward the ocean, picking up my pace both because it's cold and damp and because I want as much distance as possible between me and that stage.

Kiernan catches up to me before I'm even a block away and tosses me the lace cape. "Well, that was an interesting spectacle."

I catch the cape and pull it over my shoulders, glaring at him the entire time. "He has your damned note. Are you happy? I hate being on stage. *Hate* it."

"Really?" He looks genuinely surprised. More to the point, for that brief moment, he looks *genuine*. He looks like the Kiernan I know.

"I've hated it since I was a kid. What—your Kate never told you that?"

He doesn't answer, making me wonder if his Kate somehow dodged stage fright. Maybe she didn't stumble over her lines in that stupid play—or maybe the other kid never got the flu in the first place.

It's a rare occasion for me to mention something about myself that Kiernan doesn't already know, and it's clearly caught him off guard. And while his mask is down, I want some answers.

"Okay, I did my part. Now it's your turn. What have you been up to for the past six years?" I'm tempted to add that he should start with whatever it was that turned him into a total jerk, but I decide to keep that bit to myself.

"You're not done yet, Kate. You still have to convince him to give us the bloody key. That was the final act of the show, so you need to get over to the Queen's Hotel and—"

"You mean *we* need to get over there. You're coming with, right?"

"No. As I said before, he's more likely to give it to you than to me. His guards and I already had a run-in in Edinburgh. That's why I stayed at the back tonight. It's why I'm wearing this stupid mustache."

"I don't think he's using the key, Kiernan. The light—it never disappeared, even for a moment, when he did the escape behind the curtain. And you're the one who's been researching him. If you expected me to do this alone, why not bring me in earlier so you could brief me?"

"Playing triple agent doesn't leave much time. You knew Houdini was coming up, so why didn't you bother to research him yourself?"

"When? *When* could I have done that, Kiernan? You may have had six years, but things have been kind of hectic the past few days—and yes, it's still days for me since we were at Norumbega. On top of that, I've only had a few hours of not-exactly-peaceful sleep since I left you in Georgia."

I draw in a deep breath, planning to continue my rant, but I stop mid-inhale and stare at him, adding together the bits of odd behavior he's displayed since showing up outside Mom's hotel room. There's only one reason for him to have cut things this close. He needs help getting the key, and he doesn't want to spend any more time with me than absolutely necessary. But why?

I know we need to get Houdini's key, but I can't fully trust Kiernan until I figure out why he's acting so strangely. And there's no way I'm going into this meeting without more information. Kiernan seems convinced that Houdini is using the key. I'm less convinced. I'd also like a better sense of when and where he got the damned thing.

"So that's all you're going to tell me? All the information you're going to give me before you expect me to walk in alone to a meeting with a man that you've admitted has armed bodyguards?"

"I'll be nearby—"

"To do what? Patch me up after his security guys shoot me?"

I give him one last angry look and speed ahead of him, ducking into an alley between two weathered wooden buildings, and yank on the velvet ribbon at the back of my neck. My CHRONOS key falls into the palm of my hand. When I pull up the display

I see Trey on the phone in his hotel room ordering dinner. The messenger bag with his laptop rests near his feet. The information I can get with that computer might not be the firsthand research Kiernan has been conducting, but since he doesn't seem inclined to share that, it will have to do.

"What are you doing?" Kiernan asks.

I check the time—9:52—and flick my thumb to set a local point. "You hang tight. I'll be back."

"Kate—"

∞ 7 ∞

PARK PLAZA, LONDON
September 10, 9:14 p.m.

Trey breaks off his conversation with room service when I blink in, stifling a laugh. He stops when he sees my expression, even though it's not him I'm angry at.

I'm not even sure why he's laughing until I glance down and realize I'm still in the stupid 1905 evening dress.

"Sorry," he says, although I don't know if he's apologizing to me or to the person taking our order.

He hangs up a few seconds later and smiles. "That was quick. You look very pretty. But I didn't know this dinner was going to be formal."

"It's not. In fact, it's going to be a working dinner. I really hope you have a spare shirt or pj's or something, because I can't work in this horrible thing."

Five hours later, we have a growing Houdini dossier, between the various online articles, a few fan sites, and three e-books I downloaded. We're curled up in our usual position on the couch, and I'm happy to discover that we work very well as a research team, with me skimming the material on my tablet and Trey typing and organizing my "notes" on his laptop.

I didn't read the books thoroughly, but just browsed through looking for things that seemed relevant. The first book argued that Houdini was some sort of spy during World War I. While I wasn't entirely convinced on that point, the author presented some fairly solid evidence to support the assertion. Book number two covered Houdini's friendship with Arthur Conan Doyle, the guy who wrote the Sherlock Holmes books, and their mutual fascination with the possibility of communicating with the dead. The final book was actually written by Houdini, but I'm a little suspicious of any autobiography, especially one written by a celebrity. How much is true and how much is simply what Houdini, as an entertainer, wanted his adoring public to believe?

Between the various sources, there are three different stories about how he met his wife, Bess. A half-dozen accounts, all differing on key points, tell about the encounter with a fan that may or may not have led to Houdini's death. And there are any number of theories about how he managed some of his more daring escapes.

The one thing that sticks out for me is the fact that Houdini worked on the Midway Plaisance at the 1893 World's Fair. He wasn't a headliner or anything, just one teenage magician among many. Depending on which source you believe, he was either performing as part of The Brothers Houdini or he was a street magician, in disguise as a Hindu fakir. One source says he probably did both, working the streets during the day and then doing his trademark Metamorphosis trick as part of The Brothers Houdini act in the evenings.

Trey reads the passage I point out and hands the tablet back. "It could be another coincidence, Kate. They do happen—take the bit you read a minute ago about Houdini and this Harry Kellar. Almost the same name as your dad, but there's no connection.

They just share slightly different versions of a common name. Like you said before, the Exposition drew a lot of performers. Anyone who could afford the trip to Chicago went, because that's where they'd stand the best chance of making money in a tight economy."

I nod reluctantly. He's right, but . . .

"It was also a big draw for those who traveled with CHRONOS keys," I argue. "Mostly Katherine and Saul, but Katherine said a few other CHRONOS agents trained there, both during her time and before. And then you have CHRONOS The Next Generation. I was there. Kiernan was there. So was his dad, and Prudence, and Simon. I'm thinking maybe someone lost a key. It's the most logical answer to how it ended up in Houdini's hands."

"So Houdini found it? And he just happened to be one of a handful of people on earth who inherited the gene that allows him to use it? I don't know. That seems like an even bigger coincidence to me than the possibility that Houdini is descended from one of the stranded CHRONOS agents. Or maybe one of the historians fooled around with Houdini's mom, or his grandma, and she swiped the guy's spare key as a memento?"

That sounds crazy to me, but he's right. It's not any crazier than someone losing a key at the World's Fair and Houdini just happening to have inherited the gene that would allow him to use it.

"The actual CHRONOS agents didn't carry spares," I say. "I remember Katherine being all bent out of shape because I had two keys when we were stuck in Hotel Hell. So if someone lost a spare key, it was one of their descendants."

I push the tray with the remains of our dinner to the side so that I can put the computers on the coffee table. Then I lean my head on Trey's shoulder. It's nearly 2 a.m., and the lack of sleep is hitting both of us.

"I guess it doesn't really matter how or where Houdini got the key. Not unless I plan to go back and prevent him from getting it. And I don't. It would be almost impossible to pinpoint the date or location, especially if he didn't get the key at the Expo. But I want to check Katherine's library before I do anything else, see if there are any differences between the timelines."

"So Kiernan's plan to confront him in Eastbourne still makes the most sense, right?"

"Yes," I admit, "but I don't believe for a second that Houdini's going to hand the key over without a fight. The guy has body-guards, plural. I'm not willing to shoot anyone to get the key, and Kiernan isn't going to be at the meeting, so—"

"Why not?"

"He says that they'll recognize him. That we'll have a better chance of getting the key if I go in alone."

Trey raises his eyebrows. "But you don't believe him."

I shrug. "Kiernan may be right about that. He's been in their face for several weeks. He was wearing a truly stupid-looking mustache tonight as a disguise and stayed near the back of the theater, so I think he's trying to avoid Houdini's people connecting me to him. It's more . . . it's just . . ." I let out a long sigh of frustration. "I can't put my finger on it, but something's wrong, Trey. He's different. Not just older, but . . . fundamentally different."

"So you don't think it's the same Kiernan? Are you thinking this is like a different version of him, from some other timeline, or . . . ?"

"I guess that's not *impossible*, but no, I don't think so. There's this scar on his forehead that's the same—I mean, it's older now, and faded, but the same spot. It's more that his personality is different."

I try to think of some way to phrase this diplomatically, in a way that won't hurt Trey's feelings, but I'm exhausted, and nothing is coming to mind, so I just blurt it out. "He was in love with me before, Trey. It was obvious in everything he did and said, in the way he looked at me. And while I'm glad he's moved on, it's like he can't bear to be around me. Like he hates me."

Trey shakes his head. "Nope. I didn't get that at all. And in case you didn't notice, I was paying pretty close attention when he was around. I think a more obvious explanation is that it bothered him to see me here, in London with you. And maybe he's pushing you away to keep from getting hurt even more."

I consider this, and on the surface, Trey may be right. Still, I can't shake the feeling that something deeper is going on. I just hope it's not what Julia thinks.

"Okay," Trey says. "Enough about Kiernan. When is your meeting with Julia?"

"Tomorrow morning. Nine o'clock." My voice very clearly conveys my lack of enthusiasm.

"I'd happily go with you, if not for the fact that I'll be somewhere over the Atlantic," he says. "My flight leaves at eight thirty, and even with the time zone difference, I'm still not scheduled to land until early afternoon."

"You're not going to get much sleep. And even if you were back in time, they've only given me coordinates. I don't have a physical address. But I'll make it clear that you're included from here on out."

"What about Tilson?"

"I don't know if he'll be at the meeting or not. All I know is Julia had his name, along with Charlayne's, and said that she pulled them both into the group to make me feel 'safe and cozy.'"

"No. I was wondering about the sample. Did you get a chance to talk to Katherine and Connor about getting it to him?"

"Remember? The walls have ears—our computers could be bugged as well. We're going to have to resort to scribbling notes to each other."

"Not good. I've seen your handwriting." I dig my elbow into his ribs and he laughs. "Just . . . tell Katherine and Connor that I'm not pushing Tilson. I didn't give him any specific information about what we needed. I think he can be trusted—I mean, you heard him at the barbecue . . ." He shakes his head, and I know the dual memory is bothering him.

"Yeah. And I also *didn't* hear him. Let's just try not to think about it."

"Works for me. Anyway, what I mean to say is that if Tilson is with Julia and you decide you don't trust her . . ."

"Then what? We put an ad in the paper: *Scientist needed to analyze dangerous substance. No Cyrists allowed*?" A yawn hits me, and I cover my face with my hands and nestle into that curve between his shoulder and his chest that seems tailor-made for my head. "You were right to call Tilson. He's our best bet. And if he was telling you the truth about meeting me in the 1990s, then I'm pretty sure the die is already cast."

∞

BETHESDA, MARYLAND
September 10, 9:00 p.m.

I woke up a few minutes ago on the couch in Trey's hotel room with my head on a pillow rather than his chest. We must have both crashed there, because the bed was undisturbed, aside from the missing pillow. I have a vague memory of him getting up, but that's it. A little note was leaning against a water glass on the coffee table:

Didn't want to wake you, but had to leave early to catch the first flight back to DC. Love you—will call when I land at Dulles. Trey

So I gathered up the dress I wore to the Hippodrome and jumped from 8:22 a.m. London time back to 9 p.m. last night, Bethesda time, really wishing that Trey could have taken the same shortcut.

I was really tempted to jump back to morning so that I'd be on the same schedule as the rest of the world. But I have several hours of work to do before I meet with Julia, and I'd rather be on time. If she's under a key, would she have a double memory if I missed the meeting but jumped back in order to attend? I'm not sure, but thinking about it gives me enough of a headache that I'd prefer to just avoid the problem if possible.

I change out of the clothes I borrowed from Trey and walk down the hall to the library. A profuse blue light fills the room, both from the keys at the center and from the lighted tubes that run up the walls between the bookshelves. I don't know how it works, but this contraption of Connor's keeps the keys in a state of perpetual activation and magnifies the CHRONOS field so that we're theoretically safe without a key anywhere in the house and most of the yard. I say *theoretically*, because it's really more of a backup system now. I wear a key even in the shower, and I suspect that Connor and Katherine do the same. The device here in the library emits a faint hum that I rarely notice unless the room is quiet, like it is now. It's enough to keep Daphne out, despite the fact that there are always lots of tasty crumbs under Connor's chair.

Connor is at the computer now, focusing closely on the screen. He has his headphones on, so he doesn't hear me come in. I'm pretty sure that he's playing one of his strategy games until I get closer and see the spreadsheet he's looking at.

I toss the formal dress from 1905 onto the chair next to him. He glances up, removing the headphones.

"Did you decide to do a bit of shopping in London?"

I give him a wry smile. "Does this look like something I'd buy? Your great-grandfather picked it out. I just need you to stash it with the other costumes for a while." I nod toward the screen. "What's this?"

He slides a bit to the side, and I pull up Katherine's chair so that I can see. "It's an updated—well, partially updated—version of the spreadsheet Trey's father put together with summaries of the various Cyrist financial holdings. It's . . . kind of puzzling."

"How so?"

"Well, the existence of this—" Connor breaks off. He just stares at me for a minute, then mutters a curse under his breath. "Come on. I need some fresh air."

I give him a baffled look and follow him downstairs, through the kitchen.

When I see the patio door, Connor's motivation hits me—he can't talk because of the surveillance.

I follow him into the backyard. I'm still barefoot, and the grass is wet, so I'm guessing we had an early evening shower. The bench swing is covered with droplets, too. Connor wipes the seat with the bottom of his shirt, and we both plop down.

"This is a pain in the ass," he says softly. "I've ordered something that will counteract any conventional means they're using to monitor the house. I'm going to check the post office box in the morning and see if it's arrived. Anyway . . . what I was about to say. The existence of this Fifth Column kind of had me hoping that Cyrist International would be weaker. That they'd have been doing something from the inside. I mean, that's sort of the point of a fifth column, right?"

I nod, and he goes on. "But from what I can tell, the Cyrists are stronger than ever. I'd say maybe ten percent larger, in terms of membership, and maybe twenty percent richer. Their revenues exceed the GDP of some countries—decent-sized countries at that. Unlike a lot of other religions, that wealth is fairly concentrated at the central level."

"And you're wondering why that's still the case, even after the Fifth Column?"

"No," he says. "I'm wondering why it's *even more the case* than before. That doesn't make a lot of sense to me." He shrugs. "Anyway, I take it you found your mom? And Trey found you?"

"Yes to both. But the situation with Mom is complicated. Where's Katherine?"

"She went to bed a little early, but I doubt she's asleep yet. I'll go get her." He pushes himself up off the swing. "There's coffee, if you'd like. The weak froofy stuff you and Harry seem to enjoy."

I snort, following him. "It's not weak. We just prefer something that won't eat a hole in the mug."

Ten minutes later, I'm back on the swing with my coffee and a banana muffin that's too stale to be very good, but I'm hungry and didn't want to rummage around for anything else. Daphne comes bounding across the lawn, followed by Katherine, and Connor, who's carrying a couple of chairs from the patio.

Daphne puts her head in my lap, along with one damp, grass-covered paw, so I use petting her as momentary excuse to avoid looking at Katherine. This is the second time in the past few days that I've come back from a mission with a sense of failure—first, failing to get the keys from Abel and Delia and now not convincing Mom to come back to DC. I can only hope that there will be a silver lining to this cloud as well, although Connor's comment about the current strength levels of Cyrist International has me wondering whether that first silver lining is real.

This entire Fifth Column thing could be a trap. Maybe it's Julia who can't be trusted instead of Kiernan? Or maybe I can't trust either of them.

I push all of that aside for now. Katherine is sitting across from me, holding the tablet and diary from my meeting with Julia in her lap, along with some papers and a green file folder with *KATE'S HOMEWORK* scrawled across the front in Connor's handwriting. That brings a little smile to my lips, but it quickly disappears when I look back up at Katherine's face.

"So," she says, "when is Deborah coming home?"

"I told her everything. She's not coming back."

Katherine's expression barely changes, but I can see the little light of hope in her eyes flicker out.

"She isn't siding against us. It's just . . . Mom thinks she can be of more use there, with Prudence, than she'll be here. And she may be right."

I spend the next few minutes recounting the events in Julia's office, in London, my brief jump to 1905, and Kiernan's odd behavior.

Katherine, who has been silent the entire time, finally speaks up when I get to the part about Kiernan. "Do you still trust him?"

"I . . . *want* to trust him. And I think I do, deep down. Were you able to pull up the video of Delia from the diary?"

Katherine shakes her head, looking a little embarrassed, and hands me the tablet and the diary. "I tried, but . . . I think the medicines interfere. Or maybe Fred himself."

"Fred?"

"The tumor. I named it after the rabbiroo I had as a kid. Just like this tumor, he was a wicked little devil with a tendency to bite."

Okay. I don't really have a response to that, other than to ask what in hell a *rabbiroo* is. As that question seems likely to lead us away from the topic at hand, I just nod.

"No problem. I just thought you might be able to pick up something I didn't, but the message was pretty straightforward. Delia said to trust my heart where Kiernan is concerned. Julia blames him for the death of her son—Max's dad—so she's not really seeing things in an unbiased fashion. And Trey thinks . . ."

I pause and glance at Katherine, unsure how she'll react to me pulling in his assessment of the situation. But she just looks at me, eyebrows slightly raised, waiting for me to go on.

"Trey thinks we can trust him. He says he watched Kiernan the entire time we were at tea with Prudence, and he doesn't believe Kiernan would do anything to hurt me. And yes, he's basing that on just one meeting, but . . ."

"If anyone had an incentive to want you *not* to trust Kiernan, it would be Trey," Connor says. "And he might be a better judge in this than you are, Kate. Trey isn't comparing Kiernan to before. He's looking at what's there, what meets the eye now." He wads up his empty chip bag and shoves it into his pocket. "I'm probably not the best judge either because I really don't want to go back to thinking that my great-grandfather was . . . or is . . . an ass. So I hope Trey's right."

"Well, then," Katherine says, "what's next? Are you going back to Eastbourne to get the key from Houdini?"

I haven't actually decided that yet, so I look up at the moths that are circling around the light by the garage door and take a moment to think it through. Maybe Trey is right and I should trust the inner voice that tells me Kiernan is still on our side. But I want more information about what's been going on with the Fifth Column before I face him again. And I think I need a little more time to process the idea that, whether friend or foe, he's no longer the person I knew. And the delay won't make any difference to Kiernan, since when I do go back, it will be to the same moment that I left. He's not standing around on the sidewalk waiting for me to arrive, although there's a part of me that would be perfectly okay with that. Let Kiernan see how *he* likes being left hanging for a change.

"Not yet," I say. "I'll wait until after this meeting with Julia. Before I go, I want to dig into some of the files in the library—previous timeline stuff about Houdini."

Katherine presses her lips into a tight line. "Do you think Julia will know you didn't keep the promise about London?"

"I don't know. She's already annoyed at me anyway. I think she believed we'd just hand over the keys we've collected. On the video, Delia said they only have the one, so I guess that's the one Max had last night. Let's just say Julia wasn't too happy when I told her we'd destroyed most of them."

Connor is about to say something when a noise comes from his shirt pocket. It takes a moment, but I recognize it as the theme from *Jaws*. He pulls out his phone and glances at the screen, frowns, then puts it back.

"What was that?" I ask.

"The news alert I set up for when there's a Cyrist-related event in the press. Nothing major—just one of Patterson's judicial appointments confirmed by the Senate. What was I about to say?"

Katherine and I shake our heads, and then Connor remembers. "Oh. The medallions. I kept back two spares, like I said I would, if you think we're better off with Julia under a key. If nothing else, it would be a peace offering in case she's pissed."

"Not a bad idea. But hey, if she knows about London and she's angry, then she's angry. Lying to her might not be the best foot to start out on, but she practically kidnapped me the other night, so she hasn't been on her best behavior, either. Or maybe that *is* her best behavior. It's kind of hard to say, when I know almost nothing about her."

"I think I can help you there," Connor says, taking the file folder and other items Katherine's holding. "You can read the full file, but to sum up, Julia Morrell Waters is a big deal. Cyrist government liaison for two administrations prior to President

Patterson—who's now on her second term, by the way. Defeated the incumbent the first time she ran, instead of getting trounced. Waters is on the board of half a dozen foundations and frequent speaker at congressional hearings. She was also an ambassador during Patterson's first term, but she's retired now."

I flip open the folder and pull out a picture of Julia, seated in front of an American flag. A tight semi-smile is the only break in her otherwise stern face.

I stare at the photograph, and again I feel a twinge of anxiety. I decide to give it voice and see what Katherine and Connor think.

"Here's the thing that bothers me. Julia . . . she doesn't seem like a nice person. Even her own mom kind of admitted that. Did you read the liability waiver she wants me to sign? Why would she include something to protect Cyrist International?"

"Maybe it was just a standard form?" Connor suggests. "One that she's used for years, and she forgot to zap the Cyrist portion? You didn't sign it, did you?"

"No! And I'm not going to. I'm not enlisting in her private army, and this isn't a job. I just can't help but wonder whether it goes deeper. Maybe she sold out? Maybe this Fifth Column thing is a trap?"

"Maybe," Connor says. "Although it would be really, really dumb for her to leave the words 'Cyrist International' in the middle of that legal mumbo-jumbo if she's working for them, wouldn't it? She'd have to know that would put you on alert."

"That's true," Katherine says. "Although, either way, it raises red flags for me, too." She takes Julia's picture from me and stares at it, like I did, as though a printout of an 8 by 10 photo could provide a glimpse into the woman's soul.

After a moment, she shakes her head and hands it back to me. "Let's look at this another way. If this Fifth Column is a trap, where does that leave us? From what Connor has told me, the Cyrists are stronger than ever, and we have no other allies. It won't matter whether we walk into the trap or we wait until they bring the fight to us. Either way, the pooch is screwed."

It's such a totally un-Katherine-like thing to say that I choke on my coffee, trying to hold in a laugh. Connor doesn't even bother to hold it in.

"What?" Katherine asks. "You disagree?"

"Nope," Connor says, still smiling. "You're right. If this is a trap, that pretty much sums it up."

"Then why on earth would you find that amusing?" She shakes her head and looks at both of us before getting up to head back into the house. "You two have the strangest sense of humor sometimes."

Connor doesn't follow her. His smile fades very quickly, and I can tell that something is bothering him.

"What is it?"

He shakes his head, but turns on the tablet. "I've backed all of these up, so you can return their tablet. I couldn't do anything with the diary, of course."

Once the icons come up, he clicks to open the timeline. "It's probably nothing. I was just thinking about these dates—the ones labeled *Deadline*? One's 2024, then 2025, and 2034. I'm thinking those are probably—"

"Their best guesses on the date Saul set for the Culling."

"Yeah." Connor clicks to open the timeline chart. "So I was kind of curious about the strike-throughs here—when they crossed out those dates and why. And as much as I usually hate the whole track changes feature, it's actually useful this time. The first two must have already been crossed out before they turned on track changes, but the last two edits are a lot more recent."

He goes into the review panel and changes it from *Final* to *Final Showing Markup*, and a number of little balloons pop up in the side margin. Some of them are pink and labeled *JMW*. Others are green and labeled *KPK*.

"I used your initials," Connor says. "So she won't know you outsourced your homework."

Two of the changes deal with the *Deadlines* box. One, made by JMW, is the strike-through for the 2034 date. Connor taps that balloon, and a date pops up showing when the edit was made—three days ago, just before my meeting with Julia.

It's the second balloon that's interesting, however. It was edited by JMW at the same time, but instead of the four question marks that are now showing, it once held a specific date: *12252015*.

I give Connor a nervous glance. "Saul can't use the key. And from everything I've seen, I really do think he'd want to be there to survey his handiwork in person. Maybe Julia removed that date because she realized he couldn't possibly be planning for the Culling to happen that quickly."

Connor must hear the hopeful note in my voice, because his eyes soften. "Maybe. Or maybe she's worried it's going to happen sooner."

∞

Connor and Katherine go to bed around eleven, and I spend the next few hours in Katherine's library combing through the books and files that have been protected by a CHRONOS field. There's a good deal of information about Houdini's life in the pre-Cyrist timeline, most of it identical to what Trey and I found last night on the web. The only thing that stands out as markedly different is a description of the book on the friendship between Houdini and Arthur Conan Doyle. Katherine doesn't have an actual copy, just a review published in a history journal, but it mentions a falling out between Houdini and Doyle that wrecked their friendship. It's supposedly a key point of the book, and I'm certain the sections I skimmed last night said they remained very close.

I spend the rest of my time poring over files that Connor collected. He found nothing about a "Fifth Column" in conjunction with the Cyrists, only generic mentions of fifth columns in various wars and in some TV series about aliens. A few rumors exist about an anti-Cyrist alliance within the government, but mostly on conspiracy theory websites, next to stories claiming the moon landing was fake, UFOs control our minds through microwave signals, and the Illuminati control everything else.

I open file 4, the Mega Future-Wiki, and start reading the section labeled *2100–2199 (Government):*

> *As the century opened, the U.S. government, like most governments around the world, was still dealing with the repercussions of 2092. Efforts to rebuild damaged alliances—*

I pull my eyes away from the screen. Maybe it's Katherine's influence, but reading this info feels inherently *wrong* and spoilerish, especially when she was adamant that I didn't need to know about whatever happened in 2092. I'll wait until I know for certain what Julia is proposing before opening that particular Pandora's box.

Or maybe my tired brain was just looking for an excuse to drift off. My phone vibrates on the nightstand at a quarter after seven, awakening me from a three-hour nap. Another text from Charlayne, reminding me of our "internship meeting" at nine. Why is she being coy about it now? If anyone is monitoring our communications, her earlier text welcoming me to the Fifth Column pretty much ripped the lid off.

I wonder how much has changed for her in this timeline?

My memories of the Carrington Day barbecue are decidedly dual. Mostly I remember talking to Charlayne and Dr. Tilson, who was enraged to learn that his retirement party was being held in Cyrist Central. But there's a tiny part of my brain that insists we never went to that barbecue.

The same goes for my first day of school. I remember one version where Charlayne and I talked between classes and at lunch. And another where I saw Charlayne hanging out on the periphery of Eve's little clique, chatting with the girls she called the Evelettes.

Which version does Charlayne remember? The changes that resulted in the Fifth Column seem to have occurred gradually, over decades, so I don't see how she can remember me at all unless she's been under a CHRONOS field.

The only thing I know for sure is that I'm not going to get answers sitting here. I splash some water on my face and find some slightly less wrinkled clothes.

I'm digging through my drawer for matching socks when I feel the unmistakable gut punch of a time shift. I clutch the edge of the drawer as I go down. There's a faint snap, and the drawer comes with me, socks raining down around my head.

The room finally stops spinning, and I no longer feel like I'm going to vomit all over the carpet. I push myself up and lean back against the side of the bed.

This shift packed a wallop bigger than the others, even when I wasn't under the CHRONOS field. What could have triggered a time shift that massive?

"Kate?" Connor raps on the door. "Are you okay?"

"Yeah. Did you feel it?"

"A twinge. I'd have passed it off as a bad breakfast burrito, but it hit Katherine like a Mack truck. I got her to lie down, told her I'd come check on you."

I pull myself up and open the door. "I'm better, but, yeah, that was fierce." My eyes slide reluctantly toward the library. "I'm not even sure I want to know what caused it."

Unfortunately, my wish for blissful ignorance is granted. An hour later, we still don't know. Even Connor's automated program that tracks discrepancies between history and news online and data points from the protected files here in the library can't find any sort of anomaly.

Katherine pushes away from the computer, rubbing her eyes. "The only logical conclusion is that the impact of whatever jolted the timeline is delayed. The course of action has been set, but the actual changes aren't showing up yet."

"How . . . is that possible? I mean, how could we feel it if the shift was triggered by changes that haven't happened yet?"

"Because the sequence of events has been set in motion. What we felt was the . . ." She stops, acting like she's searching for a word, then looks at Connor with a wry smile. "Care to help me out?"

"I'll try," he says. "What we felt was our time train jumping the tracks. Maybe jumping several tracks. They're all heading in the same direction, more or less. Only, the track we're currently on has a cement wall somewhere down the line. We haven't hit the wall yet, we can't even see the wall, but the CHRONOS keys detected the disturbance. That's why we felt the shift . . . why Kiernan, for example, will probably have felt it at the same time, from our perspective, even though he's in 1905 or whenever. Does that make sense?"

I say no at the same moment Katherine is saying yes, and they both turn to look at me.

"Well, it *doesn't* make sense! I'll take Connor's word for it, but I'm not going to lie and say I understand it. So . . . you're saying we need to find a way to stop the train before it hits that wall?"

"Well, no," Katherine says. "You can't *stop* time. It's going to keep right on rolling. You simply have to push the train back onto the correct track."

Simply?

∞8∞

FIFTH COLUMN HQ
September 11, 9:00 a.m.

Charlayne startles when I blink in, and then she smiles. It's more of a nice-to-meet-you smile than an I'm-glad-you're-back, so there's one answer right off the bat. Charlayne wasn't under a CHRONOS field, which means we'll be starting from square one. Again.

"You're Kate, right?" Charlayne rolls her brown eyes, looking embarrassed. "Okay, that was dumb. Of *course* you're Kate. You just caught me off guard. I've only seen that appearing-out-of-nowhere thing once before when Max . . . oh, crap." She lowers her voice. "Don't tell him I told you that, okay? I don't think I was supposed to see, and he's . . . well . . ." She smiles and sighs. "I don't want Max mad at me."

I can't help but smile back. This Charlayne doesn't even know me, and it still took her less than ten seconds to spill about some guy she's crushing on. It's comforting that certain things do remain the same in any timeline.

"Julia was supposed to meet you, but something came up. I'm Charlayne." She sticks out her hand, with the pink lotus tattoo still on the back. She's wearing jeans and a T-shirt, however, so maybe this iteration is a bit closer to my former best friend.

When I let go of her hand, she uses it to face-palm. "And that was equally dumb. I've read your entire file, so I know you already know me—well, at least the me from BFC."

"It's okay. I'm getting kind of used to people forgetting me. What's BFC?"

"Before Fifth Column. That's what Ben calls it. And then there's BCI—Before Cyrist International—but even Julia can't remember that timeline."

"Ben? Do you mean Bensen?"

Her eyebrows shoot up. "Oh. You know Ben, too? That wasn't in the file."

"You introduced us in the last timeline. At Briar Hill."

"Okay. I'll update that. And . . . could you maybe not let Ben know I mentioned Max? I'm not *really* interested in him, it's just that he's hot, you know?"

I nod, even though Max doesn't fit my definition of *hot*. Charlayne seems to need a little more assurance than a nod, however, because she's giving me an imploring look.

"Max is practically married, and anyway, I love Ben way too much to want him feeling jealous."

I try to keep my mouth closed, but it takes a conscious effort, because I'm having a hard time processing the idea of Charlayne and Bensen as a couple. I mean, I don't think it's a bad thing. In fact, Charlayne's tendency to be completely superficial in her choice of boyfriends—including the ones she tried to select for me—was one of the few things I found annoying. But even if it was a flaw, it was *her* flaw, something I learned to expect. Part of the package. The concept of a Charlayne who's in love with a nice, smart, sweet, but absolutely not-hot guy will take some getting used to.

My slightly stunned expression clearly has Charlayne worried, so I try to reassure her. "I won't tell. There's no harm in looking, right? But shouldn't you and Ben be at school?"

Technically, I should be at school, too, but they don't have a CHRONOS key that will let them jump back and make up the days they've missed if and when life returns to normal.

"Um . . . this takes priority." Her voice goes up at the end, almost like it's a question, and she gives me an incredulous look. "We've all been preparing for this day for a very long time."

Okay. I really don't know what to say to that, so I just give her a weak smile and follow as she begins to work her way through a maze of empty cubicles toward the back of the room.

"The others are waiting in conference room four. Do you want something to drink before we join them? Soda, water? The file said you like coffee, too, but I don't think you'd like the stuff they have here. It's awful."

"If you have a Diet—"

"Dr Pepper?" Charlayne asks with a bright smile.

"Yes. Was that in my file, too?" I try to sound like I'm mildly curious rather than mildly creeped out, but she looks a little apologetic, so I must have failed.

"I'm sorry. This must be really strange for you. Do you still want the soda?"

"Sure."

We walk through several more rows of cubicles toward a break room at the back. Charlayne opens the fridge, grabs my soda and a bottle of water for herself, and points back to the exit where a carved Cyrist symbol hangs just above the door. It's an odd hybrid of an ankh and a cross, with a lotus flower in the middle and an infinity sign tacked on for good measure.

Bad things tend to happen to me in buildings displaying that symbol.

"Exactly where are we, Charlayne? Max just gave me the coordinates. I'm not even sure what city."

"Officially these are the offices of the Cyrist Interfaith Alliance." She opens the break room door and waits for me to go through. "Ben calls it Langley. Get it—CIA? But we're actually near Silver Spring. Ben and I have internships this semester, so the school is pretty forgiving about missed classes."

I look around the cubicles as we walk by, most of them barren aside from a stray Post-it note or thumbtack stuck in the dividing wall. "The place looks abandoned."

"Yeah. Most workers were reassigned a while back. An assistant comes in to handle some of Julia's correspondence a few days a week—she and Julia have offices down from the break room. The Fifth Column only meets on the days the assistant isn't here. And we'll have to find a new place soon. The lease is up in two months. Cyrists aren't really doing that much interfaith alliancing right now," she adds wryly. "Is *alliancing* a word?"

"I don't think so."

We're at the conference room now, so I don't have time to ask anything else. There are six people inside, gathered around a long table. Three faces aren't familiar. A stout man with glasses and a receding hairline is facing the wall. Next to him is a slightly built African American man wearing a bow tie. They're both in suits, as is the aging blonde across the table, although hers isn't the typical office gray. It's a horrid shade of electric blue that hurts my eyes. A faded lotus tattoo decorates the back of her hand. She's checking something on her phone and wears an expression that says she has far more important places to be.

I recognize the two people closest to the door—Charlayne's more-than-just-friend Bensen and Max.

Max looks like he's had a rough night. He's in crumpled clothes and doesn't appear to have slept well. His gaze wanders down to my chest and then back up to my eyes. There's absolutely nothing sexual in it—I'm pretty sure he's looking for the medallion, not taking in the scenery. And then I realize why. Unlike the others in the room, Max would have felt the "train derailment," too.

I also recognize the man walking toward me, although I'm surprised to see him *walking*. It's Dr. Tilson, former Briar Hill science teacher. He was in a wheelchair last time I saw him, but he's using forearm crutches now, and moving fairly well. Tilson is definitely not a member of the Cyrist fan club, so I'm a bit surprised to see him in a building they seem to own.

"Miss Keller," he says, extending his hand. "Or do you go by Pierce-Keller?"

"Kate will be fine, Dr. Tilson."

"Very well. It's a pleasure to see you again." I give him a puzzled smile in return, because I'm not sure why he added the word *again*. Trey said Tilson doesn't remember meeting us at the barbecue. "I'd hoped young Mr. Coleman could join us this morning, too, but his father said he was called out of town on a personal matter. Can I count on you to fill him in—discreetly, of course—when he returns?"

Tilson seems different as well. His speech is still formal, but he's smiling, and the grumpy old man vibe is missing.

"Yes, sir," I tell him. "I'd be happy to."

"Thank you. I believe Mr. Raji has reserved seats for you."

Charlayne tugs on my sleeve, and I follow her to the empty chairs next to Bensen. I take the seat at the end, facing Tilson, who's busy connecting a laptop to a projector.

I put my soda, the tablet, and the diary on the table in front of me. Max's eyebrows shoot up and he shakes his head.

My first thought is that he's saying I'm not supposed to have a drink in here. There actually *is* a sign above the whiteboard that reads *No Food or Drink*, but the blond woman next to him has a

Dean & Deluca travel mug and a mostly eaten pastry in front of her, so that rule is obviously being ignored.

Then I realize he's worried about the diary. What did he think I was going to do—slide it across the table and say thanks for slipping me secret information? Like all CHRONOS diaries, it appears to be nothing more than an old book, and it's stacked under the tablet. No one would give it a second glance. But I pull it into my lap and shoot Max an are-you-happy-now look. Apparently he isn't. He just continues to glare at me, so I purposefully turn my attention to the other end of the table.

The wall behind Tilson lights up. He slides his chair to the left so that his head isn't blocking the screen.

I lean toward Charlayne and whisper, "Are we waiting for Julia?"

"She's not coming. We'll probably see her later."

"Who is the woman next to Max?"

"Selene Ellicott," she whispers back. "Senator."

"She's also Cyrist—she has the tattoo."

Charlayne gives me a reproachful smile and holds up her own hand. Her tattoo is fresher, the pink more vivid than the one on Ellicott's hand. It also looks slightly different than before, although I can't place what's changed. "We're all Cyrists. *New* Cyrist, but still—"

A Cyrist is a Cyrist is a Cyrist. I don't actually say what I'm thinking, however, both because I don't want to insult Charlayne and because I realize it's probably not true anymore. And maybe it was never entirely true. As Kiernan noted back in Georgia, people joined the Cyrists for many different reasons.

"Can everyone see? And hear?" Tilson asks in a voice that seems too loud for such a small room.

There are general noises of consensus, and then Julia speaks from Tilson's laptop. "We're fine here."

Ah. So she's being conferenced in.

The image Tilson projects onto the wall behind him looks like a Koosh Ball, with multicolored spokes coming out from the core. Apparently we're diving straight into the briefing with no introductions.

"This is what we're up against," he says. "There's some similarity to H5N1, which some of you may know better as the avian flu, but also some rather striking differences. I won't pretend I fully understand how it works. My epidemiologist colleague understands a bit more, but this isn't a naturally occurring virus. It was manufactured to be highly lethal and spread quickly through the water supply or through contact with bodily fluids. Once inside a host, it mutates rapidly. There is a ninety-seven percent infection rate, and in fifty percent of the test subjects it shifted to airborne transmission—that is, via sneezing and coughing—within two days."

He pauses a moment to let that sink in. "It has excellent potential as a weaponized virus because in its original, unmutated form, it's not particularly dangerous, assuming it's handled with care. The survival time outside of a host is relatively short—an hour at most on dry surfaces. A high concentration of bleach or other medical-strength disinfectant can kill it. And the survivor sample suggests it's preventable by vaccination with no obvious adverse effects."

Just looking at the thing causes a tight fist to clench around my stomach. I'm hesitant to interrupt him, but to the best of my knowledge, the water sample I brought back from Six Bridges is in a refrigerated safe at Katherine's house. Connor didn't say anything about giving it to Tilson. And I have no clue what he means by *survivor sample*.

"Excuse me, Dr. Tilson, but... how did you get these samples?"

There's a short pause, and then Julia answers via the computer, "That hasn't happened for her yet."

"Oh." Tilson looks at me apologetically. "Apparently we have a scheduling issue. I'll sort it out with you afterward."

Well, at least that explains how he knew me.

He clicks to move on to the next slide, and the fist that was clenching my stomach pulls back and punches it. The image on the screen is the newspaper photo of Six Bridges, larger than I've seen it before because it's being projected. The kid's arm hanging over the edge of the pew is almost life-sized. I flash back to Kiernan's words as Jackson and Vernon ran down the path to the chapel. *Ghosts, think of them as ghosts.*

Doing that isn't any easier now than it was then. And I'm clearly not alone in my reaction to the photo. The others at the table look sickened, and some avert their eyes from the screen at the sight of dozens of corpses, the skin strangely mottled and the bodies emaciated, almost like someone squeezed them dry.

"This is what the virus does. Most subjects died within a day. This image was taken by local authorities in 1911."

I want to ask where he got the picture, but I already know—Future-Me will give it to him along with the samples.

A voice from the computer asks, "How do we know this was the result of the virus?"

Tilson answers, "The sample was taken from the village well."

He clicks again, and I brace for another image, but it's a map, one that I recognize as the regional map for Cyrist International. It's divided into six sections: North America, Latin America, Europe, Africa, East Asia, and SoCeAsia, which must mean South Central Asia. A major city in each area is designated with a star and the name of the regional Templar. The North American star is over DC and the name next to it is Franklin Randall. That's odd—I thought Patrick Conwell was the regional Templar? I don't recognize any of the other names, although I remember Kiernan mentioning someone named Edna, and there's an Edna Sowah listed by the star near the Horn of Africa.

"Our working assumption," Tilson says, "is that Cyrist operatives use the six regional headquarters as distribution points to disseminate both the virus and the vaccine to the various national and local temples. All members have been vaccinated—"

"Excuse me." The woman's voice coming from the computer sounds vaguely familiar, but it's definitely not Julia. "There've been a few regional immunization programs in temples located in less-developed countries, but that's the only . . ."

The voice fades as Tilson turns the computer toward Ben, Charlayne, and Max, who are holding up their right hands with the lotus tattoo pointed forward.

"The tattoos?" she says. "Really?"

Tilson nods and continues. "As I was saying, members were vaccinated via intradermal DNA tattoos at their local temples during their initiation ceremonies. At some later point, those same regional and local Templars will introduce the virus into local water supplies. The tainted water will only reach a small percentage of the population, but at that point, given the rapid mutation, it will be impossible to—"

The woman's voice cuts back in. "Surely you're not saying all *six* regional Templars are involved? And local Templars, too? My understanding was that it's only a small group within the inner circle . . ."

There's a moment of silence, then several others at the table chime in with similar comments. Finally Tilson clears his throat, and the noise gradually dies down.

"It's entirely possible that the local Templars, and possibly some of the regional leaders as well, have no clue what they're doing. They'll simply be following orders from above. Let's hope that's the case, otherwise we're dealing with evil on a far more massive scale than I wish to contemplate. But we don't know how deep the conspiracy runs, and we don't know *which* Templars are involved. With so much at stake, we have to assume the worst, wouldn't you agree?"

There's more mumbling, but no one disagrees explicitly. Then the mystery woman speaks again. "What about the children? Cyrists don't receive their tattoos until they become Acolytes. That's usually around age ten, sometimes even later."

Tilson sighs. "Children who haven't been tattooed—and yes, that's pretty much all of them under age ten—are unprotected. Babies have some degree of immunity from their mothers, but our model, based on the limited animal studies that were performed, suggests eighty percent mortality even among newborn and nursing infants."

"But that's . . . monstrous." The woman's voice is soft. She sounds close to tears. "How could anyone think people would remain loyal if you saved their lives but not the lives of their children?"

There's a long silence, so I take the opportunity to whisper a question to Charlayne. "Who is that speaking?"

She shrugs. "Don't know. Julia's boss, I think."

That confuses me even more, since I didn't realize Julia *had* a boss.

"Monstrous, indeed," Tilson says. "I should also add that the immunization status of anyone who received their tattoo at a New Cyrist temple is suspect. Miss Singleton and Mr. Raji, for example, showed no trace of immunity."

Ellicott looks down at the tattoo on her hand and gulps. The two men glance at theirs as well, so I think I know where they got their tattoos.

Tilson clicks to advance to the next slide. Two images of a CHRONOS key appear side by side. One is intact, but the other image shows two metal disks split apart, with what Connor calls the "time travel guts" open to view. Apparently Tilson has tools at his disposal that Connor doesn't, because all Connor has been able to do is separate the sides enough to get some sulfuric acid inside, rendering the key inactive.

Tilson clicks on the split key and zooms in for a closer look. It's like a bunch of little dots, but in the center is an area that reminds me of this ball my dad used to have in his office. If you touched the outside, it changed color, with little arcs of electricity shooting up toward the inside surface of the ball near your fingers.

"That's the plasma battery," Ben says.

He's whispering, but Tilson must have pretty good hearing, because he clears his throat again and says, "Perhaps you'd like to take over, Mr. Raji?"

"No, sir." Ben slumps down and looks back at the screen.

"Our young friend is correct. One of my former students, a professor at MIT, helped me analyze the device, which CHRONOS historians called a *key*. She confirmed that it is indeed powered by a plasma battery. We know, based on experimentation, that the device has a mechanism for detecting the genetic makeup of the individual holding it. I cannot operate the key, for example, while Miss Keller and others who inherited the CHRONOS gene can. Aside from that, the only thing we've been able to decipher is that one of the chips manages a counter that flips every twenty-four hours. Mr. Raji proposed, and I believe he may be correct, that the counter marks the actual age of the device—that is, how many days have elapsed since it was created around 2250."

Senator Ellicott exchanges an amused look with one of the two men sitting across the table, who's shaking his head and chuckling silently. They're obviously not buying any of this.

When Tilson clicks the pointer again, the screen displays a big question mark.

"This is to visually remind you that everything else I'm about to tell you is largely conjecture, based on the information that we have at hand. It may not be accurate."

Ellicott laughs. "That slide belongs at the beginning of your presentation."

Tilson gives her a brief glance, but doesn't take the bait. For the next few minutes, he explains how the CHRONOS key works. I understand virtually none of what he's saying. The only physics I've studied was in general science class, and we didn't discuss anything temporal. I do follow some of what he says about the many-worlds theory—the idea that every action we take could spin off a new reality. Katherine and Connor mentioned this notion, and it's one that I kind of like because it means that Dad's other kids that I met briefly might still exist. On the other hand, Trey isn't as big a fan of that theory, since it means that my saving Katherine at the Expo spun off some alternate universe where he was simply left behind.

". . . tend to believe spinning off countless alternate universes is simply unmanageable . . ."

". . . more plausible option might lie in something known as string theory . . ."

My eyes glaze over at some point. Tilson must have that uncanny teacher's ability to hone in on the student whose brain has left the building, because the next thing I hear is him saying, ". . . would you agree, Miss Keller?"

Why couldn't he have picked on Senator Ellicott? I was just sitting here, and she was actually texting while he talked.

I give Tilson a pained smile. "Could you repeat the question, please?"

"Certainly. I was asking whether your experience conforms more to the many-worlds hypothesis, with infinite parallel universes, or to string theory, which suggests that they are limited. Do smaller changes result in a time shift?"

"Um . . ." I stop and take a sip of my soda. "No. Any time I make a jump, any time one of the original historians made a jump, there were *small* changes. I step off the sidewalk in front of someone, causing him to miss his taxi and therefore miss a meeting or whatever—that's a change, right? And even the changes that resulted in the creation of the Fifth Column seemed . . . I don't know . . . localized, maybe? I felt something, but it wasn't the same sensation those of us with the CHRONOS gene felt on three occasions when there were massive changes."

Except there have now been *four* massive changes, the latest one leaving the others in the dust. But out of everyone else in the room, I'm pretty sure only Max felt it, and I'm not sure how much information Julia wants me to share with the others.

"I'd guess maybe small changes don't spin off a new reality," I say, "or if they do, that reality merges back with the other one. But the string theory part . . . no idea."

"So," Bensen says, "you're saying temporal inertia? Time sort of mends itself if the rift isn't major?" The question is for me, but all he gets back is a clueless look. "Like on *Doctor Who* or *Star Trek*? Time resists being changed."

Selene Ellicott snickers. "In case you don't know, those are science *fiction* shows. Pretend. Make-believe. Not real."

Bensen's right eyebrow quirks upward a few millimeters. This is actually a pretty strong reaction from him. I swear, it's like someone botoxed the guy's entire face.

"The people who built the CHRONOS equipment are more than two hundred years in our future," Bensen says. "If you go back a mere hundred and fifty years from today, someone—especially someone with limited imagination—would say the same thing about airplanes, helicopters, rockets, nuclear weapons . . . not to mention the device you just used to check email."

Ellicott rolls her eyes but doesn't respond.

Tilson looks at Ben, nodding slowly. His mind must still be on what Ben asked before Ellicott's interruption. "It could be. It could very well be that only massive change triggers a full timeline shift—or spins off a new world, whatever you want to call it. The CHRONOS key creates something of a bubble around the key holder, assuming that person has the gene."

"The field works on others, too," I say. "They can't use the equipment, but if someone without the gene is inside the field when a change occurs, they'll remember both timelines. It's not a pleasant sensation, and it seems even rougher on them than on those with the gene. But to get back to what Bensen was asking, I don't know if it's like time mends itself. It's more like the new stuff overwrites the minor history. The scenery changes a bit, but the train stays on the same track. But that could just be the way we perceive it."

Ellicott leans back in her chair, arms crossed, clearly not buying anything we've said. Maybe it's the jaw-clenching color of her jacket, the heavily lacquered platinum-blond hair, the tattoo on her hand, or all of the above, but Ellicott gives me a bad vibe. I can't help but feel that Julia or whoever vetted the members of the Fifth Column made a mistake including her.

Tilson must be thinking something similar. "I believe we need to address the time travel skeptics in the room before going any further."

He slides a folded section of the *Washington Post* toward the middle of the table. "September 17th. Pass it around so all three of you can find the ad you submitted. One of you was a bit of a comedian, so I spotted yours right away—it's circled in blue. *Lost dog. Doberman. Answers to Pincher. Reward if returned to Sixteenth Street Temple.*"

The guy next to Tilson picks up the paper and examines it for a moment, then mutters a curse before sliding it to Bow Tie. "You didn't happen to bring the stock pages, did you? Or maybe the sports section?"

"I did not. In fact, I put most of the paper through the shredder without reading it. But those of you who are current or former members of the temple should now have a good idea why Cyrist investment portfolios are so solid."

"Could explain a lot of things," Bow Tie says. He casts a sideways look at Senator Ellicott as he pushes the paper toward her. "Like why they've had such good luck in recent elections. And getting their bills through Congress."

"That's a good point." Ellicott turns to me. "Cyrist International has a sweet deal right now. Why cause a global catastrophe when they can do almost anything they want with impunity? A majority of Congress is in their pocket."

"Not to mention the *presidency*," Max says.

Ellicott seems taken aback for a moment, although I'm not sure why. "Yes. Of course. The Supreme Court hasn't ruled against them on any important case in years. And it's not just the U.S.—most world governments have become exceptionally Cyrist friendly in the past decade. Why give that up?"

She's clearly expecting me to provide an answer, but I don't have one, at least not one that would appeal to her sense of reason. All I can see is Saul's face in the chapel at Six Bridges. Or the look in the eyes of the woman in the stable at Estero as she slit her own throat. Their expressions were very similar—joyful, almost peaceful.

"Are you asking me to provide you with a logical explanation for genocide?" I ask. "Has any rational group ever engineered a genocide? I'm sure the leaders and members think they're acting rationally, but no one else sees it that way."

Ellicott apparently found the ad she was hunting for, because she shoves the paper toward Tilson. "So what? This proves nothing. You could be tapping our phones or monitoring our computers. You could be colluding with someone at the *Post*. I want firsthand evidence that she can time travel."

"Such as?" Tilson asks.

"Make it something easy, if you like. Have her go back fifteen minutes and interrupt the meeting."

"No," I say. "I was in the room then, and I won't interact directly with myself. It sets up this feedback loop in your brain. I've seen what it did to my aunt, so I avoid it. And it might not be easy on the rest of you, either. It messes with your head."

"What do you mean?" Tilson asks.

"In my experience, when people without the CHRONOS gene see something that's . . . inconsistent . . . their head hurts. They feel queasy for several minutes. Trey thinks it's like motion sickness. The brain can't process the discordant images or memories, so it takes it out on your stomach."

Ellicott gives me a patronizing smile. "I think we can handle a little discomfort, Miss Keller."

"Yeah, well for you it might just be one little memory. But the fact that you saw me earlier will change little things about the conversation we've been having. You won't remember that. I will." I glance at the mug in front of her. "What time were you at Dean & DeLuca?"

"Around eight-ten," she says warily.

"On M Street?"

"Yes. Why?"

I take my phone from my pocket, switch to the camera app, and snap her picture. Then I pull out my CHRONOS key and jump.

∞

When I helped Mom get ready for her research trip, one of my chores was moving books from her office back to the townhouse so she could pack them up and ship them to Italy. History professors have an insane number of books, all of them heavy. Rather than renting a truck, Mom decided it was cheaper and easier—for *her*, at least—if I carted the boxes downstairs and hailed a cab a few times.

Given that Mom was tied up in meetings and I was spending a good twelve hours each day on CHRONOS-related research, I decided it would be an even better idea to skip the part about lugging boxes and hailing cabs. I set a local point in her on-campus office, packed up the boxes, and jumped back to the stable point in our living room. I was done in half an hour.

Now I'm doubly glad I took that shortcut. No one is in Mom's building at 7:40 in the morning. A few minutes later I'm across Copley Lawn, stepping onto the sidewalk at O Street, and I'm at Dean & DeLuca before eight. I'd have been there even earlier, but I ducked into this place I like better over on O to snag coffee and a biscotti.

Not an indulgence—well, except for the biscotti. The coffee is an integral part of my plan.

It's more like 8:15 when a black sedan pulls up in front of the shop. The driver lets Ellicott out and heads down the block, taking a left at Wisconsin. A few minutes later, the car has circled around the block so that it's on Potomac Street, right across from the café.

I lean against the brick wall and wait. Several minutes later, Ellicott exits the shop in her horribly vivid blue suit, holding coffee and her little white bag of unhealthy breakfast. She doesn't notice me until the last 20 percent of my coffee—now lukewarm—connects with the front of her jacket.

Even then, she doesn't look me in the eye. I mutter an apology and she mutters an expletive. By that time, her car is at the curb. She pulls off the jacket once she's in the backseat and starts dabbing it with a napkin as the sedan drives away.

I walk down the other side of Potomac until I spot an alley between a yoga studio and an office building. Then I pull out the key and jump back to the conference room, thirty seconds after I left.

∞

FIFTH COLUMN HQ
September 11, 9:42 a.m.

Everyone is where they were when I blinked out. Selene Ellicott wears the same perturbed expression, same blond hair helmet, same impeccable manicure. The only thing marring her otherwise spotless look is a brown splotch near her shoulder.

"Sorry about your jacket."

I take my phone out of my pocket and pull up the photo I snapped before leaving. Then I walk around the table and show it to everyone, making sure they get a good look. "This phone has been in my possession since I disappeared, under a CHRONOS field the entire time. As you see, Senator Ellicott's jacket wasn't stained when I left. I went back and bumped into her with my coffee—"

Her eyes narrow. "And I'll be sending you the bill. This jacket is Max Mara!"

"Sorry," I repeat, but even to my own ears it doesn't sound genuine. "I needed something that wouldn't affect everyone . . . that wouldn't change the course of the meeting. This was the best I could come up with on short notice."

"You could have done that with Photoshop," Ellicott says, nodding at the phone.

"What about her disappearing?" Charlayne says. "And reappearing? Was that Photoshop, too?"

"The fact that she disappeared doesn't mean she was time traveling. She could have been cloaked or something."

I sigh.

So does Max. "Come on! We're facing a major disaster that could happen at any time. You know it's the truth—Tilson proved it with the newspaper, and now she's proved it again with the coffee. If you're not convinced, go home and stay out of our way. We don't have time for this shit."

Max ranks high on my jerk list after barging into Katherine's house and generally giving me a hard time. I'm about to award him brownie points for this until he glares at me again. He isn't out to do me any favors. He's just tired of wasting time.

There's a moment of silence, then the balding guy says, "I still want to know how that medallion works before I make any—"

"Unfortunately," Tilson says, "we have neither the ability to determine exactly how it works nor how to replicate it." He stresses the last two words, and the other man's mouth twitches downward. "And while this goes against my general belief that knowledge is never a bad thing, our government lacked the wisdom to safeguard this knowledge three hundred years from now. It would be a mistake to believe we possess that wisdom today."

He clicks to the next slide, and the top half of the *Washington Post* fills the screen. *Mystery Virus Sweeps Through Major Cities Here and Abroad.* The image below the headline is a street strewn with bodies, some holding children. A worker who seems to be checking a woman in the foreground for vital signs wears bio-gear that looks a lot like the suits Kiernan and I wore to Six Bridges. The sign in the background behind her reads *Hôpital Necker-Enfants Malades.*

My throat tightens and panic starts to set in as I glance up to confirm the date.

September 17th. Less than one week from today.

"As you can see, this is the front page from the paper you viewed earlier. Not exactly what we expected when Ma—" Tilson clears his throat. "When Miss Keller brought the newspaper this morning."

I glance over at Max, because I'm pretty sure that Tilson was about to say his name before he caught himself. That explains why Max looks like death warmed over. It wasn't just because he felt that jolt to the timeline. He already knew what caused it. I just don't get why they're hiding the fact that he can use the key, when that should be counted in the asset column.

A voice comes from the computer. This time it's Julia. "Each of you in the room today is here because you will be needed within the next few days, either to provide a service or to help us gain access to a required facility. Your loyalty to our faith isn't in question, nor is your loyalty to our government, else you wouldn't be in attendance. But I must stress that this is not a matter to be discussed outside this room. The usual penalty will apply for traitors to the Fifth Column."

She pauses briefly, apparently to let this sink in. I think it does, because the color drains from several of the faces in the room. Then she continues, "Our goal is to prevent this crisis before it occurs.

If we succeed, no other action will be required from you. Ellicott, West, and Pearson can go now. If you're in, let me know through the usual channels within the next twelve hours. There's no penalty should you choose not to assist, as long as you stay silent and out of our way. Although, quite frankly, if our preventive measures fail and any of you back out, I think there's a decent chance the virus will ensure you aren't around long enough to worry about penalties."

∞ 9 ∞

Fifth Column HQ
September 11, 10:05 a.m.

"How long have you known the date?" I ask Tilson after Senator Ellicott and the two men leave.

"Since Max showed up on my doorstep with the paper this morning."

"And when did I bring you the sample from Six Bridges?"

"I'm not sure I should tell you that. It would have made much more sense to have that meeting first. Anything I say now might change something."

"She *should* have met with you first," Julia announces, closing the conference room door behind her as she enters the room, taking a seat near Tilson at the front of the table. "That was the original plan. Our deadline has moved forward, however, and I had to juggle things at the last minute."

Julia glances down the conference table to where Charlayne, Ben, and I are seated. "Why don't the three of you move up, rather than sitting at the back of the classroom?" She doesn't mention Max, but he shifts into the seat that Ellicott vacated.

Once we're all settled, she continues. "Max will transfer the coordinates for Tilson's house to your key when we're done here, Kate. My father contacted Tilson years before you'll arrive, so there's no need for discussion when you get there. Just give him the samples and leave."

"Okay, you both keep using the word *samples*, plural. We collected a single sample from the well. Please tell me I don't have to go back to Six Bridges."

"You also brought a blood sample," Tilson says. "From the girl who survived . . . ?"

"Martha." The idea of drawing someone's blood makes me feel faint, but it's infinitely better than going back to that village.

My squeamishness must show, because Tilson says, a bit hesitantly, "I could try and get a sample from someone just after they were tattooed at one of the Orthodox temples, but it might raise suspicions."

"But that's not what you did before," I say. "So I'd have to go back to whenever and tell you to get that sample, and who knows how many ripples that might cause—or whether it would even work. It's okay. I can take the sample, but I'll need the equipment and some instructions. How much blood? Does it matter when it's taken?"

"You brought two vials, drawn approximately forty-eight hours after she received the vaccine. Or at least that's what you said when . . ." He glances at Julia. "What will changing the order of her visit do to my memory? Am I going to remember two versions?"

"No," she says. "You're not under a CHRONOS key. This memory will just overwrite that one. You won't have any idea we skipped all that deliberation."

Tilson looks a bit unnerved, and I can't say I blame him. As much as I hate the dual memories, I also don't like knowing that not so long ago, two different time shifts changed the entire world around me and I didn't know it. Having the CHRONOS gene meant I knew *something* happened, but I had no clue what. As awful as that experience was, it still might be better than knowing that changes could happen and you'd be totally and completely oblivious.

A tap on my shoulder snaps me out of my thoughts. Julia is behind me, her hand out. "The tablet and diary, please?"

I give her the tablet and dig into my jeans pocket for the spare key Connor gave me, hoping that it will appease her and maybe take her mind off the diary.

"Only one?" she asks, her mouth twisting downward.

"Connor disabled most of them. This is all we can spare."

She doesn't seem to believe me, but it's mostly true. Connor kept back three to guard the house along with the ones that he and Katherine wear whenever they go outside, one with my dad, one with my mom, one with Trey, two for me (a primary and a spare), and one that's attached to Daphne's collar. I suspect that Julia would argue that several of those should be given to her, especially the one for Daphne, but we've got enough stress right now without risking our dog disappearing if she's chasing a squirrel the next time the Cyrists start screwing around with reality.

Julia slips the medallion into a pocket, then holds out her hand again. "The diary?"

"This belongs to Katherine."

"No, it belonged to my mother. I want it back."

I give Max an apologetic look and give it to Julia. She slides the diary across the table to Max.

"Put that back with my mother's things, Max. Yes, I know all about her message. I watched it the day after she died. I didn't delete it, and I didn't interfere with you giving it to Kate because, like you, I loved her enough to honor her final wishes. I'm not pleased that you lied to me, although I guess that was part of her final wishes, too, so . . ." She shrugs. "And speaking of lies, how was London, Kate?"

I'm not surprised that she knows, but I feel my face flushing at being called out in front of everyone.

"It was okay. My mom knows everything now. And while I couldn't convince her to return with me, she's important to Prudence. She might be able to influence her. That means we have someone on the inside—"

"On the inside with a woman who'll have little to no impact on the events that are about to transpire." Julia shakes her head. "Prudence is irrelevant, Kate, except for her role in motivating rank-and-file members to action. She is the kinder, gentler face Cyrus shows to the masses. We have that face—or at least a close approximation—as long as we have you."

Julia settles into the chair at the head of the table. "And now we also have an approximate date. I suspected, based on my sources, that the Culling would occur on a date significant to Saul, but he seems to have eschewed sentimentality in favor of speeding things up."

"You just *had* to go to London, didn't you?" Max says. "I'll bet anything something you did tipped them off and—"

"Enough, Max," Julia interrupts. "While it's possible that Kate's actions tipped someone off, it's also possible these events would have been triggered if she'd followed my directions and stayed put. While the date is sooner than I'd hoped, it's still better than not knowing at all. Not knowing meant the Culling could start at any time, that they could be spreading the virus this very moment."

"But couldn't that still be true?" I ask. "We don't know for certain how long it would take to spread—"

Charlayne nods. "I thought about that, too. Today is September 11th. It seems like the kind of anniversary someone might target."

Tilson shakes his head. "The computer model suggests otherwise. I'd be happier if we had the models the CDC uses, but Julia says that's not possible, at least not yet, and we can't afford to wait."

"And this model is from the center at Penn State," Ben says, "which has an excellent reputation in the field. Based on the model, within twenty-four hours of release in any urban area, about eighty percent of that population would be infected. Within forty-eight hours, it would be close to total. If people are still moving around in DC on the 17th—and they'd have to be in order to print a newspaper—then we've got at least three days." He stops and glances over at Dr. Tilson. "Except we're dealing with time travelers who could always go back and change things. The models can't account for that."

Julia pulls several newspapers out of her backpack. "Max retrieved these prior to the meeting. They don't factor in time travel, but they could help fine-tune the model. The first report of the illness comes from Europe, late in the evening of the 15th, so it isn't reported until the next day."

She hands the papers to Tilson, who glances at the dates and then passes them down to Bensen.

"But we're going to stop the attack before it occurs. We have a plan, and we have people capable of carrying it out, so I don't want to spend too much time harping on what might happen if we fail. Kate, I take it you've studied the files I gave you?"

"Yes," I say cautiously. "But I need more time to go over the information in the file on 2305."

"I'm sure. It's a large file, and I know you've been busy with travel." Julia's voice is saccharine sweet, and she flashes me a tiny smile that doesn't go anywhere near her eyes.

"It may take a while to go through everything," I say with a look I hope conveys that I don't suffer smart-asses gladly. "Fortunately

I can jump back a few days so we're not inconvenienced. In fact, if it's vital to our current discussion, I can do that right now."

"There's no rush. As long as you do it soon." Julia spreads her hands out and says, "This is your cell, the portion of the Fifth Column you'll be working with directly. Feel free to consult the other people you mentioned, but they won't be part of our meetings. I'm not sure how you'd arrange it anyway. Your house is bugged, and your movements are being monitored. Since Katherine rarely travels outside, any change in that regard would be noted."

"We're aware of that. Maybe we could move on to discussing this plan?"

Over the next half hour, they spell out the details. Boiling it down to bare essentials, they expect me to jump into the static-filled, unstable stable point that's all that remains of CHRONOS headquarters, locate the keys, and bring them back so we can destroy them.

Max seems to think he's going, too. And while he's not my ideal traveling companion, this isn't a jump I want to do alone. His coming along appears to be a point of contention, however, based on the look Julia gives him each time he mentions it.

Julia's "plan" has me worried from the beginning, but I have to admit that they're fairly well prepared, thanks to the records her parents left behind. I have a hard time getting a clear answer out of Katherine about anything to do with CHRONOS. For one thing, she'd really like to forget what happened and her role in it—the fact that she didn't report Saul's suspicious actions earlier gnaws at her conscience. But Katherine was also stranded for fifteen years before she realized that her past life might be relevant to her future. And even then, we've only very recently realized that things like the layout of the headquarters building, not to mention twenty-fourth-century history and culture, might be important for me to learn.

Delia and Abel, however, heard Kiernan's theory that Saul's people are using the keys that were left behind in the future when we were in Martha's living room back in 1938. They started building a file on CHRONOS and the year 2305 while everything was fresh in their minds.

Ben is talking us through a map of the headquarters building, which is projected on the wall behind him. The first screen is a rough sketch of the exterior, with each story numbered—nine in all. The top five floors are labeled *Living Quarters*, and the bottom four are labeled *HQ*. Two additional floors below ground level appear to be maintenance and a network of tunnels.

"Based on Julia's parents' memories of the force of the explosion," Ben says, "the floors directly above and below the jump room were probably destroyed. It's quite possible the entire building is gone."

He clicks to advance, and I see a map of the fourth floor, with a "jump room" in the center, taking up maybe a third of the floor. A circular launch pad and twelve smaller circles are arranged around the perimeter.

"Wait a minute," I say. "The jump room is on the fourth floor? So the stable point is, what—a hundred feet from ground level? Assuming ground level is even there and it doesn't drop another forty feet or so below ground. Do you think Prudence jumped into something like that and *survived*?"

There's a short silence, and then Ben says, "We have to assume that she did, based on the evidence we have. It's possible that she just got . . . lucky."

I stare at him and then at Julia.

"It's also possible," Tilson adds, "that she was injured, possibly even seriously, but received medical care."

"And what do you think my chances are of completing this mission if I'm injured-possibly-even-seriously?"

Julia shakes her head. "That won't happen. You'll be airborne. You'll have about twenty seconds of lift, giving you time to lower yourself to the ground safely."

"*Airborne?* What the . . ."

Tilson and Bensen exchange an uneasy glance.

Max also looks a bit hesitant, but Julia is staring at him, so he nods. "It's a rocket belt."

I scan the faces at the table, not at all encouraged by what I'm seeing. Charlayne is the only one who seems enthusiastic, but this doesn't surprise me. We once went to a carnival together where they had this ride called Zero-G, shaped like a giant, hollow doughnut where everyone lines up against the cushions along the edges. Daredevil Charlayne whooped and wriggled her bottom upward so that her legs dangled several feet above where the floor should have been. Not me. I had to close my eyes to block out the whirling lights and fragmented images. Even with my eyes closed, the corn dog and funnel cake I'd eaten were threatening to jump ship by the time the ride ended.

"You're kidding," I say. Because I'm really kind of hoping they *are* kidding.

"No," Charlayne says. "It's awesome. This guy down in Mexico makes them. Max looked like Buzz Lightyear when he tested it. Well, minus the wings, but still . . ."

Bensen's mouth tightens a bit, but I'm not sure if it's because Charlayne mentioned Max or because he doubts the merits of the solution. "They're jet packs, really. A little hard to manage at first. Charlayne's gone up three times now." He shoots her a look. "She landed really hard the first time, although she seems to have forgotten that. So did Max. We'll need to work with you a bit out at Tilson's place."

"Have you tried using it at the same time as a key, Max? In the middle of a time jump?"

"No," he admits. "Not yet. We thought there'd be more time to iron out the wrinkles."

"We're working on a way to free up your hands for the key," Tilson says. "You currently need both hands to operate the jet pack."

"But those are just technicalities, right?" Julia asks, looking around at the others. "You told me you had people working on it."

"And I do," Tilson says, a bit defensively. "But as Max noted, the schedule was accelerated. More to the point, your insistence that we keep the time travel component secret, not to mention the entire Culling thing, doesn't make it easy. I can find scientists who oppose the Cyrists, but it's hard to explain why tweaking a jet pack is a critical element in fighting them."

"I'm not opposed to learning how to operate this thing as a fall-back option," I say, "but getting me into what's left of CHRONOS HQ without breaking my neck isn't enough. We have no idea how long Prudence was there. How she got the keys. How or even when she gets back to Saul. I don't think I'll have much luck following her around for days on end, especially when the location will be . . . foreign to me."

"Which is why you need to—" Julia begins.

"Yes. I *know*. Read the background file thoroughly. And I will. But unless I missed a category in my admittedly brief scan, there's nothing about what happens to Pru when she gets there. My cover won't hold for long, no matter how many times I read your file." I take a deep breath, because I don't really like what I'm about to say. "The obvious solution, the only one with any real chance of work-ing, is to find Prudence in the wreckage and keep her from getting the keys. From getting to Saul. I bring her home before this begins. She used the key to get there accidentally. I'll show her how to use it to come home."

"And you'll change the entire timeline, all of history, if you do that!" Julia says. "Not to mention erasing yourself in the process, along with Max and myself."

"I know. I don't particularly like the erasing-me part. I'm guessing you don't care for the me-erasing-you part, either, but if that's the price for stopping the Culling and erasing Cyrist International, then . . ."

Julia's eyes widen. "Why do you assume those two goals are linked? Stop the Culling, yes. But I have no intention of erasing Cyrist International. None of us do."

My jaw drops. I look around the table and see that Charlayne, Ben, and Max clearly agree with her. There's hesitation in Tilson's eyes, however, so I hold his gaze for a moment, hoping for a little support.

"I'm actually okay with that," Tilson says reluctantly, giving Julia an apologetic look. "You've known my views on organized religion in general and the Cyrists in particular from the very beginning. I wouldn't mind seeing the world without their influence."

"But you've worked with us for the past twenty years, Harvey! I thought your prejudice on that point was long gone."

Tilson bristles and looks like he's about to give an angry retort—quite possibly the same one he gave at the barbecue about it not being prejudice if the belief is based on factual evidence. Instead, he stares down at the table for a few seconds and takes a deep breath before responding.

When he finally looks back up, his eyes pause on each of their faces in turn as he speaks. "There are many, many good people among the Cyrists, especially the New Cyrists. I hold those individuals, including the ones at this table, in the highest regard. I even freely admit that Cyrist International has done much good in the world. That's the case for most other major organized religions, too, I would venture. But I don't believe the good they've done outweighs the harm caused through the centuries. I'd like to leave it at that, because I don't think I should have to justify my personal religious views or lack thereof to any of you. I happily work with any and all allies in stopping this Culling. I don't have to embrace your religious views in order to do it."

He adjusts the steel-rimmed glasses on his nose and turns to me. "As I was saying, Kate, I agreed to compromise on this point for the greater good. It took Julia's parents a while to convince me, but I'm glad I listened. I think it's for the best that we focus on the Culling and let history determine the fate of Cyricism."

I turn to Charlayne. "You said 'New Cyrist' earlier. So did Tilson just now. Exactly what does that mean?"

"Well, we're all Cyrist. But you have Orthodox Cyrists who've been around forever—back to the fifteenth century. The New Cyrists are an offshoot starting in the 1950s, so we're really quite new. Orthodox Cyrists focus on both the *Book of Prophesy* and the *Book of Cyrus*. We focus more on the *Book of Cyrus*. There's a lot of wisdom in there if you take the time to read it. We don't require the tithe, although it's still encouraged. And we've gotten rid of some of the silly stuff, like arranged marriages and no sex until you're forty."

"It's twenty, not forty," Julia corrects drily. "Hyperbole aside, however, Charlayne has given an accurate summary of the differences."

"I'm kind of stuck between the two," Charlayne says with a shy smile, seemingly pleased at Julia's half compliment. "Dad is Orthodox. Mom is New Rite. I followed her, and so did two of my brothers. The other one goes to Dad's church."

Julia nods. "Officially Max and I are Orthodox Rite, although that's only for appearances. Cyrist International accepted that growth might require a certain degree of compromise, so rather than exclude those who sought a more . . . relaxed . . . form of worship, they were allowed to continue as an adjunct group. They've provided a decent cover for the Fifth Column, especially once I was assigned as head of the Interfaith Alliance, which is—or perhaps I should say was—as much about coordinating activities between New and Orthodox as it was between the Cyrists and Christians, Muslims, Buddhists, and so forth."

"What about your parents?" I ask. "Did Delia and Abel want the Cyrists to continue?"

"They were at temple several times a week."

"That doesn't answer my question."

"Because the answer doesn't matter. They're gone. And even if they were here, you'd be dealing with me. My goal at the end of this is as little change to the timeline as possible. Destroy the keys, ditch most of the miracles, which we all know to be false anyway. Ditch the *Book of Prophecy*. The *Book of Cyrus* stays. What we'll end up with is closer to New Rite than Old, with no Culling. We all still exist, and it's far more likely that we'll recognize the world we live in."

"But the *Book of Cy*—" I'm planning to say that the *Book of Cyrus* is as bogus as the *Book of Prophecy*. It's a mostly plagiarized volume of platitudes cobbled together from every religious text and self-help book on the planet, and it shouldn't exist at all.

But Tilson's expression is practically yelling for me to back away from that comment, so I change subjects. "Fine. If I'm not going to stop Prudence from joining Saul, then we need to know more about what happens to her when she lands in 2305 *before* we make this jump."

Max snorts. "And how do you plan to find that out? Just stroll up to her and ask?"

"Maybe." My voice sounds as hesitant as I feel because there are so many ways this could go wrong. "It might work if I can find the younger Pru, before they turned her mind to mush. Kiernan says there was a period when she rebelled, when she hated Saul. If I can talk to her then, before—"

"Based on what I've seen and heard," Julia says, "she's hated Saul most of her life. But as I told you before, any information you get from Kiernan Dunne is suspect. I'd have said the same thing before my son died, no matter what my mother believed. You ignored my warning about London, but you need to take my advice about Kiernan seriously. Otherwise you'll put our entire plan in jeopardy."

"What about Houdini's key? Kiernan and I were working together on that."

"Do you even know for certain Houdini has a key?"

I decide it might be a bad idea to admit I've now seen that key, since it sort of confirms that I've also seen Kiernan. I don't want to open that can of worms right now.

"Other-Kate, the me in the previous timeline? She was certain."

"Focus on getting the keys from CHRONOS HQ. Once we destroy those, I think there's a better than even chance that Houdini will have no key and no career. We'll be saying 'Houdini who?'" Julia is clearly pleased with her lame joke, and glances around the table to make sure it was properly appreciated.

Charlayne and Max both give a silent chuckle. Ben even gives a little lip twitch. Tilson and I are apparently the only people in the room who aren't total suck-ups.

But I feel oddly protective of Houdini, who isn't here to shield his reputation from this new group of challengers. "He *had* a CHRONOS key, but I'm not convinced he needed it. Houdini had a career before the time shifts. Before Cyrist International even existed."

That wipes the smirk from Julia's face. "How exactly would you know that?"

"I read it in one of Katherine's books. A book that's been under a CHRONOS key."

Julia's eyes narrow. "I wasn't aware that Katherine was such an avid librarian. What's the point in keeping track of timelines so radically different from our own?"

"It's . . . history," I say.

"Not anymore. And either way, you won't be solving the mystery of whether or not Houdini has a key right now. We have bigger fish to fry."

Truthfully, I probably *will* wait and finish up with Houdini once everything else is resolved. But I can't shake the feeling that his key is important.

I flash Julia a one-second smile that she seems to accept as agreement. I'd rather avoid making more promises that I may or may not keep.

∞

BOGART, GEORGIA
September 15, 1911, 11:45 p.m.

The moment I enter this set of coordinates into the key, the significance of the date hits me. When Julia was thinking of dates special to Saul that he might use for the Culling, she forgot a very important one—September 15th, the anniversary of his successful test run at Six Bridges.

Kiernan's cabin is dark when I blink in and totally quiet aside from the crickets, or maybe they're frogs, engaged in a raucous chorus outside. The sound reminds me of the little machine my mom uses when she has trouble sleeping. I guess this is nature's version of white noise.

The meeting at Fifth Column headquarters ended over an hour ago, but I had to jump forward to meet Julia later in the day so she could give me the blood collection kit I'm holding. It apparently isn't something you can pick up off the shelf at the local CVS, which meant Julia had to contact some doctor she knows.

Fortunately, the kit has little wings on the needle that make it easier to hold than the ones I've seen previously. Even so, I didn't want to show up in the middle of the night and start jabbing holes into a girl who's just been traumatized without some sort of practice. I was going to poke my own arm, but Julia thought that was a bad idea and offered Max as a pincushion.

If Max didn't hate me before, he definitely does now. Once I finally punctured the vein and drew a sample, he stormed out. While I'd have preferred to practice a few more times, his arms already sported four Band-Aids, and one glance at his face told me not to push my luck.

Before jumping in at Kiernan's, I scanned the key to find a time when they were both sleeping. Martha sat huddled in a sad little ball on the couch for most of the evening, dressed in the odd split-skirt bicycling costume I wore the first time we visited her village. Kiernan tried to get her to eat something and did his best to comfort her, but comfort doesn't come easily to a fifteen-year-old who's just witnessed the murder of her entire family and narrowly avoided being killed herself. At one point, Martha broke down. Kiernan held her head against his shoulder, just patting her back and looking helpless.

He finally convinced her to eat a sandwich and drink a small glass of something. I couldn't read the label, but I'm pretty sure it was alcoholic, because Kiernan tossed back an even bigger glass himself once Martha was settled in the guest room. Then, a little over an hour ago, he went upstairs to the loft where he usually sleeps.

I hate to wake them. Sleep can't have come easily. The first time I closed my eyes after our trip to Six Bridges, my mind flashed a rapid-fire montage of images—the bodies in the pews, Saul dragging Martha through the door with that sick blissful smile on his face. Even though I was exhausted, it took ages to fall asleep.

But waking them can't be helped, so I grab the bottle from the table as soon as I jump in to the cabin. It's whiskey—Old Grand-Dad, to be precise—and there's a good two-thirds of it left. I tuck it under my arm and tiptoe to the ladder, using the glow of the CHRONOS key to light my way so that I can climb to the loft. Kiernan is sprawled across the bed on his stomach, shirtless, the sheets wrapped around him in a tangle. His left arm is unmarked, the nasty scar still somewhere in his future. As much as I'm tempted to warn him, Julia emphasized that I can't do anything to change the path he's on because I don't know how that might impact either of us or the Fifth Column.

In fact, Julia didn't want me talking to him at all. If she had her way, I'd be sneaking into Martha's room like a vampire and stealing her blood, with Kiernan none the wiser. But I know he's got a gun under his mattress. He might shoot first and ask questions later if he saw someone prowling around the cabin, especially if Martha screamed. And if anyone knows when and where I can find Prudence—the younger, saner version—it's Kiernan.

I kneel down beside the bed and nudge his shoulder. "Kiernan, it's Kate."

"Mmm." He smiles, his eyes still closed, and his arm circles my waist, pulling me toward him. "Kate. Missed you."

"No, Kiernan." I pull his arm away—gently, but it's enough that he opens his eyes. "I need to talk to you."

He pushes himself up onto his elbows, huffing out a breath that would've confirmed my guess about the whiskey even if I hadn't found the bottle. After the day he's had, I don't blame him.

"This couldn't wait 'til morning?" He doesn't sound angry, though, and he gives me a slightly groggy version of his usual grin. It stirs up the memory of him sitting in the chair at Eastbourne last night, looking out at the ocean. His tiny, perfunctory smile when he finally turned to greet me.

My expression must change with the memory, because Kiernan frowns. "What's wrong?"

I shake my head. "Nothing. I just . . . I have to get a blood sample from Martha. They need it . . . for the vaccine. Oh, and the photo from the newspaper, so they can see the effects."

"You've found someone already?"

"Yes," I say, deciding to steer clear of the details. "The sample needs to be taken within forty-eight hours, and I'm not sure when Saul gave it to her."

"I wish you'd come before Martha fell asleep." Kiernan reaches under the bed as he's talking and pulls out the shoe box. The article with the photo is on top. "She's really torn up about this, and now she'll have to—" He starts to swing his legs over the side of the bed, but I hold him back.

"I'll get the sample in a minute, but you should stay in bed. I came when you were asleep because I have to ask some questions."

Realization dawns in his eyes. "Oh. You're from . . . later."

"Yes. The less you remember about me being here, the better. For both of us." I hold up the bottle of Old Grand-Dad and hand it to him. "I'm sorry."

"Me, too. I'm gonna have a wicked headache in the morning." He removes the stopper and chugs from the bottle. A shudder runs through him, and then he asks, "What do you need to know?"

"A time and place I'm likely to find Pru by herself. Young Pru, back when she was angry at Saul."

"Why—"

"Kiernan, the less you know, the better. You're always telling me to just trust you and do what you're asking, and I do—"

He snorts. "When it suits you."

"Okay, but I do when it seems important. And this is really, really important. I was thinking maybe the Seneca Falls Convention? That's when she changed the document—the one that Katherine noticed—by adding her signature."

"Pru wasn't there. We tried that before, in the other timeline."

"But . . . her name's on the document. Maybe—"

"I didn't go to the convention with you—sorry, with my Kate— but I remember that trip very well. We spent some time in a cabin on the Finger Lakes near there. Kate didn't find Pru at the meeting. She decided Pru prob'ly never even went. Just bribed the printer to add her name later on."

He takes another swig. "Victoria Woodhull. Pru worked for her presidential campaign."

"I've heard the name. Something to do with 'free love,' so must've been the sixties or seventies, right?"

"Yeah. 1872."

I was thinking more like *1972*. Women couldn't even vote in 1872, so how did one end up running for president? But I just nod. Getting him off on a tangent will only wake him up further.

"Kate's backup plan was snatching Pru's key in 1872," he continues, "assuming she couldn't lure her back to the same time as your mom. Woodhull gave this big speech in New York. Pru was probably there. She was about your age, right after the baby was born. Simon mentioned it once. Said Pru freaked out over something Saul did and disappeared for a few days, but Pru said she was there a lot longer than that."

"Did she know about you and your Kate then?"

"Not . . . directly. Pru and I weren't ever together until she was eighteen, nearly nineteen. Older Pru might have told her something about it, though. Anyway, if Pru's not at the speech, I *know* she's there when Woodhull gets jailed for the Beecher article. Nearly got herself arrested, too."

"I'm not following any of this, you know. Beecher who?"

"Henry Ward Beecher." Another slug from the bottle. "He's a preacher. Hey, that rhymes."

Well, that answers any questions about whether the alcohol is working.

"Okay . . ." I motion for him to continue.

"Beecher spoke out against Woodhull's free love speech, but he'd been foolin' around with a married woman. Woodhull called him a hypocrite, got hit with an obscenity charge. Was all over the papers."

He hands me back the bottle, which is down to about a quarter. "Any more of that an' I'm gonna blow chunks."

I have to smile, wondering where in time he picked up that bit of slang.

"See if you can get Martha to drink a bit more. Help her sleep." He slumps back down onto his pillow. "An' don't nag me about corruptin' a minor. Sleepin' meds in 1905 have some scary ingredients. Bourbon's safer."

"Kiernan—when you see me next, don't mention this. And you can't follow me like you did in Australia. Really and truly you can't."

"'Kay."

He said okay last time and still wound up killing a crocodile out of some misguided determination to protect me, so I nudge his shoulder. "No, Kiernan. Not okay. You have to *promise* me."

"I promise." With half-closed eyes, he reaches out and grabs a handful of my T-shirt, pulling me toward him. "*Mo ghrá thú.*"

Kiernan's bourbon-scented kiss is half on my cheek, half on my lips, but I feel the same stirring I always do, followed by the same flood of guilt. I push him gently back onto the pillow and kiss his forehead, next to the scar that's nearly healed.

A sleepy smile spreads across his face. "Night, Katie."

∞10∞

BETHESDA, MARYLAND
September 11, 1:35 p.m.

Connor is at the computer when I blink in. He's squinting, but I can't tell if it's from what he's reading or the fact that he needs to be wearing his reading glasses.

He glances over when I sit down. "Everything go okay with Tilson?"

Connor is certain the devices he installed shield the house from any sort of eavesdropping equipment, but I'm still nervous about talking inside. He's right, though—we can't keep hiking out to the backyard every time we need to discuss things, and I'll freely admit that he knows much more about electronics than I ever will.

Still, I keep my voice low. "Yeah. Someone must have prearranged the date and time. Tilson was waiting at the door. I just handed him the samples and the article and blinked back."

I omit the part about my hand clutching the handle of the cooler a little too long. Tilson gave me a sympathetic look, so I think he understood why I might have a few qualms about handing over a deadly virus to someone I hardly know. I had to remind myself that Trey's dad and Trey's granddad have known Tilson for decades and hold him in high esteem, and also remind myself that in a slightly different timeline, an older version of the man in front of me would refer to the Cyrists as "lotus-wearing parasites." I just hope that Tilson and his colleague at MIT are really able to come up with a vaccine based on the blood and water samples inside the case. Although I guess they already have, based on what Tilson said at the meeting.

Martha barely opened her eyes. I'd like to think it was my newfound skill as a phlebotomist, but I suspect it was due more to the dose of bourbon Kiernan gave her earlier and lingering shock. She nodded a few times as I spoke and winced slightly when the needle went in, but she was back asleep before I even finished bandaging her arm.

"Any luck on Woodhull?" I ask.

Connor is reading a digitized version of *Harper's Weekly* from February 17, 1872. The highlight of the page is a cartoon entitled "Get Thee Behind Me, (Mrs.) Satan!" At the forefront is a woman— Victoria Woodhull, I guess—with horns protruding from her hair and bat wings attached to her back. In her hands is a sheet of paper: *Be Saved by Free Love.* Another woman trudging along the rocky terrain in the background, with children strapped to her body and a drunken man on her back, claims she'd rather be shackled in the worst possible marriage than follow Woodhull's path.

He rubs his eyes. "The problem isn't a lack of information. It's the exact opposite. I wish you'd asked Kiernan *which* speech. The woman gave a lot of speeches. Aside from what she made publishing the paper, most of her income was from public speaking. My best guess? He's talking about her acceptance speech at the Equal Rights Party convention on May 11th. But it could also be the one in September that starts the whole Beecher scandal, or one to the Spiritualist Association. Could you go back and ask him to clarify?"

"Not a good idea. He wasn't even positive Prudence was there for the speech, so let's focus on the arrest."

"Again," he says dryly, "*which* arrest?"

"Oh."

Connor types something in, and a picture of a stout, balding man with puffy whiskers pops up. "Wait, that's him when he's older," he mutters. A few clicks later, and he taps an image of a slightly thinner guy with a narrow mustache.

"This one's closer to Anthony Comstock in 1872. Fortunately it's a headshot so you don't see the gigantic stick up his ass. This jerk dragged Victoria and her sister into jail every few days during November. As soon as her lawyer could spring them, he'd find some reason to haul them back in."

"Was he police chief or something?"

"No. The weird thing is he didn't have any actual authority, but everyone acted like he did. He used the Woodhull case to draw national attention and eventually landed a position as postal inspector, where he spent the next forty years tracking down so-called pornographic material. It got so bad medical schools couldn't even send anatomy textbooks through the mail."

"Woodhull was innocent, then?"

"Well . . . Woodhull and her sister weren't angels. They clearly didn't mind a bit of blackmail. Or fraud. But Comstock keeps jailing them because of the issue claiming Beecher was having the affair with Elizabeth. Tilton included another article that used the word *virginity*."

Katherine comes in, holding a dress over one arm. It looks like the pale-green dress I wore at Houdini's show, but she's tweaked it a bit. "The obscenity charge was just an excuse to get Woodhull out of the way," she says. "I did a two-month study of the Beecher-Tilton trial before they teamed me up with Saul. Beecher's people were behind the arrests. I doubt they paid Comstock off—he was such a stickler for propriety he probably wouldn't have accepted a bribe— but it's funny how the complaints against Woodhull and her crew evaporated the moment Beecher's church decided the charges against him merited closer examination."

"So Beecher and the Tilton woman sued Woodhull for libel?" I ask. "Or is it slander?"

"Libel," Connor responds, "since it was in print. But no. Beecher and Tilton never sued Woodhull. The case was brought by Theodore Tilton, Elizabeth's husband, against Beecher. This is a few years after the article. Theodore—who was, coinciden- tally, sleeping with Victoria Woodhull at pretty much the same time Beecher fooled around with Elizabeth—decided that Beecher might actually have harmed him by having sex with his wife. So he sued Beecher for alienation of affection."

"Why would he sue Beecher if he was cheating, too? Are you sure this isn't a plot on *Days of Our Lives*?"

"It was a very different era," Katherine says, sitting down next to Connor. "Husbands cheated frequently and with impunity. Wives did not. Divorce was a scandal, especially for a woman, not to mention an enormous risk. She lost all rights to marital prop- erty and to her children in most states. That's a large part of what Woodhull was protesting. Her plea for 'free love' was less about sexual promiscuity—although there was a touch of that as well— than about the double standard for women. As for it being a soap opera, you're absolutely right. The so-called 'scandal issue' of *Woodhull and Claflin's Weekly* where they exposed Beecher's affair sold for as much as forty dollars on the streets a week later—over seven hundred dollars in today's money. Victoria Woodhull and her sister were the 1870s equivalent of the Kardashian sisters."

Connor shakes his head. "Bad analogy. The Kardashians started out with money. Woodhull is more like Honey Boo Boo. Or maybe *Duck Dynasty*. Just smarter."

"True," Katherine says. "Victoria and Tennie started from nothing, and their family was . . . colorful, to say the least. Long before Victoria ran for president, the sisters were on stage. They worked as spiritualists, they were the first female stockbrokers, and they claimed to be the first female newspaper publishers, although that's not accurate. Several other women ran newspapers long before, including Elizabeth Timothy back in—"

Connor clears his throat, interrupting her. "And yes, students, we'll be learning all about that in tomorrow's lecture."

Katherine shoots him a perturbed look, but pulls herself back on topic. "Anyway, I've done the best I can with this dress. I'd have gone with something less flashy, but this is what we have on hand, unless you'd like to jump back to last week and give me some notice?"

"I'd rather not twist your memories or mine any more than we have to. This will be fine."

She frowns, making a tsking sound. "Even with the lace in the front, the bodice is a bit . . . well, just don't go outside the hall if you can help it. I don't think it will be a problem at this particular convention—many women wore less. I tried to replicate the Dolly Varden dress that was in vogue for younger women. There were some truly crazy variations, so you may be able to pull it off. I padded the back with some spare pillows since we don't have a hoop."

She holds up the dress, and I see she's made a rather large split down the middle of the skirt, tying the fabric back with ribbons. Beneath this outer apron is a flounced skirt of darker green, which looks like fabric left over from my trip to 1893. The back poofs up like a partially deflated balloon. Bits of lace from the bolero cape thingy are stitched around the neckline.

Katherine's also holding a very familiar pair of white kidskin boots, which I will *not* be wearing, and one of the rattan placemats from the breakfast nook that she's fashioned into some sort of bonnet. It used to be a natural straw color, but now it's a very familiar shade of mojito green. It smells familiar, too—sort of acrylic-y.

"Did you use all of my nail polish?" I ask.

"Yes. I thinned it out with a bit of polish remover and used it to stain the bonnet. The color is quite close. Beautiful, isn't it?"

Beautiful is not the word I would have used, but then I'm not a hat person. She's stitched two strips of the lace from the bolero to the edges of her creation—I guess so I can tie it onto my head. Leaves and berries that I'm pretty sure came from the holly tree outside are clustered on one side. It looks like someone ate a Christmas wreath and then threw up on top of a large green pancake.

"It looks very nice," I say, hoping that my lying face is in proper working order, "but please put the boots away."

"I know. They're not era appropriate. But they're the closest we have. This style heel is—"

"Who cares whether they're historically accurate? They blistered my feet in Chicago, and I can't move in them. I'll wear my black ballet flats."

"Women didn't wear—"

"Or I can wear these." I smile, pointing to the blood-red Vans currently on my feet. "Your choice."

Katherine sighs, tossing the torture shoes under the desk. "Ballet flats it is, although I'll warn you, the skirt may drag a bit without a heel."

"Not a problem. I'll hike it up if I need to run." I think it's more likely I'll strip down to the shorts I'll be wearing underneath. My patience with historical accuracy is wearing thin, especially with future history teetering on the brink.

"Very well," Katherine says. "There's a stable point near the back of the theater, tucked away in a little alcove. And you'll be fine in this outfit as long as you stay in Apollo Hall. The people I talked to outside the hall were much more conservative and—"

"Wait." Connor and I say the word in unison. He nods for me to continue, so I finish the sentence without him. "You were there?"

"Well, *yes*." Her expression clearly indicates that this is a stupid question. "I could hardly do a proper study of the trial and Woodhull without attending *that* event. Even if I hadn't been focusing on Woodhull, I studied women's movements. She was being nominated for president. By a fringe party, admittedly, but it was an historic moment. Of course I was there. Only twice, but—"

"Twice." I give Connor a sick look. "Can you remember where you were? What you did? I need to avoid you."

"You certainly do." Katherine drops the dress into my lap and steps over to the bookshelves, pulling out a CHRONOS diary. "While I have a vague memory of both trips, I'm sure there are full details in here somewhere."

I hold up my hands. "Unless you really think it's important, I need to settle for the vague memories. My afternoon is booked. Going back and carving out extra hours isn't a good idea, either. I'm running out of times I won't run into myself or an earlier one of you. I'd rather not mix things up any more than necessary."

Katherine looks like she's about to argue, but she nods. "You're right. The first trip, I wore a dress like that one—except in the gaudiest floral print imaginable. I was near the front, with the more ardent Woodhull groupies. The second trip, I spent most of my time outside talking to the men and women who were looking down their no . . . ses—"

We both turn to stare at Connor's computer, which is now emitting the same ominous *bom-bom, bom-bom, bom-bom, bom-bom* his phone made in the backyard last night.

"What?" He turns back to face his screen. "I needed a Cyrist alert. It was either *Jaws* or Darth Vader mouth breathing, and this one's easier to hear if there are other things going on." He plugs in his headphones, and the noise disappears.

"As I was saying," Katherine continues, with a slight roll of her eyes, "I was outside with the self-righteous types—the *Mrs. Grundys*, as Woodhull's advocates called them—during the second jump, and made up to look at least twenty years older. I never visited Woodhull's offices. The positive side is that you won't run into me there, but there's also no stable point. So you really need to contact her at Apollo Hall if possible. Steer clear of the very front and don't go outside, and you'll avoid both of me."

"I don't suppose you remember seeing anyone who looked like Prudence?"

"Unfortunately not, although I wasn't really looking for someone who might resemble a teenage daughter I might have at some unspecified point in the future." She stops and pulls in a sharp breath, closing her eyes.

"Katherine? Are you okay?"

She holds up one hand. Her eyes are squeezed tight, and it's clear she's in pain.

"Katherine!"

"Shh." She opens her eyes slightly, glancing at Connor, and seems relieved that he's still engrossed in whatever triggered his shark alert. "It's fading. Give me a minute."

A few deep breaths later, she gives me a shaky smile. "I'm okay. It happens sometimes. Just Fred taking another nibble."

I want to tell her that's not funny, but if she needs gallows humor to get through this, is it my place to criticize? "Can I get you anything?"

"No, dear. Still another hour before my next pill. I'm better now, really. As I was saying, even if I saw Prudence at Apollo Hall,

I doubt she'd have stuck out in my mind unless she did something bizarre—"

"Hey," Connor interrupts, unplugging the headphones. "You both need to watch this."

A network logo flashes at the center of his screen—Cyrist International Network's pink-and-blue lotus with the letters CIN across the center petal. A wire-frame globe spins slowly behind the lotus.

Breaking-news music—a faster, higher-pitched version of Connor's shark-alert tone—builds the dramatic tension, and then a woman's voice cuts in. "World leaders discuss global warming in Geneva." An image of Paula Patterson standing next to someone I vaguely recognize—maybe the British prime minister?—flashes up in a square frame and then shifts to the background as a financial ticker takes the center square. "Making the most of your *Book of Prophecy* forecasts." A doctor and patient appear next. "Exercising your constitutional right to a Cyrist physician. These stories and more this hour on *Cyrist International News*."

The newscaster appears, a young Asian woman with carefully styled hair, seated at a curved black desk. "Hello. I'm Mindy Casey, in today for Parker Phillips. Before our featured stories, we have breaking news from Brazil—a rare public appearance by Sister Prudence at Rio's Templo do Caminho. For details, we go to Alan Mabrey, live on location at Morro da Urca in Rio."

The picture freezes momentarily on the landscape in Rio. Dark clouds hang in the sky, and there's a slight drizzle in the air. A mountain with a huge statue of Jesus, his arms spread wide, is in the foreground on the right side. On the left, in sharper focus, is a gigantic temple perched on another mountain. It looks as though a second, higher peak rises from the top of the temple, but I think that's just the camera angle—it's probably behind the building. At the apex of that third, tallest mountain is a Cyrist symbol, even larger than the one on the Sixteenth Street Temple.

The camera shifts to a man standing in front of a massive white temple on the middle peak. "Alan Mabrey, at Rio's Templo do Caminho, the central temple for Latin America and the Caribbean, where we've had a weather delay, Mindy." One bit of hair keeps blowing across his forehead. "Sister Prudence was supposed to speak an hour ago, but nature hasn't cooperated."

Behind him, a crowd is gathered around the base of the temple. Most are looking up toward a rectangular balcony jutting out over the main entrance, lined with balusters and surrounded by TV cameras. A microphone is placed in the center, with another one off to the right.

"This is the first public appearance by Sister Prudence since her brief stop at the Cyrist Inaugural Ball after the last election, and—" He stops and presses his finger to his ear. "She's coming out."

The doors open, and four men step outside, all dressed in dark suits. Two of them carry rifles. They move toward the balcony's edge, looking out over the crowd. One motions with his hand, and several people on the periphery, also armed, move in a little closer.

The guy closest to the door wears shades, despite the gloomy weather. He looks familiar. As the cameras zoom in closer, I see that it's Patrick Conwell.

Conwell reaches behind him to open the door again, and Prudence steps out, followed by a short, dark man in clerical garb who scurries over to the microphone on the right. Having just seen Prudence in London, I'm expecting the older version, but this girl can't be more than twenty. She wears a white toga-style dress that reminds me of the one she wore at Estero the night Kiernan and I watched her "miraculously" transform into the new incarnation of Cyrus.

Except she's very pregnant. Seven months, possibly more. And her expression isn't alive like it was that night at Estero—it's flat, almost vacant, similar to when I saw her with Simon during Kiernan's show at Norumbega.

I glance over at Katherine. A tear slides down her cheek and lodges in one of the lines near her mouth. I reach for her hand, but she moves closer to the screen.

Prudence stands at the center microphone, head down. Her hair is longer than I've seen it, except in some of the paintings online, and the dark curls partially shadow her face. She's thin—her collarbones and shoulders look like they could slice through her skin, making the belly in front even more noticeable.

She gives Conwell a nervous glance, then starts to speak. I can't see her hands, but she's looking down, like she's reading a script. Her voice is softer than I remember, more hesitant, but then I've never spoken with her when she was this young.

"I come here today with a prophecy, but those who walk in The Way know it is more than prediction. It is truth." She pauses, and the small man at the other microphone begins to translate.

When he finishes, Prudence continues, "The *Book of Cyrus* tells us there will come a time when the earth rises up to punish her careless stewards, those who borrow her resources but fail to invest wisely, those who refuse to follow the . . ." She stops, swallows, and starts again. "Those who refuse to follow The Way of Cyrus."

Another pause for translation, then she continues in a flat voice, "Already there are signs, even here in Brazil, where you felt the earthquake and suffered the worst drought in memory. There is still time, but the hours are few. Those who do not repent will face the wrath of Cyrus, for the day of the Culling draws near."

When the translator finishes, Conwell grabs Prudence's arm, but she pulls away and looks out at the crowd. Her face comes alive for the first time. "Go!" she screams, her voice pleading. "Go to the temple and ask for the—"

The last few words are yelled over her shoulder as one of the men reaches out and cuts off the microphone. Conwell grabs her by both arms. She tries to wrench away, but he drags her through the doorway. There's a faint flash of blue and another man joins Conwell to help subdue her.

The camera shifts back to the translator, who's looking down at the paper in his hands. The written speech must not include the last words she screamed, because he looks confused. *"Ir! Ir ao templo e imp—"*

One of the security guards taps him on the arm. *"Perdão,"* he says softly, hurrying back into the temple.

The camera shifts back to the newscaster, who starts recapping the event.

"Stop," Katherine says, her voice almost a whisper. She's crouching next to the desk, her eyes fixed on the monitor. "Rewind it. Back to just before she warns the crowd."

Connor does, and we once again hear ". . . the day of the Culling is near."

As her face turns toward the camera, Katherine says, "Pause it. Pause it and zoom in."

Connor stops at the point where Conwell drags Prudence through the door. "I can't really zoom in. I'll make it full screen."

I see a flash of blue and tap the screen. "Can you see this, Connor?"

"Conwell's head snapping back? Maybe she landed a punch."

"I see it," Katherine says. "Only it's not blue, it's orange. Someone came in with a key. But that's not what I'm looking for. Go back a little more. I need to see her face."

Connor plays around with it until he gets to the clearest, closest view of her face.

Katherine stares at it, and I move closer to the monitor so I can do the same. My mouth falls open, stunned, because now I see it, too.

"It's not Prudence," Katherine says.

And she's right.

The differences are subtle, but still enough to be noticed by a mother. Or grandmother.

A lotus tattoo is on the back of the hand trying to push Conwell away, but the knuckles on that hand are reddened and raw. The nose is a little longer, the face slightly thinner, the lips fuller. The eyes are not the blue-gray that Pru inherited from Katherine.

They're green.

The girl staring back at us isn't Prudence. She's me.

∞ 11 ∞

APOLLO HALL, NEW YORK CITY
May 10, 1872, 8:45 p.m.

"King George III and his Parliament denied our forefathers the right to make their own laws. They rebelled, they won, and they inaugurated the government we have today. But men do not seem to comprehend that they are now pursuing toward women the very *same* despotic course that King George pursued toward the American colonies."

The hall is packed with hundreds of people, well over half of them female. They're a motley group. Some are plainly dressed, clearly working class. Others wear more expensive, fashionable attire—including Dolly Varden dresses like mine—as though they're out for an evening at the theater.

In some ways, I guess they are. Victoria Woodhull is very much in command of her audience—petite, pretty, and quite feminine, despite the austere black dress. She paces as she speaks, her hands shaping her words. Every eye in the house follows her.

Colorful banners line the walls with slogans that aren't quite on the same page, although I guess they might be from the same general book on reform. One argues for government to protect and provide from cradle to grave, while others advocate for the abolition of interest and for direct democracy where all laws are made by the people. Still others are biblical—"Neither said any that what he possessed was his own, but they held all things in common" and "Jesus said unto him, go sell all thou hath and give to the poor." These two verses, which I'm certain Saul never considered for his *Book of Cyrus*, are emblazoned in gold letters on the blue banners near the stage.

I stand on tiptoe a few yards from the stable point, trying to get a better look at the women near the front of the hall. The goal is to spot Katherine, so that I can steer clear of her, and Prudence, so that I can get her off to the side for a private chat. But between the horrid hat creations that fill the hall and the fact that I'm somewhat vertically challenged, it soon becomes evident that the only way I'll ever see who's at the front is to be at the front.

For the next ten minutes, I inch forward. Victoria is now talking about social justice and the need for unity among reformers. I'm wishing I'd jumped in a little earlier because she seems to be building toward a climax.

I don't realize the woman in front of me is Katherine until someone behind me pushes and I stumble into her. She's wearing a dress of yellow and black, with three different floral patterns. Daisies and black-eyed Susans decorate one side of a straw hat that actually does look a bit like the monstrosity on my own head. The entire costume brings to mind a bumblebee in a field of flowers. I fully understand why Katherine hated it.

Fortunately, she barely gives me a second glance when I mumble an apology. She's engaged in conversation with three other girls about my age—about her age as well, since she's in her early twenties or very late teens here.

I know I need to get away and avoid interaction, but I can't resist watching Katherine for a moment. Was this before she was assigned as Saul's partner, before she fell in love with him? I remember the video entry in her diary, after he used her face as a punching bag, and wish, as I often do, that things were simpler. I'd pull her aside and tell her to steer clear of Saul at all costs, that his supposedly charming exterior is cover for a psychopath.

Of course, I can't. There's no guarantee doing that would stop the events now in motion and every chance that it would leave no one in position to prevent them. I send a mental apology in her direction and turn away, but as I do I see another girl who's also watching Katherine.

It's Prudence. Her dress is dark and shapeless, with no hint of the bustles and frills the fashionable women in the hall wear. At first I think it's navy blue, until I realize the black fabric is slightly altered by the medallion she's wearing beneath it. Her shoes are men's work boots, and I'm guessing she's raised more than a few eyebrows with her hair, which is so short it barely covers her ears. I know Pru doesn't have the CHRONOS costuming team—or any sort of team, for that matter—but it looks like she's wearing whatever she could snatch from an unattended clothesline.

Her expression, a strange mix of forlorn and angry, leaves no doubt that she knows she's watching a younger version of her mother. Combined with the haircut, it makes her look far younger than seventeen.

I'm even more certain, looking at her now, that the pregnant girl at the Rio temple was not Prudence. The last few minutes here in Apollo Hall were the first time I've had any degree of success with forgetting that scene, but now the anxiety and questions come flooding back. As much as I want to convince myself that I'm wrong, that it was the lighting or the camera angle, I know better. That was me in Rio.

I just don't understand *how*. From everything we know, Saul's plan for rebooting the world begins in a few days. Even if the pregnancy was one of those pillow things—and I don't think it was, given the way the toga was draped—that girl was thinner than I've ever been. Older, too. While I find it comforting to think that I'm alive beyond this next week, that girl looked haunted. Who else that she loves didn't make it? And whose baby is she—am *I*—carrying?

I'm jolted out of my thoughts when the entire auditorium breaks into thunderous applause. Well, almost. The exception is Prudence, who's giving me a very odd look. My CHRONOS key is under several layers of fabric and inside the leather case. There's no way she can see the glow, so she's either staring because I'm the only person not applauding or because she's noticed the family resemblance.

I immediately start clapping and shift behind the two women to my left, hoping Pru will forget me once I'm out of sight. Talking to her here would be a bad idea with Katherine so close.

Unfortunately, I can't move. One of my human shields stumbles backward into me as a tall, stout man pushes past several layers of people and hauls himself onto the platform. It takes him a few tries to be heard over the crowd, even though his voice, when it finally comes through, is booming.

". . . the hearty concurrence of every member of this convention. I therefore nominate, as the choice of the Equal Rights Party for president of the United States, Victoria C. Woodhull."

The applause this time is even more enthusiastic. The women next to me are cheering and crying at the same time. In the tiny space between their shoulders and swooping hats, I see Prudence, still staring at me. Ours are the only eyes not fixed on the stage.

Unable to move left, right, forward, or back, I sink down, yanking out my medallion as I go. Buffered by a sea of skirts, I pull up Plan B and blink out.

∞

CITY HALL PARK, NEW YORK
November 2, 1872, 11:00 a.m.

The closest stable point to Woodhull's office is 10 Broad Street, the New York Stock Exchange. But as Katherine pointed out before I left, that one has a little *No Women* icon at the bottom. She says it's never wise to ignore that.

The nearest equal opportunity stable point is at City Hall Park, by the fountain, about a ten-minute walk from my destination. It's Saturday, so the park is rather crowded, and the location is more exposed than I'd like. There's a hedge for shelter in one direction and the enormous fountain in the other, leaving two sides open. I'm glad I took the time before I left Katherine's to pinpoint a moment where I could blink in relatively unobserved.

I arrive in the same crouched position as when I left Apollo Hall and glance around to be sure no one sees me. A young couple strolls by a few seconds after I land, but they're too interested in each other to pay attention to the gaudily dressed girl trying to dislodge her skirt from the hedge.

Once I pull free, I look around to get my bearings. With City Hall in front of me, I take a left onto the path and then another left when I reach Broadway. I've only been to New York once, when I was eight and totally obsessed with *Beauty and the Beast*. A souvenir magnet from the show—the magical rose inside a snow globe— is still on our fridge at the townhouse. Mom and Dad split up later that year, so it was the last vacation we took together. We rode a taxi down this way, but the only things I remember are Dad pointing out Ground Zero where the World Trade Center's twin towers once stood and eating sandwiches in a place I dubbed Zucchini

Park. It was near an ancient church—gigantic, gorgeous, and gothic—with tall spires, statues, and odd sculpted heads sticking out of the building. It probably wouldn't have made an impression except for the fact that I was excited beyond belief about seeing the play that evening, and the church reminded me of the Beast's castle.

I did my usual cyber-sleuthing before this jump, but Google Street View isn't quite as helpful when 140 years have lapsed between the time you land and the time their car rolls through with its big camera on top. Still, this part of New York City was well established by 1872, and the vast majority of the changes around me are cosmetic. The trees in the park seem smaller, and there are fewer tall buildings nearby. City Hall, across from the fountain, gained a few additions over the years, but the architecture is largely the same. So is the general layout of the streets around the park.

Broadway itself, which is paved with something similar to cobblestone, only more regular in size and shape, isn't especially crowded. The sidewalks are, however, perhaps because it's quite nice for November, with just a slight nip in the air. Less pleasant weather would've been better. The foot traffic makes me nervous. It's harder to avoid conversation with someone walking next to you than with someone riding past in a carriage.

There are few unescorted women. Most are with men or strolling together in small groups. They're dressed in brown and black, with the occasional daring soul in navy blue. Either this isn't the most fashionable area of town or Katherine was right about the dress being a bit much for daytime wear. I pull the shawl around my shoulders and lower my head.

A newsboy is hawking papers at the corner a few blocks down. I give him a three-cent nickel—yes, that's a thing in 1872—and tuck the paper under my arm. Hopefully I'll be less conspicuous hanging around outside Woodhull's office if I'm occupied.

Halfway down the block, I have to step into the street to avoid the hindquarters of a dead horse blocking the sidewalk. There aren't many horses on the roads, which seems strange. Most of the carriages and carts are drawn by oxen.

A large cemetery across the street catches my eye just as I'm about to turn onto Wall Street, and I get a sudden flash of déjà vu. We walked down this street. I remember running my finger along the metal rails on that cemetery fence and pointing up at the church—the one that reminded me of the castle in *Beauty and the Beast.*

The cemetery looks the same, but the church is gone. In its place is a Cyrist temple. It's not as awe-inspiring as the previous building, but it's equally massive and shiny white like all Cyrist buildings. How many people does it take to keep it that clean when everything around is stained by smoke and soot?

The temple gives me a shiver of unease, and I keep my eyes on its doors as I approach the corner. That's a mistake because I collide with a kid who can't be more than ten. His grungy face is level with my chest, something that appears to embarrass him at first, but he recovers quickly, grinning and wagging his eyebrows as he backs up toward the shoeshine stand where several other boys are gathered. He whistles a few bars of a tune I don't recognize as I walk away. It must mean something to his buddies, however, because they howl with laughter and clap him on the back.

I give the preteen Romeo an annoyed look and turn onto Wall Street, picking up my pace. The kids don't worry me. They're just goofing around. It's that temple that has the hairs on my neck at attention. Wall Street dead-ends directly across from the temple's entrance. The therapist I saw last year would say I'm projecting my fears onto an inanimate building, and maybe that's true, but as I glance back over my shoulder, the entrance looks like an open mouth and the windows look like eyes. I feel like it's watching me, and I don't breathe easily until I turn onto Broad Street, two blocks down.

Broad Street is more crowded than Broadway, but I don't see any women. Men huddle in clusters along the sidewalk, and from the few bits of conversation I pick up, they're making business deals. Maybe illegal deals, given the way their eyes dart about.

One of them, a tall, husky guy in a poorly fitting suit, notices me, and when I pause halfway down the block, trying to find number 48, he flicks his cigar out into the street and steps in front of me. His eyes travel from head to toe, taking leisurely stops in strategic locations along the way. I feel the blood rising to my cheeks.

"Need some help?" he says.

"No, thank you. I see the office I'm looking for. My friends are waiting for me."

He laughs. "I'd say your *sister* is waiting for you. Except you're the prettier of the two. And maybe smarter as well, since you know it's better for business to keep the goods out for customers to view."

I'm still on edge from seeing the temple and have no patience for this creep, especially when what he just said pretty much confirms that Prudence is here.

I step to one side and he follows.

One of the other men says, "Aw, Hank, she don't want nothin' to do with you. You ain't got enough money to buy one of the girls at Molly's place, let alone someone hangin' out with The Woodhull."

Hank ignores his buddy and slides one of his beefy hands around my waist. Four or five other guys are watching, and I'm not sure how they'd react, so I clench my teeth and resist the urge to give him a kick that would wipe all lecherous thoughts from his mind.

Instead, I just smile and force myself to move a step closer. "Why don't you hold on to my newspaper while I go chat with my sister? And then maybe we could . . ." I shrug and smile again.

"Sure," he says, a little surprised. "Hey, your sister can come, too. Tell her to bring Woodhull and Tennie C., if you want. We'll have a party."

The other guys laugh, and I hurry toward the doorway.

He must realize as I'm leaving that my mood changed too quickly, because there's an edge in his voice as he says, "I'll be waiting right outside, sweetheart, and I can see down the alley. Don't go sneakin' out the back."

"I won't." And that's true. I have no intention of sneaking out the back door, assuming there is one. I also don't plan on leaving this way, either, which means he's going to have a nice, long wait.

I ring the bell and stand there uncomfortably for a bit before ringing again. The men along the curb go back to whatever they're negotiating, except Hank, who leans against a lamppost watching me.

A young girl of around nine or ten finally answers the door. She has solemn eyes and light brown ringlets that frame her round face.

"Hello. I'm Miss Keller. I have a message for Mrs. Woodhull from Mrs. Hooker. May I come in?"

According to Katherine, suffrage activist Isabella Beecher Hooker is one of Victoria's staunchest allies. She also happens to be the half sister of Henry Ward Beecher, the minister whose affair Victoria has just exposed in her paper.

I still think there's a good chance I'm stuck in a soap opera. Everyone is sleeping around, engaged in blackmail, or planning revenge. If I run into anyone with amnesia, I'll have the full set of plot devices.

The girl doesn't return my smile. "Mother isn't home, and she already has one visitor waiting. Do you have a calling card?"

"No, I'm sorry. I'm afraid I've run out."

"All right. I'll ask the Colonel. Wait here."

I nod, and the girl starts to close the door, but then she sees the men behind me. Her lips press together in a knowing expression that looks much too old for her years. "No. You can wait inside. The Curb Market isn't the best place for a lady."

I step inside, grateful to be away from Hank and his companions. "The Curb Market?"

The girl cocks her head to the side. "Are you from out of town?"

"Yes . . . why?"

"I thought so," she says matter-of-factly. "Those men are brokers, or at least most of them are, but they're not the type of gentlemen allowed onto the floor of the Exchange. So they trade on the curb. That man outside the door says rude things to my mama and Aunt Tennie." She nods toward a small bench near the door. "I'm Zulu. You can sit over there."

I'm about to sit, and then I remember Katherine's warning about the padding at the back of the dress. "That's okay. I'll stand."

Halfway up the stairs, she turns back, giving me a shy smile. "I like your hat."

After a few minutes, Zulu comes halfway down. She looks over the railing at me, perplexed, then dashes back upstairs.

I'm just thinking I may try my luck sitting down and risk whatever damage it causes the dress when I hear footsteps.

Zulu, again. "Colonel Blood said you need to stay down here since we don't know you. The other lady used to work with my mama. That's why I let her go upstairs. She looks just like you, except she's not dressed as nice. She's not even wearing a hat."

"Lucky her," I mutter under my breath, but the girl catches it.

"If you don't like your hat, why do you wear it?"

I laugh. "Apparently it's the proper thing to do."

Her expression grows very serious. "Proper isn't always right," she says as she comes back down to the waiting area. "Mama thinks women should be able to dress as they please. She says by the time

I'm grown up, women will be able to wear breeches if they want. Do you think that's true?"

I *think* her estimate is off by about sixty years, but I say, "Let's hope so."

Zulu parks herself on the bench near the door, swinging her feet in front of her. "Breeches are okay, but I wouldn't want to wear them all the time. I like pretty things, too." She looks up at my hat again.

"Would you like to wear my hat?"

Her eyes widen. "Really?"

"Sure. Why not?" I pull the lace ribbons loose and remove the hatpin that anchors the thing to my hair.

"Did you know my mama is going to be president one day?" she asks as I position the hat on her head.

"I've heard something along those lines."

"It may not happen this election because only the men can vote, but Mama says one day women will vote as well. It's our constitutional right. Do you think that's true?"

"I do, indeed." Zulu's hair is down, so I have to tie the ribbons under her chin rather than behind the neck as Katherine did for me. "There! It looks much better on you than it does on me. You should keep it."

"May I really? Thank you! I have to go show the Colonel!"

Zulu is only four or five steps up when we both hear raised voices and a door slamming above us. She slowly reverses course and sits back down on the bench.

"I told you she doesn't have it!" a man's voice exclaims. "How dare you come into our place of business and accuse my wife of theft? She found you work and a place to stay, and this is how you thank her?"

"I never said she stole anything. Please, I have a little money now." I'm pretty sure the voice is Prudence's. I take a step toward the staircase, but I can't see either of them. "I'll pay you—"

"You need to leave. Victoria would tell you the same thing. Do I have to call the police?"

"Fine, I'll go. But I'm coming back. Maybe Victoria will listen to reason."

I hear footsteps, and then Prudence rounds the corner landing. Her hair is longer than when I saw her at Apollo Hall, pulled back in a knot. She's in the same dress and boots, both of which look slightly worse for wear.

Pru pauses when she sees me. Her face shifts from confused to relieved and then back to confused again. "Who are—"

Her voice is drowned out by a loud rapping. "Open the door. Federal marshal!"

She turns back to look up the staircase. "You already called the police?"

A tall, thin man comes barreling down the stairs, pushing Prudence aside with his elbow. His beard is that odd style Hugh Jackman wears when he plays Wolverine, except it's bushier around the edges. He runs one hand through his dark hair, then crouches down so that his face is at the same level as Zulu's. I assume this is Woodhull's second husband, Colonel James Blood—which again sounds like a soap opera name to me.

"Zulu Maude," he says quietly, "go to the office and get your brother. Take him to the attic and lock the door behind you. Do not open the door or speak to anyone until your mother, your aunt, or I come for you. And keep Byron quiet. Do you understand?"

"Yes, sir." Zulu scurries up the stairs, the green hat slipping down to her shoulders as she runs.

Another knock, even louder. "Mrs. Woodhull, open the door."

I glance out the window. The man who's knocking isn't visible from this angle, but two uniformed officers stand behind him on the sidewalk. Another man, not in uniform, sits on the driver's seat of an enclosed carriage. The reins he's holding are attached to a long board connecting the horns of two oxen. Again, where are the horses? Are they all dead or dying in this timeline? And if so, why?

On the plus side, Hank and his buddies have vanished.

Colonel Blood glances at me and then back at Prudence.

"Zulu said you had a message from Mrs. Hooker?" he says, his voice barely above a whisper.

I nod and start to speak, but he holds up his hand.

"I don't care what the message is. Deliver this reply. It's too late for her hypocritical brother to cooperate. The entire nation will know his story by the time we're through. And if there's any justice in the world, the police will soon be knocking on his door as well." He glances back at Prudence and shakes his head in annoyance. "Both of you go upstairs and wait in the outer office."

I don't like the way he's ordering me around, and from the look on Prudence's face, neither does she. I gladly comply, however, since it gives us a chance to talk. She must be thinking the same thing, because she also goes upstairs without comment.

I hear the door open behind us as we reach the second floor.

"Good afternoon, gentlemen. How may I help you?"

"Special Agent Anthony Comstock here with Deputy Marshal Colfax and his partner. We have a federal warrant for the arrest of Mrs. Victoria Woodhull, Miss Tennessee Claflin, and other employees of the publication known as *Woodhull and Claflin's Weekly.*"

"I'm sorry. Mrs. Woodhull and her sister are not here at the moment. I'm not an employee of her paper, nor am I an owner. That's strictly my wife's enterprise."

Comstock says, "You were talking with someone."

"Yes. Two visitors are here to speak with my wife. I told them they could wait in the office upstairs until she returns, but I suspect it will be several hours, possibly longer."

Pru tugs on my sleeve to pull me into the office, a large open room with high windows. Two desks are positioned in the corners, and a sofa and two chairs line the wall behind me near several bookcases. There's a closed door on the other side of the room. The two blue banners with Bible verses that I saw at Apollo Hall hang vertically on either side.

"Listen," I begin, but Pru holds up her hand.

"Shh. I need to hear what they're saying."

So we both listen.

". . . mind if we check upstairs?"

"Not at all," Blood replies, and they all clunk their way up the steps.

I was hoping to be out of here before Comstock and his crew arrived. While there are plenty of historical figures I'd like to meet, Comstock isn't one of them, and Kiernan's comment that Prudence was nearly arrested echoes in my head. If worst comes to worst, Prudence and I can take the CHRONOS exit. I'd rather not do it in a room full of people, but if the alternative is jail . . .

Comstock's portly frame is the first through the door. He looks like a groundhog, with the same atrocious facial hair as the Colonel, only in ginger. The two officers come in behind him, followed by Blood.

"Who are you?" Comstock asks. His pinched expression suggests that he's already decided *what* we are and is simply seeking names to attach to our profession.

"Who are *you*?" Prudence snaps back.

For the very first time, I kind of like my aunt.

"I am Special Agent Anthony Comstock."

"Special Agent of what?" I ask. From what Connor said earlier, he's nothing more than a vigilante at this point.

Comstock lifts his chin proudly. "Special Agent for the YMCA Committee for the Suppression of Vice." Prudence and I exchange an amused look that he either doesn't notice or ignores. "Are you employees of Mrs. Woodhull?"

We both say no, but Colonel Blood disagrees. "The young woman in green is telling the truth. I have no idea who she is. I'm afraid the other one isn't being entirely honest, however. Her name is Prudence Pierce, and she's worked for my wife for the past several months, helping with the campaign and, more recently, with distribution of the *Weekly*."

"That's a lie!" Prudence jumps to her feet and takes several angry steps toward Blood. "I never worked for the paper, only for her campaign."

Comstock holds up his hand. "I'll deal with you presently, miss." He glances at me again, taking in my dress. His nostrils flare like he's caught a whiff of something nasty, but he doesn't say anything, just turns his attention to the closed door across from us. "Would you be so kind as to open that, Mr. Blood?"

"It's *Colonel* Blood. The office door is unlocked."

The marshal closest to the door opens it, and the three of them step inside. Blood hovers in the doorway, his back to us, watching them.

"We need to talk," I whisper.

"Yes," Prudence hisses back through clenched teeth. "I thought you were one of me at first. Who the hell are you?"

I take a deep breath. "I'm your daughter."

Katherine and Connor both thought she might be more willing to believe my story from a daughter than from a niece. We're still unsure exactly what Saul told Pru that convinced her to stay away from Katherine and Deborah. And I certainly look enough like her for the story to be plausible.

"What's your name?"

I catch a note of challenge in her voice just before I'm about to say Kate. I doubt Prudence or Saul would have named a child after Katherine. Even Mom wouldn't have added the Katherine part if it hadn't been Pru's middle name—she simply named me after the sister she lost. And I'm guessing Pru might have done the same, given the chance.

"Deborah. You named me Deborah."

"Middle name?"

"Marie."

The look in her eyes tells me I was right, and then shifts to panic. I'm not sure why, until she says, "But you're born from a surrogate, right? I told Saul no more pregnancies . . ."

I nod quickly to reassure her. "Yes. I was born at the Farm. I met you later, and we . . . talked. Sometimes." My insides are clenching. I'm improvising at this point and well aware that anything I say could trip me up. On top of that, how much am I changing with each word? How much of this will Prudence remember later? Is the version of her currently with my mom sane enough for this conversation to even matter?

The tension drains from Pru's face, replaced by confusion. "He let me name you?"

"Yes. You told me Saul said it was . . . a birthday present."

Lame as hell.

"And you and I are . . . friends?" Her expression is skeptical, but I can see that she wants to believe it.

"We're friends. You asked me to come back and get information to stop Saul. He's pushing you out, doesn't want to share control."

"Why didn't I come myself?" she asks, eyes narrowing. "That's how this usually goes. Older-Me shows up and starts giving orders, just like Simon or Philippa."

"You . . . can't. You're having trouble using the key. And you're worried about the dual memories."

"Hmph. Must be an older, wiser me, because that last part never stopped her before. What—"

She halts abruptly as the men come back into the outer office.

"When do you expect your *wife*, Mr. Blood?" You can almost hear quotation marks around *wife* when Comstock says it.

Blood doesn't comment on the man's tone or the failure to address him by his rank, but his spine stiffens and he practically spits his answer. "As I said, it could be hours."

Comstock gives a smug smile, then plops his behind on the couch. "We'll wait. Colfax, Adams—sit."

The younger deputy, who must be Adams, gives an uncomfortable look in our direction before taking a chair by the door. I'm not sure why he hesitated, but then I realize he feels odd sitting when Prudence and I are not.

Colfax takes the chair next to the couch and pulls a cigar out of his coat pocket.

"Do you mind if I smoke?" he asks Colonel Blood.

"Not at all."

He's reaching back into his pocket, probably for a match, when Comstock chimes in. "Put that nasty thing away. You're on duty as an officer of the federal government. Tobacco in all its forms is a vile, ungodly habit."

Colfax tucks the cigar back into his jacket with a resigned expression.

Pleased that he's struck another blow against the forces of immorality, Comstock turns his gaze to Prudence and me. "Along those same lines, I must ask you two . . . ladies . . . to wait in the inner office. And close the door. Your clothing and demeanor are indecent and unfit for mixed company."

I want to knock that pompous expression right off his face. This dress is tacky and even a bit revealing for the era, but it's hardly indecent. And the only flesh exposed on Prudence is above the collarbone and below the elbow. While her dress doesn't sweep the ground and her ankles peek out a little beneath the hem, calling it indecent defies reason. Then again, I doubt Comstock and reason have more than a passing acquaintance.

Prudence is clearly fighting the same impulse. She's already taken one menacing step in his direction when I reach out and grab her arm.

"Come *on*. We didn't want to stay in here anyway."

Pru yanks her arm away, glaring first at me and then back at Comstock. But she starts walking toward the inner office, and I follow.

"What I want to know," Pru mutters, "is why federal marshals take orders from a dinky little barf bag from the YMCA."

Adams holds open the door for us. I doubt he knows what a barf bag is, but his expression suggests that he's wondering the exact same thing.

∞12∞

48 Broad Street, New York City
November 2, 1872, 12:15 p.m.

Pru sits on top of a large desk facing the door. The wooden desktop shows through in rectangular patches, interspersed with triangles of dust, suggesting someone just cleared the office of its contents. There's not a single scrap of paper or book in sight. Someone must have tipped them off about the pending arrest.

"Saul wants to keep you from getting the keys at CHRONOS headquarters." Talking to Pru feels like walking on ice. I need to move carefully, measuring each step. "From what you've told me, he's planning to send someone to prevent you or anyone allied with you from accessing them without his permission."

"Who's he sending? Simon?" The sneer in her voice makes it clear that, at least on the issue of Simon, my aunt and I are simpatico.

I want to say *yes, Saul is sending Simon*, because he probably is. But when Katherine and I went over this earlier, we decided to keep things vague. The less I say, the less likely I'll slip.

So I opt for good old need-to-know. "You said not to tell you that."

Pru rolls her eyes and huffs. "Major surprise."

"I need to know what happened on that jump—when and where you grabbed the keys, if anyone helped you, and so forth. And we need to hurry. Woodhull will be back soon, and we have to get out of here or the marshals—"

"In case Future-Me failed to mention it, that last part is going to be a problem. I can't get out of here *until* Woodhull gets back. She's got my damn key!"

Oh.

"How did she get it?"

Pru's face flushes, and she says, "I woke one morning and it was gone."

"You don't have a spare?"

"If I had a *spare*, would I have been stuck in this place for the past six months? I didn't suspect it was Vicky until last week—I mean, why would she want it? But then the Beecher story hit, and Teddy began ranting about how Vicky was making him look like a fool in public. Right in the middle, he starts laughing about how she's the foolish one if she believes my ugly old pendant is a conduit to the next world."

The name *Teddy* pulls up an immediate visual for me. I'm pretty sure it's wrong, but I have to ask. "Not Teddy . . . Roosevelt?"

"No, you idiot. Theodore Tilton."

I decide I don't want to know why she's on familiar enough terms to call him *Teddy*. For one thing, he's still married. More importantly, my mind is trying to make a connection to her comment about the key being a conduit to the next world. I can feel it just out of reach, but then Pru starts talking again and it slips away.

"Vicky must've seen me use it once, even though I was really careful." She shakes her head. "It was a release, you know? Coming here and helping with the campaign was something I could do when I needed to get away from Saul and from her to clear my head for a while."

I'm about to ask who she means by *her* when I realize she's talking about her older self.

"They were on my case constantly—jump here, do this, do that. I could never get a minute's peace. Back here, with the campaign, I thought I might actually make a difference. Woodhull's ideas—have you read her speeches? What if they'd actually paid attention to her in 1872? If her views on birth control, poverty, the abolition of war . . . well, almost everything, were taken seriously?"

Her eyes are more animated now than I've ever seen them, and I get the feeling she's not simply talking fast because she knows we could be interrupted. She reminds me a bit of Woodhull herself when she was on stage at the Apollo, but also of this kid from my second-grade class who was really, really into dinosaurs. He could name every species, and he'd keep going forever once he got wound up. I want to steer her back to when and where she got the keys, but she doesn't pause long enough for me to get a word in.

"I mean, do you remember hearing about her in school?" I start to respond, but she barrels on. "Sorry. I forgot. Cyrist tutors for you, right? Anyway, they never mentioned her in my school. Or if they did, they did a piss-poor job, because I don't remember it. I wanted to see if I could make them pay attention. I tweaked a few things, gave her a few stock tips to help juice up the campaign. Not for her to win. Just to be *remembered*, you know? To show that these ideas weren't new. That people have been talking about ending war and controlling the population for a very long time. So they'd see we can't just keep spinning our wheels if we want to avoid catastrophe. And then I could do the same with the environmental movement, and . . ." She trails off and shrugs. "Then maybe people would wake up? Maybe we could avoid Saul's way. It was worth a try, you know?"

A door closes and we hear footsteps, but then everything is silent.

"If Older-Me is telling you to go up against Saul, you aren't safe, either. He doesn't *just* kill puppies, you know."

I'm positive there's a truly awful story behind that comment and equally positive I don't want to hear it. "And if I don't go up against him," I say, "neither of us is safe. No one is."

"But you saw them, too. All the bodies, little kids even. Stacked up in piles to be torched."

It's the same thing Kiernan talked about. An all-time-greatest-hits mash-up of man's inhumanity to man. Glimpses of war and famine and genocide. But all I see in my mind is Saul's own contribution, a chapel full of bodies and one little arm hanging over the edge of the pew.

"Yes. But I don't believe Saul is trying to stop those atrocities. Later on, you won't believe that, either."

What I've said must ring true, because Pru starts talking again, this time finally on the topic of the keys that were at CHRONOS—or at least in the general ballpark.

"The bombing reopens the entire debate about CHRONOS. Not just the time travel, but the laws on genetic alteration. Because CHRONOS agents didn't just get a single tweak like others did. They altered appearance, intelligence, memory, almost everything, in addition to the bits that let them use the key. Tate said that revived the debate about cloning, lifespan exten—"

"Wait, wait. You're going too fast for me to remember any of this."

I have only a vague memory of Katherine talking about the laws on genetic alteration—"chosen gifts," as she called them. CHRONOS may have enhanced the memory of all four of my grandparents, but only a smidgen of that trickled down to me. I'd rather place my faith in a recording. I open my bag, slide my thumb across my phone to *Utilities*, then click the *Voice Memo* app. "Okay, go ahead. First, who is Tate?"

Pru starts again, with a slightly annoyed edge to her voice. "Tate was Saul's roommate, back before Saul and Mother moved in together. Saul sent him a message that got him out of the building the day of the attack. I guess even the devil himself has one good deed in him. Anyway, the government closed CHRONOS for good and reopened the building as an archive and museum. There's this huge educational exhibit about how it was a mistake for humans to time travel, but on the bright side, there's all this info about the past we gained—oh, this is in 2306 that they open the museum. April 27th. One year after the explosion. They've got this exhibit showing how terrorists from the past destroyed CHRONOS. I guess they decided not to reveal my dear mother's role in the whole mess."

I fight to keep my expression neutral. She thinks *Katherine* bombed CHRONOS?

"How long were you there after you accidentally used the key? Or rather, how long were you *then*?" I shake my head to clear it. "In 2305?"

"A little over a year, then maybe another year on and off after I found Saul. The first four months I could barely move. Medical technology is pretty sweet in the future, but one thing hasn't changed. Physical therapy still hurts like hell. They had this one machine that—"

Interrupting seems risky, but it sounds like she's headed off on a tangent. "Yeah, you mentioned before that it really hurt. What happened after?"

"Well, once they decided I was telling the truth that my arrival was an accident and not some plan Mother cooked up, they put me to work at the new museum, talking about what it was like to be a kid in the olden days." She grins. "Those visitors got some interesting quote-unquote history. They were okay people, though, at CHRONOS. They wouldn't let me keep my key because they were worried I might actually figure out how to use it again, but they kept me under a CHRONOS field just in case not being under it would make me . . . you know." She snaps her fingers. "Pop into the reality next door or whatever. Even after what my mother did, most of them just acted like I was one of the historians who survived the attack, like Tate. But it was much worse on him than it was on me. They stuck him at one of the exhibits, just talking about the Vikings. Tate is a doer, not a talker."

There's a new gleam in her eyes as she says that, and I'm pretty sure she's imagining this Tate guy doing, not talking.

I cast a nervous glance at the door, and she shifts back on topic.

"Anyway, Tate and I both realized the keys in the exhibit weren't real. They were glowing, but all the same color, and *everyone* could see the light. Tate found out the actual keys were in the archives. There was one guard—one *old* guard—on that floor. The fake medallions in the exhibit were better guarded. I guess they assumed no one could use them without the equipment, and they didn't rebuild that. So when Saul decided we needed those keys for all of the little Cyrist babies he was planning, I convinced Tate to help me. We'd change things, get his job back so he could go do Viking stuff again. So he'd be happy. Tate took care of the guard, I returned Campbell's key, and then I was out of there. Piece of cake."

"Campbell's key?"

"Yeah. A friend of Saul's. No clue why he had a key, since he doesn't have the CHRONOS gene. Simon says Saul told him it was all about a bet, but Saul never mentioned that to me. I guess you have to be his drinking buddy to get that info. Anyway, Campbell's the one who loaned me the key in the first place. So that I could find Saul. Tate showed me how to use it."

She's hopping from one subject to the next so much that I'm having trouble keeping everything straight. I can't help but wonder if her brain isn't already too jumbled to trust, but what alternative do I have at this point? "Okay," I say, "so you find Saul, and he eventually decides he wants those keys. When you jumped back again to get them did you go to the same stable point as the first time?"

Pru gives me a look like I'm too dumb to live. "No. Shattering my back and legs a second time seemed like a *bad* idea. I set a stable point in the museum before I left."

From what Katherine told me, historians didn't have the ability to set local stable points after 2150. It was a purposeful safety built into the system because CHRONOS didn't want them changing things in their own lives or the lives of others. They could set local stable points in historical locations to make things easier on future jumps to that same place and time, but the system blocked anything after the period when time travel technology was created.

This must be another second-generation glitch. The original historians' genetic code was locked in when the system was destroyed, rendering the equipment useless for them, but that data wasn't in the system for those of us who inherited the gene. There was a similar safeguard preventing historians from jumping from one location to the next without going back to HQ—the limitation Saul assumed would be lifted if he destroyed their home base. But the only thing blocking me from jumping from Point A to Point B to Point C, ad infinitum, is the fact that it wears me out and confuses the hell out of me.

"Of course," I say, pasting on a silly-me expression. "Don't know what I was thinking. It's been a long day. I don't suppose you *remember* those coordinates at the museum?"

Prudence snorts, as I expected she would. The geographic coordinates alone are more than twenty digits, so the best I can hope for is a date and approximate time.

"Not likely. But I'll transfer them straight to your key if we ever get mine back from that thieving bitch."

Well, that's a game changer.

If I have *that* medallion—the one with the exact coordinates that Pru used on the jump when she retrieved the other CHRONOS keys from the future—everything becomes much, much simpler. No jet pack jumps into crumbling buildings required. No wandering around trying to figure out when and where they grab the keys. Just pop in and grab them. Like she said before, *piece of cake.*

Maybe it's the accumulated weight of all my dumb questions or maybe something in my expression shifted while I was thinking all of that through. Either way, when I glance back at Pru, her eyes have narrowed into little slivers of suspicion. I can almost hear the gates clanging down around me.

"So, riddle me this, Batgirl. How do I know *you're* not the person Saul's sending to stop me from getting the keys? Hmm?"

"I'm not—" I begin, but apparently the question was rhetorical, because Pru keeps talking.

"It would make perfect sense from Saul's perspective. You look like me. Saul might even think Tate won't know the difference. But he most *definitely* will. Saul doesn't know half as much as he thinks he does about me or about Tate."

"Prudence, I'm not—"

"Lips zipped. Not telling you *anything* else."

Pru pushes off the desk and crosses to the window. She lifts back the curtain, looks outside, then curses and kicks the baseboard. I walk over and see it's a straight drop of about thirty feet to a brick courtyard. If she was thinking of the window as a possible escape route, it's not going to happen.

"I'm not with Saul."

"Yeah, well, prove it." When I don't respond instantly, mostly because I'm trying to think of *how* I might prove it, she takes it as confirmation. "I have no reason to trust you and no time to waste. Vicky could be back any minute, and as soon as she walks in that door, that d-bag out there is going to cart all of us off to the Tombs."

"It's not the Tombs until later in the month. Ludlow Street Jail today."

"Who cares? Jail is jail."

From what I read, that's not true. The Tombs was hell on earth, with few accommodations for celebrity guests. Ludlow Street is more like house arrest. Zulu will visit Victoria and Tennie there tomorrow, along with half a dozen journalists, friends, and associates.

"Either way," I say, "Comstock won't be taking you. From what you told me—"

"Yeah, well, whatever I told you was what happened *before* you showed up. Are you basing your jail-or-no-jail predictions on that?" Pru arches an eyebrow. "Thought so. I'd have been out the door before the cops arrived if Zulu hadn't kept bopping up and down the stairs to ask questions."

I get a sick feeling in the pit of my stomach. It's partly because she could very easily be right, partly because she could also be completely wrong, but mostly because I have no way of telling the difference.

Is my being here the reason she escapes or the reason she doesn't?

Ack!

I rub my eyes and look at Pru, who is again staring out at the bricks below the window. Time travel conundrums aside, my best chance for getting Prudence's key is to get her out of here and handle Woodhull myself. Pru won't be worried about the key Victoria has if she has my spare—at least she won't be worried about it immediately—and I won't need extensive information on who helped her, when, where, and how. I can just jump in, use a bit of brute force if necessary on this Tate guy, and take what I need. I generally prefer finesse to brute force, but I make exceptions when the clock is quite literally ticking.

I unfasten the back of my dress. "Let me put this another way. Comstock won't be taking *you* to jail. Hopefully he won't be taking me either. I'll stay here and get the other medallion from Vicky. You . . . you've done enough. If I give you my spare key, you can get back to the Farm, right?"

Pru stands there gaping for a moment, then kicks off her shoes. "You have a frickin' spare? Why didn't you say so earlier?" She starts stripping out of the grungy stockings. "But you should leave, too. I mean, we look alike, but not that much alike. Comstock—"

"Comstock's not a problem. Did he look at your face? Because he barely glanced at mine. Colonel Blood might notice the difference, or one of the others, but Comstock? No way."

Several minutes later, I'm in Prudence's black dress and stockings. Her shoes, however, are nearly two sizes smaller than mine, and I can't squeeze into them. My black ballet flats are more obvious beneath this slightly shorter skirt, but we don't have another option.

Prudence doesn't even bother to put on my dress. She flings it and her boots over one arm and stands there in a very modern-looking bra and pale-blue panties with a Smurf face on the front.

"Tell them I jumped," she says, tugging on the window.

"Are you kidding? No one could walk away from that jump."

"Fine. Tell them I used a time key and went back to the frickin' future. Your choice."

She snaps to attention. I hear it, too—voices. Downstairs. Female voices.

"They're back. I need to go. Give me the damn key!"

My hand wraps instinctively around the spare key, and I have to force myself to drop it into her hand. This could be a huge, gigantic, enormous mistake.

Prudence smiles and hugs me. I stiffen at first, but make myself hug her back. It's not as hard as it was in London. This Pru has some rough edges, but she wasn't nearly as horrid as a teen. It's a little easier to see why Kiernan was attracted to her.

"I'll see you back at the Farm," she says. "But when?"

"You said—"

"Never mind. You can't tell me that." Pru sighs. "Believe me, I've heard it before. Is the Farm even on this key?"

No, no, no. I didn't think about that.

"I don't know! You gave it to me. Just go somewhere that's not here!"

At almost the exact moment Pru disappears, the door swings open, and a woman steps into the office. "I need a few minutes to gather my things."

I recognize her from the photos. It's Woodhull's sister, Tennessee Claflin—or Tennie C., as she's usually known. Her dress is similar to the one Victoria wore at Apollo Hall—like a women's version of a business suit, with a black jacket and skirt, a crisp white shirt with a narrow row of ruffles down the front, and a purple ribbon at her throat. It fits her differently, however—she's much more curvaceous than her sister.

"Prudence!" I get the sense that she was expecting to see someone in the office, but not me.

"Blood sent Zulu to the attic," I whisper.

She nods, then says, "How unfortunate that you were caught up in this. But with any luck, our attorney will have us—"

Comstock pushes through the door, with Victoria and Colonel Blood just behind. Judging from the sisters' expressions, not to mention Colonel Blood's casual attitude earlier and the stripped-clean state of this office, they expected the arrest. It's good publicity—the price for a copy of the paper will skyrocket over the next few days, and I suspect they're savvy enough to have ensured that most of the money comes their way.

"Where's the other one?" Comstock demands. "Where's your sister?"

"What sister?" Victoria asks.

"She jumped." I glance over my shoulder at the open window.

"Oh dear God!" Tennie rushes to the window, probably expecting to see a body on the bricks below.

"I don't think she was hurt," I say. "At least not badly. She walked away."

Comstock yells into the outer office. "Colfax! Adams! One of them escaped through the window. The one in that . . . that *dress*. She can't have gotten far. Go after her!"

"Why?" Colfax asks. "From what Colonel Blood said, that girl wasn't involved with the paper."

"Perhaps not, but she's engaged in immoral activities. You heard the man outside. She propositioned him . . . in broad daylight."

I'm definitely wishing I'd kicked him now, no matter how many people were watching.

"Sorry. Unless she's advertising her services through the mail, she's committed no crime under my jurisdiction as a federal agent." Colfax delivers this line with an air of satisfaction that I suspect is directly related to the unsmoked cigar in his pocket.

Comstock sputters, then points to Woodhull and Blood. "Then grab these two and toss them in the wagon."

"You don't need to *grab* or *toss* us," Victoria says in a very gracious tone as she and Blood walk into the outer office. "We'll go peacefully. This is a clear violation of our rights under the First

Amendment. My attorney will have us out by nightfall. Is your wagon covered, Officer? I believe we're in for a bit of rain."

I'm sure Comstock imagined this scene playing out differently, with the wicked Woodhull being dragged from her office screaming obscenities. Yet here she is strolling out with Adams, calmly chatting about the weather. He stares for a moment, looking disgusted by the whole situation, then steps forward to grab Tennie's arm.

She jerks away. "I'll also come willingly, but I need a moment alone first."

"No," Comstock says. "You might jump, too."

"Hardly. The things I need are upstairs, in my personal quarters. It's difficult to imagine someone jumping from here without injury. I'd hardly take that risk from the top floor."

"No," Comstock repeats, gripping her arm harder this time, and though she tries to wrench away, she can't. "Colfax, take the other one."

Colfax steps into the office, and Tennie looks at him imploringly. "I hope you are more reasonable than this gentleman, sir. I need a moment alone to attend to a *personal* matter." She pauses and then adds, "Of a *feminine* nature."

Colfax's face turns slightly red. Comstock's eyes bug out, and he drops Tennie's arm like it's on fire, brushing his hand against his jacket.

"I have to go with her," I say. "Same reason."

"Of course," Colfax stammers, moving away from the door. "We'll . . . um . . . just . . . wait. In the stairwell. Until you're . . . done."

Comstock doesn't speak. He's still trying to pull in a breath, and his face is turning a rather alarming shade of purple.

I follow Tennie, who's wearing a pleased grin. "Works every time," she says as she unlocks the attic door, "especially with the pious types. But why did you follow me? I just need to speak with Zulu—"

"And I need to speak with you."

The attic room is dark except for the sunlight coming through a single window, partially blocked by the shoulders of a young man looking outside. Several cots are on the floor, along with a bed and two chairs. Stacks of papers are everywhere, scattered among the books and office equipment.

Zulu comes running over and hugs her aunt. The green hat is still hanging on her back. The young man follows her, making strange noises. This must be Byron, Victoria's older child who was born with brain damage.

Tennie pulls him into the hug, too. "It's all right, Byron," she says, rubbing his back. "But we still need to be very, very quiet and stay in the chair. Can you do that for Aunt Tennie?"

Byron nods and put his finger to mouth, making a *shh* sound. He then goes back to his chair near the window, still holding the finger to his lips.

"Zulu, once everyone has gone, get Byron to Aunt Utica."

Her face falls. "Can't we just stay here? I can take care of him, you know I can! Utica's mean as a snake—"

"I know you can take care of him. But I suspect the police may come back to search after we're gone. I don't want you dealing with them if we can help it. Roxy and Papa Buck are at Utica's. Byron will be okay with them overnight. You both will."

Neither Tennessee nor Zulu look convinced by the statement, but Zulu says, "Yes, Aunt Tennie." Then she looks at me. "Did you come up because you want your hat back?"

I glance down at the dress. "How did you know it was me?"

"Your eyes. And the pink spot on your neck."

My hand flies up to my right jawline. The scar is barely noticeable now, just a slightly discolored patch.

"Why did you swap clothes? The other dress was much prettier."

I give her a weak smile. "You can keep the hat. And you have sharp eyes."

"I do," Zulu says. "Mama and Aunt Tennie say I'll make a good writer for the newspaper in a few years."

At the word *newspaper*, Tennie scans the stacks of papers and equipment along the edges of the room and sighs.

Zulu picks up on that, too. "Do you want me and Byron to take the papers with us?"

"No, sweetheart. We got two cartloads of them onto the streets before that foul little man arrived. That will have to do. Every word on those pages is truth, and we have the right to print them. We have a friend across town who'll print another run tonight. You just watch out for Byron and yourself."

Then Tennie turns to me with a piercing look. "So who exactly are you? Why would you swap places with Prudence if you knew those men planned to arrest her?"

"We're after the same thing, Ms. Claflin. Your sister took something that belongs to us. We need it back."

"Is this about that ugly hourglass pendant? Prudence *gave* that to Vickie. That's what she told me, and my sister always tells me the truth."

I start to object, but she holds up a hand and leans down to Zulu. "We have to go now. Keep Byron away from the window, okay? Someone might spot him. Mama and I will see you tomorrow at the very, very latest."

Zulu nods and goes over to her brother, watching wistfully as we leave.

"Comstock is probably already headed to the courthouse," Tennie says. "I thought his head was going to explode. But they're probably getting impatient, and even if you aren't actually

Prudence, you'll have to come with us. Otherwise they'll come looking for you, and they'll find Zulu and Byron."

"It's okay. I have to talk to Victoria anyway. I'd be happy to pay her for the pendant."

She laughs, heading down the stairs in front of me. "Too late for that. Vickie sold the dreadful thing weeks ago—along with almost everything else we owned, trying to scrape up the rent."

"Sold it? To whom?"

She doesn't answer. Marshal Colfax is on the landing, alone. I glance into the office as we pass by, but I don't see Comstock anywhere, so Tennie may have been right.

"Hello, Mr. Colfax," Tennie says. She slips her hand into the crook of his arm and smiles coquettishly up at him. "I'm ready to go now. Shall we?"

Ten minutes later, I'm squeezed into a carriage between Tennie and Adams, the younger marshal. Woodhull and Blood are across from us. Comstock is long gone, and Colfax opted to ride up top with the driver.

Tennie squeezes closer to the window. "They should have let us walk to the courthouse. It would be faster than these oxen move. More comfortable, too."

I really want to ask about the lack of horses, but I bite my tongue. Everyone else seems to know what's going on, and confessing my ignorance on this point won't do anything to improve my current situation.

"Since we're going to be in here for a while," I say to Victoria, "perhaps we could talk about my medallion. The one you *borrowed*?"

She sniffs. "I understood that was a gift, Miss Pierce. A token of appreciation after my nomination for the presidency."

My arm is pressed against Adams's side, so I feel his ribs move as he struggles to hold in a chuckle. His poker face must need work, too, because Victoria gives him a knowing look.

"Do you doubt the government would be a better place if women were involved, Officer Adams? Would your mother allow the level of corruption we see in this city? Would she vote for leaders who let children starve in the streets while the wealthy live in splendor? Or would she demand accountability?"

Adams doesn't respond. She's winding up to speak again, but I cut her off.

"It wasn't a gift. I was trying to be polite, but you took it without permission. And I need it back."

"I tell you what," Vicky says. "I'll have my attorney represent you so you don't have to spend more than, oh, let's say a week or so in jail. Surely that's adequate payment for such a paltry trinket?"

"It was my grandmother's. I don't want to stay in this city—there's no work for me here—but I can't return home without the pendant. My grandfather will be furious, and . . . he isn't a kind man."

There's a bit of truth in the mix, but Victoria isn't buying it. "Demosthenes says the medallion isn't even yours."

I have no idea who this Demosthenes person is, but she's talking like I should know him. "Then Demosthenes is lying."

Victoria draws back like I've just slapped her. "The spirits cannot lie! I know exactly why you want the pendant, but something like that belongs in the hands of someone capable of communing with the spirits. And I no longer have it, anyway. I couldn't figure out how to work . . . the clasp. So I sold it."

"To whom?"

"An acquaintance who deals in such items. I thought he might be able to make it work, and he was willing to give me six bits."

Seventy-five cents? She didn't even hold out for a dollar. "Would you give me his name and address? I'll gladly pay him double that—"

The mention of cash jolts Colonel Blood awake. "Since when do you have money? Last I heard you were sleeping on a rooftop outside Molly's place. Can't see why she wouldn't let you have one of the beds."

Victoria and Blood both laugh. I don't get the joke until I remember the jerk outside their office—one of his friends said something about "Molly's girls."

"That's not funny," Tennie snaps. I'm not sure why she's taking my side, but it's clear their little joke didn't sit well with her. "Is that the job you recommended her for? A brothel?"

Victoria glances at the marshal and gives her sister a cautionary look. "Of course not, Tennie. Molly needed another girl to work in her kitchen. The job only paid room and board, however." She gives my bag another pointed look.

"My mother sent me money to come home," I say through clenched teeth. "Not much. Just enough for a ticket and maybe some food. I'll walk home if I have to, but I can't go back without the medallion."

"I'm sorry. I can't help you, Miss Pierce."

Tennie looks at her reproachfully, then goes back to staring out the carriage window. We've just turned onto Broadway, clomping slowly past the shoeshine stand, where the group of boys is still gathered.

The trees along the edge of City Hall Park have just come into view when Tennie says, "The man is Ira Davenport. Or possibly his brother, William. Ira was in Boston for the meeting of the American Spiritualist Association back in September."

"Tennessee Claflin! How dare you!" Victoria whacks her sister's knee with her handbag.

"Oh, be still, Vicky. You're being petty. I told you I didn't detect anything connected to spirits when I held the stupid thing. It couldn't possibly transport anyone to the spirit realm."

The connection my mind was trying to make earlier finally snaps into place—Houdini's interest in spiritualism. And while it could be wishful thinking, I'm fairly certain I saw the name Davenport in the books about Houdini.

"Thank you," I say. Tennie nods, but doesn't look my way.

The carriage draws to a stop outside the courthouse. Word of the arrest seems to have spread quickly. The sidewalks are packed, with people spilling over into the park. Comstock stands on the steps, waiting to take credit for his latest effort to protect the city's virtue.

"I doubt the information will do you any good," Victoria says, straightening the blue tie at her neck. "The Davenports are currently on tour. And even if I decide to ask our attorney to represent you—and I'm not at all certain that I shall—there's still the matter of bail. Did your mother send enough for that?" She smiles, moving toward the door. "I suspect you'll be here a lot longer than we will."

And you'd be dead wrong, I think.

Colonel Blood holds out his hand to help Vicky out of the carriage. Tennie follows, and while her skirts are blocking the door, I pull out my key and vanish.

∞ 13 ∞

Kiernan's exactly where I left him when I jump back into the alley near the Hippodrome.

"How long were you gone?" he asks, his voice tinged with suspicion.

"Long enough to get the information I need."

"Where did you get that?" He's looking at the 1905 dress I'm wearing.

I don't answer because he knows perfectly well where I got it—from the guest room closet at his cabin in Georgia. Prudence is off somewhere in time with the mutilated remains of the dress he bought, and the clothing options at Katherine's are nearly depleted, so I didn't have much choice.

"You should have asked."

"Why? From what you've told me, it's my dress."

Kiernan's jaw tightens, and for a moment it looks like he's going to disagree. "Perhaps. But when last I checked, it was inside *my* house."

He has a point. Our relationship has changed a lot since he said the room was mine whenever I needed it. No big shock, I guess, when it's been six years for him. And I'm glad that he's moved past the point of building a cabin in the woods for a girl who'll never live there.

But I miss his friendship. Maybe he never really thought of me that way—as a friend, even if we couldn't be more than that—but it was nice to feel I wasn't entirely alone in all of this.

"Fine, Kiernan. I'll keep *my* dress in *my* closet from now on. Would you like to erase your cottage's stable point from my key while we're establishing boundaries?"

I try to keep the snarky tone to a minimum, but it's definitely still in the mix.

He stomps off down the sidewalk without responding. I follow at my own speed, making no special effort to keep up with his longer stride. I can just as easily not talk to him from ten paces behind.

It's a clear night, and the reflection of the moon and stars on the ocean's surface reminds me of the lights from the boardwalk on the Thames when I was with Trey. Was it really last night? It seems longer. I'm not certain how many hours it's been since I slept.

The breeze carries the same damp chill as it will in London a century in the future, except I don't have Trey's arm around me to ward off the shivers. His flight has probably landed and he's back in DC by now . . . or is the correct term *by then*? I just wish he was here and now.

Kiernan is waiting by the entrance when I arrive at the Queen's Hotel. "I'll be in the lobby. The bar is over there, through the double doors. Houdini should be here soon. If you need me—"

"I won't."

That's not true, unfortunately. Less than a minute later, I discover that I need him in order to even get a table.

The maître d' informs me that unescorted women are not allowed in the bar. In fact, he says with an imperious look, unescorted women aren't even allowed in the restaurant.

"You can't be serious!" I stand on tiptoe and look around to see if Houdini has, by some chance, arrived ahead of me, but there are no familiar faces among the mostly male diners. "How are female travelers expected to eat?"

The guy draws himself up to full height, which really isn't necessarily since he's easily a foot taller than me, and shoves a menu into my hands. "Please lower your voice, miss. Choose something from the menu and I will have the plate delivered to your room."

"No. Someone is meeting me here." His face is a closed door, so I adopt a tone I've heard Mom use. "I'd like to speak with your manager, please."

"The manager is busy, and our policy is absolute. No respectable establishment—" The man breaks off in midsentence about the time I feel a hand on my elbow.

Kiernan leans in and plants a quick kiss on my cheek. "So sorry to leave you stranded, dearest. You were right—my notecase was lying on the bed, right where I left it. Don't they have a table?"

The maître d' lets out a relieved sigh. "My apologies, sir. Your . . . wife . . . failed to tell me you would be joining her. Please follow me."

"I do hope she wasn't battering you with the whole women's rights routine. If so, you have my sympathies. I hear it day in and day out."

Two middle-aged men at the table we're walking past seem to find Kiernan's comment amusing. One barks out a cloud of foul-smelling smoke as he laughs.

There's this scene in an old martial arts film I watched with Charlayne once upon a time in that faraway reality where the Cyrists and CHRONOS were of no concern. Jackie Chan, or maybe it was Bruce Lee, single-handedly took out every man in the restaurant. While I'm under no illusions that I could actually do that, the feminist inside me would dearly love to try right now.

I wave smoke out of my face and follow Kiernan. Our less-than-gracious host is now explaining why it would be best if we were seated in the restaurant rather than the bar.

"Very well," Kiernan says with a touch of annoyance. "But we're waiting for a business associate who expects to meet us at the bar. So when Mr. Houdini arrives, please show him to our table."

If the maître d' recognizes the name, he doesn't show it. He just gives a deep nod that borders on a bow. "By all means, sir."

Kiernan reaches to pull out my chair, but I beat him to it and then nudge the chair across from me out about six inches with my foot.

He pulls it out the rest of the way and says, "Thank you, dearest," in a droll tone before retreating behind the menu.

I scan the menu simply for something to do while we wait. I'm really not hungry. Connor and I finished off some leftover pizza after I got back from 1872. I think we both needed comfort food. Neither of us is sure I did the right thing by giving Prudence my spare key, and we're both worried about Katherine. Connor says headaches like the one that hit her in the library earlier are becoming fiercer and more frequent.

Kiernan still has his nose in the menu. It's mostly in French, and it's a single handwritten sheet, so I suspect he's using it to avoid talking to me.

"Do you know what you want?" he says as the waiter approaches.

"Yes. To get the key and get the hell out of here."

"I meant to eat."

"I know what you meant. I'm not hungry."

"Fine. I'll order for you."

I give him a scathing look and glance back at the menu.

"I'll have the salmon with potatoes and haricots verts. A pint of bitter. The lady will have the same."

"No." I hand the waiter my menu. "The lady will have the cherry . . . tart?"

He nods, so my layman's interpretation of *tartes cherise chantilly* must be correct.

"And to drink, madam?"

"Tea. Earl Grey. Hot."

Yes, it's stupid, but it gives me a perverse pleasure to see that the joke is lost on both of them.

"Of course, *hot*," Kiernan says under his breath as the waiter heads back to the kitchen. "The British don't serve tea over ice, even in your time."

"I actually know that. Why don't you just go back into silent mode?" I think about that for a moment. "No, on second thought, who knows when Houdini will arrive, if he arrives at all. I have questions. Answer them or I walk out, because I think I can get this key on my own now. It doesn't have to be here. My first question is what in hell happened in the past six years to make you hate me?"

"I don't *hate* you, Kate. Although I can't say I'm particularly fond of your tendency toward adolescent drama."

"Okay, I'll rephrase. What happened in the past six years to turn you into a total ass? It can't be anything I've done, since I've lived . . . oh, let's see . . . maybe seventy-two hours in that time, and no more than three of those in your presence."

He doesn't answer, so I latch onto his wrist and flip his arm over. A tiny sliver of the scar shows beneath the cuff. "Then let's start here. What happened to your arm? I don't think it's a coincidence that this scar is in the same spot as Prudence's extra key."

And I really *don't* think it's a coincidence, even though the similarity didn't dawn on me until I looked down at his arm.

"It's not," he admits. "I went along when Pru had the upgrade. A black market operation in a hotel room in Philly."

"When?"

"Fall of 2152," he says in a whisper. "Or about four years ago, if you're asking about my own personal calendar. But this isn't the time or place to—"

"You had the chance to answer my questions in private. So here and now works fine for me." I nod at his arm. "Why?"

"Wasn't my idea. I woke up one morning with the bloody thing grafted onto my arm. Pru's idea of a gift. She said we were twinsies now." His sneer, both physical and vocal, makes it clear what he thinks of that term.

"How did it get . . . out . . . of your arm?"

"Got infected. It was a long jump for me. Pru left the day after the operation—she wouldn't stay put long enough to wait for my batteries to recharge. Said the doctor would check back in on me, but he didn't. I spent about a week with a raging fever in a flea-bitten hotel room. When the owner finally called the cops, the temporary visa Prudence gave me didn't hold up to closer scrutiny. They moved me to a detention center for illegals. One of the more zealous guards decided to remove the key on his own."

The waiter chooses that exact moment to appear with our food. He slides the plate in front of me—blood-red cherries inside a flesh-colored crust—and my stomach churns. I wait until he leaves and push the tart away.

"I'm sorry, Kiernan." The words seem insufficient, and the scar along my right jaw tingles for a moment. If not for Kiernan's help in Chicago, I'd be even more visibly scarred than he is.

He shrugs, cutting into the salmon with the side of his fork. "It was a long time ago. Pru finally remembered to come looking for me. She paid a hefty bribe to a guard at the detention center to return my key. And she hasn't let me forget it since."

"Couldn't she have just jumped back and stopped them from apprehending you?"

"Could've," he says, taking another bite. "But didn't. Said it would teach me to be more careful in the future." He flashes a brief, chilly smile and pops a forkful of green beans into his mouth.

I know this is the older Pru, not the one I just left in New York. But given that someone—me—helped her avoid jail in the past, it would've been nice if she'd had the decency to pay it forward.

"How long were you stranded?"

"A while." Something about the way he says it makes me shiver.

"And they couldn't fix it? I mean, they have doctors at the Farm, don't they?"

Kiernan doesn't answer, just takes another bite. He seems intent on polishing off his dinner in record time.

I'm about to repeat the question when he says, "By the time I got back, it had scarred over. June said she could cut away the scar tissue and stitch it up proper, but I didn't see the point in getting cut up again."

"Do you still have the stable point in your key?" My voice is hesitant. I know what he'll say, but I can't *not* offer. "I could go back . . . or forward, I guess . . . and get you out of there."

He doesn't look at me, but his expression softens. It's only for a moment, however, and then the mask is back up.

"No, Kate. You couldn't. So . . . is that it? I'd like to finish my dinner so I can move to the bar before Houdini arrives. I still think it's best if he doesn't see us together."

"I think you're lying."

"About what?"

"About why you're wolfing down your food and retreating to the bar. Houdini will be annoyed either way. It won't matter whether he knows you're behind this or thinks I'm in it alone. And both of us together would have a better chance of convincing him.

I think you just don't want to spend any more time with me than absolutely necessary."

He raises an eyebrow. "And you always said I was the one with the ego."

I ignore him and continue. "What I don't know is why. Julia would say it's because you've been with Saul and Simon all along. She thinks you were involved with the death of her son—"

"Anthony." Kiernan's mouth twitches downward. "What? You think I killed him?"

"No." And I really don't. Whatever else is going on, I still have a hard time buying Kiernan, even this older, harsher version, as a cold-blooded killer. "But the way you're acting isn't really helping your case."

"Anthony was stupid." While Kiernan's words are more callous, it's pretty much the same thing Delia said in the video. "Why he thought it would be safe to let Saul know he could use the key is beyond me. He'd just split up with his wife—she moved out and took the kid. Maybe he thought he had something to prove. Or nothing to lose. All I know is that he got hold of a key and showed up at Estero in 2028 thinking Saul and Simon would welcome him into the club. And they do—shake his hand, slap him on the back, and say it's great to have him on board."

He takes a long drink from his beer. "Two days later, Anthony's walking out of a convenience store back in 1997. Car zips around the corner, and he catches a bullet in the head. Next time I see Abel—he's nearly a hundred by then, using one of those metal walkers—anyway, he starts waving his fist at me, screaming I killed his grandson. Simon's right there next to me, and I can promise you that if Simon didn't shoot the man, he paid for the bullets. But Abel doesn't say a damn thing to him. Just me."

Kiernan stabs a potato with a bit more force than necessary. "And I still had to talk Simon down, tell him Abel was old and senile. Otherwise Abel would've been dead. Delia, too, most likely. Maybe even Julia. It only bought Abel and Delia a few more years, but at least they went from natural causes. Yet they paint me as the bloody villain."

"No one expects Simon to have a conscience, Kiernan. And when you're hanging around with him, acting like old friends, well . . ." Some of the old vulnerability is in Kiernan's eyes when he looks up at me, but I continue anyway. "It's hard not to lump you together is all. Why did you lie to me in Georgia?"

"I explained that."

"You explained *part* of it. But I watched the two of you through the key that night. Before you got into the car. You and Simon . . . it's like watching two brothers argue. And before I went back to save Martha, you promised you'd tell me everything you know. You promised on the ring I saw in that picture. The one you drew onto your Kate's finger."

Kiernan shakes his head. "You're reading more into that sketch than you should. It was drawn by a lovesick kid, the equivalent of a schoolgirl writing *Mrs. Johnny Jones* over and over in the margins of her paper. Wishful thinking."

He scoops the last bit of fish into his mouth. "And now I've told you what I know. Once we're done with Houdini, we'll go forward, get the keys at CHRONOS, and let Connor work his magic on them. That's going to shake up the Cyrist world, to say the least. We stop the Culling, you go back to your life, and I go back to my cabin."

"Does Prudence get the keys before or after she takes the *Book of Cyrus* and *Book of Prophecy* to the past?"

"After," he says. "She drops off the books about six months after she finds Saul and—"

"How does she even find him? What happened to her when she landed in the future?"

I've already heard Prudence's abbreviated version. Will I get the same version from Kiernan that I got from her? And if I don't, who's lying?

"Why didn't you ask her yourself?" He looks a bit smug about having caught me off guard. "Yeah, I remember you stopping by the cabin, Kate. I probably wouldn't have if Martha hadn't mentioned you taking a blood sample. So when you start talking about me keeping secrets, just remember that you started it first."

"I did not! That was just last night . . . no. Not last night. It was earlier *today*. Which means it was after you lied to me in Georgia, after I saw you in London, and after you acted like a jerk at Houdini's show."

He stares at me like he's waiting for me to catch on, and I do, after a moment.

"Okay. Fine. *Technically*, it was before all of those things for you, if it triggered a double memory, but—"

"I couldn't remember everything we said. Everything was fuzzy, probably because of the mostly empty bottle of Old Grand-Dad on my kitchen table. But I remembered you saying something about talking to Younger Pru, back when she was mad at Saul. Not sure what else we said, but it occurred to me that next morning that pretty much any time I ever talked to Pru, she was mad at Saul. And that got me to thinking about how I could use that to our advantage."

"So you deciding to play double agent . . . or triple agent, whatever . . . is my fault?"

He flashes a quick grin. "Maybe. Partly."

"Whatever. I'll take the blame. And yes, I talked to Prudence, but we didn't have much time. I know she was injured when she landed at CHRONOS."

He nods. "She never talked much about it, but I think she dreams about it sometimes, or at least she did when she was younger. Simon got some of the story from Saul, and I got some of the story from Simon when he was drunk. Pru jumped into that black . . . static. I don't know if she did it on purpose or if it was an accident, but there was nothing below her aside from a gaping hole that went clear down to the basement. This Tate guy found Pru. She was the only one alive in the rubble. And it wasn't just people who were at the headquarters the day it was bombed. Four or five historians who were stranded in the field were found down there, too."

"Oh my God. Grant? He was staring at that stable point that night at Martha's—"

"No clue. But that confirms my suspicion about the stable point still being there, just not being very reliable. Anyway, Tate gets the medics in there and they get Pru to the hospital. Most of her bones were shattered. She wasn't doing any talking at that point, but her blood did the talking for her. They'd figured out whose daughter she was by the time she came to. Kept her quarantined, confiscated her CHRONOS key, but eventually someone slipped her another key, helped her get to Saul. Maybe the Tate guy, maybe—"

I'm so focused on what he's saying that I don't even notice Houdini until his hand is clutching Kiernan's collar.

"Just as I thought. Sal said you were lurking around tonight." Houdini's expression isn't nearly as friendly as it was on stage. He must realize that people are staring, however, because he drops Kiernan's collar and laughs like it's a big joke, slapping him on the back. "Good to see you again, my friend!"

He pulls out the chair next to me and steps to the side. I'm not sure why until I see Bess a few feet behind him. Houdini's not much taller than I am, but Bess is so tiny that his frame completely blocked her from view. She slides into the chair, and Houdini takes the seat across from her.

The waiter hurries back over when he sees them. Houdini starts to wave him away, saying they've already eaten, but then he glances over at Bess, giving her a soft smile that crinkles his eyes.

"Unless you'd care for something, Mike? Some champagne, perhaps?"

It must be a nickname, because Bess shakes her head.

Houdini leans back in his chair after the waiter leaves, looking first at Kiernan and then at me. "I think introductions are in order. I won't bother with our side, since you very clearly know who we are. So who are you?"

"Kate Pierce-Keller. This is Kiernan Dunne."

"I won't say it's a pleasure," Houdini says, "because it's not. I'm here because Bess wonders why you wear a medallion identical to my good-luck charm." He narrows his eyes and looks at my face again. "And I can't shake the feeling I've seen you before. Otherwise I'd simply have sent Smith, so he could convince your friend here to adopt a more original stage name."

"But . . ." I say, "you took your own stage name from another magician. Robert Houdin?"

Bess sniffs indignantly. "It's not the same thing. Mr. Houdin died before Harry was even born. Taking that name was an homage. Mr. Boudini, on the other hand, is a competitor trying to profit from our hard work."

Kiernan shakes his head. "I'm really not a competitor, ma'am. I've done a few shows . . ." He looks confused for a moment, and I realize he's trying to sort out whether we're before or after the shows he did at Norumbega. "I also . . . have a contract to do some shows in Boston in early July, and I'll need to honor it. But that will be the end of The Amazing Boudini. The entire purpose was to get your attention so we could discuss this."

He pulls the CHRONOS key out of his vest pocket and nods for me to do the same. "We tried to contact you several other ways, but we failed. My creation of Boudini was a last-ditch effort."

"Your medallion was stolen from my aunt," I say. "As you can see, it's part of a matching set. My grandmother is dying, and her last wish is to see all of them back where they belong. If you can tell us where you bought it and how much you paid, we'd be happy to reimburse you."

I'm pretty pleased with that as a bare-bones cover story. Every word of it is true, and it's kind of nice not lying, especially since I suck at it.

The sincerity seems to have some impact on Houdini, because his face softens a bit. "My sympathies to you on your grandmother's illness. But I'm afraid I cannot help you. There's only one reason I wear this, and it's the same reason no amount of money could convince me to part with it. I saw this charm in a case at Ira Davenport's home back in 1899 and told Bess it reminded me of something I'd seen in Chicago just before I met her. Bess went back later and asked if he'd sell the piece, but he said it wasn't especially valuable. He presented it to her as a gift. And she gave it to me."

"He got his big break the *very next day*." Bess taps the table three times to emphasize each word, and that's when I see the tattoo. It's faded, barely noticeable, but definitely a lotus. "We played a full season in Omaha, and we've been booked solid ever since. It's brought us wonderful luck."

I glance over at Kiernan and direct his eye to her hands, which are back in her lap before he looks over.

Houdini laughs. "I suspect that's mere coincidence. Nevertheless, I do know my wife worries less about my safety when I wear this. I'm not superstitious. Bess, on the other hand . . ."

I sigh. Time to add the next layer to the story. And since Houdini claims he's not the superstitious one, I aim it at Bess.

"My grandmother's request isn't just sentimental, Mrs. Houdini. You may consider it a good-luck charm, but my family has found it to be the reverse. There are some individuals who can use these medallions to . . . harm people. We're trying to prevent that. We're also concerned they might try and take it from you by force."

Again, all of that's true, but it sounds overly dramatic, even to me. I'm not surprised when Houdini laughs.

"This is merely a piece of metal, Miss Keller. If it has any effect on me at all, it's because wearing it reminds me that my wife worries about me. I take fewer risks."

"What did Ira Davenport think? Didn't he believe it could transport him to the spirit world?"

"If Davenport thought this item was in any way connected to another world, I doubt he'd have given it to Bess."

"Did he know it was stolen property?"

He shrugs. "I don't know him well enough to say for certain, but the Davenport brothers are respectable men. I can't imagine either of them knowingly dealing in stolen goods."

Bess gives me a challenging look. "Are you saying it was stolen from *you*?"

"No. It was taken from my aunt, in 1873, by Victoria Woodhull, although Woodhull claimed it was a gift. When my aunt tried to get it back, she learned it was sold to Mr. Davenport."

Kiernan's eyebrows go up, so he clearly didn't know Houdini's key originally belonged to Prudence. Houdini and Bess don't look surprised, however, so they must have heard at least some of the story from Davenport.

"Mrs. Woodhull believed it had magical powers," I say. "That it could transport her to the spirit realm if she learned to use it. When she couldn't make it work, she sold it to Davenport."

Kiernan leans forward. "I'm guessing that's because you *can* make it work, Mr. Houdini. Maybe that's how you manage . . ." He pauses when my kick lands on his shin, but finishes the sentence anyway. ". . . some of your more elaborate escapes."

Houdini pushes back his chair and starts to leave.

"No! He doesn't use it, Kiernan. Like I said earlier, the light never went out. And he's . . . in Katherine's books. From before. I think they're telling the truth. He wears it for good luck."

Houdini drops back into his chair. "What do you mean, the light never went out?"

"The escape behind the curtain. I could see a bright blue light above and below. I can see it now, coming from your key . . . your medallion . . . from all three of them. So can he." I nod my head at Kiernan. "If you'd been using the key to help with your escape, it would have flickered out for a moment. And it didn't."

"What did I tell you?" Bess says excitedly. "It's an aura."

"It *might* look like an aura. I've never seen those. But it's not related to spirits. It's more . . . scientific. The medallion reacts to something in the blood of certain families."

Bess nods. "The ability to commune with spirits runs in families, too."

Houdini sighs. "Because families are better at sharing and keeping each other's secrets, sweetness. They're less likely to turn a so-called medium in to the authorities for bilking a client out of her life's savings."

Bess gives him a sassy look. "I've never claimed they're all genuine. Obviously some of them are fakes, but you've a long way to go before you'll convince me they're all swindlers, and your mother would agree."

That seems to silence Houdini, and Bess turns back to me. "Mrs. Woodhull told Mr. Davenport that the girl who gave her the medallion could disappear into thin air just by waving her hand above it. She said the girl told her it was a spirit device and that it had a bright green aura for her. If that was your aunt, maybe she wasn't being truthful. Perhaps she really did give it away. You see, I've read Mr. Grumbine's treatise on auras, and while it does depend on the shade, a green aura can be a mark of deception or dishonesty."

I shoot Kiernan a smug glance. While I'm certain this aura stuff is total bunk, he and Prudence both see the light as green. "Does this Mr. Grumbine say anything about blue auras?"

"Again, it depends on the shade. But it's usually associated with truth." Her eyes widen, and she looks at Houdini. "What if she's telling the truth? What if the charm is like that play we saw last year in London? About the monkey's paw? Yes, it's brought good luck so far, but . . ."

Houdini's lips press into a firm line, and he looks annoyed, not so much at Bess as at me. It's a see-what-you've-started-now sort of expression.

"I don't think it's brought any sort of luck, Mrs. Houdini," I say quickly. "Good or bad. It's like your husband said earlier. Just coincidence."

"But he also said he's seen you before! He told me tonight when he saw your face in the audience that you were there the first time he saw the charm. You're the girl he saw vanish at the World's Fair! Is that also coincidence?"

Kiernan gives him a suspicious look. "You performed at the Expo?"

"Yes," Bess answers. "Along with his brother, Dash. They head-lined as The Brothers Houdini on the Midway Plaisance."

"Really?" Kiernan shakes his head. "I was there as well. For the *entire* run. I knew every headliner on the Midway."

Houdini eyes shift slightly. "Well, we weren't exactly headlin-ers, but yes, we did perform at the Fair." He turns to Bess. "And I said it looked like her, sweetness. But it can't be. She'd have been a child twelve years ago."

Kiernan glances around the restaurant and leans forward so he can speak more softly. "It wasn't twelve years ago for her, Mr. Houdini. The medallion is a time travel device. I thought perhaps you were using it in your act, to help you escape."

He holds up a hand when Houdini starts to protest. "If Kate says you're not, I believe her, but there really are people who'll be coming for that medallion. We'd like to keep it from falling into their hands, but we're also concerned for your safety. They've killed at least one person who didn't hand it over freely."

Bess grows pale, and she reaches for Houdini's hand across the table. "Give it to him. It's cursed. I don't want you—"

"Mr. . . ." He flounders about for Kiernan's name and then spits out, "Boudini. You have upset my wife. And now you ask me to hand over a gift she gave me. A gift I've worn and cherished for over ten years. Come on, Bess. These people are engaged in a confidence scheme, and we are far too smart to fall for it."

"You're Cyrist," I say to Bess. "The tattoo?"

She raises her eyebrows. "No. My parents were Cyrists. I tried it as a kid, but it didn't take. Too many restrictions. My mother was scandalized that I went onstage and married a performer, not to mention a *Jewish* performer."

"What has that to do with anything?" Houdini asks.

"The people we mentioned are Cyrist, too. The entire religion is a . . . what you said before. A confidence scheme. Created by people with these keys. We're trying to stop it."

His mouth tightens. "Nice try, Miss Keller. Here's an idea for you. If this really is a time travel device, when do I die? Do you know?"

I can't remember the exact day, but I do know the year—1926. He has a little over twenty years left, according to the histories I read—both the ones from this timeline and the ones in Katherine's library. His star will continue to rise, his name will be a household word in most of the world. Then, at the height of his fame, he'll insist on doing a show when he's far too ill to perform.

I open my mouth to explain why I can't tell him, but he holds up his hand.

"Don't tell me!" He leans across the table and says the words so forcefully that I feel specks of saliva hit my cheek. "Just remember it, because the day that I die is when I'll be done with this gift from my wife. I will leave it in her hands, to do with as she pleases. Until then, do not come near either of us. Have I made myself clear to both of you?"

Houdini stomps around the table, grabs Bess's hand, and then they're gone.

"Well, that went well," Kiernan says after a few seconds. He nods toward my cherry tart. "Are you going to eat that?"

I shake my head, and Kiernan pulls the plate toward him.

"He dies in 1926. I'll find out the exact—" I halt when I realize the man at the table across from us is listening in. "Let's go back to your room. The neighbors are nosy."

Kiernan stops in midbite when I mention his room and once again looks uncomfortable.

"Really?" I hiss under my breath. "You act like I'm going to pounce on you the second we're behind closed doors."

And since when would he consider it a bad thing if I did?

"No," he says quietly. "I'd just . . . maybe a walk on the beach instead?"

"Whatever. I'll meet you outside."

The ocean breeze hits my face as soon as I step out the door. I breathe deeply, hoping it will clear my head. The wind whips my hair around, pulling strands from the loose knot at the back of my head. For the first time quite possibly in forever, I wish I was wearing a hat.

The longer I'm around Kiernan, the more I wonder how much I can trust him. If he's on our side, he needs to know the Culling has a definite and impending launch date—at least for everyone in my time who can't escape into the past. The fact that there's no tattoo on Kiernan's hand worries me. It seems odd that Simon would leave his dear old chum unprotected, but thinking back, I don't remember seeing one on Simon's hand, and it's a very safe bet that he's protected from the virus.

I take a seat on the same log where I saw the couple earlier when we were walking to the Hippodrome. The temperature seems to have dropped ten degrees in the past hour, although it could just be that I'm closer to the water. After a few minutes, Kiernan sits down on the log next to me.

We're both quiet for a moment, just looking out at the half-moon on the waves.

"Houdini dies in 1926," I say. "I'm not sure of the date, but it was very well documented. I'll check it when I get back to Katherine's. If Bess will give the key to me after he's gone, fine. If not, I'll jump back a few days and take it."

"Bodyguards," Kiernan says. "Usually armed."

"Then I'll go back to the spiritualist meeting, or whatever it was, and keep Woodhull from giving it to the Davenport guy."

"How did Woodhull get it in the first place?"

"Someone stole it off Pru when she was asleep. She seemed a bit . . . embarrassed about it, so I'm guessing she'd either been drinking or she wasn't sleeping alone. Maybe it was the Theodore Tilton guy? She'd have been carted off to jail with Woodhull and the rest of them if I hadn't given her my spare key."

"Do you think that was a good idea?"

"That's exactly what your great-grandson asked when I got back to Katherine's. And I'll tell you what I told him—I have no idea, but I couldn't see another option. You said she didn't go to jail, and my being there seemed to have changed that."

"What did you tell her?"

"That I was her daughter from one of the surrogates. That she'd asked me to go back and get information on when and how she got the keys from CHRONOS HQ because Saul is trying to prevent it. That her memory is Swiss cheese by the time she's thirty, which she already knew from encounters with her older self. I kept it as vague as I could. Does it . . . feel like she changed to you?"

His forehead creases. I'm pretty sure he's sorting through his growing collection of double memories. Finally he shakes his head.

I look out at the water again for a long time, debating how much more I should tell him. He's quiet, too, either because he doesn't have anything else to say or maybe because he can just tell that I'm thinking. Does he know the date they've set for the Culling? Does he know that at some point I'll be under Simon's control?

"I need to know what you're hiding from me before I can tell you anything else," I say. "I want to trust you, but you've changed so much. I told Julia to kiss off when she said you were a traitor, but a lot of other people's lives are on the line here. You need to meet me halfway."

"Kate, look at me." When I do, he holds my gaze for a moment, then says, "I'm sorry for being an ass. I'm just not . . . comfortable around you. Before, I believed you were still my Kate or that I could change you into her, given the time and opportunity. But over the past six years, I've . . ."

He stops, staring at toe of his shoe as he runs it back and forth a few times in the sand, and then he gives me a pained smile. "I've come to accept that you're really not her. I thought I'd made my peace with it, until our paths crossed again, and . . ." He gives a wry laugh and rolls up his sleeve. "Being near you is like this scar. While I'll admit the wound didn't heal cleanly, I don't want to go through the pain of opening it back up."

I feel tears come to my eyes. "You're sure that's it? You haven't gone over to the Dark Side?"

"Kate told me once that they have cookies on this Dark Side. But no. I'm in this to the end."

I'm pretty sure he's being truthful on that part. Still, I can't shake this niggling feeling he's not telling me everything.

But can I really ask that? Doesn't he have the right to some secrets?

Once again, I'm left with the same decision. Either I trust Kiernan, despite my doubts, or I push ahead alone. I might have this Fifth Column behind me now, but none of them can help me on a jump. Who do I trust more in a matter of life or death, Max or this angry, older Kiernan?

The answer is still Kiernan.

"Okay, then. Back to Houdini. We need that key before we do anything else. It's Pru's key, and it has a stable point that will keep me from having to operate a rocket belt."

He gives a quiet chuckle. "I'm not even going to ask."

"What's your best estimate for when they'll do the Culling?"

Kiernan looks surprised. "The date? Um . . . I've heard some guesses, but I don't think anyone knows for sure. I'm not even sure Saul has decided. Simon joked once that we were on a ten-year plan—basically the ten-year anniversary of Saul's arrival. So I'd say 2034."

"They've pushed things forward a bit." I unfold a Xerox copy of the news article from September 17th stashed in my pocket. It's too dark to read, so I hold my CHRONOS key close to the paper so that he can see.

Kiernan skims the article, then looks back at the date. "How far away is this for you? I mean, what day—"

"September 11th. So less than a week." I wave the medallion back and forth. "But plenty of time when you've got these, right?"

"Maybe, if the enemy didn't have them, too. Kate, they know about the Fifth Column. I don't know how much, but I've heard rumblings. I mean, things changed. Suddenly you've got this moderate group that wasn't there before. Saul's not an idiot. Neither is Simon. They both connected it to Delia and Abel. To me being back in the fold. I think I've convinced Simon I'm not a threat, but . . . they *are* watching the group." He runs a hand through his hair, and that reminds me about the tattoos.

"Tilson believes that they've inoculated Cyrists—at least the Orthodox variety—through the tattoos. Some sort of subdermal . . . something." He gives me a look. "I'm sorry. It's been a long day and I've heard a lot of technobabble."

"And where are they in terms of an antidote?"

"Not an antidote. A vaccine. And we have one. But I have no idea how we'll disseminate it. Tilson thinks the virus will be spread by the Cyrist regional and local Templars. And they've already started with official speeches about The End and the wrath of nature. Prudence made an appearance today in Rio. Except . . ."

"Except what?"

I hesitate, not because I don't trust him with this, but because suddenly I feel very exposed here on the beach. If someone were to kidnap me in the past, that would leave plenty of time for me to lose twenty pounds or so and become noticeably pregnant before the speech in Rio.

Kiernan grips my arm. "Katie. Except *what*?"

"Except it wasn't Prudence." I'm shaking now, both from the chill and from fear. "It was me. A very thin, very *pregnant* me, trying to scream out a warning to the crowd."

He's off the log now and on his knees in the sand in front of me. His hands are holding both of my arms and his eyes are wide. "Where in Rio? Do you know the exact time?"

"No. It was this afternoon. The Templo . . . something . . . something. I can't remember. We watched it on the Cyrist news. On the computer." I wriggle my shoulders, but he just grips tighter. "Kiernan, let go. You're hurting me."

He lets go and sits back, his eyes darting around to various spots on the sand in front of him, like he's trying to figure something out. "Do you need my help with Houdini?"

"I don't think so. I mean, it'll be Bess, assuming Houdini keeps his word. I can handle Bess."

"She may have bodyguards . . ."

"If I can't handle it, I'll let you know."

He nods and then holds out his hand. "Give me your medallion. I'll set a time for us to meet at the cabin. Get Houdini's key, and we'll leave from there for CHRONOS."

"Kiernan . . . are you sure you can make that jump? I'm not Pru. I won't leave you behind to be arrested and tortured, so if you can't make it there *and* back, I should go alone."

"I'll be smarter this time." He gives back my key, but holds my hand for a moment longer. "Are you okay?"

I nod, but it must not be convincing, because he pulls me forward into a hug. The whiskers feel odd against my skin, but his arms are safe and reassuring. When he pulls away, his dark eyes lock onto mine.

"Just remember that what you saw isn't . . ." He stops and sighs. "It's not necessarily *your* fate, okay? We can fix this. We can fix *all* of it."

∞14∞

BETHESDA, MARYLAND
September 11, 5:37 p.m.

"Your phone rang," Connor says. "Twice. One was your dad, so I answered. The other was Trey, so I answered."

"You do know there's this fancy new invention called voice mail, right? It lets callers leave a message for me so I can call them back."

"Yeah. I think I've heard of it." He clicks off his monitor and spins the computer chair around to face me. "But they're both worried about you, and they'd be more worried if they got kicked to voice mail. And I thought I'd save you a little time by bringing both of them up to speed."

Valid points, but I still take my phone off the desk and stick it into my pocket. "Thanks, I think."

Connor gives me a cheeky grin. "Always happy to do my part. Harry had to take your granddad to the doctor this afternoon. They've got some sort of home health care worker coming in first thing tomorrow morning, then he'll head back here. Trey is on his way over now. He said to tell you he loves you madly and he's missed you every single second."

"He did not." I hesitate for a moment and then ask, "Did you tell them about the video from Rio?"

His jaw twitches. "Not Harry. He's stuck there overnight, and . . . I couldn't. I gave Trey the link, though. But I told him we couldn't be certain of anything, because we can't. That girl didn't look exactly like you to me. I still think it could be Prudence."

"You've never met Prudence."

"I've seen photographs. It looks as much like her as it does you."

I shake my head. As much as I'd like to believe he's right, I know better, and denying it won't change what I saw. The only thing that will change it is me ending this nightmare, and to do that, I need to find Bess Houdini.

"Is there anything in the costume trunk that might work for 1926?"

Connor glances down at his flannel shirt and faded jeans. "You're seriously asking me? Anything I've told you about historical fashion has been passed along from Katherine. Speaking of, she's awake, but the light makes her head worse. I told her we'd stop by her room."

He flicks off his monitor, and I follow him downstairs. I've never actually been in Katherine's bedroom, at least in part because Connor stays there most nights, and Katherine's still pretending no one else knows that. It's silly to act like I'm a little kid who'd be shocked, but it seems we always have more pressing matters to chat about than their relationship status. And if it would stress her out for me to know, I don't mind playing ignorant.

The lamp on Katherine's bedside table has one of those really dim night-light bulbs. The CHRONOS key in Connor's pocket is almost as bright. Daphne hops down from the foot of the bed where she's been snoozing and squeezes through the door before Connor pulls it shut.

"Kate." I expect Katherine's voice to be weak, but it sounds normal. "I told Connor I could just put on some sunglasses and meet you out there, but—"

"We can just as easily talk in here. Right, Kate?" Connor pulls up a chair from the corner, and I sit on the edge of the bed. A faint medicinal smell permeates the room, although I think that's due more to the half-full cup of herbal tea on the nightstand than the bottles of pills next to it.

"Connor briefed me on everything except your visit with Houdini. Did he cooperate?"

"No. At first he said we could pry it out of his cold, dead hands. Then he amended that slightly, saying Bess could take it from his cold, dead hands and give it to us. So my next stop is 1926. Costume ideas?"

"Hospital, funeral, or house?"

"Haven't gotten that far. I'll check my notes on Trey's laptop when he gets here and see which is closest to a stable point."

"Well, either way, I have a black drop-waist dress in the closet. It's not ideal, but it should fit you well enough, and the length is about right. If you have some closed-toe heels, you'll be fine except for the hair. Unless you want to cut it, I'd advise shoving it under the cloche hat—"

"Which I had to ditch behind a jail toilet in 1938 Georgia."

"Or you can be the only teenage girl in the late 1920s who resisted the stupid craze of bobbed hair."

I smile. "I think I prefer that option."

"Do you think Bess will actually give you the key?" Connor asks.

"Maybe. She's kind of superstitious. Kiernan and I had her convinced the key was bad juju. She begged Houdini to hand it over to us then and there. But that seemed to set him off. Bess will be a total wreck when he dies. I hate to bother her at a time like that, but if I wait too long, we risk her getting rid of it."

The doorbell rings, and Daphne sounds off a second later. It's not her stranger bark, so it must be Trey. I start to get up, but Katherine holds me back.

"Let Connor get it. We need to talk for a moment."

"Sure." I swallow hard and turn to face her, scared that this is a just-in-case-I-die-before-you-get-back talk. I can't deal with that yet.

"Don't look so worried. I'm okay."

"No, no. I'm not worried."

"You're a lousy liar, my dear, even in the nearly dark. But we're not quite to the part where I start in with tearful goodbyes. It's just . . . I've watched it again." She takes the phone from the nightstand, taps the screen, and hands it to me. The video at the temple in Rio is paused at the point where I'm screaming the warning to the crowd. "In fact, I've watched it more than once, because it bothers me on several levels. Saul's plan goes into action in a matter of days. And from everything we've seen, Prudence has been pushed aside. Why would he need you posing as her at this stage of the game?"

"Maybe Saul has run out of hours in the day that he can steal from Younger Pru? Like Julia said at the meeting yesterday . . ." I stop, trying to remember whether that was yesterday or earlier today, and then decide it doesn't matter. "Julia called Prudence the human face of Cyrist International. Or something like that. And unfortunately, her face is pretty close to my face."

Katherine nods slowly. "True. Prudence's face *is* the one on their religious art, at least most of it. She's the one their people recognize. Their fertility goddess, their symbol of the future. Their constant."

"And even if the Cyrists are spared the brunt of the Culling," I say, "they'll lose friends, family members. I don't see how you could lose that much of the population and not risk the social structure and economic system breaking down. Maybe Saul thinks they need the image of Prudence to keep the survivors centered. To keep them focused on rebuilding this new future in the way he wants."

She takes the phone back and stares at the screen for a moment. "How many months ahead would you say this is?"

"Six?"

"I'd guess closer to seven. I saw Deborah several times when she was pregnant with you. She was dreadfully thin. Poor Harry kept enough ice cream in the house to start his own Ben & Jerry's, but anything she ate came right back up until around six months."

Kiernan said pretty much the same about Prudence when she was pregnant, but I'm not sure Katherine needs to hear the details. It won't make her feel better to think about the fate she couldn't protect her teenage daughter from. And since all signs are pointing in that direction for me right now, I don't want to dwell on it either.

"Well, on the plus side, my scar continues to fade."

Katherine waves her hand. "It's barely noticeable now if you wear makeup. And I wish you wouldn't make light of the situation, Kate. You need to be very, very careful. I know you don't . . . *usually* don't . . . take reckless chances, but this video tells us that in the course of events as they currently stand, the Cyrists will grab you at some point and take you back—"

"I know, Katherine!"

It comes out more sharply than I intended, and I hear the thrum-thrum of my pulse revving up. I draw a deep breath through my nose and release it very slowly before continuing, trying to keep my voice calm.

"I know. And that idea terrifies the freakin' hell out of me. If locking myself in the closet for the duration was an option, that's exactly what I'd do. But it's *not* an option, and if I'm going to get through this, I need to avoid dwelling on the thing that terrifies me."

"I'm sorry." Her voice is quiet and frail, and her eyes fill almost instantly with tears.

And mine, of course, instantly follow suit.

"No! I'm the one who should be saying sorry. I didn't mean to upset you. It's just . . ."

Katherine reaches out and pulls me toward her fiercely. Her grip is almost painful, and I can't help but feel she's trying to give me what strength she has left to help me get through this. And that starts me crying—big, wet, noisy sobs—because the other thing that terrifies me is knowing that even if by some miracle I stop the Culling, even if I never become the girl in this stupid video, my time with Katherine is drawing to a close.

When I finally look up, Katherine gives me a tender smile and reaches for a tissue, then shakes her head. "On second thought, this isn't going to suffice. Go into my bathroom and grab a wet cloth. Cold. I'm afraid none of the Shaw women 'cry pretty,' but in my experience a cold compress will solve the worst of it."

I do as I'm told and then lie back down across the foot of her bed, holding the cloth against my eyes.

We're both silent for several minutes, and then Katherine asks, "Did you figure out what's going on with Kiernan?"

Her usual crisp, no-nonsense, down-to-business voice has returned. I'm relieved to hear it. I needed the cry, needed the release, but I can't afford to dwell on my fears right now. And neither can she.

"I think so," I say, propping myself up on my elbows. "He's says he's having trouble being around me again, after so long."

"You don't sound convinced."

"No, I believe him. It's just . . . I still get a feeling there's something he's not telling me."

"Do you trust him?"

It's the second time she's asked me that in the past few days. I sigh, because the answer is still more complicated than I'd like. "I trust that he's not with Saul. That's he's still in this fight. And that's all that really matters. Everyone needs their secrets, I guess. But I'm not sure how much help he'll be anyway. I don't know if he's overusing it, or if his ability with the key is deteriorating, but I'm not sure he'll be able to make a jump to CHRONOS and back in rapid succession. I'm worried he'll get stranded . . . again. It's happened once already. Pru just left him somewhere, and I couldn't do that."

I take a deep breath. "And speaking of Prudence, she thinks you were responsible for the sabotage of CHRONOS. Not sure exactly what Saul told her, but . . ."

Katherine doesn't look surprised. "Well, I knew he must have told her something. That son of a bitch. What I wouldn't give to use that key one last time." She squeezes my hand. "Go. Trey is waiting."

I get up and toss the washcloth into the sink. "One more thing. Pru mentioned someone named Tate. He wasn't on the list, but he's CHRONOS, right?"

"Yes. Tate Poulsen. Nice enough guy. Studied the Vikings, a few other primitive warrior societies. He was Saul's roommate the year I was in field training. Seemed more brawn than brains, but Saul said that wasn't true once you got to know him. Why?"

"Do you think he was in on Saul's plan?"

She thinks for a moment. "If he was, why would Saul have left him in the future? We usually jumped in cohorts, organized roughly around the eras we studied. But there were exceptions. I took a few jumps to the medieval era during training and studied a few women's groups in the 2100s as well. Saul could've found a time when Tate was in the field with him, if that's what he wanted. Why did Prudence mention him?"

"I think they were friendly. Possibly . . . very friendly. Kiernan said Tate was responsible for rescuing Pru from the CHRONOS wreckage and probably for connecting her with Saul."

"From the frying pan to the fire." Katherine sighs. "I'll see if I can dredge up anything else on Poulsen later this afternoon. Now go. I'll bring the dress out in a few minutes."

"No, I'll just come back after—"

"Oh, would you stop it, Kate! I am not a total invalid. I'll tell you the same thing I told Connor. There's no way I'm checking out until this whole damned thing is finished."

I muster up a return smile, even though I can't help but worry she's jinxing herself.

The aroma of coffee hits my still-stuffy nose as I walk into the kitchen. Trey sits at the breakfast nook near Daphne, who has a new toy—a bone decorated with the Union Jack—wedged between her paws.

"Somebody likes her souvenir."

Trey hands me a round candy tin with pictures of London tourist spots. "You have to share the toffee with Connor and Katherine. And me. But this guy . . ." He reaches behind him and pulls out a Paddington Bear, complete with his blue coat and red hat. "He's all yours."

I smile and hug the bear. "Was your flight okay?"

He must catch the hint of guilt in my voice because he pulls me closer. "The flight—both ways—was totally worth it. Connor says you've been busy."

"You could say that. We have less than a week, Trey. And Victoria Woodhull is kind of a bitch. Houdini could be a bit more reasonable, too. And . . ." I stop and just look at him. I don't have the words to talk to Trey about Rio.

Apparently he doesn't have the words, either. He pulls in a long breath through clenched teeth, and then he kisses me, hard. A little too hard, but I'm okay with that.

When the kiss ends, he says, "I love you so much, and I want to tell you I won't let anyone hurt you. But . . . you're going places I can't follow and—damn it! This sucks, Kate. It totally sucks."

I don't say anything, because that pretty much sums it up.

His voice is flat when he continues. "I watched the video in the cab coming from the airport. I've never had the urge to kill anyone, Kate, but when I saw that guy grab you like that. . ." He shakes his head and says, "Kiernan's going with you, right?"

"He's going with me to get the keys at CHRONOS, but not to get the key from Bess. Houdini's wife."

As I say it, I realize that Kiernan's decision not to go on this jump is evidence of how much has changed. Kiernan has the same information that Trey does about Rio. If Trey could use the key, he wouldn't let me out of his sight. I'd have 24/7 backup. The same would've been true for six-years-ago Kiernan, even if it took him weeks to build up enough "battery power" to make the jumps.

"I could ask Max to go," I say reluctantly. "It might not be too bad, if he'd stay in the background."

"He can use the key?"

"So Connor didn't tell you everything," I say as Connor walks in, heading straight for the coffeepot.

"I hit the high spots. Anyone else want some? There's no milk . . ."

Trey passes, but I need the buzz. "I can take it black. And yeah, Max can use the key. Not very well, from what Delia said on the video, but he can use it."

"And he's the only one?" Trey asks. "The only jumper? What good is this Fifth Column if they can't back you up?"

"Well, for starters, they created a vaccine." I fill him in on the events at the Fifth Column meeting. When I'm done, he shakes his head.

"So Tilson is the only one who's done anything really meaningful—he and his colleagues. The rest of the group seems more concerned about jet packs and making sure their branch of Cyrists survives."

"Well, maybe. But the jet pack thing was to keep me from breaking my neck. And . . . they don't want to kill anybody. They want to stop the genocide."

Connor snorts as he slides my coffee in front of me. "Bravo, Fifth Column. They win *all* the gold stars." He pries open the toffee and grabs a few pieces. It smells good, but I don't have any appetite. I wave it away when he pushes the tin toward me.

"Yeah," Trey says. "If the best thing you can say about them is that they're not in favor of genocide, especially when that genocide would apparently include them, since they're New Cyrists, well . . ." He shakes his head.

What they're saying makes sense, but I can't help but feel I've painted Julia's group too cynically. "The religion is part of their heritage. Even knowing the bad side, maybe they want to salvage something. To turn those resources into a force for good?"

They nod, although I doubt either of them is convinced. I'm not even convinced. But going back to what Katherine said earlier, they're the only allies we have, and we need allies.

"Would Max help you get the key from Bess?" Trey asks. "Honestly. Don't just say what I need to hear because I'm worried."

I think for a moment. "If he stayed in the background . . . I guess. Maybe?"

"But you don't think he will?"

"No. Max seems like . . . maybe he's jealous of my ability with the key? He wants to play hero. I don't think he'd be content just providing cover. And I'm worried having him there might spook Bess. I mean, you've both seen Max."

"Yes," Connor says dryly. "If this Fifth Column gig doesn't work out, I hear they're casting for a biopic of the Rock."

I snicker because there actually is some resemblance in the face, even though Max isn't anywhere near *that* large. "The bigger issue is that Julia didn't want me going after Houdini yet. She didn't know the key he has belonged to Prudence, but she told me to wait, and I'm thinking that after defying her about London, this would just make things worse. I'll be careful. And I'll have the gun."

They both go a little pale, and I wish I hadn't reminded them about the Colt.

"What if Bess says she doesn't have the key?" Connor asks.

"Then I go back to when they left the restaurant in 1905 and take it by force. If that fails, I go back and track down Ira Davenport. Either way, I need this over and done with before tomorrow morning. We're supposed to meet at Tilson's place at eleven. I don't have the address, though. Just coordinates."

A yawn punctuates the last sentence. I glance at the clock. It's only eight, but I was up much of the night, and I'm not sure how many hours have been packed into this day.

"It's okay," Trey says. "Tilson lives maybe ten or fifteen miles north of Gaithersburg. I have his number. I'll call, get the address, and meet you there."

"Or maybe come back and pick me up here? A car ride, a little time to wake up properly, would be really, really nice."

Connor gives me a hesitant look. "Umm . . . this isn't something Julia expects Katherine and me to attend, is it? Because . . ."

"No. Julia said you should stay here. Anyone watching the place is used to seeing Trey come and go. Julia even has him listed as a student intern, in case he comes with me to her office. But you and Katherine . . ."

"Yeah. As you can tell from the fridge, I haven't even been going to the store lately. And I don't think she should be out this soon given the headaches—"

Trey clears his throat and glances toward the door.

"What Trey is trying to tell you is that *she* is standing in the doorway listening to every word you say." Katherine's sunglasses are the large, dark kind that cover half of her face. They hide the circles under her eyes, but she's still pale. A black dress—one that actually *looks* like a dress and not a disaster—is flung over her arm, along with a beaded handbag. "Julia is correct. Connor and I can do more good here, getting background information or whatever else you need."

She slides the beaded bag across the table. "This one is close to what girls carried back then, but I'll find something else if it's too small. I'd rather have people notice you for an odd handbag than because the barrel of a Colt is sticking out the side."

Katherine seems much more at ease with the idea of me carrying the gun than Connor or Trey is, which makes me wonder if this is a guy thing. Would they be less worried if Trey were the one packing heat?

I take the bag. "I'll make sure the gun will fit when I'm getting ready." Another yawn hits. "Sorry."

"How many hours since you slept?" Katherine asks with a knowing look.

"It was in London, so technically, last night." I shrug. "I'm okay. Nothing another cup of Connor's coffee won't fix."

Katherine reaches out and takes the purse back. "No. You need more sleep, not less, when doing long-distance jumps. I don't care how adept you are with that key, travel wipes you out. And I can only imagine the impact of multiple jumps to different locations in a single day. We never did that, even during training. We had a day or two off between jumps." She shakes her head. "You need your wits about you, and that's hard to manage when you're exhausted."

"But Trey just got here. I don't think I could sleep yet anyway. And we need food."

"We'll get food," Katherine says. "And Trey can stay until you wind down enough to sleep. But I'm keeping the dress until morning."

∞

278 W. 113TH STREET, NEW YORK
November 9, 1926, 3:12 p.m.

The rain is coming down hard, much harder than I'd have guessed viewing through the key. This has taken five jumps so far, and I really hope Bess is home and in a mood to talk, because I'm tired of stalking her.

My first jump this morning was to set up observation points for watching Houdini's townhome. I blinked into a stable point behind the Block House in Central Park on April 4, 1965—a clear spring morning chosen entirely at random—and walked several blocks to 113th Street, where I set up four local points to observe the comings and goings at number 278. Then I caught a cab and set a few more points near the Elks Club, where Houdini's memorial was held, and a few more outside Machpelah Cemetery.

Most of that was a total waste of time. The initial plan was to corner Bess at the memorial or the burial. According to the *New York Times*, there were over two thousand people at Houdini's services on November 4th, but having been there, I'd say that was an understatement. I was never able to get anywhere near Bess.

So I spent the next hour in the CHRONOS version of a stake-out, watching the stable points around the Houdinis' townhouse from the sofa in my room. Friends escorted Bess home, and there was a steady trail of visitors until early evening when she left for a second memorial at a nearby theater.

That's when things got interesting. The car carrying Bess had barely rounded the corner when two men appeared on the front stoop in a flash of blue light. While I couldn't see their faces, I'm pretty sure one of them was Simon. The other guy was taller, thinner, but that's all I could tell from his silhouette.

Once they were inside, there was intermittent activity on all four floors for nearly two hours. The lights stayed on until about a minute before Bess arrived home, so they were clearly watching her movements. And unless they got really lucky during that last minute, I don't think they found what they were looking for.

So . . . the Cyrists know Houdini has a key. But how long have they known? Who told them? I'm not sure, but given that they've clearly been watching the house, I'm glad I listened when Trey suggested jumping in at a random date to set these observation points.

There was a flurry of police activity at the house that night and again the next morning. I skipped forward a few days, looking for a time when scrutiny died down and Bess seemed to be alone, but after a half hour or so, I said screw it. Waiting for the precise, perfectly right moment to present itself isn't a viable option in a doomsday scenario.

And so I'm here in the rain. I duck under the umbrella as I cross the street, both to shield me from the afternoon shower and from anyone who might be watching via CHRONOS key. A middle-aged woman answers my knock almost immediately. After a quick glance at my face, she says, "Come in. Bess has been expecting you."

Both the foyer and the parlor off to the right are dark. I don't get the feeling this is simply because the house is in mourning or even due to the overcast sky. It's just a dark home—the paneling is dark and the windows are narrow. I doubt it would be bright and airy even on the nicest spring day.

We go up three flights of stairs to a library, and when the woman opens the door, I see Bess seated on the carpet. Papers are strewn everywhere, and she's replacing books on the shelves. She's older now, and mostly gray, but her features are still childlike.

"Thanks, Marie," Bess says without looking up.

As Marie closes the door, I hear an unearthly screech, followed by a high-pitched voice proclaiming, "I am the Great Houdini."

I jump, turning toward the sound. The outline of a cage against the window reveals that it's only a stupid parrot. I try to relax, but the adrenaline surge has my body on full alert, and I jump again when Bess slams another book into place.

"Mrs. Houdini," I begin, "I'm so sorry for your—"

"Did you send them?"

"Who?"

She picks up another book off the floor and waves it toward me before shoving it onto the shelf.

"No, I didn't send the men who did this. But I saw it happen. I watched through the key the night of your husband's funeral. Two men with CHRONOS keys broke into your house. I couldn't have stopped them, Mrs. Houdini—not without alerting them to the fact that I know you have the medallion. And there's far too much at stake for me to risk that. Did they find it?"

"No. And you won't, either."

My stomach sinks. "He got rid of it?"

"I didn't *say* that," she sniffs. "I just said you won't find it. You fix this . . . you bring him back to me . . . and then I'll give you the key."

Bess shoves two more books onto the shelves, thwack, thwack, and reaches for a third.

I crouch down a few feet away so that I'm at eye level with her. "I can't do that."

She's quick. The book is out of her hand and flying toward my head before I realize it. I barely have time to lift my arm. Even so, the force of the blow knocks me off balance and I land on my backside.

"You *knew* they were planning to kill him!" she screams. "Didn't you? And you did nothing to stop it! Nothing to warn us so we could take precautions."

I pick up the book that bounced off my arm—*Was Abraham Lincoln a Spiritualist?*—and move it out of her reach. She still has plenty of ammo on the other side, however, so I keep an eye on her hands.

"They didn't kill him, Mrs. Houdini. I don't know if you remember what Kiernan told you about time travel, but I've read historical accounts from this timeline and ones from when there were no Cyrists around to threaten anyone. He died the same day in the very same way both times."

"Bushwa! Then why did that guy ask him about the key? Before he punched him?"

I have to guess at what the first part means, but I have no idea how to answer her questions.

In both timelines, Houdini died from a ruptured appendix. In both timelines, insurance paid double indemnity because some guy punched him in the gut when he wasn't ready. Apparently Houdini liked to play the macho dude, something that doesn't surprise me, having met him. Several biographers said he'd go around challenging young guys to punch him in the stomach, saying he could take anything they could dish out.

And usually he could. Squirming your way out of handcuffs and straitjackets when you're suspended by your ankles requires some pretty rock-solid abs. But this time, his appendix was inflamed—or maybe it's because he'd screwed up his ankle in a trick and was reclined on a couch when it happened, so he couldn't brace himself properly. There are half a dozen different versions and at least as many theories. But it's the same half-dozen versions in both timelines.

Houdini went on to do the show that night, despite a raging fever. They eventually rushed him to the hospital and removed the appendix. He seemed to be getting better, but then he died early in the afternoon on Halloween.

Same injury, same chain of events. Both timelines . . . at least until now.

"Can you tell me exactly what happened?" I ask.

"I can tell you what he told me. Two guys in their twenties came up to him in the lobby at the Prince of Wales Hotel. He was reading his mail, and one kid asked if it was really true he could take a punch to the gut without flinching. Like always, Harry says yes. The guy punches him. Then he leans over and says real quiet that he's gonna punch him so hard it'll kill him if he doesn't hand over the key."

He's here because he wants to see a lynching.

It's Kiernan's voice I hear, explaining why Simon was in 1938. And there was something about Cincinnati once. I never got the full story, but Simon enjoys landing in the middle of chaos.

I'm guessing the guy who was supposed to hit Houdini that day—a guy named Whitehead in most of the stories—never got the chance. Simon quite literally beat him to the punch.

"But Houdini didn't give them the key?"

"He didn't *have* the key! I made him stop wearing the thing after we left the hotel in Eastbourne. It wasn't even in Montreal with us. I told him I couldn't stand the idea of him going onstage with it. I even went back to the restaurant to give it to you that night . . ."

Bess halts in midsentence, realizing she's revealed something she shouldn't have.

"I mean, I *thought* about doing that, but . . ."

I pull out my medallion, and she dives toward me, grabbing for it.

"No! You have to bring him back."

"I can't. I'm really sorry."

Bess claws at my arm, trying to get the key, and I push her backward. I don't want to hurt her, but when she comes back again, her fist is cocked, ready to punch me.

Flipping a tiny, middle-aged woman gives me zero joy, but I have no choice.

"I'm sorry," I repeat as I roll her over and pin her against the carpet. "Are you okay?"

The string of curses she slings at me suggests that her mouth and brain, at a minimum, are still in working order.

Feet are pounding up the stairs. Apparently Bess screaming is something Marie is accustomed to, but maybe not the loud thump of a body hitting the floor.

Bess hears the footsteps, too. "Marie! Call the police!"

The footsteps pause and then retreat. Almost immediately, Bess realizes she's made another mistake.

"No, wait! Marie! Help!"

The footsteps continue fading out. Either Marie didn't hear that last bit, or she's tired of running up and down the stairs.

"Bess, your husband dies on Halloween, 1926, in both timelines. I can't change that, and I need the key."

"I won't be there to give it to you! I've changed my mind—"

It takes me three tries to lock in the stable point because Bess wriggling beneath me keeps jarring my arm and breaking my focus. Finally I lock in on the 1905 dress that belonged to Other-Kate right where I left it, flung over the footboard of my bed.

"I really *am* sorry," I say one last time, and then I blink out.

∞

Eastbourne, Great Britain
April 26, 1905, 10:13 p.m.

I've only been in the hotel lobby a few minutes when Bess Houdini bursts through the front door, walking quickly toward the restaurant. The maître d' halts her at the entrance, just as he did me earlier. She plants a palm in the center of his chest and shoves him back. He sputters, reaching after her, but she dodges his hand.

The man is about to follow her until he notices me and steps forward to block my path. I decide I like Bess's approach and simply push him aside.

It feels good. Should've done that the first time.

I reach Bess just as she finds the still-uncleared table where Kiernan and I ate.

"Mrs. Houdini!"

She turns toward me. It's strange to see her face again this soon, twenty years younger, minus the tear streaks and pain of bereavement. In her right hand is a silver chain holding the medallion.

"There you are! Take this thing before my husband changes his mind. He's a sentimental old fool, but I'll buy him something else."

I take the key and stick it in my pocket. "Thank you."

"I don't want anything that's con—"

The maître d' steps up behind Bess, putting his hand on her shoulder. "Ladies, if you'd be so good as to follow me."

Bess whirls around and pokes her finger into his chest. It's a bit like watching an angry Chihuahua turn on a greyhound. The guy actually flinches, holding his hands in front of him to ward her off.

"We have no intention of being *so good*," she says, poking his chest a few more times for emphasis. "Go away and let us finish our conversation."

The man slinks off without a word, and Bess turns back to me, giving an eye roll.

"As I was saying before, if I'd known the thing had any connection to the Cyrists, I'd never have asked Davenport for it. Those people gave me the willies even when I was a girl, with all that talk about the Chosen and The Way and everyone else dying."

"You have very good instincts," I say and begin moving toward the exit. Now that I have the key, all I want to do is get out of here, especially knowing that Simon has an interest in it, too.

But Bess grabs my arm. "Last year my mother-in-law consulted a medium before we set sail for Europe. The spirits said my husband is in no any danger for at least two decades. Is that still true?"

I wonder for a moment if this psychic has a CHRONOS key, because that's pretty darn close. "I'm not a psychic, Mrs. Houdini."

She gives me a knowing look. "I saw your face earlier. I'm not asking you when he dies. I don't want that much information. Just tell me if the spirits were right."

I can give her that much.

"The spirits were right."

∞15∞

Jeans. T-shirt. Skechers on my feet, the really comfy ones that I've worn so often they're starting to look raggedy. A mostly empty frappuccino in the cup holder.

Traffic has thinned out now that we're north of Gaithersburg. The air doesn't quite have the autumn crispness I love yet, but there's a slight hint of it in the breeze coming in through the windows. And Trey's playlist is close to perfect. No deep lyrics or brooding music, just up-tempo tunes by the Arctic Monkeys, OK Go, Frattellis, Vampire Weekend, and a few neo-punk songs I don't recognize. He also has some eighties classics that make me suspect Trey and my dad would do just fine on a road trip.

That, of course, pulls my mind out of the little cave of oblivion where I've been trying to entrap it and back to the fact that Dad is currently driving home from Delaware. That's good because I really want to see him, but bad because I felt like he was safe at Grandma Keller's.

I give my head a brisk shake. If I focus hard enough, maybe some fairy godmother will take pity on me and let me stay in this moment. Even if I don't think it could actually happen, it's nice to imagine all my worries drifting upward and fading away like soap bubbles.

Although, to be fair, stranger things *have* happened pretty much every day for the past few months. An hour ago, I was in 1926, fighting with Bess Houdini. This time tomorrow, if not sooner, I'll be in 2308. I'd say that leaves fairy godmothers who grant wishes entirely within the realm of the possible.

With that thought firmly in mind, I focus on the warmth of Trey's hand against mine, the music, the blue sky outside my window . . .

And then Trey's fingers tighten around my hand. Again. Almost painfully, as though a stray thought has sneaked into his head. Am I doing the same thing to him each time I lose grip on my all-too-slippery inner bliss?

"It's not working, is it?" I say. "Beautiful day, great music, you here next to me, and I still can't clear my mind for more than thirty seconds or so before it goes running back into Nightmare Land."

Trey's mouth tightens. "I just keep seeing that video. Wish I could accept Connor's argument that it's not you, but . . ."

"I'm not even sure Connor believes it's Prudence. He's just contrary."

"Mostly because he's worried about you. And Katherine."

We're silent for a minute and then he asks, "So . . . this meeting we're going to? Who'll be there?"

"Not really sure. Why?"

Trey gives a small chuckle. "A lame attempt at changing the subject to something slightly less worrisome. And I would kind of like to know how many Cyrists will be around. I'm not even sure I trust the Cyrist Light version."

"Me either. Tilson will be there, obviously, since it's at his house."

"Actually, it's a plot of land *near* his house." He nods at a scrap of paper in the console between the seats. "The jet pack apparently isn't something they like to test too close to buildings. Something about the lack of precision."

Lack of precision. And they were planning to have me use it to jump inside a building, or at least the ruins of a building. The weight of Pru's key in my pocket is suddenly very comforting.

"I'm guessing Max, Charlayne, and Bensen will be there," I continue, "since they all seem to have been involved with previous tests of the jet pack. Julia."

I stop for a moment. At least, I *hope* Julia. It hadn't even occurred to me until this minute that she might not be there. If she's not there, I need to track her down and let her know about getting the key from Houdini, because that's going to change the entire focus of this meeting. Learning to use the jet pack is no longer a priority.

Trey turns off I-270 onto a local road. I pull out my own CHRONOS key, the one Max used when he transferred the meeting coordinates, and bring up the stable point so I can see if Julia is there.

Trey's right—the location is a big, open field that looks like it was once farmland. Not a tree in sight, just gently sloping, slightly rocky hills. No one's there yet, so I push forward to 10:57 a.m., a few minutes before we're supposed to arrive, and scan the area.

At first, I only see cars—two sedans and a white minivan with the tailgate open. Charlayne and Bensen are in the back, fiddling with some sort of harness.

I pan right and see Tilson talking on his phone.

Max is off to the left, with his arm draped around a blonde. Her head is tipped up toward him. Must be the girlfriend Charlayne mentioned.

My opinion of Fifth Column security plummets to a new low. They escorted me and Trey to meet Julia at a secret location, in a car with dark-tinted windows, but Max's girlfriend is invited to watch me make a fool of myself as I try out the jet pack for the first time?

Then she turns toward the stable point, and I see her face.

I'm so surprised that I nearly blink myself into the location. That wouldn't have ended well, since I'm currently moving at about forty miles an hour.

"Trey, pull off and call Tilson."

"Julia's not there?"

"No, but Eve Conwell is."

Trey is silent for a moment. "Maybe . . . she's Fifth Column?" He doesn't remember Eve as well as I do, but his voice sounds doubtful. "I mean, I know her dad's a Templar, but maybe that's changed, too. Maybe they're New Cyrist?"

"Trey, that was Eve's dad in the video. Patrick Conwell was the man who dragged me back into the temple."

His hands tighten on the wheel. "My phone's in the console. Tilson was the last call I made."

"I think I'm going to need to set a local stable point after you call him. And that doesn't work so well in a moving car."

About a half mile down, I spot a small garage and convenience store combo off to the right. Two patrons are at the gas pumps, so Trey drives around and parks facing the trees.

I pull out my phone. "I need to do a little cyber-sleuthing. Call Tilson. Tell him you're running late. Ask who's coming. Make it sound like you're a little nervous about meeting everyone. If he mentions Eve, try to feel him out. See if you can find out how long she's been around. And if Julia isn't going to be there at all, see if he knows where she is."

He grins. "And I should do all this without being obvious?"

"If Tilson suspects you're prodding for info, I'm not too worried. I trust him more than any of them. As much as I hate to say it, maybe even more than Charlayne. I mean . . . I don't think she's a bad person, but she has mixed motives. All of them do, except Tilson. And maybe Ben, but he's with Charlayne now, so . . ."

"Like *with* with?" Trey asks, and I realize I haven't filled him in on that bit of info. When I nod, he says, "Way to go, Ben."

Trey starts dialing, and I pull up the browser on my phone. Wikipedia shows that the Sixteenth Street Temple is still the regional headquarters for North America, led by someone named Frank Morton. I can't remember if Kiernan ever mentioned that name, but the picture leaves no doubt that he's one of my Cyrist cousins. He looks like Pru, if she had short hair and a square jaw. And he's older—even older than Older Pru. And yes, I know he was born from a surrogate who knows when, but that fact is still disturbing.

Trey asks Tilson about Julia as I click through a few links trying to locate Conwell. He's no longer a high-profile televangelist, just the minister of a smaller congregation in Alexandria that converted from Orthodox to Reformed Rite in 1972. The church website says Conwell was appointed in late 2012, after the sudden death of the previous minister.

I half follow Trey's conversation with Tilson while searching, but he fills in the details when he hangs up. "Julia might be there later. He hasn't talked to her since last night, but he said she had a meeting scheduled earlier this morning at . . . did he say *Langley*?"

I laugh. "Ben's code name for the headquarters building in Silver Spring. Cyrist Interfaith Alliance. CIA."

"Oh. Ha." Trey rolls his eyes and continues, "As for Eve—Tilson says she's been with Max as long as he's known him, but he'd only seen him a few times before this year. He says Eve can't use the key."

"Kiernan says otherwise, although she has less luck with it than he does. When you talked to Tilson about the dual memory—about meeting him before at the barbecue, did you mention anything about Eve? Or Patrick Conwell? Or where the party was held?"

"I doubt it. I barely remembered the names. I guess it would have made a bigger impression on the version of me that got chased by Dobermans, but I'm pretty sure I just said it was held at some Cyrist's house. Oh, and Tilson sounded really suspicious by the end. Ben and Charlayne were there when he was talking to me, so . . ."

"It's okay. I don't think Tilson would say anything to Max. They didn't look like the best of pals. And Bensen definitely won't."

Which leaves Charlayne, who's never been a stellar secret keeper. I mean, she never leaked anything that I told her, but we were besties, and she dished plenty of dirt on others when I knew her at Roosevelt High.

My forehead is starting to tighten, so I stretch my eyebrows up to relieve it. Then Trey turns my face toward him and gives me a long, deep kiss. For the next minute—or is it five?—my mind empties of everything except his hands, one wrapped in my hair and the other at the small of my back, and his mouth on mine. The sound of his breathing fills my ears, and I close my eyes, shutting out everything that isn't Trey.

When he pulls away, the rest of the world gradually comes back into focus.

"What was that for?"

"You were looking like I was feeling. Stressed, confused, maybe a little bit whack." He presses his lips against my hair. "We both needed to reboot. So, what's the game plan?"

"Find Julia and tell her what I know."

Trey starts the engine, but I grab his hand. "No, just me. It'll take forever to drive there, and we don't have the time. I have a stable point set at Langley."

Trey's gray eyes darken. "Okay. That may be the quickest route, but I keep seeing your face from that video in Rio. I don't want you going alone."

"I won't be . . . exactly." I give him an apologetic look and unzip my backpack, pulling out the Colt.

"That's still alone. Just alone and armed."

"Better than alone and unarmed, right?"

He sighs. "I can't talk you out of this, can I?"

"Unfortunately, no." I slip Prudence's key out of my pocket and into the backpack. I still have my own medallion and a spare tucked into the band of my bra. I'm just a little leery about taking Pru's key with me, especially when I don't know who Julia might be meeting.

I pull up the current time at the Langley stable point. The chair where Charlayne sat yesterday morning is empty now and the room is dim, with just indirect sunlight coming in through the windows. I skim backward in one-minute increments for one hour, and then another, but I never see lights come on. I try again, going back as early as 7 a.m. The room gradually grows dimmer and dimmer as less sunlight illuminates the rows of cubicles. Still no sign of anyone coming into the building.

There must be another entrance. I was hoping to catch Julia coming in so I didn't have to walk around looking for her, but apparently that's not going to happen.

I check the stable point I set in the conference room when I jumped back after dumping coffee on Senator Ellicott, but the room is completely black. It's much closer to the break room, however, and Charlayne said Julia's offices were nearby. Since I'm not sure which is creepier—jumping into a room with rows of (probably) abandoned, dimly lit cubicles or jumping into a pitch-black conference room—I opt for proximity.

Trey's eyes are dubious as I double check the safety and tuck the Colt into the waistband of my jeans. I give him a quick kiss and open the car door, setting a local point outside. "I won't make you worry long—back in ten seconds."

The conference room that seemed pitch-black is now illuminated by the blue glow of my medallion. A song I liked as a kid about the blue canary in the outlet by the light switch runs through my head, and I hold back a nervous laugh.

Then I see a faint blue glow at the opposite end of the room, and it's all I can do to hold back a scream.

When I duck behind one of the conference chairs, the glow disappears, too. Feeling foolish, I cautiously lean back out. Sure enough, it's my own key reflecting off the whiteboard. I clutch the back of the chair for a moment to give my heart a chance to work its way back down from my throat, then head for the door.

Before I step into the hallway, I tuck the key back into its leather holder. That reflection scared the hell out of me, but it also reminded me that if anyone with the CHRONOS gene is roaming around the building, having this key out in a dim room is the equivalent of a big red arrow pointing out my location.

And again because that reflection scared the hell out of me, I draw the gun, holding it by my side.

The building is quiet, except for a faint hum from the break room. It's probably the fridge. As I turn down the corridor toward the offices, I see a shaft of light coming from a cracked door two rooms down.

I tap lightly. "Julia?"

No response. I push the door open to reveal a sparsely furnished office. Julia is behind the desk, slumped forward across the keyboard.

The coppery tang of blood hits my nose before I see the pool spreading onto the carpet. I suspect it's too late, but I reach out to check for her pulse. When I do, my knee bumps the edge of the office chair, and her body shifts toward me, throwing me off balance.

Which, as it turns out, is a very good thing.

I don't even hear the shot until it hits the wall, sending specks of plaster in all directions. Crawling under the desk, I jerk the cover off my key. A cool wetness soaks through my jeans as my knees press into the bloody carpet. Julia's body slides out of the chair, and as it does, I catch my first glimpse of her face. If the shot to her neck wasn't fatal, the one to the head definitely was.

Somehow I manage to lock in the stable point. I'm at a lower angle than when I set it, so I have no idea how this will work, but I can see the open car door and Trey's feet. A bullet pings against the desk, followed by footsteps. And then my eyes open to see gravel beneath Trey's car.

"I'm okay! It's not my blood!" The words are out before I realize that might be a bad thing to yell when there are people within earshot and a pistol in my hand.

I'm already up and moving toward the car when Trey reaches me. My knees are wobbly, and I'm about to sink down into the seat when I remember that my jeans are a gruesome mix of dirt, gravel, and blood.

"Is there something I can sit on? I don't want to get—"

"I'm not worried about the damned car, Kate." He cups my face in his hands. "Are you okay?"

"Yes . . . it's Julia's blood." His eyes slide down to the gun. "No! I didn't shoot her. But since she was very clearly murdered, I think it's a bad idea to get her blood inside your car."

"Hold on." He grabs a rain poncho from the trunk and spreads it across the seat, then tosses two reusable grocery bags onto the floorboard.

"I could just jump back home."

"Not until we're out of here. We're getting odd looks from that guy at the pump. No—don't look at him! Let's just go."

Once we're back on the road, he asks, "Are we still going to Tilson's?"

"Not yet. Find somewhere else to pull off while we think about what to do. I need to call him."

I'm glad my hands weren't shaking this badly in Julia's office or I'd probably be as dead as she is. That thought doesn't exactly steady me, but I manage to dial anyway.

"Hello, Trey," Tilson answers.

"No, Dr. Tilson. It's Kate. Are Max and Eve there yet?"

"Not yet. Is there a problem? You sound—"

"Yes. I jumped back to earlier this morning, to Julia's office. I needed to talk to her before the meeting, and . . ." I take a deep breath. I don't get the sense that he and Julia were especially close, but he's still very old and this may come as a shock. "Are you sitting down? Because . . ."

"Oh my God. How?"

"She was shot. Twice."

"And you're certain—"

"Positive. The gunman was either still there or, more likely, he's a jumper who was monitoring the office, because he fired at me, too."

Trey says, "You skipped that part earlier, Kate!" at the same moment Tilson asks if I was hit.

I give Trey an apologetic look and tell Tilson, "No. I had to dive under her desk. But listen, I'm very, very concerned that Eve Conwell's there. I can't imagine any scenario where she's on our side in this. Her father is Cyrist inner circle. In the timeline I remember, he was regional Templar for North America. And Eve . . . she was a self-centered bitch, so unless she's had a radical personality change . . ."

"No," Tilson says, "that's still a fairly accurate description. Max would even admit that most days."

Trey pulls off at a small park, backing in so that we're facing the lake.

"Your house could be bugged," I tell Tilson. "For that matter, I don't even know if this phone is safe, but . . . I had to let you know."

"I don't think we're bugged. I've taken precautions in that regard—" He stops, and I suspect he's thinking the same thing I'm about to say, so I just wait. "But I suppose Julia did, too."

"I'm sure she did. You, Charlayne, and Ben need to get out of there before Eve arrives. I don't know about Max . . . can he be trusted?"

Tilson sighs. "I think so. I'll find a way to get a message to him about . . . all of this. Hopefully without alerting anyone else."

"You might want to wait on that. I'm—" I pause because Trey's not going to like this. "I'm going back in to see if I can save her."

Trey shakes his head vehemently, and Tilson says, "No. You're not."

"I'll be careful. I can't just let her—"

"Kate," Tilson says, "please take a look at the papers you signed when you joined the Fifth Column. The rules are absolute. No time alteration for any reason not directly related to preventing the Culling. Julia made it clear that this included preventing member deaths, even her own. There are no exceptions . . ." He pauses like he's about to add something, then just repeats, "No exceptions."

I know Tilson's right in terms of the big picture, but it feels so wrong not to even try. "I actually never signed those papers. And Julia's gone. There's no one to enforce those rules anymore."

A long, rather ominous silence follows. "Don't count on that, Kate. You've only seen the surface of the Fifth Column. And you're sensible enough to realize there's more at stake here than one person's life."

I'm tempted to tell him it's easier to say that when you're not drenched in that one person's blood. But I don't.

"Hold on. I'm going to give the phone to Trey."

I press mute and hand Trey the phone. "Back in a few seconds. Try to figure out a meeting place without telegraphing it to anyone who might be listening."

When I lean forward to kiss him goodbye, he grabs my arm. "You're not going back there, right? Please tell me you're not going back there."

"I'm not going back there."

He starts to smile and then it fades. "Are you just telling me that because I asked you to, or . . ."

"No. Tilson's right. This is just another of those cases where all the choices suck. But I'll keep my focus on the big picture. I'm going to shower, change, and come right back. Promise."

∞

BETHESDA, MARYLAND
September 12, 10:47 a.m.

I peel off my jeans in the bathroom and toss them, along with the poncho, into the sink. This entire situation reminds me of jumping back from Georgia with Delia's blood all over my sweater. And then just before that, jumping back from Six Bridges in the containment suit when Kiernan and I got the virus sample. Maybe I should set a stable point inside the shower to save time.

While the water runs over my body, I take deep breaths and try to center my mind so I can devise a game plan. But I keep seeing Julia's face.

Smoke hits my nose as I'm tugging on a clean pair of jeans. The detector in the hall goes off the same second, as if my noticing the smoke reminded it to do its job already.

Whatever calm I found in the shower shatters instantly. I snatch a T-shirt from the closet and grab my phone as I run to the door, remembering at the last second to see if the handle is hot before opening it.

It's cool, but smoke is pouring from the library, and I see flames in the corner. Books are pulled off the shelves, dumped onto the floor, and their dry, brittle pages are perfect kindling.

"Katherine! Connor!"

No response.

I run to the railing and look down over the living room. It's empty except for Daphne, who's at the door, whimpering. She moves toward the stairs as I run down, dragging one back leg.

"Oh my God! What happened, girl? Where are Connor and Katherine?"

I dial 911, then scoop Daphne into my arms. She yelps when I lift her, but I can't stop now to see where she's hurt.

The emergency worker answers as I reach the backyard. Once I've given the address, they tell me to stay clear of the house. Sound advice, even though I can't follow it until I find Connor and Katherine.

"Daphne, stay!" I command, setting her down near the bench swing. "Stay!" She whimpers, but doesn't follow.

The garage door is open, which is unusual. I reach inside the door to grab the fire extinguisher, only to find it missing. Then I head back inside, despite the voice in my head screaming that it's a very, very bad idea. The smell of smoke alone has me looking over my shoulder, half expecting to see H. H. Holmes following me.

The fire extinguisher inside the pantry is gone, too.

I check Katherine's room, and Connor and Katherine aren't there. That leaves upstairs. I run to Connor's rooms, Dad's, and then the attic. Between my shrieking and the smoke alarm, they should have heard me by now unless they're unconscious.

Or unless . . . they're *in* the library?

I fly down the attic stairs, hitting the last few steps on a skid. Smoke billows from the library. I pull my T-shirt over my face and am about to plunge in when it occurs to me that I'm approaching this, as Kiernan would say, far too linearly.

I yank out my key, set a stable point outside the library, and roll the time back ten minutes to when I was in the shower. I may go back further and prevent the fire eventually—Julia's Fifth Column rules be damned. But for now, I need to see what we're up against and, most importantly, locate Connor and Katherine.

Through the CHRONOS display, I see the fire was pretty much out ten minutes ago, so they must have had it nearly under control and then it blazed up again. The windows are open and spirals of smoke drift outward. White dust, possibly from a fire extinguisher, coats the bookshelves, walls, and carpet. Connor is sprawled on the floor, one canister in his hand and another near his head.

Maybe he and Katherine were overcome by smoke trying to put out the fire? But where's Katherine?

I jump in. As I approach Connor, one of the monitors lights up, startling me. My movements must have jarred the mouse, pulling the computer out of sleep mode. I press my fingers to Connor's neck to check for a pulse, giving a short prayer of thanks when I find it.

I'm just turning around to search for Katherine when I hear Simon. "Well, hello, Katie."

I whirl toward the sound, cursing myself for leaving the gun in Trey's car. But unless I was planning to shoot Connor's computer, it doesn't matter. Simon's face is in close-up on the screen until he moves a bit back from the camera. He's older, thinner, sitting in the back of a large car . . . a limo, maybe? He wears jeans and an antique-looking New York Yankees jersey with several jagged rips running down the front. There's a makeshift bandage the same color as the jersey on his left forearm.

He slips the CHRONOS key back into his pocket and looks up at the camera. "Yes, I've been watching you through the stable point to see when you'd come in. Ain't technology grand?"

I give him a foul look and grab my own key.

"Nuh-uh-uh. Drop it."

The location at Trey's car is locked in. I scan forward ten minutes to the current time and see he's still there.

I'm about to blink away when Simon says, "Drop it, Kate. Otherwise I'll have to start winnowing down hostages, and I hate doing that so early in the game. It just ruins the suspense."

I drop the key as soon as I hear the word *hostages* and take another look around the library. Katherine's not here, so I'm not really surprised when Simon shifts the camera to show her, gagged and tied to the seat next to him.

"Katherine, are you okay?"

He shifts the camera back to his face. "She's fine. Just a bit of excitement, right, Grandma? She was playing fireman with your buddy on the floor when I dropped in. I was beginning to worry the fire would gobble him up before you finished your shower." A slow grin spreads across his face. "Did you enjoy it? I certainly did."

Simon lets that comment sink in. My shiver of revulsion must show on my face because he laughs.

"I'm glad you ducked out of the way at Julia's office. Not only because I enjoyed the view just now—although I really did enjoy the view—but because you and I have a common goal. We can *work* together. I just needed to find the right incentive to . . . motivate you."

I tell him exactly what I think of him and his incentives.

He laughs. "You talk like that in front of our grandmother? Sheesh. But on that last part, we're in agreement. We both know my mother, and yes, she *can* be a bitch."

I snatch my medallion up again, and he stops laughing abruptly.

"I'm not stupid, Kate, and I'm under a key, too. If you're thinking you'll go back and change things, make sure I don't grab Katherine, that would be a very *bad* idea."

The next thing I see is him holding up an image. Mom. She's in the same position as Katherine, except she's unconscious. I think she's in a hotel room, although it doesn't look like the one in London. The barrel of a pistol is wedged under her throat.

I can't breathe. It's not just the smoke. Mom looks helpless, totally at the mercy of Simon's thug. My first thought is that I should never, ever have let her stay in London. But I'm not sure what I could have done short of kidnapping to get her home. And maybe home isn't any safer, since Simon has Katherine, too.

"Prudence should be right there with her, but she can be a slippery one. My point is, if you change anything about this sequence of events, I'll know. So don't go splitting any of my memories if you want these two ladies alive."

"What do—" I stop, coughing as a bit of smoke catches in my throat. "What do you want?"

"The same thing you do. Pru can't get her hands on the other keys. You bring them to me—intact—and I'll let them go."

"Why don't you get the keys yourself?"

He shrugs. "Easier to let you do it. Yes, I could jump in there and get Pru's key from you, but I really don't look much like her, and then I'd have to fight the guy, find the keys—"

"And you expect me to just trust that you'll release them?"

"You don't have any choice, Kate. And hell, I'm a nice guy. Give me what I want, and maybe I'll even protect all of you from our little . . . event . . . that's coming up. And the aftermath. I've looked ahead, and it's going to be *interesting* for a few years."

So he knows we know about the Culling.

But he doesn't know we have a vaccine. Not if he's offering to give it to us. One tiny island of good news in a sea of catastrophe.

"Why would you give us protection?"

"Who said anything about *giving* it to you? Consider it a trade. The flock is going to freak a bit while things are . . . leveling out. I need a spare Sister Pru to help them stay calm. The one I've got isn't very reliable. You help me, and we'll find a nice safe spot for the fam. Maybe even the boyfriend, although he's got a little payback coming for this scar on my forehead." Simon runs one finger across the spot where Trey whacked him with a tire iron in the previous timeline.

And this is how I end up in Rio.

Simon knows I won't just walk away—not when he has Mom. Not when he has Katherine. Not when he's threatening everyone I care about.

I won't simply offer up the keys. There's too much at stake. But what if we can't stop him? If we're stuck with a world where Cyrists call the shots, I'll do anything I can to keep those I love alive and safe within that nightmare.

"If I agree to this, you'll bring both of them to the same place. I give you the keys, I come with you, and you let Mom and Katherine go."

"Sounds fair."

"Where?"

Simon looks confused, so I repeat it, spitting the word at the camera as another wave of coughing hits me.

"Oh, don't worry. I'll find you. But . . . Katie, you really might want to take care of that fire. Looks like it could get out of hand."

The monitor goes dark.

Simon's last words are an understatement. The carpet near the books is once again ablaze, and Connor is only a few feet away. The fire extinguisher near his head is empty. Wrenching the other one out of his hand, I point the nozzle toward the carpet near the burning books. It blasts for a few seconds, and then it's empty. Hopefully the fire department will arrive soon, because there's no way I can get Connor downstairs on my own.

I can, however, get him out of this room. I'm just grabbing his feet when I hear, "Katherine! Connor!"

My voice comes from the other side of the house, followed by the fire alarm in the hallway, and I remember no one has actually *called* the fire department yet.

I look at the gadgets in this room and beyond them at myself in the hallway. Was calling the fire department a good idea? The jeans in my sink are covered in the blood of a woman the police will soon find murdered in her office. And how would we explain this library? The odd contraptions? Or the information on the computers they're likely to find if this is treated as arson, which I suspect it will be.

"Oh my God! What happened, girl? Where are Connor and Katherine?" I watch the earlier version of me run downstairs and get a queasy feeling totally unrelated to the smoke.

Because I'm about to do what Katherine told me to avoid at all costs.

I drag Connor to the doorway and run to the banister. Earlier-Kate is almost to the kitchen. Daphne's in her arms, looking pathetic, and my mind suddenly connects her injured leg to Simon's bandage and the rips in his jersey.

Good girl, Daph.

"Kate! Don't call 911! And don't . . . turn around." I should have said the last part first, although I'm not sure it would have mattered. The double memory starts coming in, coupled with the strangest sensation, sort of like a feedback loop.

Pulling my eyes away from the me below, I say, "Get Daphne outside! Don't call 911. When you're done, get up here and keep pulling Connor toward the stairs. Simon has Katherine. He also has Mom. I'm going to get help."

I pull my phone out of my pocket—*the phone she's also holding right now*—and call Dad.

"Hey, sweetie, what's up?" R.E.M.'s "We Walk" is in the background, the song Dad always sang to me as a kid when he was trying to lure me up the stairs and into bed.

"Dad, turn around and go back to Grandma Keller's house, okay? Stay there until I call."

The music clicks off. "What's happened?"

"They've got Mom. Katherine, too. Julia—with the Fifth Column group I mentioned?—she's been killed. And someone's set fire to Katherine's library. I've called the fire department . . ."

Which is true, although I've just uncalled them, so I guess it's also a lie.

"You won't be safe here, Dad. I've got less than six days to fix this. I just need to know you're *safe*."

"I understand."

I breathe a big sigh of relief, followed immediately by a coughing fit, because any deep breath right now means a lungful of smoke.

"Get out of there, Katie."

"I will. Love you."

Earlier-Me is standing in the kitchen doorway looking up at This-Me. It hurts to look at her, so I pull my eyes away. But then I realize she's holding a fire extinguisher.

"Where did you get that?"

"On the patio. By the grill?"

How did I miss it the first time? Maybe I was looking down at the phone?

"I'm going for help. See what you can do while I'm gone."

Will she still be here when I get back?

I have no idea. It's killing my head to even think about it.

∞

Near Damascus, Maryland
September 12, 10:48 a.m.

"—you could take Estella and go back to Punta Cana? Or down to—"

Trey takes one look at me and says, "I'll call you back, Dad."

"Simon has Katherine. And Mom. I need fire extinguishers. The biggest you can find."

Trey nods, cranks the car, and is already halfway out of the parking lot when I blink to Kiernan's cabin.

∞

BOGART, GEORGIA
December 11, 1912, 11:03 a.m.

"I spent the past six months hiding out here in the cabin, trying to store up enough . . . I don't know . . . jump juice, whatever the hell you want to call it, so that I can make the trip to 2305. And now we have a side trip because of a fire? Who set it?"

"Uh . . . Simon?" It seems pretty obvious to me, so I'm not sure why Kiernan even asked. "But it's okay. I'll handle it without you."

I try to sound more confident than I feel, but I don't think it's working. "The other me . . . and this me. The two of me will get Connor downstairs. And then we'll put out the fire."

He shakes his head and looks up at the ceiling. Then he pulls me into a hug. I kind of wish he hadn't, because tears sting the back of my eyelids. I bite my lip, willing them away.

"They're okay, love. They'll *be* okay."

"You can't know that."

I told him Simon has Mom and Katherine as soon as I blinked in. And about Julia. What I didn't mention was Simon's bit about needing a new Sister Prudence. I won't be mentioning that to Trey, either. Or Dad, or Connor—so yeah, not to anyone. It's partly because I know they'd try to stop me, but also because I'm not willing to admit out loud that I'm considering it as a last-ditch option. The fact that some future version of me was there in Rio, with Simon, is like a drop of acid slowly eating away at my last sliver of optimism.

"You smell like smoke. Again." Kiernan's fingers trace the scar along my jaw, and he looks lost for a moment. "We'll get them back, Kate. But the first stage of your plan has a major flaw. There's only going to be *one* of you in a few minutes. If not when you get back, then definitely before you'd be able to get Connor downstairs and put out the fire."

"How do you know?"

"Watched it happen a few times. I never did it on purpose, but Simon got a kick out of it when we were first fooling around with the keys. The deal is you didn't spin off an entirely new timeline. You just created this tiny . . . splinter. Kind of like a shard of ice that melts away. That earlier you only exists up to the point where you chipped away at your own personal course of action. She's wearing the same key as you, so she'll disappear. You're the original one, right?"

"What?"

He repeats in a slow voice, like he's explaining to a child, "Are you the one who jumped back and created the splinter, or are you the splinter that was created?"

"Okay. I get it. I'm the original one."

"Then she'll vanish. I don't know if it's something to do with two copies of the same key coexisting in the same space and time, or if the timeline sort of . . . repairs . . . or what, but she's only temporary."

I feel a rather unreasonable sense of relief that this me is the one that doesn't vanish. I mean, that other one is still me, so it shouldn't matter. But it kind of does. I'm . . . unique. I'm the one who *didn't* see the fire extinguisher by the grill. The one who called the fire department.

Neither of those facts seems to suggest that the continuation of this me and the disappearance of that me is survival of the fittest. But she had the advantage of my warning. Right?

"If she disappears, I'll jump back and go find some neighbors—"

"Who will call the fire department. Wait. Except the neighbor who lives in the green house. The one with the blue van."

"The one you hired to spy on us?"

"That would be the one." Kiernan finds a piece of paper, scribbles something on it, and folds it. "Give this to him. I can't understand why he didn't intervene when Simon grabbed Katherine."

"Why would he?"

Kiernan doesn't answer. He gives me a strange look—sad, maybe a little disappointed. "Just give him the note. And if you can't find him or he can't help for some reason, come back. Six more months in this cabin won't kill me."

∞

NEAR DAMASCUS, MARYLAND
September 12, 11:26 a.m.

The parking lot is still mercifully empty when Trey pulls in and parks under the tree. He pops the trunk, and I see six big, fat fire extinguishers.

"Did you know I love you?" I ask.

He gives me a shaky smile. "You'd better."

∞

BETHESDA, MARYLAND
September 12, 10:58 a.m.

Two fire extinguishers stand at attention along the wall when I blink in with the last three. That means one is missing. I hear a whooshing noise in the library, so my double must have grabbed it to fight the flames. The smoke seems worse now, and I hear a symphony of fire alarms throughout the house, including one downstairs that repeats "Fire . . . Fire" in a robotic monotone.

I reach down to check Connor's pulse again. It's strong, but I can't help worrying. It feels like he's been out a long time.

I rush downstairs in search of the mystery guy in the van. Kiernan's note is just a single nonsense word—Skaneateles. It must be a password of some sort.

The blue van is across from the woods separating Katherine's house from the next lot. No one is inside, so I hurry up the sidewalk to the door of the green house. I ring the bell twice, but there's no answer.

I'm running back to Katherine's when it occurs to me that the man could be in the rear of the van, monitoring surveillance feeds. I run back across the street and tap on the side door, tilting my head to the left to peek in the driver side window.

The man is slumped across the seat. I can't see the wound, but there's a dark stain beneath his head. And now that I'm closer I see a tiny hole in the passenger side window with a halo of spiderweb cracks around it.

I try to open the driver side door to see if he's still alive, but it's locked. So is the sliding door.

"Damn it!" I kick the tire and yank out my CHRONOS key, preparing to jump back to Kiernan. But then the battered Subaru that Dad and I fondly refer to as the Gray Ghost pulls into view.

I don't know whether to laugh or cry.

Dad is already inside when I catch up with him.

"Connor's upstairs. We need to get him out."

When we reach the landing, Dad hoists Connor's upper body and we begin working our way down the stairs.

"You said you were going back to Delaware!"

"No, I said I *understood*. Katherine's gone. Deborah—" He shakes his head. "Dear God, Kate! Even if I hadn't been less than ten minutes from here, there's no way I'd leave you alone with this mess."

I'm so very happy to see him. And so very angry that he didn't turn around and go back to Delaware as I asked.

"I love you." My voice sounds as conflicted as I feel—happy, sad, pissed off.

"Love you, too, kiddo."

Daphne's right where I left her. She whimpers and limps toward us when we lay Connor on the grass. "Stay with Connor. We'll be right back. And you're a good, good girl."

"What happened to her leg?" Dad asks as we run back toward the house.

"Simon. I think she attacked him when he took Katherine. He must have kicked her. I haven't had a chance to examine it."

We snag the last two canisters from against the wall. The second me is no longer in the library, so apparently Kiernan was right that we'd . . . merge or whatever. I'm glad, but it raises new headache-inducing questions. Where did that other version go? I know she's me, and I'm here, but . . .

Although the smoke is still thick, the fire looks like it's nearly out. Of course, it looked like it was nearly out before, back when

Simon's face appeared on the computer, so I don't want to take chances. We crouch low, spraying in a wide arc. I had no idea the extinguishers emptied that quickly—they spew white gunk for about fifteen seconds and that's it.

Dad's hair and clothes are flecked with white. Mine, too, probably, but I'll be staying that way unless I spray off with the hose. No way am I showering in this house after Simon's comment.

We head down to check on Connor. I grab two bags of frozen vegetables from the freezer. Dad tilts Connor's head gently to one side, revealing a large red lump behind his ear, split slightly near the middle. He moans when Dad presses the makeshift ice pack to the lump, so maybe he's beginning to come around.

Daphne rests her muzzle on Connor's stomach. I check her fur carefully, but there's no visible wound. My guess that Simon kicked her is probably a good one. I feel a slight twinge of guilt about kicking the Cyrist Doberman at the Sixteenth Street Temple. He was protecting his owners the same way Daphne tried to protect Connor and Katherine. Of course, his owners are pure evil, and he'd been trained to do maximum damage, whereas poor Daphne . . .

She's not interested in the frozen corn cold pack, except as something to sniff, so I just rub her ears and pull her closer. "It's okay, girl. We'll get Katherine back. And I'll make Simon pay for hurting you and Connor." She responds by giving my chin a gentle lick and then settles down with her head on my lap until she hears Connor's voice.

"Harry. Where's Kate? Katherine? What . . ." He tries to prop himself up and decides it's not a good idea. I slide over so he can see me without moving. Daphne follows, nuzzling his face.

"I'm fine, Connor. You took a blow to the head. Simon."

"Kath—"

"He's got Katherine," Dad says. "Deborah, too."

"The fire—"

He struggles again, but Dad holds him steady. "You should stay put for a bit, Connor."

"Yeah. You were unconscious for . . ." I stop and think, but given the way I was jumping back and adding an extra minute here and five extra minutes there, I have no idea. "For a while. The fire is out. You nearly had it out before Simon showed up. He dialed in through your computer after he left with Katherine, so I think it's safe to say the network isn't secure."

I start to tell him about Julia. And the dead guy in the van. But he still looks disoriented, so maybe I'll hold off on more bad news.

"We were trying to put out the fire . . . I didn't even hear him come in."

"It's okay, Connor. We'll get them back."

He glances down at the key around my neck, and I shake my head. "Not that way. I can't. He's got Mom. Claims he tried to get Prudence, too, but she slipped away. Anyway, Simon's wearing a key, and he'll know if I change anything to stop him from grabbing Katherine. I have to do what he asks—or at least make him think I'm doing it."

"What does he want?" Dad asks.

"He wants me to get the keys from CHRONOS headquarters. Instead of Pru. Simon and Saul don't want any control in her hands."

Connor's face falls even further. "Ah, damn it, Kate. That's how you end up in Rio, isn't—"

I make a little kill motion. He squelches pretty quickly for someone who's just taken a whack to the head. But it's too late.

Dad's eyes move from Connor to me. "Rio?"

∞16∞

A large plate of cheese fries sits in the center of the table. There are a few fries missing from the side facing Charlayne and Ben, but otherwise it's untouched. They look good, smell good, and I probably should be hungry, but none of us has much appetite. Tilson just felt we should order something besides beverages to justify taking up a table for six. And we *will* be six if Max ever arrives.

We had to meet somewhere, and the only reasonably safe option that anyone could think of at this point was somewhere public. I would have preferred *random* and public, instead of this spot that Max and Tilson have used in the past, but I wasn't in on that part of the arrangements.

I lean back into the padded bench and pull up the stable point in Katherine's library while we wait, watching Dad and Connor clear away the soggy mess in the center of the room. Connor still seemed a little shaky when I left, so I'm glad to see him sitting down, going through the books to see if any are salvageable.

Dad was pretty shaky, too, mostly from seeing the video of me in Rio. He took the same tack Connor had at first, claiming it wasn't me. But I think he knows better, because he really wasn't acting like himself. We had a shouting match over my decision to leave the gun with him and Connor, and I can't remember when Dad has ever shouted at me. I finally won because I told him I could get another one much more easily than they could. And now that I know Simon has been in the house, leaving the two of them there with no protection other than Daphne and the kitchen knives was unthinkable.

I wanted Dad and Connor to get into the car with Daphne and get the hell out of there. It scares me to think that Simon could be watching them at this very moment, just like I am, maybe planning to take a few extra bits of insurance by grabbing them, too. But Connor was adamant about staying behind to keep an eye on Katherine's library. He kept referring to it that way, as Katherine's library. And since we couldn't leave him there alone, they're there and I'm here, and . . .

Trey can't see the display, but he can see my expression. "Are they okay?"

I nod. "Yeah. For now."

He pushes a strand of still-damp hair back behind my ear. Hosing off outside and changing in the hall closet wasn't fun, but it was immensely preferable to showering upstairs where Simon the Creeper might see.

Trey looks like he's going to say something—probably tell me not to worry. Again. But he just pulls me closer.

We've been waiting the past ten minutes or so for Max. Tilson left a message on his phone, using a code Julia devised. I'm not sure telling him where we're meeting, even in a code Tilson says Eve won't understand, was a good idea. I have a tough time believing he'd be okay with killing his own grandmother. But then again, he's apparently been with Eve for over a year. Who knows how much nasty has rubbed off?

Tilson's eyes dart toward the door for about the dozenth time. He glances down at his phone again and shakes his head. "We should probably start. I can fill Max in later."

Everyone's eyes shift to me, so apparently I'm tasked with running this meeting. Between finding Julia's body, learning that Simon has Mom and Katherine, and playing firefighter, my thoughts are flying in so many directions that what I really want to do is hide in a dark room and scream.

I try to take a sip of my coffee, but it's full and I'm shaky, so I wrap both hands around the base. The mug is much too hot to hold this way, but I grip it tighter. The painful twinge in my palms seems to calm the chaos in my brain.

"So . . . the Houdini key that Julia said I should wait on? Well, we now have it, and it's going to make things a lot easier. That's what I'd planned to tell Julia when I went to her office. Before Houdini had this key, it belonged to Prudence. She set some local stable points in DC after CHRONOS headquarters was destroyed. I haven't had time to go through them yet, between Julia and the fire and . . ." I press my palms against the hot mug again and take a deep breath. "Anyway, the good news is we can skip the jet pack, although I guess that's a mix of good *and* bad news given how much time you guys put into it."

Charlayne and Ben exchange glances, and she says, "The suit's okay for tooling around in the backyard . . ." She stops when Ben snorts. "That is, in a backyard that doesn't have a flimsy storage shed in the middle. Max wasn't any better. He hit the house when he used it."

"I've never been completely convinced you'll be able to fire the thing up quickly enough to beat gravity when you jump in," Ben says. "It's just the only thing we had that *might* work. If you have a better way, it's a win all around."

"Okay, that's good." I give him a quick smile, even though I can't help wishing they'd voiced those reservations earlier. "I assume you're all aware of what's happened with my mom and Katherine. What you may not yet be aware of is *why* they were taken. Simon doesn't want the keys housed at CHRONOS to end up with Pru."

Charlayne gives me a nervous look. "You're not considering . . . actually giving them to him, are you?"

"No. But I *am* planning to let him think that I will until I can get my mom and Katherine back. Don't tell me you wouldn't do the same if it was your family, because we both know better."

"Hmph. Depends on which members of my family." Charlayne snags another fry and takes a vicious chomp out of it.

My Charlayne would never have made that sort of comment about any of the Singleton clan. Even though she'd grumble occasionally about Joseph, the oldest, getting special treatment, it was good-natured griping. She loved her mom, her dad, and even the brothers who delighted in tormenting their baby sister. What happened?

"So you'll do some sort of bait and switch," Tilson says. "Do you think it will work?"

Probably not, but I don't want to admit that. "Yes, I think so. But we need to come up with a reasonably safe location for me to jump back to after I get the keys. Not Langley, not Katherine's, and not your place, either. I don't think we can assume any location Eve knew about is secure."

There are no disagreements on that point, so I go on. "Julia referred to this as a cell, so I'm guessing information is pretty compartmentalized, right? Do any of you know how this cell connects to the rest of the Fifth Column?"

Tilson, Ben, and Charlayne exchange glances, and I don't especially like what I'm reading in their eyes.

"Oh, that's just great—"

"No, no." Tilson holds up his hand. "It's just . . . Julia's backup for that kind of information is Max, and he's not here."

I sigh. And though I'm not sure I like that any better than the information having died with Julia, I nod and say, "Okay. Next—the vaccine. Is it in a safe location?"

Tilson nods, and this time he looks confident about the answer. "It's not at my house, and I'm fairly certain that no one, not even Max, knows the location."

"Did Julia know?"

"Yes." His expression grows grim. "You're thinking she may have given that information up."

"Actually, no. Simon said something that . . . well . . . I don't think he knows about the vaccine. To be honest, I'm more worried she told Max."

Tilson considers this for a moment. "Unlikely. Max was Julia's backup for political and bureaucratic connections. I was her backup for scientific connections. Senator Ellicott and the others were at the meeting yesterday because they're at the nexus of those worlds. Ellicott is on some Senate health committee. Powers is with the CDC, and West is Homeland Security."

"Speaking of the vaccine," Charlayne says, rummaging through her backpack. After a brief search, she pulls out a clear Ziploc bag containing two squat cylinders of some sort—one pink, one blue.

"What are those?" I ask, eyeing the tubes with suspicion.

"The vaccine. It's like a rubber stamp. Doesn't hurt a bit. I re-inked mine and Ben's yesterday, which is why they're both a little blurry. It was hard to line up with the original tattoo."

"This ink is temporary," Bensen adds. "It's intradermal, like the vaccine. And this is the same application device they've been using at the initiation ceremony for Acolytes since around 1940. Before that, everyone sat around waiting while someone actually tattooed your hand, but now they do that part a few days later. In private. In case you're a wuss about needles, like Charlayne."

"Says the guy who squealed like a baby before the needles even touched his skin." Charlayne reaches across the table for Trey's hand.

"Wait!" I grab her wrist. "You're sure it's safe?"

"I used it on myself back in 2002," Tilson says. "Right after they finished the last round of tests on rhesus monkeys. No side effects, other than irritation around the site for a few days."

I glance down at Tilson's hand, which doesn't have a tattoo.

"The ink is only temporary," Ben repeats. "It fades away in a few days."

"But . . . why use the ink at all?" Trey asks. "Couldn't you give the vaccine without it?"

Tilson shrugs. "Yes. But it was easier to simply re-create what the Cyrists did. And Julia thought we could pass this off as a recommitment ceremony for New Cyrists, once we learned their original tattoos didn't carry the vaccine. It's probably too late for that to matter now, but if this preemptive strike fails, it's part of the backup plan."

Trey slides his hand forward, and Charlayne stamps it quickly. He pulls it back and says, "Would you mind making Kate's blue as well?"

His eyes are troubled, and I know what he's thinking. A pink lotus tattoo on my hand takes me one step closer to being the girl in the Rio video. But if what they're claiming is true, this temporary ink will be gone long before I could be either as emaciated as that girl or as pregnant. If she's me, and I can't see how she isn't, this doesn't change anything. And as much as I don't want the nasty thing on my hand, Pru has one. If I'm impersonating her, we need to match.

I give Trey's knee a reassuring squeeze under the table and wink at Charlayne, like it's a joke. "No way. I want to be a girly-girl. Gimme the pink."

The device barely touches my skin. "That's it?"

"Yep. Easy-peasy."

I'm not sure that's the phrase I'd have used, because seeing the pink flower on my hand makes my stomach very *un*easy. But it's a done deal.

Then Charlayne slides a small white box toward me. "You'll need these at some point. The color isn't exactly the same as Prudence's in the picture I have, but it should be close enough."

"Um . . . I've never worn contacts. Will they fit?"

"One size fits all. I had a pair that looked like cat's eyes for Halloween. They were cool. And they're not hard to put in, but your eyes feel a little funny at first. You might want to start getting used to them."

I'm not looking forward to that at all. I even hate wearing mascara. But I shove them into my pocket.

The waiter stops by to see if we need refills. He glances at the barely touched cheese fries and asks if they were okay, and we assure him that they're fine.

When he moves on to the next table, I move on to the next thing we need to discuss.

"Has the rest of the Fifth Column been told about Julia?"

"I haven't told anyone except Max." Tilson's mouth twists downward. "A single word of code to convey that his only surviving family member is dead."

Charlayne rests her hand consolingly on Tilson's shoulder. "You didn't have a choice. We couldn't risk him going to Langley. He could be targeted, too."

"That brings up another thing we need to talk about. We have to assume that any of you could be targeted. Families, too."

"Not an issue for me," Tilson says. "No kids. No wife. I gave away my cats last month."

That seems like overkill at first thought, but then I remember poor Daphne's limp. Maybe not.

Bensen squeezes Charlayne's hand. "We know there's risk. No one likes it, but . . . my mom knew what I was getting into. So did Charlayne's. They both cleared out of DC yesterday, along with two of Charlayne's brothers. They were careful. I think—I *hope*—this Simon guy will have a tough time finding them."

But not Charlayne's dad or her third brother. I guess that explains her earlier comment. This Singleton family isn't quite as happy and united as the one I remember.

Charlayne catches my gaze and holds it for a moment. She seems to mistake my concern for pity, or maybe a lack of faith in their commitment, because her mouth tightens and her dark eyes are defiant. "We all knew this could happen, Kate. Ben and I have kept a packed bag in his van for months, along with . . . supplies. Like I said earlier, we've been planning for this a very long time."

"Miss Singleton is correct," Tilson says. "The three of us will find a place to stay. Trey is welcome to join us, and I think we can secure it well enough for you to use it as a jump location. Focus on what you need to accomplish and we'll—" He stops and nods toward the door. "Max."

I look over my shoulder, relieved to see that he's alone. When he spots us, he crosses over and drops into the empty chair. An annoyed huff when he sees Trey suggests Max considers him an add-on rather than true Fifth Column. But he probably thinks the same about me. Too bad we can't just step aside and let Max save the day.

"We were getting concerned," Tilson says.

"It took time to deal with Eve. I think . . ." Max's mouth tightens. "No. I don't just think. She knew about Julia."

"And where is she now?" Tilson asks.

"I took care of it," he says. "She won't be sneaking off to report on us."

Charlayne's eyes widen. "You didn't . . ."

"No." When he realizes we're not going to settle for a vague answer, he says, "Trunk of my car. That's what took so long. I had to unload some stuff to fit her in there. I want to find out what she told them, whether she was involved in . . ." For a moment, it looks like he's going to cry, then he gives his head a shake. "What did I miss?"

I give him the condensed version, ending with the fire and my conversation with Simon. "He'll kill them unless I get the keys from CHRONOS before Pru and turn them over to him."

Max is quiet for a moment, giving me a long, level stare that's clearly intended to make me uncomfortable. Then he leans back a bit in his chair and says, "Okay, first. I think you're lying. What you've said doesn't make sense. Why would Simon need *you* to get the keys? He could just stop Prudence from making that jump, right? Or go himself. And second, there's no way I'd let you hand over those keys."

I bristle, both at what he says and how he says it. He's baiting me. While I'd rather take the high ground, Trey tensed up when Max said I was lying, and even more when he got to the last bit. If I don't defend myself, Trey will feel like he should. So I guess I'll go on the offensive.

"Okay, *first*," I say, mimicking Max's snide tone, "I have no intention of giving Simon a damn thing. But I will most definitely play along and make him think I'm willing to trade. That's not even up for debate."

Max's nostrils flare, but he doesn't respond, so I go on.

"And second . . ." I point to my face, drawing an air circle around it. "Unlike Simon, I stand a decent chance of passing for Prudence. She's the one with the connection who gets her those keys. I don't even know if Simon has coordinates for that time, unless he wanted to jump into that . . . gaping pit . . . as you were expecting me to do. I now have the Houdini key, which used to be Pru's key, which means I can avoid that fiasco."

He lifts his chin combatively. "Let me guess. You got it all by yourself, without any help at all from Simon's best buddy."

"Yes. I got the key myself, Max." I put as much conviction as I can muster behind the half truth. Houdini and Bess didn't turn over the key in Eastbourne, and aside from telling me where I might find Prudence, Kiernan really wasn't all that much help.

"So, you're telling me you're not in contact with Dunne?"

Okay . . . that would require an all-out lie. Tilson, Charlayne, and Ben are all watching to see how I'll answer, and at some point, they'll know Kiernan is involved.

"I didn't say that."

Max pounds the heel of his hand against the edge of the table. A fork clatters to the floor and the pepper shaker topples. "I knew it. That kind of stupidity is why Julia's dead!"

"Maximilian Waters, lower your voice." Tilson has silenced several generations of Briar Hill students. He uses that experience to good effect now, casting a meaningful glance first at Max and then around the restaurant.

He turns to me, continuing in the same tone, "But to be blunt, Miss Keller, Max is right. You weren't authorized to contact anyone outside of this group. Dunne is a known associate of Saul and his allies—"

"Everyone at this table is a known associate of the Cyrists! That's pretty much a prerequisite for working from the inside." I jerk my head in Max's direction. "I'm not the one who brought Eve Conwell, someone I know beyond any doubt to be—"

I bite back what I really want to say, which is that it's far more likely Max's association with Eve is what got Julia killed. Playing the blame game won't bring her back and will make it even harder to work with Max. And I think everyone gets my point without me saying it.

"Listen, Max," I continue in a softer tone. "I'm sorry about what happened to Julia. I wanted to go back and stop it from happening, but Dr. Tilson said—"

"And he's right," Max says. "The rules are clear. But since when have you paid attention to rules?"

"I didn't play a part in making those rules, Max. And I know . . . I'm absolutely certain . . . that Kiernan had no role in Julia's death. Or your father's. Have you forgotten that he saved your great-grandparents' lives? He's as passionate about stopping the Cyrists as anyone here. If we're going to work together, you'll have to take my word on that, because I *will* be working with Kiernan."

No one openly objects, so I go on. "Kiernan will be going on the jump with me to CHRONOS. I need backup and—"

"I'm going, too," Max says.

"No. That's not what Julia wanted."

He gives me a scathing look. "You met her twice, Kate. Don't presume to tell *me* what Julia wanted."

∞

Bogart, Georgia
March 1, 1913, 7:12 p.m.

Connor and Dad are doing exactly the same thing they were doing last time I checked. If I lived in a logical universe, I guess that would be obvious because I'm looking at the same time and the same location I watched earlier today at the diner—the time when I agreed to jump back in. But since my own personal universe is a far-from-logical place where Simon or Pru or some second-cousin-twice-removed could jump in and change this reality at any moment, the fact that they are still where I left them comes as a huge relief.

Kiernan's cabin is a bit on the chilly side tonight, so I tug up the quilt before using the key to check on Trey and Charlayne. They are also when and where I left them—a quarter after five in the evening in one of the hotel rooms Tilson rented just north of Silver Spring. They'll serve as a temporary base for the Fifth Column, or at least this particular cell, since we can't assume any of our houses are safe. Trey's on his phone, probably trying to convince his dad to leave town again.

Charlayne sits on the bed, cleaning a rifle. That ranks high on the list of things I never, ever expected to see Charlayne doing. Of course, I also never expected to see this lotus tattoo on the back of my right hand, but it's there. The center is puffy, and it's starting to itch a little. I don't know if that's just the normal reaction to ink and teeny tiny needles or something to do with the vaccination, but I resist the urge to scratch.

Since I don't see Max, Ben, and Tilson, I'm guessing they're hanging out in the other room a few doors down. I didn't set a stable point there, mostly because I didn't want to watch Max glowering. He's angry that I wouldn't give him the stable point for CHRONOS headquarters before I left, even though I was being totally honest when I told him that I don't yet know which one it is. Pru has dozens of local points on this key that are active in 2308, and this afternoon, here at Kiernan's cabin, is the first chance I've had to go through them.

I told Max I'd jump back and give him the coordinates once I pinpoint them. But I'm not sure I will, and I think he knows it. Unless I have a major change of heart, I don't trust Max enough to want him following me to 2308.

Each time I think about his arm around Eve, my resolve to exclude Max from this jump strengthens.

Kiernan is currently combing through the Future-Wiki that the Fifth Column put together. Every few minutes he gives a huff and jots something in his notebook. He's sitting in the same spot where I saw him with Prudence. It's not the first time that memory has sneaked into my brain in the past hour.

And each time I think about Pru on his lap, my resolve to include Kiernan on this jump weakens.

That's probably not fair—to either Max or Kiernan—but I have little reason to trust Max. And Kiernan has stretched my trust almost to the breaking point over and over in the past few days.

I tuck my own CHRONOS key back inside my T-shirt and pick up the other key I'm wearing—Prudence's key, which hangs from a long silver chain. My eyes are tired and itchy, partly thanks to these stupid contacts, but I need to keep working. I've spent the past hour looking through a lot of Pru's local points, most of which make absolutely no sense. On the whole, my first glimpses of the future have been very anticlimactic. Quite a few of the locations seem to be black holes, and not just at night. They're perpetual black spaces, like the one at the remains of CHRONOS headquarters, minus the staticky feedback.

Pru wasn't exactly diligent about labeling the points she set—not that I can fault her for that, since I've never labeled any of the points I've set on my own key. Still, I can't tell why she set any of these locations, and that worries me.

Because the thing about local points is that they haven't been tested for stability. I mean, I can set a point at any time and place, but there's nothing to indicate that it's going to be a good jump site two years later—or two years before, for that matter. Someone could build a highway through that point tomorrow.

The locations in the CHRONOS *Log of Stable Points* all include a range of dates when a specific point is viable. The same is true for the commonly used jump locations that are hardwired into each medallion. But with points that individuals set on their own personal key, it's basically a crapshoot.

For every one of Prudence's local points that's black, there's another that's worthless in terms of stealth. And many more just don't make sense. A dozen or so are inside the bedroom of an elderly couple, most of them centered on their bed. At least, I'm pretty sure it's a bed—it's more like a small, partially enclosed platform that they climb into at night.

"Kiernan?"

"Mmm-hmm?" He doesn't look up from his writing.

"I need a second opinion. Bring your key."

I transfer four of Pru's stable points to his medallion. And yes, it would be quicker to just hand it to him—I'm still covered by my own key, so there's no risk. But he might jump away with it. He clearly knows why I won't let him handle it, just as Max did. Unlike Max, however, Kiernan doesn't complain.

"Why would Pru watch that couple?" I ask. "They're ordinary, other than being really old. The woman has mobility issues when she first gets up, at least until she's dressed. Otherwise they seem unremarkable. The cat, on the other hand, is bizarre. It does normal cat stuff when they're awake, but when they crawl into bed, it goes straight to its own bed and . . . I think it shuts down. Sometimes it stays there all day, unless they come back and point at it. Then it gets up and starts being a cat again."

"The cat isn't too surprising," he says. "They had similar pets when I was stuck in 2152. Although this guy looks a lot more like a cat than the so-called dogs I saw on the street. Never understood people walking the bloody things. The whole purpose was to own a pet they didn't *have* to walk, but they'd still take them out and show 'em off, let them sniff each other at the park. But yeah, the old couple—no clue. The number of stable points at their place seems almost . . . voyeuristic?"

My brain wanders off in search of a logical explanation. I'm about to ask whether they might be Katherine's parents, or maybe Saul's, when Kiernan says, "But maybe she wasn't watching them. Maybe she was watching someone else? Did you scan through the whole period when she was using these locations?"

"I skimmed the full two-year span, picking random dates. They occupy this apartment the entire time."

"Then this could be another change. Come over to the table. Might as well show you now."

Something about his tone makes me reluctant to follow, but I do. He slides the notebook across the table, and I see a long list, divided into the same categories as the Future-Wiki. "Someone in the Fifth Column spent a lot of time compiling this information, but a lot of it doesn't synch up with what I've heard or seen."

"But you haven't been to 2308."

"No. I haven't been to *any* point past 2152. But you can extrapolate some things about the future from the past. The people in 2308—and I mean the people *currently* in 2308—had a very different past than what they've got recorded here. Different from the one Abel and Delia remember. Or Katherine and Saul, for that matter."

Kiernan picks up the tablet and scrolls down to the section for 2100–2220 and the subsection *Government*. "Like I said, I've only seen to the halfway point of that century, but the government they describe here is nothing like the one I experienced. And keep in mind that was before the latest shift and the Culling, so I'd imagine the changes are even more extreme. One government controls the entire continent—North and South America as a whole—by 2308, based on what Pru told me. The mergers start happening around 2050, and there were only a few pockets of resistance by 2152, when I visited. The government gives a few nods to religious freedom, but everyone in power is Cyrist."

He paces back over to the table. "And that's the point whoever put this together is missing. Scroll through and you won't see a single mention of Cyrists. The war in Africa I told you about—the one where I suspect Saul got the toxin he used at Six Bridges? Still happens, but not the same way. There's a centralized government for the African continent as well, although it's showing some signs of strain in the 2150s. Europe and Asia are a bit more fractured. And the environmental issues. Those affect society as well. To name just one, what impact would killing off most of the population have on the sea level? Pru said half the landmarks in DC were partly underwater when she first arrived . . . but who knows if that's true now, with fewer people and lower emission levels or whatever."

The panic engine was already cranking up inside me when he started speaking, and by the time he gets to the end of his future history lesson, it's roaring full speed. "So the file is garbage?"

"Pretty much. I'm guessing the stuff about the Objectivist Club is worth a look because of Saul's bet with Campbell. If that's really why he's doing all of this, and Simon seemed certain it is, then Saul would make damned sure Campbell knows he won. But other than that . . ." He sighs, rubbing his temples. "Think about it this way, Kate. Each time there's been a shift, you've noticed small changes, and you don't even remember the timeline before the Cyrists. Those little changes spread out, and before long, you've got a very different history. Very different government. Different cities, different culture, different pretty much everything."

"And the train track we're riding on hits a cement wall in a few days," I say. "Well, in a few days from my perspective. The Culling changes everything. That's why these stable points are screwed up. The geographical and chronological coordinates are still the same, but everything else has changed. There may not even *be* a CHRONOS! Maybe it was never created, maybe there aren't even any keys to—*ugh!*" I pound both fists into my thighs, hard, but it doesn't even begin to vent the frustration.

Kiernan leans forward and grabs my wrists. "I don't think so, Kate. Unless someone opened them up and gave them an acid bath like the ones Connor had, the keys wouldn't be affected. They're a constant. They're inside a CHRONOS field. Even if everything changes around them, those keys existed in some timeline, so they exist in this one, too."

He's right. At least I *think* he is.

"Okay. But where? And how do we grab the keys before Prudence does, if she got them in some other timeline that doesn't even exist anymore?"

∞

This is the first time I've been awakened by rooster.

I don't like it.

He yanked me out of a deep, dreamless sleep, and I almost slip back into it, until he starts up again. The creature clearly takes his alarm clock duty far too seriously, and there's no way to turn him off or press snooze. Even pulling a pillow over my head doesn't block his racket. No wonder people went to bed early in these days. They knew they'd be jolted wide awake at the crack of dawn.

I vaguely remember moving to the guest room after the third time I drifted off on Kiernan's sofa. Keeping your eyes open is kind of important when scanning stable points. I was starting to worry that the next time I opened my eyes I'd find I blinked myself into the future.

Everyone is still where they're supposed to be when I check in via the medallion. I know my constant checking is bordering on obsession, but there's something comforting about the routine. If I had a stable point for Mom and Katherine, it would be so easy to get stuck in this loop where I circle endlessly, making sure everyone I love is safe in this one block of time.

But that would be crazy.

And speaking of crazy, the glow stars, the ones Kiernan brought here from his room in Boston, are still on the ceiling. Those stars nagged at me when I saw them in his room in Boston. They still bother me, and I finally realize why. The stars shouldn't exist. Kiernan said her other things vanished. I have to keep the 1905 dress—the one that belonged to her—under a CHRONOS field or it will vanish, too. If Other-Kate put those stars on his ceiling, they should've blinked out of existence when she did. Right?

I check the nightstand near the bed for a CHRONOS diary inside, but there isn't one. While Kiernan does have a diary in the loft and the field *might* extend that far, I doubt it.

Did Kiernan jump to the closest time and place with a Spencer Gifts and buy more? It's the only thing that makes sense. If so, it's sad. In fact, it's borderline creepy-obsessive, and I'm not comfortable putting Kiernan in that category.

I pull on the jeans, sweater, and socks I discarded before climbing under the quilt last night because the cabin is chilly this morning, and the 2308 costume Kiernan nabbed from Prudence's closet doesn't look very warm. It also smells funny . . . a musky, spicy scent he says Pru wore when she was younger.

I've mentally tagged the outfit "Seven of Nine." It's one of those catsuit things—stretchy, shiny, and grayish-purple. It reminds me of this cyborg character on one of the *Star Trek* shows Dad used to watch. I don't think he really liked the show itself, but he definitely paid attention when the catsuit woman was on-screen. Even though I won't fill it out as impressively as she did, it wins the best jump costume hands down.

I also put the contacts back in, reluctantly, scratching my eyelid in the process. Charlayne swears I'll get used to the lenses after a while. I can't understand why anyone would wear these for fun.

It's much warmer in the main cabin, thanks to a roaring fire. Kiernan's already up with a cup of coffee, reading something on my tablet.

"Is there more of that?" I ask.

"Of course. You're here, so I knew to make a full pot." He pushes his chair back and goes to the kitchen. "Are you hungry?"

"Yes. I'm thinking Kentucky Fried Rooster."

There's another chorus of cock-a-doodle-doo just as I finish speaking, and he laughs. "Henry's just doing his job, love."

Kiernan seems almost cheerful, in stark contrast to last night. This may be the first time he's called me *love* since we were with Abel and Delia in Martha's cellar. I have mixed feelings about that part, but if it means he's not snapping and muttering constantly, I'll consider it a fair trade.

He comes back into the room with a full mug and a plate of what looks and smells like banana bread. "Did you sleep well?"

"Better than I'd have thought, but I'm still exhausted. In fact, if you want to track down Henry and pop a bag over his head, I'll go back for five or six hours more."

"I could do that, but you'd just lie there and worry about everything that needs doing, so you might as well get back to it." Kiernan speaks as though this is a given fact, which it probably is. And that irks me, because it's one of those things he shouldn't know but still does.

And that's probably why I decide to ask the question that's been bugging me since I was in his apartment in Boston, even though I'm fairly certain it's going to wreck his pleasant mood.

"So . . . the stars on the ceiling in the guest room. You said they belonged to your Kate. But they couldn't, could they? The dress . . . you said it would've disappeared if you left it at Jess's store without the CHRONOS field from your grandfather's diary. Why would those stars be any different?"

I was right. Kiernan's eyes take on the guarded look that's pretty much the norm these days and he looks away. I instantly regret pushing the point, but he's hiding something, and I can't help thinking those silly stars are part of it.

He goes to the fireplace and pokes it vigorously a few times, even though it's blazing quite nicely and doesn't need the attention.

Then he walks over to the couch, leans his head back, and closes his eyes.

I think he's ignoring me, but just as I'm opening my mouth to repeat the question, he sighs and starts talking.

"When my Kate disappeared, the stars went with her." The lilt in his voice is gone, and he sounds tired. "Some time later, I came back to the apartment, and the stars were back. They weren't stuck on in quite the same spots, and I think this batch may be from another company because the color seems more yellow this time. At first I thought it was one of Pru's jokes. Then I thought it was you . . . *this* you. That you made a jump back and put those stars in our sky as a sign. To tell me I shouldn't give up. So I brought them along when I moved. Now . . ." He shrugs, still avoiding my gaze. "I don't have an answer to give you, Kate. If they bother you, take 'em down."

I don't have an answer to give you, Kate.

I think his wording is intentional. Not *I don't have an answer*, because I'm pretty sure that would be an outright lie. And whatever else is going on with him, Kiernan still doesn't like lying to me.

"No," I say. "I just wondered. Seemed odd."

And it does seem odd, but Kiernan's closed expression makes it crystal clear I won't get anything else out of him. So I pick up the key and start scanning stable points again.

Like the old folks' apartment yesterday, the first few visual thumbnails seem similar enough in color and lighting that I believe they're set in a single room, even though the angle varies a bit. I select one that appears to be looking down on a party from a balcony. The room looks like it could be part of a museum. It's very posh, with dark paneling and upholstered chairs that would probably seem antique even to Kiernan. An immense fireplace takes up much of one wall, but people stand too close to it for me to believe it's an actual fire. More likely a video screen. Framed portraits hang above the mantel. The one closest to me is a woman with short gray hair. There's an inscription above the pictures, but the room isn't well lit enough for me to make it out.

The crowd is maybe three-quarters male. Some wear suits a bit like tuxedos—they appear to be servers. Two men are in attire that looks Elizabethan, and several other historical eras are represented. This is either CHRONOS or a costume party.

I'm leaning toward the latter. Directly in front of the stable point is a woman whose dress scoops low in the back to highlight her assets, by which I mean not only her shapely behind, but also her *wings*.

They don't look large enough to be functional—maybe two feet long—so I'm thinking costume. But they seem to rise straight out from the skin of her shoulder blades, and she uses them as she talks to emphasize her points, much the way I use my hands. The wings are delicate, gossamer-looking confections of white and seafoam green, with feathers tipped in a gold a few shades lighter than her dress.

The winged woman is by far the most stunning creature in the room, but the man at the far end of the table also draws my eye. While he isn't obese, he's definitely well cushioned, in stark contrast with every other person in the room. They all seem extraordinarily fit . . . almost too fit. The large guy appears isolated from the others. They're clustered around him, but talking to each other. It's almost like he's on display.

The man's eyes dart around nervously. A dog, also well cushioned and clearly past its prime, sleeps near his feet. The man keeps one hand on the animal, like he needs constant reassurance that his pet—a sad-looking parody of the lean, mean Dobies at the Sixteenth Street Temple—hasn't wandered away.

Campbell's dog . . . that gassy old Doberman named Cyrus.

If that's Campbell, and I'm pretty sure it is, this must be the Objectivist Club. I don't believe it's inside CHRONOS headquarters, from what Katherine and Grant said. But who knows if there even is a CHRONOS anymore? It's a reasonably safe location where I could jump in. Better than arriving by rocket belt.

I grab Kiernan's notepad and jot that location down as one to transfer to his key, then move to the next stable point. The geographic coordinates are so close to the last one that it might be the same building. But it's the date stamp that catches my eye after I click it: 10022308_2200. That's near enough to the estimated date for Pru's jump to CHRONOS HQ that I decide to study this one closely.

A gargantuan pool takes up the center of the room, with several smaller pools scattered about at one end. People wander in and out of the area during the day, swimming and soaking up the sun. At some point, most of them enter one of the small white doors lined in a row along the far wall.

Clothing appears optional, more for decoration than decorum. And the groupings are . . . odd. I've yet to see a woman stroll in without a man, although several groups of men have wandered in without women.

At first I think the place is outside, because it's sunlit part of the day and there's a sky when I pivot upward. But as I skim through several days, the patterns seem too regular to be natural. Each day is aggressively bright and sunny, with just a few wispy clouds. The sky fades gradually beginning at 5 p.m. with a uniformly spectacular sunset promptly at 5:45. There's a full moon every night, and regardless of the time of day, the wall of doors at the back remains fully lit until midnight. Then everything shuts down until six the next morning. The moon, the stars, and even the little reflecting lights along the edge of the pool go out.

When I hit the midnight blackout period after three iterations of this loop, I decide to zip through more quickly, thinking it may be time to move on to something new. But then I notice an odd flicker of white in the darkness.

It looks like a flashlight. Whoever's holding it turns left, walking around the pool toward the stable point I'm viewing. As the person gets closer, I pick up a second source of light, fainter, but very clearly the vivid blue of a CHRONOS key.

After a moment, the man—he's definitely a man, and a rather large one, too—comes closer to the stable point. He tosses a small bag onto the ground and puts the flashlight down beside it with the beam pointing upward. He's tall and very muscular, in his early to midtwenties, with long hair that's either blond or light brown, and a slightly darker beard.

The guy turns and stares directly at the stable point. And even though he's hundreds of years into the future, I know exactly what that expression means.

I'm waiting. Where the hell are you?

∞17∞

He looks like Thor.

Kiernan says that's just projection on my part, because this must be Tate Poulsen, who was a Viking historian, and Thor is what comes to mind when I think of Vikings.

But Kiernan has never seen the movies. I think it's much more likely that whichever CHRONOS scientist landed the task of tweaking Tate Poulsen's genetic makeup *had* seen those movies and decided to create this guy as an homage.

Because he looks like Thor. Tangled blond hair, mustache, beard. Give him a hammer and a red cape and he'd be a decent movie double . . . except he might be a little *too* large.

One thing Kiernan and I did agree on is that Thor doesn't look happy. He looks confused. Frazzled. There may even be some crazy in the mix.

So I'm very glad Kiernan is hiding in the shadows as backup. He jumped in first—my new, nonnegotiable rule for any trips we take—and he'll stay in the background unless I'm in clear danger.

Which could be instantly, judging from Tate's clenched fists and that twitchy little vein near his temple.

I wait until he steps away from the stable point, then take a deep breath and blink in.

He grabs my shoulders before I can get my bearings and lifts me several inches off the ground.

"What in God's name have you done, Pru?" His voice is deep, but he keeps the volume low, barely above a hiss.

I stretch my legs, trying to at least touch my toes to the floor, and resist the urge to fight back. I don't think Prudence would fight him.

On the other hand, I don't think she'd care for being manhandled any more than I do. And if I don't get control of the situation pretty quickly, Kiernan will probably step in.

"Put me down, Tate! You're hurting me."

He does as I ask, and I notice the floor isn't very floorlike. My boots sink into it, almost like beach sand. But when I take a step, my footprints fill in almost instantly.

I don't know enough to take the lead in this little tango. The odds of me making a mistake increase each time I open my mouth, so I wait, hoping Tate will speak first.

He doesn't. His eyes are very busy, however. They move down my body and then back up in a way that makes me very uncomfortable. Even though there's barely an inch of flesh exposed below my collarbone, this suit leaves little to the imagination. And his eyes are familiar—I don't know why, but it's not a pleasant familiarity.

When his gaze arrives back at my face, he grabs me again, very differently this time. His left hand swallows the back of my head, his fingers twisting into my hair. His right hand pulls me from behind and scoops me up against his body.

It takes every bit of control I possess not to panic and shove him away. I try to channel Prudence, something I would normally avoid at all costs.

Pru wouldn't freak out. She wouldn't. In fact, I'm pretty sure she'd kiss him back.

So that's what I do, trying to pretend this is Trey. A very large Trey. Who has a beard. Who smells like he hasn't bathed recently.

And who is . . . *crying*?

Yeah. Definitely crying.

He sinks downward, taking me with him. I brace myself against the floor with my hand, and it *is* like beach sand, only . . . not granular. It's solid, slightly warm. A little like the memory-foam thing that Dad put on the pull-out sofa at his place, only I suspect this stuff would actually have kept me from feeling that stupid bar in the middle.

Tate's shoulders stop shaking after a moment, and he leans back on one elbow, the other arm still clutching me to his body.

"I thought you'd come back before . . . when it all went crazy. I looked for you everywhere. This was my last shot, my last . . ."

He doesn't finish the sentence, just burrows his face into my neck, breathing deeply. I tense automatically, and it's almost like the tension flows from my body to his.

"What's wrong?" he asks.

"You're holding me too tight. I can't breathe."

Tate loosens his hold, but he's still looking at me strangely. I force myself to kiss him and then say, "My key was swiped. I couldn't get back, Tate. What happened?"

"Maybe you should tell *me* what happened? I got out of the building and headed back to my place to wait. Like we agreed. Only I'm in the hallway when I suddenly feel like I'm going to heave my guts out. Everything . . . changed around me." He slumps back into the fake sand, his hand remaining possessively on my thigh. "I go to my door, but I can't get in. Some ancient hag called building security. I had to dismember the guard to avoid winding up in a holding center, and the damn thing still sent out an alert before I crushed its comm unit."

I let out the breath I sucked in when he said *dismember the guard*, very relieved to hear that the guard is an *it*. Because that means not human . . . right?

"That old couple has lived there since before I was born. Excuse me, since before I should have been born, because from everything I can tell, I wasn't. My credits don't exist, CHRONOS still doesn't exist, but this time it's not that they shut it down, Pru. It never existed at all. If I have parents, I can't find them. No one knows who I am . . . except for Campbell, of course, but he's completely flaked."

"Campbell was under a key then?"

"Yeah. The one you brought *back* to him?" His eyes are narrowed now, and I finally place why he looks familiar—aside from the whole Thor vibe. The eyes are Simon's. In fact, if this guy never exercised, never went outdoors, and was shrunk down about a foot . . .

That realization sets my pulse racing, but I fake a smile and raise my eyebrows, like he's the one saying something stupid. "Well, obviously. I was asking whether he *still* has it."

Tate's eyes remain wary as he shakes his head. "They let him keep the key long enough for a tour of the EC, so he could see the mess for himself. After that, they took it. Said he could go anywhere he wants inside the OC. If he steps outside . . . adios, Campbell. Same for the dog. They don't exist any more than I do."

He punches the sand-stuff, and his fist sinks down nearly to the wrist. "God almighty, Pru! This isn't what I agreed to! You were supposed to restore CHRONOS and *fix* the mess Saul made, not make it worse."

"I'm trying! Don't you think I'm trying?" That line is 100 percent sincere, and it must ring true, because his expression softens.

Unfortunately, that means he pulls me close to him again. "How long for you? Since you went back? You look . . . different. Rounder."

I take a moment to think about my response. A few years' distance might help explain any lapses of memory. Also, I'm pretty sure Pru wouldn't like his last comment.

"Just over two years. And did you just call me fat?"

"No. Rounder is good." He squeezes my thigh and adds in a voice that is almost a growl, "I *like*. You were so thin last time I saw you. But, babes, things are . . . different. Wearing that could complicate matters once we're outside the club."

"It was all I could find. How long has it been for you?"

I know this is a loaded question. Prudence should know the date she got the keys. But since I don't know the date, I need to play stupid.

He rolls his eyes. "Um . . . non-time traveler? September 20th to October 14th is still right at three weeks for those who are chronologically grounded. It took me nearly two weeks to figure out a way to get in here. This is the only stable point I could think of that you might check and that might possibly still be active."

"I have to go back and fix this."

"No kidding. I know I said before that I'd go crazy if I was stuck here, stuck at a desk. If I couldn't jump. And I'm still not sure I could take it. But this? I can't . . . I can't imagine staying in this place, Pru. It's infinitely worse than—"

Something rattles in the darkness. Tate squeezes my thigh again and says, "Shh."

"I don't hear anything," I lie, since I'm pretty sure the noise was Kiernan.

"No, there was something. We should get out of here either way. Come on." He pulls me up and then reaches down to grab his pack and flashlight. "They have sensors at the exits, but security is programmed to keep people from getting in, not out. We should be okay."

"So how did you get in?"

He hesitates. I think maybe he's blushing. "Hid in one of the old-style Juvapods no one uses. I can see why. You can barely breathe in there."

I don't think that tells me how he got into the building, although maybe it does, since I have no idea what a Juvapod is. But since Prudence might know, I just follow him, wishing I could catch a glimpse of Kiernan before we leave. I don't know how much he's heard, and he needs to get out, too, preferably before we set off a sensor.

There's a movement from the shadows to the right of the row of doors. Tate must see it, too, because he mutters a curse and takes a half step in that direction. Then he changes his mind and reverses course. Scooping me up under his arm, he takes off past the rows of doors into a dark hallway beyond.

"Put me down, Tate!" It's the second time I've had to tell him that in less than five minutes, and I'm beginning to feel like I'm dealing with King Kong. "I can run, you know."

"Not as fast as I can."

I open my mouth to argue, but . . . yeah. He's moving fast—almost *unnaturally* fast—especially when you consider that he's lugging an extra hundred and twenty pounds of me.

A glowing red X in a square box comes into view as he rounds the corner. The X just hangs in the darkness, and I have a sudden strong feeling that we shouldn't continue this way, but that could be because there's *a large red X* in front of us. As we get closer, I see that the X is above a doorway, so maybe EXIT signs lost a few letters over the centuries?

The rim around the door starts to glow the same red as the X when we're a few paces away.

"Damn it!" Tate shoves the door with his shoulder, barely breaking stride as we go through. "Something triggered security already!"

I crane my neck around to see if Kiernan is behind us, but the door slams shut. The building rises up at least ten floors, maybe more, white and immaculate like one of the Cyrist temples. I don't see a Cyrist symbol, but the place is massive, and we're too close for me to view the top.

I also don't see the door open again, and that has me very worried about Kiernan.

The streets are nearly deserted, with no cars, buses, or any other form of transportation. I scan for street signs, but I don't see any. There's a park across the street and a statue that looks vaguely familiar. Commodore Something-or-Other. I think that means we're near McPherson Square, or at least where it used to be.

Two people cross the road a few blocks down. They're moving quickly, at a smooth, even pace that doesn't look natural. The only other signs of life are an oversized rat that slips into a drainage pipe and a man huddled in an alley between two buildings—both of which could fit in my present-day DC.

I nearly miss it, given Tate's need for speed, but as we zip by the guy in the alley, I catch a brief glimpse of his face.

It's Kiernan. How did he get out before we did when he was behind us?

A few seconds after we pass, Kiernan darts out of the alley, but he can't keep up. Usain Bolt couldn't keep up with Tate.

The difference between the building we were just inside and the rest of the neighborhood is striking, even in the dark. The entire area is in shambles, nearly deserted. There are a few newer-looking buildings, or at least buildings that are still intact, scattered around here and there, and a few lit windows about a quarter mile up the hill.

"Can you slow down, please?" My voice is tentative, more like Kate than Prudence, so I add, in a sharper tone, "You're crushing my frickin' ribs, Tate! I need to stop and breathe."

He rounds the next corner and ducks into the recessed doorway of one of the less dilapidated buildings.

"Past curfew." At least he's breathing heavy after that sprint. I was beginning to wonder if he's actually human. "Had to get you out of there. You'll attract attention, especially in that."

"Why? I mean, it's tight, but the women inside that place wore far less. Some of them weren't wearing anything."

"Well, yes. But . . . they belong to members. Or they're hired companions. They'll be safe if they stay inside."

"Wait . . . they *belong* to members?"

"Uh . . . well, not property. Some are family members. Others are registered to them sort of like. . . pets?" He says the last word hesitantly, as if he expects me to explode, but I'm rendered totally speechless.

He shakes his head. "That's not quite right either, but like I said before, a lot of things are different. I haven't pieced all of it together, but whatever this was that happened a few years before 2020, it was massive. History now tells us the only reason anyone survived the Great Plague is because the Cyrists issued a warning. Those who listened and believed lived. But I get a feeling that's not quite how it went down, is it?"

"Not quite. They called it the Culling. Saul—"

"Did you . . ." Tate grabs my shoulders, and his expression is conflicted. "Tell me you didn't help them, Pru. Not with something like that."

"No." I twist to loosen his grip and look away because I don't really know the extent to which Prudence helped with the Culling. I can't imagine Younger Pru, the one that I met in New York, the one that this guy was involved with, knowingly assisting Saul with something that massively evil. But Older Pru?

"That why I'm here, Tate." He looks a little hurt, so I reach up and run my hand along his neck. "The *other* reason I'm here."

"Did you find him?" One hand slides down from my shoulder to rest on my abdomen. "Is he safe?"

I have no idea how to answer that. Is who safe? The only thing I can think to do is shake my head.

"And it's been two years? That's just wrong, Pru . . . a babe should have his mother. Maybe when you find him, you can go back, make up the time."

I'm really glad it's dark, because I'm pretty sure my cover would be totally blown if Tate could see my face right now.

"You'll find him, Pru. You will. Is there any news of Patrek?" He says it oddly, almost like *pot-wreck*, with a slight accent on the second syllable.

"Patrick?" I ask.

"Is he part of this . . . Culling?"

I can tell he's hoping I'll tell him no, although I've no idea why. But I tell him the truth. "Yes. He's helping Saul."

"Then that's my fault, too." He looks like he's going to cry again, but he just presses his lips to my palm, then turns my hand over to trace his finger over the tattoo. "You let them tat you. I liked the other one better."

No clue what other one he's talking about, so I just give him a tiny smile and change the subject. "Only you and Campbell remember the other timeline?"

He's quiet for a moment. "There could be others, but I don't think so. There were rumors before—when I was CHRONOS—that someone in the administration was under a key. Some people said the president, others said the vice president. But I think they'd have started up the program again if someone in power remembered about CHRONOS, if they knew some historians were behind a plague that wiped out nearly a billion people. I think they'd try and stop it. Don't you?"

Nearly a billion people.

My first emotion is relief—not even a billion! The models Tilson and Ben mentioned predicted at least triple that number.

That's followed by the realization that it's still *nearly a billion people.* And whatever the number, the changes were radical enough to create this reality, which is a far cry from the future Katherine, Delia, and Abel knew. Grant, too. Would he have wanted to return to this version of his future?

"But maybe . . ." I'm about to say that maybe someone in power is in the process of doing exactly that, at this moment, but I catch myself. It's one of those odd conundrums that twists my brain into a pretzel. The fact that this plague *did* happen would seem to suggest that he's right. No one in a position to reinstate a time travel program knows about Saul's role in this "Great Plague," because if they did, they'd have found a way to be sure Saul's Culling never happened. The newspaper headlines Tilson showed me would never have been written.

But. Here comes the bendy-twisty part. That same logic could be applied to me, since I'm also currently trying to prevent that catastrophe. Does the fact that I'm here in the future, seeing evidence that it happened in the past, mean that I fail?

No, no, no, no. Stop it, Kate.

"Okay," I say. "Let's go on the assumption that it's just you and Campbell. Do you think he can help us? *Will* help us?"

"I don't know. All of the changes sort of . . . undid him. He's drinking a lot. Last time I was there he went on and on about

CHRONOS history and other things . . . other people . . . that used to exist. I think he's taking some strong mood drugs. Or it might just be how much he's drinking. Anyway, I had an hour with him that first day, and he was coherent maybe fifteen minutes, total. It wasn't much better last time. All I managed to find out is that he was inside the club when everything shifted. The next thing he remembers, someone hands him a sealed box, saying it's from Brother Cyrus, and shows him to his quarters."

"What was in the box?"

"A blank CHRONOS diary, which I'm guessing was included only for the CHRONOS field. Copies of Saul's two little books. And a note, which Campbell says was in Saul's handwriting, on some really old paper. Two words: *I win*."

Tate sucks in a breath and then slams his fist into the side of the building. The punch meets only slight resistance before the wall swallows his hand, kind of like the sand-stuff did earlier.

"The books were a *joke!* We were both nuked half the time when we were writing them. Saul was going to give them to Campbell at the holiday party. Then he moved in with Katherine. I guess she convinced him they were a work of genius."

I'd love to know what evidence Saul left behind that convinced everyone Katherine was the mastermind who destroyed CHRONOS. I mean, it's a moot point in this timeline, since CHRONOS never existed, but I'd bet it was at the heart of Prudence's decision to stay with Saul. Mom said Pru was always the more rebellious twin, always eager to butt heads with Katherine. But even though Mom herself would never have nominated Katherine for Mother of the Year, would she have believed Katherine was evil enough to commit an act of terrorism that killed God knows how many people? I think the evidence would have had to be very, very convincing for her to accept that.

But whatever the evidence was, Pru did believe it. And asking questions at this point seems ill-advised, especially when Tate is already wound up.

"If I could use this damned key, I'd track both of them down and separate their heads from their necks."

I watch as the dent Tate punched in the wall finishes filling back in. When everything is going to hell around you, it's kind of comforting to see something repairing itself. To see something humans invented that's useful rather than destructive.

"I'll take care of Saul and Katherine, Tate. But first, we have to come up with a plan for getting the CHRONOS keys."

Tate stares at me blankly. "But . . . we did that. You have the keys. Getting the keys made things worse."

"Saul has the keys . . . or at least most of them."

"Then why are you here? Go back to . . . whenever . . . and get them from Saul."

I was really, really hoping Tate would already understand what Kiernan told me earlier about the keys existing even if the rest of the timeline didn't. That maybe this type of discussion was part of CHRONOS Agent Training 101. But Katherine's knowledge on these issues seems pretty sketchy, so there's no reason to assume the other historians are any more inclined toward perverse temporal logistics. CHRONOS never planned for historians to change timelines, and they even took precautions, faulty though they may have been, to make sure that they couldn't. Maybe they didn't want them even thinking about how it might be done and the possible ramifications.

"Saul would kill me before giving them over, Tate." That's true, as far as it goes. I'm just leaving out the bit about not knowing when and where the transfer happened. "I need to stop . . . myself from giving the keys to Saul in the first place. As you keep saying, everything changed. CHRONOS never existed. But despite that, you're still wearing a key, right? So am I. The keys are a permanent fixture. They have their own CHRONOS field, so alterations to the timeline don't affect them. The existence of the keys is the only constant. Somewhere and when there's a whole box of unassigned CHRONOS keys—the only link between this reality and the others. *When* is easy—before Prudence got them." My mouth goes suddenly dry as I realize what I've just said. "That is, before the younger me got them. *Where* might be tougher. I'm guessing someone—"

I stop in midsentence and resist the urge to thwack myself in the forehead. "They took Campbell's key, but he's okay if he stays inside the OC. Do you mean the entire building?"

"Yeah . . ."

Connor's rig in the library takes three keys, and the range extends the CHRONOS field to the rest of the house and most of the yard. That club building takes up a full city block, and it's at least ten stories high. While it's entirely possible they've found a way to amplify the field far beyond Connor's twenty-first-century limitations, we do know they have at least one key—the one they took from Campbell.

It's a start.

"Tate, tell me again how you got into the Objectivist Club. And this time, I need specifics."

∞

OBJECTIVIST CLUB
WASHINGTON, EC
October 15, 2308, 4:45 a.m.

Kiernan jumps into the stable point as soon as I step aside. He looks annoyed and tired.

"How did you get away from Thor?"

Sure. Last night he calls the nickname stupid, but now that he's seen the guy in person, he steals it.

"He's joining me later. Since he can't use the key, he'll have to take another route."

We sit down in the sand-stuff, and I bring him up to speed about Campbell and the fact that this entire building is, based on what Tate told me, under a CHRONOS field. Then I pull up the observation point I set outside the building around daybreak and scan ahead a few hours to show Kiernan the line that stretches around the building. It isn't moving yet, so apparently the screeners got a late start.

"They're all day laborers. Tate said there are rarely fewer than two hundred candidates waiting, even though the screeners never choose more than fifty on a weekday, evenly split between servers and companions."

"Companions?"

"Yeah. Paid escorts. Or—"

His nose wrinkles slightly. "I get the point."

"Tate's near the front of the line because he has a blue chip they scan as he comes in the door. The chip means you're a regular or a special request. Or both."

"Which is he?"

"Special request, I think?"

"No. Server or companion?"

"He's listed as companion, although he seems embarrassed about that. Campbell requests him, just to have someone to talk to, and Campbell has special status with the group running the place. Tate says they treat him and the dog kind of like mascots. Check out the girl just behind him. Does she look familiar?"

"Um . . . no. Should she?"

"I think she's the one with the wings. That we saw watching the stable point set at that party. See the way her cloak sticks up in the back?"

"What's with all the cloaks anyway? It's kind of hot."

"You joked about the propriety police back in 1905? Apparently that's a *thing* in this reality. Red cloaks for the women applying for escort positions. The female server candidates—there aren't many of those, because they usually hire men—are in the black cloaks."

I don't point out that there's a double standard—no cloaks for the men. Most are in tuxedos, applying for server positions, but some near the middle of the line are shirtless and oiled like bodybuilders, probably hoping to catch the eye of a screener and steal an escort spot from someone like Tate near the front. Tate is still in jeans—which look identical to men's jeans in my time—but he traded his T-shirt for a gold mesh tank top clearly designed to draw attention to his chest and abs, so I don't think he's as confident about getting back into the building as he pretended. He said the shirt—what little there was—would give him an edge, but it's clearly not his preferred attire, judging from the Simonesque sneer when he pulled it out of his pack.

"Tate's part of the Cyrist gene pool, isn't he? He looks like . . . what Simon could have looked like, if things went right. Except his nose, but that's familiar, too, for some reason."

"June's the only one who knows for sure," Kiernan says, "except maybe Saul. The nose looks like Conwell to me, except it doesn't look quite as oversized on Thor's face."

"Yeah. He mentioned Patrick, but I didn't understand it. And he asked Pru if she'd found some baby. I got the sense from what you said before that she didn't want anything to do with motherhood."

"With the surrogate babies, I know that was the case. But . . . maybe she felt differently about that first one. And I'd say it's a safe bet that Tate was directly involved in that pregnancy from the way his hands were traveling all over you last night."

The last words are clipped, his mouth firm and judgmental.

"Hey! I'm walking a very thin line here. Do you think—"

"No. I'm sorry." He actually does sound a little apologetic. "If anything, you probably need to be a little more enthusiastic. Because Pru would be."

"I thought *you* were the one Pru was interested in?"

"Convenience," he says, with a little shake of his head. "I was there, easy access. But I wasn't her first. Never asked who was because I was worried the answer might be Saul, and if so, that's a scar I didn't want to disturb, you know? But sometimes, during . . . well, I got the feeling she was imagining I was someone else. Fair enough, since I was doing the same."

I don't really want to meet his eyes after that, so I pull up the local point outside the club. Tate's still in line.

"You think you can trust Tate?"

"To help us fix this? Oh, yes," I say. "Absolutely. He doesn't want to stay in this reality. Do you still have the tux you wore as Boudini?"

"It's in the loft at the cabin. Why?"

"You'll need it in order to pose as a server. Unless you'd rather be a male companion?"

"No thanks."

An evil little part of me is dying to say he has more experience as a companion, given his time with Prudence, but I bat it down.

Five minutes later, he's dressed in the tux. That involved me jumping back to the cabin twice because I couldn't find his stupid shoes. The cut isn't identical to the tuxedos I saw on the prospective workers outside, and I'm certain it's not the same fabric, but unless someone decides to give it a thorough inspection, it's close enough.

We walk around the pool to the row of doors on the other side. For some reason it doesn't feel like it's a swimming pool to me. Maybe it's the lack of chlorine smell. Usually with an indoor pool this size the fumes are really noticeable, but I can't really smell anything.

"So we wait in the dressing rooms?" Kiernan asks. "Do they lock?"

"They're not exactly dressing rooms. Tate called them . . . Juvapods? And I don't know if they lock, but I viewed ahead and we'll be fine. A cleaning crew—automated, not human—comes through in about an hour. But they don't clean inside the pods. Tate said they're self-maintaining."

"So if they have robotic cleaning crews, why not robotic servers?"

It's a good question, and one I asked Tate earlier.

"Tate says it's a class thing, and it's apparently not something new to this timeline. It was the tradition here at the club since the beginning, over a hundred years ago. Anyone can be waited on by robots, and there are also robots with AI who can serve as companions, or escorts, or whatever you want to call them. But some people prefer to boss real live humans around. And from what Tate's seen, jobs are scarce throughout the East Coast—or EC, as they call it now. It's one big economic region, not separate states.

There are plenty of people who'll take whatever work they can find, so they're willing to put up with a lot of crap from the patrons."

He huffs and glances around the room. "I guess it's not as much fun to degrade a machine."

"Yeah." We're now in front of the door at the end of the row—a *Juvapod Delux*, based on the label. I set an observation point directly in front of it, and Kiernan does the same so we can keep watch, just in case. And that way, I'll see when Tate is coming, too—he said around nine, but that line still isn't moving. And there's no guarantee he'll get in. Once Tate picks me up, Kiernan will find a moment when he can step out unobserved and head to one of the dining halls to see what information he can uncover.

I touch the door to my pod, and it slides upward to reveal an oval-shaped interior about the size of a broom closet. It reminds me of a sarcophagus, except it's padded with a thick layer of gelatinous-looking goop. The back wall is formed into a chair and there are two shelflike nooks carved into the walls. A slight warmth radiates outward. The walls look blue, although I think that's the reflection from our CHRONOS keys. Only the floor looks normal . . . well, if you consider the sand-stuff under our feet normal.

"And you're sure no one uses these?" Kiernan reaches a tentative finger toward the wall, but I pull his hand back.

"Don't touch the inside. Tate said that's how you activate the pod, and it's connected to the computer system. And no, these are empty until later in the day. People take the newer models first."

"Not sure I'd want to touch them anyway." Kiernan drags the toe of his shoe through the faux sand beneath our feet. "It looks a bit like this crud, just wet and shiny. Like a big green mouth . . . or stomach."

The fact that he said green rather than blue confirms my guess that the walls are just reflecting the light from the CHRONOS key.

And he's kind of right about it looking like a mouth. That ramps up my anxiety about entering the thing by several levels.

I paste on a brave grin. "Into the belly of the beast, I guess. Be careful, okay?"

Kiernan grabs my arm, a worried expression in his eyes. "You be careful, too, Kate. I'm not entirely sure I . . . like . . . you walking around with everyone assuming you're for hire. It sounds . . . risky."

His voice is hesitant, as well it should be. I'm so close to saying I don't really care what he *likes*. His attitude over the past few days is beyond baffling. I never know if I'm going to get the worried friend-who'd-like-to-be-more or the aggressively indifferent colleague. His mood swings are worse than Katherine's.

But I bite my tongue.

"I'll be with Tate. If anyone questions us, he'll say I'm part of a . . . package request. From Campbell. And you've seen Tate. I don't think anyone would dare approach me if he's nearby."

Kiernan looks like he's going to say something else, but I push his hand off my arm. The door slides between us, and I flip the latch to secure it.

To be honest, I think my bigger challenge may be keeping Tate's hands to himself. His relationship with Prudence was most definitely not platonic, and he wasn't happy when I rebuffed some of his more fervent advances earlier. The multitude of stable points in the old couple's bedroom—which used to be Tate's bedroom— make a lot more sense now. Pru was watching him. Was she spying on him? Or maybe it's just her version of having Tate's picture on her phone?

And then Woodhull snatched her key with this set of stable points, severing her link to Tate and essentially ending whatever plans they were making to fix the mess she'd helped Saul create. Assuming that Prudence ever really planned to fix anything.

Tate clearly believes she intended to restore a future that included CHRONOS, but would she have done that if it entirely erased the Cyrists? And where does this mystery kid he mentioned fit into the picture?

I sit cross-legged on the floor, being careful to avoid the sides, and jump forward a few hours to 9 a.m. No point sitting here in this hot box any longer than necessary. A quick check of the observation point outside my pod shows a number of people in various stages of undress swimming, "sunning," and chatting with friends. The stable point outside shows Tate, waiting in the line that hasn't budged. Maybe the alarm going off last night means tighter security?

And even though I try really hard to resist the urge, I check on Trey at the hotel, and Dad and Connor back at Katherine's.

All still safe.

After fifteen minutes inside the Juvapod, the goop isn't the only thing sweating. It's wicked hot. No wonder Tate smelled like week-old gym clothes when he greeted me last night. I feel like I'm going to melt. A bead of sweat trickles down the side of my nose, tickling my nostril. I reach up to flick it away, but before I can, it triggers a sneeze.

And instantly, the pod springs to life. The walls glow a bright, sterile white that's almost painful to the eyes. "Welcome, guest! I'm Alisa. Please survey the treatment menu while I pull your account information." The voice has a bubbly, too-cheerful quality, like the actress who played Glinda in *Wicked*.

A holographic "Treatment Menu" pops up in front of me. Choices include *Vitamin Infusion, Skin Resurfacing, Stress Reduction, Weight Mitigation, Eye Correction, Hair Restoration, Hair Coloring,* and maybe a dozen others. A few seem to be trademarked, because I haven't the slightest clue what the words mean. The ones that puzzle me most are *Aerobic Conditioning* and *Muscle Tone*. Does the goop just reach out and whip you into shape?

The chipper voice is back. "I'm sorry. I can't locate your client record. Now scanning DNA for family membership."

DNA? I didn't touch the walls. Other than the latch on the door, I haven't touched anything. How did I manage to activate this thing, let alone give it DNA?

Oh.

The drop of sweat.

The sneeze.

Damn, damn, *damn.*

The discovery that someone with DNA not in the system is in one of their Juvapods is bound to trigger an alarm of some sort, so I need to hide somewhere else until Tate arrives.

I search the menu for a cancel button. No luck—just the menu items and a line at the bottom, *Powered by ALISA.* So I shove upward on the door. It's also lined with the goo, which actually isn't wet to the touch, just warm and pliant like bread dough.

"The door must remain locked until treatment cycle is complete."

I shove again.

"I *said*, door must remain locked until tre—" The voice halts abruptly, and then continues in a less annoyed tone, "Client DNA linked with a sixty-one percent probability to account Rand02. If this is correct, please state your name and disrobe for treatment."

I freeze, and for a moment, I can't even breathe. Tate said that this section of the complex is new. It didn't exist in his time, so I don't think Prudence could have had an account.

Then the voice says, "Please state your name to begin new client record."

I'm pretty sure I'm screwed no matter what I do, and I need information. "Prudence K. Rand. Account information, please."

"Welcome, Prudence! I am Alisa, and I will be your host today. Please disrobe for your treatment while I process the file."

I wait a few seconds and then repeat, "Account information, please."

"I'm processing that request. *Please wait.*"

It may be my imagination, but I'd swear Alisa's voice has taken on a decidedly snarky tone.

I wait silently, and when Alisa speaks again, her usual chirpy tone is back. "Account information Rand02. Active and in good standing."

"Thank you, Alisa. Please list members included in account."

A list pops up in place of the menu. "Account Rand02 has four primary members. Arturo Rand, Leamon Rand, Eryssa Rand, Saul Rand."

Saul? If CHRONOS never existed, then Saul couldn't either. But . . . his family could still exist. And maybe even someone named Saul? In fact, I'm pretty sure my grandfather would try to ensure that some version of himself not only continued but prospered in this brave new Cyrist-designed world.

"Account Rand02 also has nine affiliated members." The voice proceeds to reel off names in rapid succession. Most of the guest names appear to be female. The last one is the name I just gave her, *Prudence K. Rand.*

I get a sinking feeling in my stomach. It's not just that this could complicate matters. I suspect that it will, but leaving that aside, the fact that the system connected me to the Rand family at all is a blunt reminder that I inherited more than just the CHRONOS gene. I shake my head to clear it of the image of Saul standing near the altar at the Six Bridges chapel, blissfully surveying the rows of bodies before him.

"Please disrobe and select a treatment. Do you need assistance reading the menu?"

"No," I say, matching her snide tone. "I can read."

"Do you need assistance disrobing?"

"No! Account history, please."

"I don't understand. Please restate your request."

I think for a moment and then just spit out exactly what I want to know. "Are other members of account Rand02 in the club today?"

"Yes."

I wait, but apparently Alisa wasn't programmed to be forthcoming, so I prod again. "*Locate* members of account Rand02."

"Arturo Rand and Saul Rand are in the Redwing Dining Hall. Eryssa Rand has a treatment scheduled for sixteen hundred hours in Juvapod unit seven. Please disrobe and select a treatment. Other clients are waiting."

Well, that's a lie. Other clients may be waiting for the *Juvapod Ultra Mega Supreme* or whatever the spiffy newer model is called, but no one is waiting for this one. The observation point outside the pod is clear, except for a middle-aged man diving into the pool.

I wait until the diver hits the water and say, "Cancel treatment."

The door slides up, and I step out. Once I'm in the observation point outside Kiernan's pod, I wave and mouth the word *open*.

He does, and I'm surprised to see he's bare-chested, holding the shirt and jacket in his hand. I guess his pod was as hot as mine.

"Sorry. Tate's not here, so you need to stay put. My pod was triggered when I sneezed."

Kiernan gives me an exasperated look.

"I couldn't stop a sneeze, okay? Anyway, the system linked my DNA to an active account—one that includes a member named *Saul Rand*. It's probably not the same person . . . not exactly. But I didn't want you to be caught unaware. He and some other Rand, maybe his dad or grandfather, are in Redwing Dining Hall."

"Do you know where that is?"

"No. That didn't seem like a question to ask the Juvapod answer . . . person. Or bot, or whatever. Just avoid the room if you can. And close the door. Tate could be here any second."

His eyebrows shoot up. "Avoid it? I'm looking for it!"

"Why?"

"Because I'm guessing someone with the last name Rand will have a better idea than anyone as to where we'll find those bloody keys!"

∞18∞

The door to Kiernan's pod glides shut, and I stare at it, more than a little stunned at my own stupidity.

Okay, in my defense, steering clear of anything related to Saul Rand is very logical from a self-preservation standpoint. But Kiernan is right. Following Saul, even this alternate version of Saul who—as far as we know—hasn't killed anyone, seems more likely to lead us to the keys than blindly poking around the building in search of a CHRONOS field.

I take a step toward my pod, thinking it might be best to go back inside for a few minutes, even if it means another chat with Alisa. But Tate rounds the corner and motions for me to join him.

"Saul is here," I say in a soft voice when I reach him. "Or at least someone with his name is here. In one of the dining halls. Did you know that?"

Tate shrugs. "Yeah. He's a resident. One of the older Rands lives here, too. I haven't seen either of them. Campbell calls him

Pseudo-Saul. Doesn't look or act like him. His family tree would be different, since the Culling probably wiped out so many people. He probably made provisions to preserve that line and for there to be someone here with his name. But over that many generations, there was bound to be some slippage. And this Saul didn't get the specific genetic boosts from CHRONOS. He probably got a half-dozen black-market boosts, given how much his family is worth . . . but I guess those aren't black market now. Anyway, you won't recognize him."

He looks at me and huffs out an annoyed breath. "But *he'll* recognize *you*. Damn, I didn't think about that."

I start to ask why Saul would recognize me, but then I realize that's a stupid question. The same reason the woman at Norumbega recognized me. The same reason half a dozen other people have recognized me. My face is plastered all over their religion.

"Did you have trouble getting in?" I ask.

"Not really. They're more AR than usual because of last night's breach, but the blue chip meant they waved me in without much scroot."

"Great." I smile, even though there are a few words in the mix I'd like to google or whatever they call it these days.

Tate leads me down a corridor similar to the one we were in last night. There's another door at the end with a large red X, but we turn left before we reach it, onto a curved walkway surrounding a large atrium with trees, ponds, and seating areas scattered about. It's very lush and tropical, but as I look closer, I think it's the same sort of artificial environment as the recreation area. There are three or four dozen people in small clusters. A few seem to be playing a game, and others are watching something I can't see. There's a loud cheer, and the sole woman near the back reaches up to give the guy beside her a high-five.

"Stop gawking." He takes hold of my elbow, steering me away. "We need to get to Campbell's quarters quickly and avoid drawing attention."

He waves his hand in front of something that looks like the Juvapods. The logo on the door is similar, except it reads *Transpod Ultra*.

The door swoops shut once we're inside, and the Alisa voice greets us. "Tate Poulsen. On special request from account Cyrus01. Again." Her voice is snide, almost angry. "I guess you expect me to take you to his wing?"

"Yes," Tate replies in a weary voice. "And I don't want any commentary from you about it this time."

"Noted," Alisa says. "But you're disgusting, and I have every right to comment."

"You *know* her?" I ask Tate.

Before Tate can answer, Alisa says, "Hello again, Prudence K. Rand. Will you be joining your family in Redwing Hall?"

Now it's Tate's turn to shoot me an incredulous look, and I hold up a hand to tell him to save it until we're out of earshot of this Alisa thing . . . person . . . whatever. Although I'm starting to wonder now whether we're ever out of her earshot. Is she present throughout the club, or only in these pod devices?

"No, Alisa. I'll be joining Mr. Poulsen."

"I'm sorry, Prudence." She doesn't sound sorry at all. "That would be a violation of OC policy. Unescorted females may not be transported to the quarters of male members outside their family. Once I deliver Tate Poulsen to level ten, I'll take you to the dining hall, the main clubroom, the Rand family rooms, or back to the recreation area."

"She remains with me," Tate says. "At the request of Morgen Campbell."

A short pause. "My log shows no such request."

"It will, in about two minutes," Tate says in a low tone, but Alisa keeps talking over him.

"But even so, it would still violate OC policy. Prudence K. Rand is an affiliate member, and as a guest on her family's account, she shouldn't even be sharing a Transpod with a companion, let alone accomp—"

"Silence!" Tate's command is very close to a roar. Alisa stops talking, but she gives us a very audible how-dare-you sniff, and I can almost *feel* her listening, so I keep quiet.

Tate leans down and says, "Request that your record for today's session be kept private."

"Okay." I repeat the request in a louder voice.

"Request noted."

Hmph. *Noted.* I glance over at Tate and can see he doesn't find that any more reassuring than I do.

A few seconds later, the pod door slides upward, and we both step out onto a translucent platform. I make the mistake of glancing down and instantly regret it. Each floor below us is visible beneath my feet, and for once, I'm glad Tate's hand is on my arm.

"Close!" The pod door slides down after Tate speaks, and the entire unit drops back into the tube, which seals behind it.

"Can she still hear us?" I ask.

"No. Only in the pods."

"You're sure?"

"Of course I'm sure. People *live* here, Pru." He looks a little disgusted, as though I've asked why someone would use a toilet instead of just peeing in the hallways.

We turn right, and as we walk along the curved corridor, I keep my eyes trained on the walls and on the single strip of carpet that runs along the middle of the floor. Each time they stray toward those clear edges and I see the floors beneath my feet, I feel a little dizzy. Heights don't usually bother me much, but you can see the level below us, and the level below that, each one a little less clearly than the layer above. It reminds me of this M. C. Escher poster that Dad's girlfriend, Sara, has in her apartment.

"Why did the Alisa recognize you in the first place?"

"I sneezed. It activated the pod, and the DNA linked me to the Rand account. What does Alisa stand for?"

"No clue. Everyone in the club calls it *the* Alisa, so maybe it's an acronym, but I think it's just a name. Alisa was the name of Campbell's daughter. I only met her once, but from what he's told me, that's her voice you're hearing. Her personality, too, to some extent."

"How—" I stop myself before I can launch into the barrage of questions his statement just raised.

You're supposed to be Pru, remember? Maybe downloading someone's consciousness into a computer system is the norm in 2308, whether it's in this timeline or some other.

But there's also another issue . . .

"Wait."

Tate stops and turns back to look at me.

"How can that be? If Campbell doesn't exist, then his daughter never existed, so how does she end up as . . ." I nearly say the twenty-fourth-century version of Siri, but he wouldn't get it and Pru probably wouldn't either. "How does Alisa's voice end up in the system if she never existed?"

"Campbell wondered that, too. At first he thought it was really her. That she was here somewhere, protected by a key. Said he rode up and down the lift talking to her, asking questions. But he's convinced it's an AI of some sort, with her voice and speech mannerisms grafted on top."

"But again, if she never existed . . ."

"Saul knew Alisa. I think he knew her *really* well. He was a major horndog between the time he broke up with Esther and moved in with Katherine. After, too, when he could get away with it. Campbell figures he took a recording of her voice back with him. Having his people put Alisa's voice in the system when they built this club is just another of Saul's little gotchas, another way to remind Campbell he won. Didn't you hear her in the Transpod? The account that provides Campbell's room and board is in the dog's name. Almost every time we were at the club, Saul would pat old Cyrus on the head as he left and snark about him being smarter than his master. Now Campbell is symbolically dependent on his pet. It doesn't seem to bother him, but it's another echo of Saul saying he won."

"Not only won, but erased someone Campbell loved in the process."

"Eh . . . I guess. They didn't like each other, but she was still his kid, so . . ."

I can't help but think of Connor's kids, two more people who were erased by Saul, even though they weren't purposefully targeted. We're now so far from the timeline where they existed that I don't think Connor holds out much hope for getting them back. After several years, Connor seems to be at the point where it doesn't eat at him constantly, aside from fueling his determination to stop Saul, but it's still a source of pain. And could he have reached even that level of healing if every time he turned on his computer he was confronted with the virtual ghost of Andi or Chris?

"Come on," Tate says, tugging my arm. "We need to get moving. I just hope Campbell's coherent enough for us to get any info he has and get out. You being tagged as a Rand is . . . a complication. They're supposed to believe you're a companion brought in at Campbell's request. Instead, the minute one of the Rands steps into a pod, they'll get the whole story from the Alisa."

We cross an intersecting corridor and enter a wide hallway. There's a door at the far end and another one about halfway down.

The walls are a cool white, but every few yards, they're separated by a bright blue strip of light. The effect is similar to the tubes along the walls in Katherine's library, so I'm pretty sure it's from a CHRONOS key.

I pull Tate to a stop just to the left of one of the lights. "There's a key nearby. The lights are blu—"

My heart stops. Pru sees the key as green. I fake a cough to give myself a second to think how to rephrase. "The lights are blurry, but they're the same shade of green."

"These?" Tate looks at the light strips.

"Yes. We should check that smaller door. I can't tell for certain, but it looks like there's a pinpoint of light coming through, there at the bottom corner."

He crouches down to look at the door and then back up at me. His expression is . . . envious? "See? That's what I mean. The lights look pale yellow to me, just like half the lights you see in this building. Or most other buildings. Whoever set my parameters—"

Tate stands suddenly and grabs my chin, turning the right side of my face toward him. His fingers trace the scar along my jawline. "What's this?"

I applied a pretty thick coat of makeup, but given that it's been at least eight hours, and that part of the time was spent sweating like a pig in the stupid Juvapod, I'm guessing it's rubbed away.

"It's nothing really. An accident a while back."

The look on his face tells me he's not buying it. I tense up, ready to run or fight, certain my cover is blown. Unfortunately, I doubt that either fight or flight will be successful against this guy.

"That son of a bitch!" His fist connects with the light strip, which apparently isn't made of the squishy stuff, because it doesn't bend around his knuckles. It doesn't crack, either, and Tate gives his hand an annoyed shake as he pulls it back. "I told you that if he hurt you again, you should kill him, Pru. I should never have listened to Campbell. If you'd stayed here, Saul couldn't have touched you. He'd have been stuck there in the Dark Ages, stranded."

I have a hard time imagining 2024 as the Dark Ages, but he's genuinely angry, and again I see the resemblance to Simon—slight, but definitely there. Tate reaches out and crushes me to his chest, holding me a bit too tight for comfort.

"Let's just go," he says finally. "We'll find out what we can from Campbell and grab whatever is inside that room on our way out. I want to get this done and then get the hell out."

When we reach the end of the hallway, Tate presses his hand to the wall, and the larger door slides upward. No one is on the other side, but I hear a few feeble barks from somewhere within the apartment.

"Campbell?" Tate says as we step inside. It's a large room, with a single window that wraps around three sides. There are no curtains—no roof, for that matter—and I get the sense that what I'm seeing above me is the real sky and not the facsimile in the recreation area below.

The view from the windows is depressing, overlooking the ruined buildings we ran past last night. Off in the distance, I see a few familiar landmarks. The Washington Monument is still there, and closer in, the White House. Contrary to Kiernan's statement about DC in the previous timeline, most of the area around us appears to be dry land, although there are more pockets of water than I remember seeing when Trey and I took in the view from the rooftop of the hotel.

I'm still not sure precisely where this club is located, but the landmarks help orient me a bit. I think we're somewhere between Metro Center and McPherson Square. Of course, those stops—the entire Metro—didn't exist in Katherine's future. I don't know if they exist here or not, but it confirms my earlier suspicions that the building is near to where CHRONOS headquarters would have been, based both on Katherine's memory and the information in Delia and Abel's Future-Wiki.

As for the apartment itself, it brings to mind the room I viewed in the key when I saw Campbell and the winged girl. The dark paneling on the inner wall to my left and the heavy antique (or at least antique-looking) furniture and carpet seem strangely out of place next to the panoramic, if not particularly pleasant, view on my right.

One segment of the paneling slides up, and the fat Doberman trundles toward us. I tense up instantly when he sniffs me and even more when he gives me a halfhearted snarl. The few teeth he reveals, however, are so worn down I don't think they could do much damage even if he had the energy to bite. He moves on to sniffing Tate.

"Get on, you ugly beast." The words are harsh, but Tate's tone isn't malicious. The dog's stub of a tail wags a feeble greeting before he waddles over to a padded mat on the floor and flops down.

Still no sign of Campbell. Tate calls out to him again. No response.

He curses and says a bit louder, "Campbell! Get out here. We need to talk, and we don't have much time."

A long, drawn-out noise somewhere between a snore and a groan comes from the other room. Something about it pisses Tate off, because he curses again and storms across to the doorway and out of sight.

"You want to fix this?" His voice is so loud, even from the other room, that it startles me. "We've got another chance, if you get off your sloppy ass and help. Or are you gonna lie here basted and let Saul gox you again?"

There's an answer, but I can't make it out. Tate fires something back at him. While most curse words seem to have survived the centuries intact, the insults he's injecting between them have apparently evolved.

Tate sticks his head around the corner of the door. "Need a little help."

I enter reluctantly, unsure what might meet my eyes. A platform-type bed like I saw at the old couple's place takes up the center of the room. There's a white door similar to a Juvapod set into one wall.

Everything seems very dim after the brightness of the adjoining room. Campbell's sprawled belly up across the bed. His robe gapes open to reveal what looks like a pair of Speedos. He keeps grabbing at a clear tube that runs from an outlet in the wall into his upper arm.

"*Wait* a minute," Tate says, slapping his hand away. "I'll give you a jolt before you disconnect. Pru, could you get a cloth from the lav?"

I look around, confused.

"Over there?" he says, nodding toward the door, his voice clearly indicating that I should know where the lav is.

I wave my hand in front of a sensor near the door, and it glides open. It's actually fairly similar to bathrooms I'm used to, except there's another podlike inner door. A stack of cloths is on a shelf near the back. I grab one and dampen it at the sink. It doesn't feel much like a towel, but hopefully it will do.

Whatever the "jolt" was that Tate gave Campbell seems be working. I hand him the damp cloth and go back into the main room. The two of them follow a few minutes later. Campbell is still in his robe, but he's pulled on a pair of shorts under it. His legs look too thin for his body, almost like popsicle sticks, and he apparently hasn't bothered ordering the hair restoration service from the Juvapod menu because his hairline has receded so far that it's not even visible from the front. What hair he does have hangs in dark, greasy strands around his ears. He's holding a glass of something green—almost the same shade as my anticavity rinse. His other hand is angled over his brow, shielding his eyes from the sun. He plops onto one of the sofas near Cyrus, who is curled up on his mat, snoring.

"Dim light thirty percent."

The ceiling dims, but the windows seem pretty much the same to me. Apparently to Campbell, too. He scowls out at the sunlit day, giving it what Charlayne calls the "stink eye."

After about thirty seconds, he turns that same look on me. "Come to view your handiwork so you can report back to Papa, you backstabbin' little bitch?" Campbell's voice is slurred and tired, an odd contrast to the venom in his words. He sips the green stuff and waits for me to respond.

"No. I've come to try and fix—"

"Oh, yeah. *Fix* it. Isn't that what she told us when we helped her get the keys, Poulsen? 'I can fix it, I can get CHRONOS back up and running, I can get your club back, I can make everything better again.' All lies . . . well, I guess the club is back, but it sure as hell's not mine. Even this room's not mine. Belongs to the dog."

There's a laugh at the end, short and bitter.

"Shoulda never helped you get back," he says, looking out at the remnants of DC. "Then you'da been the one stuck outta your time. You'da been the fish on dry land, the anom'ly, instead of me. Or better yet, Tate shoulda left you in that wreckage."

"Shut up, Morgen. We weren't doing her any favors when we helped her go back. You knew it. I knew it." Tate turns and gives me a sad smile before looking back at Campbell. "I apologized for that when she came back. Once we knew Saul was as much a part as Katherine—"

"No."

They both look at me like I've grown another head. Maybe this is a mistake, but I'm tired of Katherine's name being dragged through the mud. Every time Tate talks about her, I keep imagining her face on some twenty-fourth-century holographic wanted poster. And I think I'm better off if both of them understand that Saul was the one responsible for destroying CHRONOS. For destroying the entire world they knew.

"It was Saul, not Katherine. Saul set her up. The evidence was planted. She only recently found out what he was up to and—"

Tate looks a little stunned. "You're certain? The investigation was pretty thorough."

Campbell laughs. "Thorough and conclusive. There was a confession." He leans his head back against the chair and peers out at me through lids that are barely open, but I still get the sense that he's watching me closely. "Katherine's prints and DNA on the case that held the device. On the tape around Angelo's head."

"And you're saying the evidence couldn't have been faked?" I ask the question of Tate, not Campbell. His scrutiny makes me uncomfortable, and I don't really like looking at him. "Saul couldn't have faked it?"

"Saul . . ." Tate shrugs. "Yeah, maybe."

"You knew Katherine, didn't you? Do you think she was capable of something like that?"

Tate tilts his head to the side like he's considering it. "Your mother was more than a little unstable when it came to Saul. You should have heard her at the New Year's Eve party. This World War II historian, Adrienne. She started coming on to Saul when Katherine was out of the room. When Katherine came in and caught them together, it took me and two other guys to get her away from there. I thought she was going to rip Adrienne's throat out."

One bit of that story doesn't line up with the version I heard from Adrienne. I think Tate has flipped around exactly which party was coming on to the other. I don't press that issue, deciding to stick with the main point.

"Jealousy is one thing. I was asking about mass murder. Stranding her pregnant self in the past? If she was so crazy about Saul and just wanted to get him to herself, wouldn't she have planned this for a jump where they'd actually be traveling together?"

He considers that and then nods. "Maybe."

Campbell tosses back the rest of the drink. "What the hell does it matter? Like I said, the evidence was conclusive. The investigators needed a culprit, and Saul gave them one ready-made. But he also gave the anti-alteration cause a boost, and I seriously doubt that would've been part of his plan. No more genetic fixes, no more CHRONOS, nature as nature intended."

He spits, thankfully into his glass, but it's still gross. "All that happy horseshit the weak use to bind the strong. The poor use to bind the rich."

Tate is staring at him. "So . . . you knew from the beginning that it was Saul? Even before this Cyrist stuff began popping up? All along?"

"What if I did?" Campbell's diction, which was slurred and indistinct only a few minutes earlier, is increasingly crisp, making me wonder what's in the glass. Or maybe what was in that "jolt" Tate gave him.

"You let her believe all of the evidence against Katherine, knowing it was false? Knowing that you were—no, since you pulled me into it as well—knowing that *we* were sending a sixteen-year-old girl into the hands of a man responsible for killing most of the people at CHRONOS? Instead of back to her own time?"

"Yes. Because she could be put to use there."

"But at what cost?" Tate asks.

"Oh, give me a break. You'd have sent her back either way if you thought she could give you your precious job back. All that whining about how you don't belong here, about how you were made for a time long past."

That hits a nerve, because Tate stands up and takes a threatening step toward the old man. "No. I wouldn't have. I ought to snap your neck for lying to me, for lying to both of us."

"Wait—" I reach out and grab Tate's arm, even though I definitely understand the sentiment and even though I'd stand zero chance of stopping him if he was determined. "We're here to talk, remember?"

Tate stands there for a good five seconds, like he's trying to decide, but he finally huffs and sits down again.

I look at Campbell. "Saul said you had a bet. Then why send me back to help him?"

Campbell pushes himself up from the sofa and goes to a small lit alcove in the wall. He shoves the glass into the light. There's a brief flash as the light grows brighter, and his glass vanishes. "Another."

A new glass appears, so this must be some sort of replicator system. Thankfully this glass isn't spit-lined like the other one, but is instead filled with more of the emerald-colored liquid.

"Would you like anything?"

Tate just snarls in his direction, which Campbell interprets as a no. I'd prefer to do the same, but my time in the pod with Alisa left me feeling dehydrated.

Campbell issues the request, and a clear glass of water appears in the dispenser. He places it on the low table in front of me and settles back into the opposite sofa before answering my question.

"Our wager was about Saul's methods. I didn't think—and still don't think—that using some bullshit religion was the best way to achieve our goals. If he'd used the keys a bit more . . . judiciously . . . he could have fixed the problems and left the basic society, the basic history, intact. Instead, he screws up everything and leaves a bunch of moralistic fools in charge who are even worse than what we had before. Just to prove he was right."

His tone is disdainful, but I think there's an underlying hint of admiration. It's a disconcerting mix.

Tate is still glowering at him, so I guess I'm taking the lead in the questioning. "What if you could help us change that? Show Saul he's not as smart as he thinks?"

Campbell rolls his eyes. "And how do you propose to do that?"

"Go back and stop him from ever getting the keys. Make the changes you're talking about, but do it your way. A . . . surgical strike. No more Cyrists."

"Says the woman whose face decorates their temples. Their money, too. Why should I believe you'd want to change that?"

I take a long sip of the water to give myself a few seconds to think. Any arguments I'd use as Kate would undoubtedly be useless in convincing Campbell. And since I'm supposed to be Prudence, I need to think about why she would be here. I'm pretty sure Tate would be part of it. I remember the look on her face in Woodhull's office when she was talking about him feeling useless without CHRONOS, and she'd be even more upset to see him as he is now. But I doubt the "twoo wuv" defense would resonate with Campbell, either.

So I go with a partial truth. It's *my* partial truth, but I'm beginning to suspect it's Pru's as well.

"Because I don't want Saul to win. And I don't mean your silly little wager. I want him to lose everything. *Everything.*" I enunciate each syllable and hold his gaze as I speak.

He watches me silently for a few moments. I don't look away, don't blink, just arch one eyebrow at him and stare back.

"And why do you think I can help you?"

Truthfully, I'm no longer sure that he *can* help. I'm thinking Kiernan's plan of finding Pseudo-Saul might be the better one. But maybe Campbell knows something.

"You've been here in the building since the time shift. Tate said they took your key. Do you know what they did with it?"

"They said they were using it to extend the field so that I could travel freely throughout the facility. Just another way of saying I'm a prisoner."

"Hmph," Tate says. "Some prison. You've seen what it's like outside. People fighting in the line and degrading themselves to get in for a day. And they won't earn enough to buy the food that Cyrus there eats each evening. You wouldn't go outside if they let you."

"Do you know *where* they took that key?" I ask.

"Why? Are you planning to carry it back to Saul and put me out of my misery?"

"No." While I'm not entirely convinced that the world would be a poorer place if Campbell went poof, mentioning that to him seems unlikely to help my case. "I don't have any quarrel with you, Campbell. I'll leave the key until things are . . . fixed. But here's the problem. I need to stop myself from giving the other keys to Saul. We got them from the CHRONOS archives, but it isn't around anymore. If our theory is correct, those keys have to be somewhere, like they were in the archives, prior to September 20th. Tate says no one knows the history of CHRONOS better than you do, so we thought you might have some ideas."

That's not exactly what Tate said, but based on the bits and pieces various people have told me about Campbell, it's clear he was obsessed with CHRONOS. And he seems like the type who might be swayed by a bit of flattery.

Campbell's expression suggests that was a misread on my part, however. He's quiet for a minute, watching me over the edge of his glass long enough to make me uncomfortable.

"You're lying about leaving the key," he says. "I doubt you can fix this. Either way, you won't risk leaving a key behind to protect me. But you're telling the truth about wanting to bring Saul down, so I'd be willing to gamble. Not existing is better than living as a ghost." He tosses back the last of the green stuff and leans forward, setting the glass on the coffee table between us. "Of course, whether I trust you is irrelevant, since I don't know what they did with the key."

Tate kicks the leg of the coffee table. It splinters, and the glass crashes to the floor. I expect it to break. Instead, it bounces, then rolls a few inches until it bumps into the dog's bed. Cyrus gives it one lazy lick and then ignores it.

The outburst surprises me. I'm not sure if I widen my eyes too much or blink too hard, but my left contact lens pops out. I glance around near me as best I can without drawing attention. I don't see it.

Campbell just laughs at Tate. "Ooh, big bad Viking temper. Sit down and let me finish. I don't know what they did with the key Saul gave me, but I *do* know Saul Rand. He's twisted, perverse, and single-minded. He's only loved one person, only trusted one person in his whole life, and that person is Saul Rand. Look at the effort he put into letting me know he won. The lives he was willing to expend to get that point across. If he set all of this up from his perch in the twenty-first century, then I can promise you he made sure one of his Cyrist lackeys found those keys."

"Yeah," I say, trying to keep my voice calm as I look about for my lens. "But which one?"

"Like I said. He trusts one person, and that's Saul Rand. He couldn't have the real deal in this timeline, so I think he'd settle for the pale imitation that lives here in the future. I've had two conversations with the man. He's boring, insipid, and has been thoroughly pampered his entire life. Would you like me to arrange a meeting?"

Tate gives Campbell an odd look. "She needs to get the keys before September 20th . . . that's in the past. What good would a meeting in the present do?"

Campbell sighs. "Don't be dim, Poulsen. Meeting Pseudo-Saul in the here and now—a meeting that she'll remember but he won't—gives her an advantage."

"Maybe. But the system has already tagged her as a Rand. It picked up on the DNA. And he'll recognize her."

"I would certainly hope so," Campbell says. "That's her biggest advantage if she plays it right. That outfit needs to go, however, if you want to play Cyrist Madonna. Use my printer to manufacture one of those white flowing monstrosities you wear in their propaganda."

Campbell tilts his head to the right, and I see a glimmer of something I don't like at all, something slightly malicious, in his eyes. "You remember how to use the printer, don't you, Prudence?"

"It's been . . . a while." I push up from the sofa slowly, taking one last chance to scan the area around me for the contact lens. No luck. "I'm sure it will come back to me."

"I'll show you where it is, then." He follows me to the door and says in a lower voice, "You might want to grab another lens before Poulsen there takes a closer look at you. And while you're fabricating a new outfit, go ahead and fabricate a new story about who you are and why you're here. Because you're not Prudence Rand."

RESIDENCE INN
BURTONSVILLE, MARYLAND
September 12, 5:15 p.m.

Charlayne startles when I arrive back at the hotel room. And that causes *me* to startle because she whips up the rifle she's cleaning and braces it against her shoulder. It looks a thousand times more dangerous than the pistol I've used, and it also looks emphatically wrong in her hands. It took me three weeks to convince Charlayne to take up karate back in my original timeline. She freaked when we were biking one day because she accidentally squished a lizard. And here she is acting like she's fresh out of boot camp.

Maybe she is, sort of. She said they'd been preparing for this for a long time. I just didn't know the preparations included advanced weapons training.

It's not loaded if she's cleaning it, I remind myself, trying to force my heartbeat back into normal range.

She lowers the gun, letting out her breath in a big whoosh. "Could you give us a warning or something?"

"No early warning system on the keys. You're going to have to get used to it."

"Maybe you could settle on a specific time?" Trey suggests, looking up from his phone. "That way, we'd know when you're coming in."

Although, now that I look closer, it's *my* phone he's holding. That's kind of odd.

"Okay," I say to Charlayne. "Next arrival at exactly five thirty. Does that work?"

"Sure." Charlayne gives me an apologetic smile. "And sorry about the gun. I'm just nervous. About all of this."

She has every reason to be jumpy. I glance from Charlayne to Trey, and a wave of guilt hits me. Both of them are here because of me. Yes, they'd still be in danger from the Culling if I'd never met them, never crossed their paths in any timeline. But they wouldn't be on the front lines. They'd be off living a normal life, blissfully ignorant of all this insanity. I can't help but feel that would be better. Kinder.

"So, something went wrong?" Trey asks.

"Sort of. Charlayne, could you get Tilson and the others in here before I start?"

Charlayne gives me a quick nod and hops up to fetch them.

Trey eyes my costume, and an amused grin spreads across his face. "Is that what women wear in 2308? Not complaining, but . . ."

"Maybe it's what they wore when Pru visited, but women's fashion has taken a rather conservative turn." I glance over at the guns on the bed. "What's with Charlayne and the heavy artillery?"

"Ben says she's actually a good shot, especially at long range. And even though I hate to say it, those guns could come in handy soon. We've . . . got a lead on your mom and Katherine."

My eyes widen. "Oh my God. Where? How?"

"Well, it's just your mom, really, but we're hoping Simon has them in the same place. Remember when I set up that geo-location app for you and your mom when we were in London?"

"Now that you mention it. I'd kind of forgotten before that."

"So had I. But then your phone buzzed—it was your dad. I answered. Hope that's okay?" I nod, and he says, "I didn't tell him where we were for . . . security reasons . . . but I told him you're okay and you'd call him soon. He seemed really nervous. Anyway, your phone's the same type as your mom's, and holding it jogged my memory of setting the geo app. This blip on the map has been moving pretty fast since I first checked, and I lose the signal every now and then. I'm thinking she's on a plane."

Trey hands me the phone, and I see the blip he's talking about, currently over the ocean, approaching DC.

"Maybe she had the phone in her pocket and they didn't check," he says. "We're just waiting for them to stop moving."

"And then?"

"Assuming you get the keys, then we take the fight to Simon. Did you know you lost a contact?"

The door opens and Charlayne and Ben enter. Tilson is behind them, followed by Max.

Attached to Max is Eve.

I stare at her, open-mouthed, unsure whether this is a trap or just stupidity on Max's part.

He catches my expression and says, "What? I couldn't leave her in the trunk indefinitely."

Okay, not a trap. Just stupidity. Complete and total stupidity.

"And she has information. We've been having a productive little chat. Turns out her dad wasn't always New Cyrist. In fact, he used to be—"

"Regional Templar? I already knew that. You may not remember the previous timeline, but I do. Eve here sicced the temple hounds on me, and I have the scars to prove it."

I expect Eve to gloat, but she's barely listening. She has Max's arm in a death grip, and her self-assured smirk is gone. In fact, she looks nervous. Extremely nervous.

Tilson says, "I still think you should have taken her back to your place, Max. She could be wearing a tracker. And what if she manages to get away?"

"I checked thoroughly," Max says defensively. "There's nothing on her body that could lead anyone to us. And she won't be running away. Will you, Evie?"

Eve doesn't answer at first. Then Max starts prying her fingers away from his arm one by one until he's holding her wrists in one hand, with the other pressed against her chest. He repeats, "*Will you*, Evie?"

"No! I won't! Please." She tries to move closer to him, her expression escalating from nervousness to sheer terror. "I won't go anywhere! I promise, Max! Don't let go . . ."

Her voice is almost a whimper at the end. This Eve is nothing like the one I knew. The Eve I met at the Cyrist temple, at her little barbecue, and even at Briar Hill, struck me as manipulative, bitchy, and quite possibly evil. But possessive and clingy? Definitely not.

And then I get it.

"You have her key, don't you?"

"Actually, Tilson has it."

"Does she exist without it?" Trey asks, glancing from Tilson to Max a little nervously.

"Don't know. Don't care." The look Max gives Eve is angry and contemptuous, but there's also a good deal of hurt in the mix. I think the bit about not caring is a bluff. To my surprise, Eve gives him an almost identical look, making me wonder whether the role she's playing became a little too real at some point, at least where Max is concerned.

"Saul's people like to alter several things at once," Max says, "probably because these shifts hit them in the gut the same way they do us. I doubt they'd wipe out Evie on purpose, but there's always a chance. Eve clearly thinks so, don't you, sweetie? I've never had a very clear answer as to what happened to her mother."

"Max, I'm not sure that any of us connected to CHRONOS exist outside a key right now, so you might . . ." I don't finish the sentence. It's hard to muster up anything close to a full serving of sympathy if Max did pull her key, when she evidently doesn't care how many people die by Cyrist hands. Still, it feels a little *wrong* to root for her extinction. The Cyrists managed to convince Kiernan that their Way was the only Way for a while. And Kiernan had the benefit of knowing people outside the Cyrist circle, people who questioned those beliefs and made him question them.

Did Eve have anyone like that in her life? Or has it been lived entirely inside a Cyrist bubble?

I catch a glimpse of Charlayne's face as I look away. She's sitting on the bed, weapons on one side, Ben on the other. Her eyes seem troubled, and I suspect she's thinking the same thing I am.

Max is asking me something, and I've missed the first part. "Sorry. Can you repeat that?"

"The keys? I take it you didn't get them, since there are clearly no pockets on that thing you're wearing."

"No. I had a minor wardrobe malfunction." I fork my fingers, pointing to my eyes. "Do we have a backup pair of lenses, Charlayne?"

She nods, and while she's searching for her handbag, I bring my little corner of the Fifth Column up to speed on the changes I witnessed in the future and the fact that most of our research is essentially worthless.

"I know Julia . . . and I guess Delia and Abel, too . . . spent a lot of time on the file, but I don't think it was even accurate before this last shift. Kiernan noted several changes that were in place as early as 2150, and—"

Max gives me a look that suggests he thinks I'm too dumb for words. "And how do you know he's not bullshitting you, Kate?"

"Because I've just been there! What is it with you? The changes I saw go well beyond what Kiernan told me, and there are actually a few things that match up with his descriptions. The biggest problem now is—"

I stop in midsentence and look at Eve. "You know, I'm not saying anything more with her here. This is insane. What if she *does* happen to escape and she doesn't vanish? It would be beyond stupid to just dish up everything I've learned on a platter. That never goes well when the villain does it in the movies, and even though we're the good guys here, I can picture so many ways it could blow up in our faces."

Max shrugs and then loops the arm that was resting on Eve's shoulders around her neck, lifting her onto her tiptoes as he squeezes the pressure points.

I know this move. I used it—twice—on Detective Beebe back in Georgia. But it's still disturbing to watch. Eve flails briefly, digging her nails into Max's arm, and then goes limp.

Max holds her there about ten seconds and then slides her down to the floor. "Talk fast."

"Fine. CHRONOS wasn't just disbanded in this timeline. It never existed. But I think we can still get the keys if I go back to the date before Pru takes them. They should still be somewhere."

I pull in a deep breath, preparing to launch into the reasons that Kiernan spelled out as to why the keys would still exist even if CHRONOS didn't in this timeline. But Tilson is already nodding.

"That's true. They should still exist."

I could hug him, because I wasn't looking forward to explaining that. Make it a group hug, because now Ben is nodding, too.

"Just a matter of figuring out where. They have their own CHRONOS field, so they should be . . . where they would have been . . . if there had been a CHRONOS in that timeline. Unless someone moved them."

Max, Trey, and Charlayne all look a little confused, but Eve is stirring, so they'll have to piece it together on their own.

Charlayne gives me the spare contacts, and I move over to the mirror inside the bathroom. Thankfully, the process of sticking these stupid things in my eyes gets a little easier each time.

Trey comes up and rests his hands on my shoulders, pulling the door closed behind him. When I catch his eyes in the reflection, he gives me a sad look. "I like the green better."

"Me, too." I'd much rather have my dad's eyes looking back from the mirror than eyes that are almost but not quite the same as Pru's. I give Trey's hands a squeeze and turn around to face him. "Can you call Dad and let him know I'm all right? Bring him up to speed on Mom, too, okay? I'm glad he's back from Delaware, but he's super stressed about all of this, and when I talk to him, his nervousness kind of . . . I don't know . . . seeps into my head, too."

"Done," he says, tipping my face upward for a kiss. "Is everything else okay there . . . in the future?"

I shrug. "Okay-*ish*. This Morgen Campbell guy figured out that I'm not Prudence. He didn't mention it to the Viking historian, the one Pru was involved with, so I think I'm safe. I'm about to meet someone named Saul Rand . . . except it's not really him, just who he would have been if the timeline hadn't changed. Kiernan thinks this Pseudo-Saul is our best shot for finding the keys."

"How about I nod and pretend I understand everything you just said? But, to be clear, it sounds a lot like one of those 'the road so far' recaps when I've missed a few episodes."

"Believe me, I know."

"You look tired. How long since you've slept?"

"Not that long. The jumps just . . . I think they wear me out a little faster when they're really long distance. I haven't paid much attention to it before, but these jumps are a bit farther out than usual."

"Be careful, okay? And hurry back." Trey's trying really hard to be nonchalant, probably because I've just told him that Dad being worried makes it tougher on me. But I can tell from his eyes that he *is* worried.

When we step back into the main room, I look over at Charlayne. "I'm back in eight minutes—at five thirty—so weapons down, okay?"

"Yes, ma'am!" She gives me a sassy salute and a grin that pulls up a memory of the two of us in my room at the townhouse, Charlayne ducking as I tossed a pillow at her for teasing me about a guy in gym class. For some reason, that memory has me close to tears. Trey is right. I'm tired. I need to wrap this up soon so I can get some rest.

I give Trey's hand a squeeze and start to pull up the stable point in the OC recreation area at 2 a.m. so I can fill Kiernan in on my progress. Before I can lock in and blink, Max yells, "Hey! You said you'd give me the coordinates."

"You're attached at the hip with Eve Conwell right now. There's no way I'm transferring these coordinates to your key."

He starts to fume, so I look around the room. "Does anyone here disagree with me on that?"

Everyone looks a little uncomfortably in Max's direction, and Tilson says, "No. I think we all agree it was a lapse in judgment, Max. And . . ." His voice softens a bit, like he's about to deliver a blow he'd rather avoid. "From everything Julia told me, I doubt you could handle a three-century jump. She was convinced you were gone a lot longer than you would admit when you made that jump to 2072 last year. That you couldn't get back at first."

Max's eyes flash, and I'm pretty sure things are about to get nasty, but Charlayne clears her throat.

"You're all missing the key reason that Max can't make this sort of jump. With Julia gone, he's needed here. Like Ben was saying earlier, you have to make sure the Fifth Column is ready to roll when the time comes. No one else can do that. We simply can't take a risk . . . any risk at all, even if it's only a tiny one . . . that you'll get stuck there."

I'm impressed. That's a pretty stellar bit of diplomacy. Charlayne just gave Max a way to save face and still look like he's in control.

But Max isn't having any of it.

"Duct tape." He reaches his hand toward Charlayne. "I know you've got some in that bag somewhere, so pull it out. I'll secure Eve in the other room . . . with the key. One of you guys can keep watch if you don't think I'm capable of securing her to a damn chair. But I have to—"

He looks around at the others as he talks, his eyes making it back to me just as I blink out.

Sorry, Max.

∞19∞

If someone told me an hour ago I'd ever be glad Morgen Campbell and I occupied the same room, I'd have called that person a dirty rotten liar. Campbell may, however, be the only reason I'm still in one piece, or at the very least still in 2308. I'm not sure whether he told Tate or Tate found the contact lens on his own. All I know is that it was on the end of the finger Tate was shoving in my face when I came back into the living room dressed in my new custom toga. Thor most definitely lost his cool when he realized he'd been tricked, and much like his colleague the Hulk, you wouldn't like him when he's angry.

On the other hand, I could get used to "clothes shopping" in the twenty-fourth century. Campbell's closet is almost entirely bare, but as soon as I stepped in, the closet lights surged a few times and I heard a brief humming noise, like I was being scanned. Then a voice—thankfully *not* the Alisa voice, but a male with a slight British accent—asked what I'd like to wear today. I requested a Greek toga costume, and a holographic menu popped up inside the niche showing several variants. After I selected one, I heard another hum, and a few seconds later, a toga dropped onto the shelf. The fabric feels a little unusual, and there's a bit less coverage than I'd like, but the fit is perfect.

So, with my contact lenses now in place and my catsuit swapped out for this shiny new toga, I wait for the arrival of Pseudo-Saul. The message that Campbell sent was vague, simply saying he needed to speak with him, privately and in person, as soon as possible. He didn't mention me. But I already know Alisa didn't even wait until the Rands reached the Transpod to spread her juicy bit of gossip. In my brief meeting with Kiernan before jumping back in, he said a message popped up at the Rand table shortly after he located the dining room. He wasn't close enough to tell what the message was or even to get a clear look at them, but both men seemed a little stunned and left immediately afterward.

Tate, still fuming, is parked on the floor next to the dog. I'm okay with the snub. It's a big improvement on murderous rage, and I don't blame him for being furious. I lied to him. Tricked him. It didn't help that Campbell not only realized it before he did, but gloated about it.

I think the reason for his mood goes deeper, however. There were several times last night and earlier today when I was sure my cover was blown. Each time, I saw the question in his eyes, and each time, he pushed it resolutely away. I think part of him already knew. He just really, really wanted to believe Pru made it back. That he wasn't alone.

"Have a drink, Poulsen, and stop pouting," Campbell says. "The one advantage of this cage is a well-stocked bar."

Unlike Tate, Campbell is delighted that I'm not Prudence. And I don't know whether it's the green stuff he's drinking or the fact he's proved himself oh-so-smart by outing me, but the man's mood has turned a complete one-eighty. The possibility that we might be able to undo this and that Saul might not win after all has him on the verge of a happy dance.

The area between the two couches shimmers slightly, and a man appears. He looks first at Campbell, then at me. His features are finely—no, *unnaturally*—chiseled, like his face was carved from stone. Campbell was right. Aside from the hair and the eyes, which are similar, this man doesn't look like the Saul I saw at the Expo or at Six Bridges.

He does, however, very closely resemble another Saul I've seen—the one in the stained glass windows at the Sixteenth Street Temple. He's even wearing the same robe. There's a CHRONOS medallion around his neck, too, but it's a replica, a dull bronze disk against the white fabric of his garment. The Pseudo-Saul nickname is dead-on. He looks manufactured, almost like a store mannequin.

I glance down at the man's feet and see a slight flicker where they should be touching the ground.

Campbell snorts. "Too lazy to come in person, Rand? We're on the same damned floor!"

"It's not safe," he says, turning to face me. "Sister Prudence, it is a great honor to meet you. If I had only myself to consider, I would be there in person. But my grandfather is old and prone to infections, and the Alisa says you carry faint traces of the Great Plague."

Tate and Campbell both look alarmed. I'm startled, too, until I remember the lotus tattoo on the back of my hand. The system probably picked up something from my recent immunization.

"Why are you here, Sister Prudence?"

I watch his face for a moment, trying to pick up clues, but it's hard to read expressions when his face is so unusual. His eyes are the only feature that look genuine. They seem curious and maybe a little frightened, although I guess that could be his concern about the plague. There's also a hint of awe, like this is a meeting he never expected.

Just toss the dice, Kate. You'll never know until you try.

I suck in a deep breath, keeping one hand on my key as I speak. If my next statement is wrong, I'll need to make a quick exit, and Kiernan and I will just jump back to some point before September 20th and start searching for a needle in a haystack.

But if it's right . . .

"I'm here to express my gratitude, and that of Brother Cyrus, for your family's role in protecting the keys over the past century. We'd like to prepare a commemorative plaque to mark the spot where the keys resided, so future generations can appreciate the sacrifice and devotion of the Rand family."

His answering smile is wide and innocent, an almost childlike expression that I can't imagine on the face of the real Saul Rand. "Thank you! My grandfather will be—" The smile fades a bit. "You mean here in the club, correct? Maybe in the main hall, near the portraits?"

"Well, no. Brother Cyrus had hoped to have the memorial in the exact location."

Pseudo-Saul nods, a little uncertain, and then smiles again. "If that's the wish of Brother Cyrus, then my grandfather will be happy to relocate. We both will. That way, you'll have the entire sector for the memorial."

Bingo.

I glance at Campbell, who's grinning like a toy monkey. Tate still isn't looking at me.

"Oh, no! I'm sure Brother Cyrus wouldn't want to inconvenience your family in that way. You've already done so much. The main hall will work just as well."

Pseudo-Saul protests that it's really no trouble, and we go back and forth for a few rounds. I'm tempted to just blink out with him standing there. I don't have anything more to say to Campbell, but I do feel I owe Tate . . . well, if not an apology, then something.

"No," I say firmly. "I've decided the main hall would be better anyway, since it's on a lower floor. I'll double check with Brother Cyrus and get back with you soon to finalize plans. Go forth . . . in The Way."

He gives me a puzzled smile and a little bow and then vanishes.

"Impressive! That was a clever strategy." Campbell seems to expect me to bask in his words of approval, but I ignore him. He gives an offended grunt and heaves himself off the sofa, empty glass in hand.

Cyrus opens one eye and gives a menacing growl as I approach. I ignore him, too, and crouch down to Tate's eye level.

"Pru wanted to return, Tate."

He's silent for a moment, and then he asks, "She's still alive, then? In your time?"

"Yes. But . . . she's crossed her own timeline on so many occasions that I don't think she's the person you knew. It took a rather nasty toll."

I decide not to add that she was nearly twenty years his senior when I saw her in London, because age is kind of relative with a CHRONOS key. The girl I saw in New York was younger than he is now. I wish I could imagine some scenario where that girl could jump back here and the two of them could find a bit of happiness, even if there's no CHRONOS in whatever final reality we end up with. But I can't even begin to imagine the ripple effects from that course of action.

"Do you know if she found the child?"

"I didn't even know she was looking for a child, Tate. The baby was . . . yours?"

352   *Time's Divide*

"Yeah. She . . ." He doesn't finish the thought, just shakes his head slowly. "Is she with her sister? Deborah?"

I go with another partial truth. "She was the last time I saw her."

He smiles, but his eyes are sad. "Part of me knew you weren't her from the beginning. She's a better kisser."

I laugh, and he says, "Promise me that you'll give your aunt a message. Tell her I'm sorry. I don't blame her—for this mess or about the baby. And . . . tell her I wish I could make her another mix tape."

"I promise, even though I have absolutely no idea what that last part means."

"You don't need to," he says, getting to his feet. "If the girl I knew is still in there somewhere, she'll know what it means. That's all that matters."

He calls out, "Later, Campbell!" as we leave, and then adds, in a softer voice, "Except I'd see you in hell first." I suspect he could have said it at full volume, because Campbell doesn't respond. I wonder if he's already hooked back up to whatever drug he was on earlier.

When we reach the small door in the hallway where we first saw the glow from the CHRONOS field, Tate presses his hand to the wall. We wait for a moment, but nothing happens. He tries again, and then I try, thinking maybe that it will open for my magical Rand DNA.

"So what now?" I say, but he's already stepping back. He launches a hard sideways kick at the area on the wall where we pressed our hands. It hums, and there are a couple of short clicks, but it doesn't open until Tate hooks his fingers under the bottom and pulls upward.

There, in the middle of a device far smaller and simpler than Connor's gizmo in Katherine's library, is one lone CHRONOS key. I reach for it, but Tate stops me.

"That could set off alarms, so you need to be ready to go as soon as you grab it." He pulls the long silver chain out of the ridiculous gold muscle shirt he's wearing and hands me his medallion. I hadn't even thought about asking for his key, even though I know we can't afford to leave any loose ends. I'd blame the lapse on exhaustion, but it's also because I don't want to think about the implications of what he's doing. It's not as bloody as the women slashing their throats at Estero, but I think there's a very good chance it's equally fatal.

Tate catches my expression and shakes his head firmly. "No. When you go back to your time, you'll take my key along with this one." His voice seems different, more solemn than before. "That's how it must be. I've seen much, learned much, fought some good battles, and loved two women well—that's more than many can say. You'll either fix this and I'll have a life worth living, or else you won't and my life is done. I don't agree with Campbell on much, but he's right about not wanting to live as a ghost. And if the only tie holding me to this earth is that medallion, a ghost is all I'll ever be."

∞

OBJECTIVIST CLUB
WASHINGTON, EC
September 20, 9:40 a.m.

A few people are lounging outside the pool or swimming laps when I blink in, but the area isn't crowded yet. I stroll confidently past the desk and through the main lobby, trying to remember which turns I made earlier when I was walking with Tate. When I step inside the Transpod, I hold my hand against the spongy side wall.

"Welcome, guest! I'm Alisa. Scanning DNA for family membership. Please wait." After a moment, she continues, "Client DNA linked with a sixty-one percent probability to account Rand02. If this is correct, please state your name and destination."

"Prudence K. Rand. Please locate members of account Rand02."

"Saul Rand and Arturo Rand are in the Rand family quarters."

"Please take me there. Level ten." I add the last bit just in case she has any questions as to whether I'm authorized, but the pod is already moving.

"My pleasure."

I'd feel better if Kiernan was along for backup, but when we discussed this earlier, we couldn't come up with any logical reason a day laborer would be in the living quarters without being logged into the system as a request.

When the pod doors open, I turn left instead of right this time. The vertigo sensation from looking down at the levels below seems worse now, probably because I'm tired. Deep-down-to-the-very-bone tired. I keep my eyes trained on that center strip of carpet so I don't feel as wobbly.

Once I arrive at the end of the hallway, I press my hand against the wall as I saw Tate do earlier. There's a faint chime, and I wait, tugging nervously at my toga.

The door slides up, and an elderly man looks out. He seems confused and glances back at Pseudo-Saul, who's a few steps behind. He also appears puzzled. I have to remind myself that even though I remember our meeting in Campbell's apartment, it still hasn't happened for him.

I paste on a smile I hope is close to the beatific one Prudence wears in most of the Cyrist art. "Arturo Rand? Saul Rand?"

"Yes! Yes, Sister Prudence." The old man bows so low that I'm scared he's going to tip over. After a moment, Pseudo-Saul bows, too.

"I am here for the medallions you've been guarding."

Arturo gives me a confused look as he pulls himself back to standing. Then he waves his hand in a shooing motion at his grandson. "Go! Bring them to me."

Pseudo-Saul nods vigorously and disappears into one of the other rooms, leaving me with the old man. The silence is odd and heavy, but I'm not sure what to say.

"You've . . . done well . . ." *Sir? My son? How would Pru address him?* "You've done well, Arturo Rand. Brother Cyrus thanks you for your service."

His smile is shaky and teary-eyed, and it suddenly occurs to me that this is my great-great-grandfather. Well, my sort-of great-great-grandfather, since there are now a few broken branches in the Rand family tree. Would that mean he's my 61 percent great-great-grandfather?

Pseudo-Saul is back now, holding a very plain white tub with a dark red top. It reminds me of this plastic cake holder Mom has, aside from the thin line of bright blue light leaking out of the seal. I take the canister and pry open the lid. The light is nearly blinding. Squinting, I tilt the container around to get a better view of the contents. There are a lot of keys in here. I almost feel like I should count them, but that would be pointless when we don't know for certain how many there are supposed to be.

Arturo seems to have picked up on my urge to count. "They're all inside." He gives his grandson a nervous look, and something in the exchange tells me they're beginning to get suspicious.

"We were told . . ." Arturo begins as I pull up the meeting place Kiernan and I established earlier—2:30 a.m. tonight, across the pool from the Juvapods.

"In the *letter*," Pseudo-Saul stresses the word. "The one from Brother Cyrus? We were told the keys would simply disappear at the appointed time."

"Brother Cyrus decided that would be unkind. You've given so much, the least I can do is come and give you my blessing."

I lock in the stable point and blink, expecting to see Kiernan's face when I open my eyes, but it's still the eerie, sculpted face of Pseudo-Saul.

Okay, aside from ruining my dramatic exit, this is scary. Not just his weird face, but the fact that I'm still here. This is the first time a blink has failed, except for a few cases when I was rushing and didn't fully lock in the stable point. I try to keep a neutral expression on my face, glad that they're too far away to hear my heart pounding.

Why now?

Katherine's comment about resting between jumps echoes in my mind. How many miles and years have I traveled in the past twenty-four hours? From the hotel to 1905 Georgia, here, back to Georgia, here, back to Georgia again for the stupid shoes, back here, back to the hotel, back here—and four or five local short hops in between. Over two thousand years . . . and at least that many miles. And that's just today . . .

I look up and add a hearty, "Brother Cyrus thanks you for your service," hoping to make it look like the delay was intentional. My hands are shaking, which makes it hard to lock in the stable point, but I finally do. And even though it's stupid and I know it has nothing to do with whether or not I get out of here, I blink extra hard.

∞

OBJECTIVIST CLUB
WASHINGTON, EC
September 20, 2308, 2:30 a.m.

This time, it *is* Kiernan I see when I open my eyes. He's a few feet away, still in his Boudini tux.

My knees buckle almost instantly, and I collapse onto the squishy sand-stuff, glad for the soft landing it provides.

"That's it?" he asks as I push myself up to sitting.

I lift up the edge of the lid so he can see the keys inside. "Kind of anticlimactic, huh? After all this, you'd think they'd be stored in the Ark of the Covenant or something more dramatic than twenty-fourth-century Tupperware."

His eyes narrow as he looks at my face. "Something happened. Did they resist? You look—"

"No. Although they seemed a little suspicious since this wasn't quite the magical disappearance outlined in the message handed down to them from Brother Cyrus."

He just stares, waiting for me to go on.

I sigh. "You remember that standing rule I insisted upon, where you always jump first, just in case?"

"Yes?"

"We might need to revisit it. The first time I tried to blink out, nothing happened."

"You're sure you had the stable point locked in?"

"I'm certain. It worked the second time."

I don't have to tell him why I'm worried. He battles this problem every time he jumps.

"Bloody hell. If you had trouble on a local jump eight hours into the past . . ." Kiernan sinks down into the sand next to me. "But you've been hopping around like a grasshopper the past few days. Has this ever—"

"No. Never. And I'm really hoping it was only a fluke. Give me your key."

He does. I transfer the stable point at the hotel that's preset for my 5:30 p.m. return.

"Do you think it's a good idea for me to meet you there?" he asks after watching the stable point for a moment. "Given Max's general lack of affection for me and the nasty-looking weapons on the bed next to your friend, I'm thinking—"

"No." I really don't want to get into a squabble with him right now, but I'm still worried about what he's hiding. I also think it's quite possible that the key will fail him, too, and I'm not about to leave him here the way Prudence did.

"We need to go to the same place," I say, "and your cabin is a longer jump, both chronologically and geographically. The hotel seems like our best bet, since Simon is watching Katherine's house. I'll jump in first, and I'll tell them you're coming before I step out of the stable point. If Max doesn't like it, I'll kick his surly ass."

"Under normal circumstances, that *might* happen, even though Max is twice your size. But you're exhausted and dressed in a toga that isn't exactly cut for kicking anything. Katherine's place might be better, Simon or no."

I can't decipher the look in his eyes—worry, definitely, but there's a smidgen of guilt, too. That's ridiculous. If the possibility I'd run out of jump juice didn't occur to me, why should it have occurred to him?

"I have backup. Trey's there, too. And no one else in the room is very happy with Max right now."

"Why?"

I look up from the stable point and fill him in on the whole Eve fiasco. "Did you know they'd planted Eve and Patrick as part of this Fifth Column?"

"No." Kiernan's lip curls slightly. "But I'm not a bit surprised. Patrick is a good little Cyrist soldier. Does what he's told, when he's told. And Eve usually does what her daddy tells her, so . . ." He gives his head a shake and says, "Fine, since you have backup. Let's jump to the hotel."

Except we don't. I try three times before Kiernan closes his hand over my key.

"If it hasn't happened yet, it's not going to, love. Voice of experience. It's kind of like a car battery. You cranking the engine over and over won't help."

I sink down onto the floor, resting my head on my bent knees as I try to steady my breathing. It doesn't work, and I decide to just let it out.

"How long?" I pound my fists into my thighs. "How long am I stuck here? I *can't* be stuck here! There's too much left to do!"

He sits down next to me. "It's not like the clock is running back home. You can jump in at the same time you planned all along. It's just a temporary setback."

"You don't know that for certain."

"I don't know anything for certain. You and I could both explode in the next two seconds. Or the swimming pool over there could have a clone of the Loch Ness monster swimmin' about on the bottom, ready to spring out and have us for a midnight snack."

He's trying to make me laugh, but I'm tired enough and jumpy enough that I cast a wary glance at the pool before looking back at him.

"But for right now, you make it back in. Keep watching past five thirty."

He's right. A few seconds after five thirty, I see myself step away from the stable point, toward Trey. I'm holding the keys.

"See? I have a lot of experience with that key failing. If it's not permanent in my case, when I can barely use the bloody thing, it won't be permanent in yours. You'll get some rest, and later today . . ."

"It could change, Kiernan. We still have several hours before I go to level ten and get these keys from Pseudo-Saul. He was looking a little suspicious by the time I blinked out. If we're still here by the pool 'later today,' someone's going to find the two of us with a bucketful of CHRONOS medallions. Then they find out I'm sixty-one percent from the family Rand, and Pseudo-Saul and my semigreat-great-granddad show up to take the keys back, and we're at square one again."

I feel panic nibbling at the back of my brain, so I breathe deeply and close my eyes. Kiernan doesn't speak, but I can feel him watching me.

"I'll rest here for the next few hours. If I can't jump before the cleaning crew comes in, I'll hide back in the damned Juvapod, and you take the keys. To the cabin, if you think it's safest. Or take them to Katherine's or the hotel. Anywhere is better than having them here. I'll follow as soon as I can."

I shove the container of keys into Kiernan's hands. "Hold on to them while I sleep."

He sucks in a breath, staring down at the container like it's a bomb, gripping the edges so tightly that I can see every vein on top of his hands. His dark eyes are angry . . . furious. I pull away from him instinctively. After a moment, he shoves the container in my direction so hard that the sand-stuff piles up in a wedge behind it. Then he storms off into the dark, cursing.

What in hell was that about?

I fall back into the sand and look up at the blackness. I really want to follow him and ask what I did to precipitate such a drama fest, but I'm too tired. When he doesn't come back after a few minutes, I roll onto my stomach, hook one arm protectively around the bucket of keys, and close my eyes.

It's still dark when I wake up. Kiernan's sitting next to me, head resting on his bent knees. I prop myself up and check the time on my CHRONOS key. A little before five.

Eventually Kiernan looks over at me. I can't tell for certain in the dim light, but I think he's been crying.

"I can't do it." His voice is filled with self-loathing. "I swore I'd do anything, but . . . I can't."

"You can't what, Kiernan?"

"I told Simon I'd make sure the keys end up with him. And you, too. He wants you as his backup—"

"His backup Sister Prudence. Yes, Kiernan. I made the same promise. I should have told you, but . . . I thought . . ."

I don't finish the statement, since what I thought was that he'd object to me making that kind of sacrifice. But apparently not, so I shift tracks.

"Simon said he'd be sure the people I care about are safe. If we can't stop this, the chaos after the virus could be just as dangerous, and . . . Simon would target them. But it's my fallback option, the very last resort, if we can't stop him. You were thinking about giving him the keys *now*? Before we even—"

"No! But I won't lie. Part of me wants to."

"So is this how I end up in Rio? You hand me and the keys over to Simon?"

His voice is barely above a whisper. "That wasn't you in Rio."

"Yes. It's me. Connor tried to argue that it could just as easily be Pru, but—"

"Not Pru. But not you either. It's my Kate."

I'm so stunned for a moment that I can't speak.

"But . . . that's . . . not possible. Is it? You said it yourself—that when you saw me on the Metro that day, you knew if I existed, she couldn't."

"You just saw this other Saul, the one you said looks like a statue or something. The other Saul Rand still exists in this time-line, too, back in 2035, right?"

"But it's not the *same* Saul! The Culling changed the time-line. A different ancestor here, a different one there, over several generations."

"And you aren't *exactly* the same Kate. Damned close. Close enough to fool me, close enough that I can't not love you, as much as I've tried. Genetically you're probably indistinguishable. But a different experience here, a different one there, over several years . . ."

"But . . . how? How could it happen?"

Kiernan runs his hands through his hair and laces his fingers behind his neck. "Some of this is just my best guess, okay? Simon and Pru will both lie if the whim strikes them, whether they've got a reason to or not. The time shift, the one where my Kate disappeared? Simon was supposed to kill her."

He stops for a moment, like he needs to bolster his courage for the next part. "I think he did kill her. I'd almost swear to it, based on what I saw through the key that night, but I took an awful whack to the head earlier, so I'm not really sure of anything that happened. I think he killed her, and afterward, as he's about to yank her key, he gets a better idea. He goes back and stops himself from killing her, 'cause he's thinking she could take over for Pru running their Cyrist errands. I mean, they were pretty much out of hours they could steal from her younger self. Simon said the plan all along was to tell me, to get Kate back to me eventually, but then . . . well, he started questioning my loyalty when he found out I was helping you."

"Okay, stop. I guess that explains how she's around, but how did we get me? This me? Did Simon know that would happen?"

"It actually wouldn't have happened if Pru had done the job Saul assigned to *her* during that time shift. Simon says she was supposed to go back and kill Katherine when she landed in 1969. But . . . it's like Pru said back at the Expo, remember? Doing that would have erased her own existence. And your mom's."

Kiernan lies back in the sand and stares up into the darkness. It looks like he needs a moment, and I'm kind of okay with that, because my brain is already reeling.

"This next part," he says, "is what I've managed to piece together from being around Pru during some of her less . . . lucid . . . moments when she doesn't realize she's letting something slip. You've seen how she is now. It's hard to tell how much is real and how much is fantasy. One night, Pru was going on and on about killing herself, and I'm saying no, you shouldn't, but she's saying she already *has* killed herself, back when she was fourteen, and she's sad about it. Wishes she hadn't. So my point is, a lot of what Pru says is just plain crazy. But . . . this is the only chain of events that makes sense."

Kiernan pauses, and I can see that he's trying to decide how best to explain all of this. I feel a time travel headache coming on just watching him. As much as I want to understand, part of me wishes I could just tell him to skip the explanations.

"Imagine for a minute," he says, "the timeline before they started inserting any of their Cyrist nonsense. Katherine landed in 1969, had the twins, Pru disappears fourteen years later. And Katherine had cancer in that timeline, just like she does now. Except there's no Connor with her because they never met, so Katherine's all alone when she gets sick. Maybe your mum never married because Katherine had no reason to set her up with your da, so there's no you, and despite their differences, your mum ends up taking Katherine in during those last few months."

He stops again, watching my face. "What? You don't think she would?"

"No. If Katherine had nowhere to go, Mom wouldn't turn her away. But she'd have been miserable."

"Apparently she was—"

"My question is . . . was Pru watching them? And if so, why didn't she let them know she was alive? I'm pretty sure she thought Katherine was behind the bombing of CHRONOS, so maybe that's why she didn't want anything to do with her, but couldn't she at least have let Mom know?"

"That part is fuzzy for me. There was something about a video . . . or a recording of some sort. With your mum. It didn't make sense to me, so it could be something else Pru's made up in her little fantasy world. Last time she had some new nonsense, talking about Deborah as her daughter rather than her sister. I've given up trying to make all the pieces fit. Anyway—"

"That last bit might be my fault. The 1872 trip? I had to tell her something to get her to trust me."

He gives me an annoyed look. "Shush, okay? I'm trying to keep all this straight, and you adding in new twists and tangles isn't helping. Anyway, Pru saw what taking care of Katherine did to your mum. So in the next timeline, after they insert the *Book of Cyrus* and the *Book of Prophecy* into the past, Pru goes back, bribes someone at the hospital in Italy that first time Katherine goes in for testing. Has them tell her everything's fine, just an infection. The pills Katherine gets aren't antibiotics, however. They're an anticancer drug Pru got from some point in the future. Katherine gets better, and then wham! Two months later, she starts training my Kate. Pru was pissed. Said she did a good deed and that's how Katherine repaid her."

"But . . . it's not like Katherine knew."

"Didn't say it was logical. Just said that's how Pru *felt*. Then Saul decides, for whatever reason, that the best bet is to reset everything."

"Maybe because he was worried you and your Kate were getting too close to stopping him?"

Kiernan shakes his head. "Pru always said Saul wasn't worried about that. Simon, too. I suspect they're right. Think about it. Saul tells Simon to snatch my Kate's key and erase my memory, knowing it means Simon is writing off our friendship. He tells Pru to kill Katherine back in 1969, knowing it means killing herself and her unborn sister, too. I think they were loyalty tests. Simon once said Saul had one of the regional Templars kill his own wife to prove his loyalty, so it wouldn't be the first time."

"So, like the story of Abraham and Isaac in the Bible?"

"Yeah, except Saul doesn't intercede and tell the guy to stop at the last minute. Anyway, neither Pru nor Simon can follow orders . . . it's not in their nature. Simon did a decent job of hiding it. Saul may still not know what Simon did with Kate. But Pru, she told Saul flat out that she didn't kill Katherine. She gave him some garbage about how she wanted Katherine to die a slow death and that she wouldn't give her the cancer treatment so that she'd be too sick to train you. But she knew that wasn't why Saul set that task for her. She's crazy, but she's not stupid."

I'm silent for a long time, trying to untangle all the threads. This stuff screws with my brain under the best of circumstances, and I already felt like crap before Kiernan started piling on the conundrums. There are at least half a dozen things that bug me about what he's just said, but I think most of them are because I'm thinking linearly. And logically, which probably isn't any better when it comes to Saul and Prudence. Maybe Simon, too.

"Why didn't you tell me this when I asked in Georgia? You knew then, didn't you?"

"I didn't know for certain. Simon told me about a month after we left Martha's. I think he was testing me. Saul taught him well, huh? But . . . the whole thing at Norumbega was bugging me. Why would Pru be there with Simon? She bloody hates him. She hated him when she was younger, too. Drugged or no, she wouldn't have stood there quietly and . . . she wouldn't have been watchin' me that way, either. Like her heart was being torn out—"

"And Simon says he'll give your Kate back in exchange for the keys and me. What if you refuse?"

"He yanks her key."

"Let's say you did hand the keys over, then what? The two of you just go back to the cabin and don't worry about the next century when nearly a billion—"

"The three of us." His tone is still low and flat as he says that, but then the next words explode out of him. "You saw her, Kate! She's with child. You saw her. It's not so simple. The baby . . ."

"But that's one child, Kiernan! How many children die in the Culling and after?"

"How many people died in World War One, Kate? World War Two? How about the other wars in the last century? Tally up those deaths, and no, it's not quite the 'nearly a billion' that you mention, but it's not so far from it. And there's plenty more to come."

"But Katherine says things get better, that they're getting better even in my time, if people would just look at things objectively. There's less hunger, less disease, fewer wars. The Future-Wiki that Delia and Abel put together, everything Grant told me, what Campbell and Tate said, too—everything points in that same direction. Even if that future wasn't perfect, I'm certain it's better than what we see here."

"I'm not arguing with that, damn it. Would you let me finish? What if someone said you could stop all of those deaths by sacrificing an innocent child? Would it be an easy choice for you? What if the child in question was your own?"

I don't know how to answer. I mean, I know it wouldn't be an *easy* choice, but could I do it? Could I sacrifice a child of my own—or any concrete, living child for that matter—to save millions? I'd like to think the answer is yes, that the good of the many outweighs the good of the few or the one, but I have to admit I'm not certain, even when the idea of having a child of my own seems distant and remote.

And while I don't have the guts to admit it out loud, I have very mixed feelings about the news that Other-Kate is alive. I'm relieved it's not me in Rio, and I'm really and truly happy for Kiernan, even though I think the odds of him getting her back safely with everything else currently on the line aren't good. There's also a touch of jealousy, however unreasonable it may be. Not over Kiernan. I care for him. Okay, yes. I love him. But not the way I love Trey.

The jealous feeling is that she's butting into *my* timeline, a timeline where she's not supposed to exist. And that's kind of scary. Maybe I'll be the one who evaporates this time, like the other Other-Me did during the library fire.

But the baby? That's a very different kettle of fish. Thinking about this baby—a baby that shares half my genes, a baby I most likely will never see even if it survives—stirs up an odd sense of protectiveness.

"Is it . . ." I try to think of a delicate way to phrase it, but there isn't one, so I just blurt it out. "Is the baby yours?"

He's quiet for a bit, and then he says, "I think so. After I left Estero, the supply of contraceptives June gave me ran out. So Kate was taking care of it, but when most of your days last longer than twenty-four hours, it's hard to stick to a schedule. I think she may have missed a few times, especially during the whole craziness with the jump to Georgia. She was going to get one of those implant things, but she never got around to it. And Simon swears it's mine. Swears he never touched her, swears Saul and the others don't even know about her, that they think she's Younger Pru. He claims his goal all along was to give her back to me, once it's all done."

"Do you believe him?"

His laugh is nervous, shaky. "The sad thing is, I really do. Why else would he bring her to watch me at Estero? Simon took the stars down that night after he and his goons grabbed Kate—probably the same goons that knocked me out in the alley. Said he was worried Pru or Saul might catch on to the fact that he didn't follow orders. But he's also the one who came back later and put the stupid things back up, to let me know I shouldn't give up hope. It's like Kate said long ago, Simon's never loved anyone other than me. No one can love Saul, it's like lovin' a damned cobra. You might try to please him, but that's mostly self-preservation. And Pru . . . there's no love lost there. Saul set the two of them against each other from day one. With no mum, no dad, he latched onto me like a brother. So, yeah, I believe him when he says the baby's mine. But there are limits. He'd feel bad about yanking Kate's key, just like he'd probably have felt bad about killing her. But he'll do it if he finds I've double-crossed him."

A defiant note comes into his voice as he continues. "But on the issue of the baby, it wouldn't matter either way, Kate. The child is indisputably hers, and . . . she is my very heart. So the child is *mine*. I won't be asking any questions of her."

Kiernan reaches into his pocket and then stretches his hand out to me, dropping something into my palm. "Sorry. I lied to you about that, too."

The gold is tinted blue in the light of the CHRONOS keys. It's still obvious that it's a wedding band. Something is engraved inside, but I can't read it.

"It was just a civil ceremony in Boston, about three months after my mum died. Jess and Amelia stood up for us. Katherine would've had a fit, and so would your mum and dad, probably—Kate had barely begun college. We had so much uncertainty in every other part of our lives, though, and I needed . . ." He shrugs. "Kate would've been just as happy to wait, but she humored me. Simon said he had to drug her to get the ring off her finger."

That image clearly riles him up. He clenches a handful of the sand-stuff and squeezes it into a firm ball, then smashes it back into the ground.

"So . . . you're pissed at yourself because you couldn't betray me—and what we're working for—to save your Kate and the baby. And you're also pissed at yourself for even thinking about doing it. Is that it?"

"Yeah," he says, still looking off in the distance. "Pretty much sums it up."

"Kiernan, would you just look at me?" I wait until he finally turns toward me. "I'm not angry. Well, maybe a little, but I *under-stand*. I just . . . I wish you'd told me. You acting like such a jerk makes a lot more sense now that I know what's been weighing you down. And we're not at odds here. We'll both do our best to stop this, but if we can't? I'll go with Simon and help him do whatever he needs to do to calm the survivors if he keeps his promise and lets Mom and Katherine go—that's my fallback option, too. This just means there are two more lives we might be able to salvage if all else fails."

It's my best effort at making peace, and I give him a hopeful smile. But if anything, he looks even angrier than before.

What did I say to set him off this time?

Kiernan struggles with whatever it is for a moment, and when he finally speaks, it's through clenched teeth. "First, let's not forget that it wasn't just a matter of trading you for her. I was toying with the idea of looking the other way, of accepting Simon's argument that all those lives are irrelevant. And second, cut the bloody martyr act. I'm not letting you sacrifice yourself. I suspect there are others who might object to that as well."

I really, really want to punch him. To hear him talk, it's like I'm one of those Koreshan women, eager to sacrifice my life for the cause. I take a few calming breaths, but my voice is still quivering when I reply.

"First—and I know this was your second point, but since it's what pissed me off the most, that's where I'm starting—if you think I plan on just giving up, that any of us plan on giving up without a fight, you are sadly mistaken. And as for your other point, *everybody* toys with the idea of walking away, Kiernan! Do you think I haven't thought of it? I haven't even seen Saul's demo reel of the collected horrors of the next few centuries. But even without seeing everything you've seen, there's a part of me that just wants to say *screw it all* and run. I want to believe that voice would never win out, but if I had the option of finding a safe corner of the past and taking the people I love with me . . . the way you can? Let's just say the temptation would be a whole lot stronger."

He doesn't respond. And that's fine, because there's only about fifteen minutes before the bots come rolling through to clean the area. Hopefully a few hours of rest were enough.

I pull up the hotel stable point, set for five thirty, as I promised. Trey is on the corner of the bed near Charlayne and Ben, watching the point where I'm really hoping I'll arrive. Eve and Max are off in the corner by the window. Her hands are duct-taped in front of her, as are her ankles. I guess Max decided to hold off on securing her to the chair since I didn't leave him coordinates.

And even though I was arguing in favor of jumping in at the hotel earlier, seeing Eve again bothers me. The idea of taking these keys into a room where she is sitting—even if she's restrained—sets off all sorts of alarm bells.

So I pull up the foyer at Katherine's. Simon's watching the library, he's watching my room, maybe even watching the kitchen. But the foyer? Maybe not. I could yell upstairs and . . . I have no idea beyond that, but I'd really love Dad's and Connor's input on the next steps.

But . . . the foyer isn't empty. Or rather, the living room, which is just *beyond* the foyer, isn't empty. Connor and Dad should still be in the library—in fact, they were still in the library at this exact moment, the last time I checked.

Something has changed. Connor and Dad are sitting in the two chairs across from the sofa. They look confused. Worried. Daphne is on the floor between them, head between her paws.

Dad says something, but not to Connor. It looks like he's talking to someone on the sofa.

They're no longer alone.

I pan to the left and suck in a sharp breath. I can't see her face, but someone with hair very much like mine is in the sofa opposite Dad, talking rapidly. She's gesturing with her hands, and my eye is drawn to the CHRONOS key embedded in the inside of her forearm.

"Kiernan? We have a complication. Pru is at Katherine's." I lean over to transfer the point to his key. "She looks kind of crazed."

He gives me a look that says *surprise, surprise*, and pulls up the stable point on his key. "She doesn't seem to be threatening them. Since Simon has Deborah . . . I don't know, maybe she's looking for help?"

"Damn it. Pru is at Katherine's. Eve is at the hotel. The freakin' Cyrists have eyes everywhere."

Kiernan thinks for a moment. "Maybe not . . . everywhere."

He reaches over and grabs my hand, his eyes imploring. "Can you still trust me, Kate? I won't blame you if the answer is no, but if we can get you back to my time, there's a spot—no, not the cabin—where you can rest up and the keys will be safe. It's the only spot I can think of where I'm sure . . . well, as sure as I can be . . . that no one is watching."

"I don't know if I can make it that far back. But yes. I still trust you."

He gives me a smile that makes him look years younger, much more like the Kiernan I remember. "Hand me your key."

Once the stable point is transferred to my medallion, I grab the tub of keys and stand up. I still feel shaky, and it's several seconds before I can even focus enough to pull up the location he transferred to my key. The stable point is pitch-black, just like this one was, although I think there's a bit of light coming in from above.

"So, where am I headed?" I ask, and then hold up my hand. "No. On second thought, you said this is the only safe spot you can think of. Tate said he didn't *believe* there's anyone in this reality who can use the CHRONOS equipment, but I'm not willing to bet the entire future on that. If I'm apprehended here before I can jump out, I can erase this stable point. I'm sure that here in 2308 there are very sophisticated methods of getting people to cough up information they'd like to hide, so I don't want to know where . . ."

Kiernan shakes his head. "Kate, I'm not leaving you here alone."

"Yes, Kiernan! You are. If this doesn't work, if I can't blink out of here, I'm crawling into one of the Juvapods until I *can* leave, and you're getting the hell out of 2308 with these keys. So . . . here goes nothing."

And, unfortunately, I'm right.

∞20∞

OBJECTIVIST CLUB
WASHINGTON, EC
September 20, 2308, 9:07 a.m.

The Juvapod is warm and humid, like a hot tub without water. It's all I can do to stay awake and upright so that I don't bump into the walls. I'm safe in here—I scanned ahead on the key, and no one uses this pod today. There's just enough space that I could lie down if I curl up into a fetal position, but I'm worried that I'll stretch out in my sleep if I get too comfortable. I'd rather avoid another discussion with Alisa.

I think I dozed off for a few, although I doubt it's enough to allow me to blink out. Since Kiernan is probably correct about "draining my battery" with too many attempts, I just take a small sip from the water bottle we found behind the information desk, and I wait. Only sixteen more hours until I can climb out of this tomb, stretch out on the sand-stuff, and get some real sleep.

Kiernan took the keys when he left. I wouldn't let him tell me where or when. While that was an enormous, gut-wrenching leap of faith, I didn't see much choice. He asked me three times if I wouldn't rather keep them here with me. I think he was scared he'd give in to temptation, but that seems much less risky than me keeping them here when I've no idea how long before I can jump.

With nothing else to do, I check on Dad and Connor. Still there. So is Pru. Watching her makes me nervous, so I pull up the hotel room, even though I've watched this scene over and over. I always stop when I see myself jump in. I don't want to see what I do next, because then I'll be thinking about what I saw myself do when I'm actually doing it, and the idea of that makes me crazy. And if I ignore Max and Eve's side of the room and just focus on Trey, it's kind of relaxing. He is talking to Ben about something, occasionally glancing over at the stable point where I'll pop in.

Several minutes pass, and I realize the mood has changed. Trey looks really nervous, and then he turns toward Max, who must have said something to piss him off.

This is new.

I should have jumped in by now.

Trey storms over like he's going to hit Max, but then I see it's Eve who made him angry. The others try to calm him down, including Max, but they look uneasy, too. Eve is the only one who's calm, staring at the stable point with a satisfied little grin that looks out of place on the face of someone sporting a duct-tape bracelet.

I don't want to look at the time stamp on my display, but I do. It's almost 5:31.

Nearly a full minute *after* I was supposed to return.

It's just one minute, except . . . you can't be late with a CHRONOS key. I could jump in at exactly 5:30 a year from now if I needed that long to recover from temporal jet lag.

So if I'm late returning, it means something's changed. It means I *won't* be returning. At all. That's why Trey looks like someone has punched him in the gut. That's why Eve is smiling.

Disregarding Kiernan's earlier warning, I try to blink in again. No luck. I feel the writhing snakes of a panic attack working their way through my body, so I focus on taking slow, even breaths. I need to stop looking at the stupid key and relax if I'm going to get to the point where I can jump back.

Except you're late, and being late means you don't make it back.

Why am I not surprised that the little voice in my head sounds just like Eve?

I pound my fists against my thighs in frustration because I can't think of a single option other than waiting here in this hot, sticky coffin until I can jump out—and the evidence in front of me says sitting and waiting isn't going to cut it.

Acting solely on impulse, I shove my hand into the wall next to me.

"Welcome, guest! I'm Alisa. Please survey the treatment menu while I pull your account information."

"Prudence K. Rand. Guest member. Account Rand02." Hopefully there will be less of a footprint on their computer system if I just give her the information.

There's a very brief pause before Alisa chirps, "DNA confirmed. Since this is your first visit to the OC, you may not be aware that clients are asked to refrain from bringing in outside food or beverage."

I'm not sure what she means until I glance down at the mostly empty bottle of water.

"Sorry," I say, gulping the last bit. "Where's the trash?"

"Pardon?"

"Where can I discard it?"

The shelf to the right flashes. I put the bottle on the shelf and it vanishes.

"Please disrobe and be seated."

I ignore her and pull up the exterior of the pod on my key. It's late morning and the place is crowded. If I tell Alisa to cancel and step out of the pod, I'll be seen, and the toga isn't exactly inconspicuous. I'd be less likely to be tagged as Sister Prudence if I follow Alisa's advice and disrobe, but that option isn't very appealing.

The chair, however—just a body-shaped indentation in the pod wall—does look appealing. So I sit.

"Some treatments cannot be given if you remain clothed. Please be assured that this is a private session."

I ignore her, trying to think what to do. She waits for a moment, but then dives into the same routine she did last time. "Do you need help reading the menu?"

"No. I just don't know what I need."

"Scanning."

I gasp as the material of the chair morphs around my body and the entire room flickers slightly, like Campbell's replicator did when taking my measurements. I panic and start to struggle, but my body says my brain is overreacting. It's like being wrapped in a soft, warm towel. Oh, yes. I could definitely sleep here.

There's a beep, followed by a male voice I haven't heard before. "Increased cortisol, epinephrine, and dopamine levels. Lowered blood glucose. Heart rate outside normal range for age and weight. Hyperhidrosis. Hypercalcemia. Dehydration. Recommendation: Stress tonic, followed by bed rest."

I start to say cancel, but then I reconsider. "Bed rest isn't possible. I have to stay alert."

"Very well. Combination stress and focus tonic."

"Can you tell me what's in it?"

The voice reels off a list of ingredients, starting with cortisol receptor something, premium neurotropic or maybe neo-tropic, a whole list of vitamins and minerals, and then concludes with a question. "Would you prefer a fruit or vegetable juice base?"

Okay, I don't recognize most of those ingredients. But I've eaten Twinkies and hot dogs. I don't recognize most of the ingredients in those, either. Is it all that different from a smoothie with those vitamin boosts? Dozens of people go in and out of these pods all day—well, not this model, but the shiny new ones at the other end. They seem perfectly okay.

"Fruit juice."

There's another flicker, and the cushiony material slides away from my body. A few seconds later, a tall, frosted glass appears on the shelf beside me. It's cold and tastes a bit like mango and reminds me that I haven't eaten in forever.

I slurp to the bottom, then push the glass back onto the shelf, where it disappears.

"Would you like another treatment?" It's Alisa again.

What I really want is another one of those mystery smoothies and a long nap in that blanket chair. "I'm thinking. Let me look at the menu for a moment. Oh . . . how long before that tonic takes effect?"

"Five to ten minutes."

I scan the list of services, wondering how long "skin resurfacing" takes and whether it hurts.

"Please make your selection. Other clients are waiting."

"I'm done. No other treatment."

"Thank you for visiting the OC, Pru—" The door starts to slide open but halts just as Alisa stops speaking. Then it starts going back down.

I shove upward on the door, but it doesn't budge.

"Door must remain locked until treatment cycle is complete."

"No. Other. Treatment." I pull upward on the door again. "Cancel treatment!"

No response. I pull out my CHRONOS key and lock in the stable point in Boston. I blink, but I know before I open my eyes that I'm still in the Juvapod, because Alisa is speaking again.

"Please wait. A security team is on its way."

"A security team? Why?"

"You are wanted for questioning in an incident on level ten. Estimated waiting time is less than thirty seconds."

Level 10.

"What time is it, Alisa?"

"The current time is nine forty-six."

Pseudo-Saul. The keys.

A few too many discrepancies from the game plan they'd been given by Brother Cyrus, I guess. So they alerted security, who will find me here in this hot and sticky gift box.

Alisa's voice chirps throughout the building. "We have a blue level security alert in the recreation center. All clients exit immediately through the front entrance. All clients exit immediately through the front entrance."

I pull up the outside of the pod on the key. The Juvapod doors slide open and about a dozen disoriented semiclothed bodies stumble out and rush toward the exit at the left. Most of the people who were lounging in the fake sun scurry out of the recreation area, although a few brave souls hang near the door so they can rubberneck. The sole exception is a swimmer in the pool—the same one I saw yesterday—who's calmly swimming laps. He seems oblivious to the chaos above water. The earbuds or whatever they use in the twenty-fourth century must be really effective.

Two dark metallic-looking . . . things . . . roll around the corner at the far end of Juvapod Row. They're about four feet high, and the bodies look a bit like the robot in this movie I watched with Dad—can't remember the name, but the words "Number Five is alive" flash through my head. These guys don't look as friendly, however.

In their wake is a woman about the same build as my former karate instructor—short, square, and solid. She doesn't appear to be armed. I'm less certain about her metal companions.

Tate said something about dismembering a security bot. I have no idea how he did it, although my best guess is sheer brute strength. Of course, he was facing just one.

Surprise is my only hope, and the odds will be much more in my favor if it's the woman in front when the door opens. I skip ahead a few seconds, and I'm relieved to see her push forward as they draw closer to the door. I move into a fighting stance and wait.

When the door is halfway open, I pull my knee up and in, then thrust a side kick into the woman's body. I was aiming for her stomach, but the pod is a few inches above ground level, and my heel connects with her sternum. She stumbles back into the first of the security bots, and they both land on the floor a few feet away from me.

It's a gentle landing, thanks to the squishy sand-stuff, and she's already pushing herself up as I turn to face the other bot. The woman hits a button on the vest she's wearing and dives into one of the open Juvapods for cover.

The second bot is indeed armed. Not with a gun, at least I don't think it's a gun. More like some sort of stun weapon. The inside of the pod sizzles when it's hit, about an inch from where I was standing a second earlier.

It's raising one of its appendages to fire again when a volley of gunfire sounds off to my right. One of those shots connects, and the security bot's head flies off, splashing into the pool a few lanes away from the oblivious swimmer.

I steal a glance down the hallway to my right, where a large masked gunman is crouching in the shadows. I can't see his face from this angle, but a CHRONOS key hangs from his neck. He motions sideways with his gun, and I press back against the pod to give him a clear line of fire as he sends several more shots into the bot that still has its head. Both of the things are now disabled.

Lights are flashing, including the ones in the pool, and I guess that's what finally broke through the swimmer's trance. He pokes his head out of the water and is already pulling himself up the ladder when he sees the scattered bot parts lining the beach area and the last few clients pushing through the exit doors. His eyes meet mine as he starts to drop back into the water, but then he freezes in midair as a voice booms out from the hallway.

"Don't move!" Max yells. "I can shoot you in the water, so do as I say. Kate, grab the guard. We need hostages."

I take a few steps sideways until I reach her. "Hands up where I can see them!" No idea why I say that, since I'm fairly certain she's not armed, and, for that matter, neither am I. It just sounds like what I'm supposed to say to someone I'm holding hostage.

Someone I'm holding hostage?

Holy crap.

"Move toward him slowly, okay? We don't want to hurt anyone, but I'm pretty sure he'll shoot if he has to."

She gives me a confused look, and we walk slowly toward Max. The swimmer pulls himself out of the pool and tries to stand, but his legs are shaking, so he just crumples next to the body of the second bot, watching nervously. Max moves the gun back and forth between the two of them with one hand and holds out a second rifle toward me with the other.

This is light-years away from the Colt, a long black automatic of some sort. "I don't know how to shoot this, Max!"

He rolls his eyes and shoves it into my hands anyway. "Point toward the swimmer. Pull the trigger if I tell you to. Safety is off."

I nearly drop the thing when he says that, but manage to maintain my grip.

"Where are the keys?" he asks.

"Safe." I say it with as much certainty as I can muster, but Max still gives me an incredulous look.

"You stupid little . . ." Max clenches his teeth and turns toward the security guard. "Take off the vest—slowly—and slide it toward me."

"We only wanted to question her," the guard says. But she does as she's told, and Max tosses the vest into the pool.

"Now both of you. Into the hallway. Keep going."

Once they're about twenty feet inside, Max slides down with his back against the wall on the right and motions for me to do the same on the opposite wall. "Keep your gun—and your eyes—on them. She had a communicator in the vest, so I think we'll have more robot friends joining us shortly. At least I hope it's just the bots."

"I didn't think you could jump this far. Julia said—"

"My dad was killed because he let people know he could use the key. Julia didn't want me to risk it. But I'm smarter than that."

"How did you know where to find me?"

"You didn't show up on schedule," he snaps, still looking toward the rec center. "Which meant you were either dead or stranded. So someone had to come save your ass."

"I thought Fifth Column rules prohibited that? When I wanted to go back and save Julia, Tilson told me—"

"Yeah, well that was going *back*. Changing history. This is going forward. It hasn't happened yet. Not the same thing. And either way, whether I like it or not, you're the one exception to that rule. If you do something stupid and get yourself killed—past, present, or future—I have to fix it."

I don't really have a response to that, and I feel a little guilty for not trusting him earlier. Oh, hell. For not trusting him *still*. Because even though he's here trying to get me out of this mess, I don't like him and I don't trust him. Mostly because he was with

Eve, but also because I know that getting Mom and Katherine back safely is pretty much rock bottom on Max's list of priorities. I could understand it being below preventing the Culling. As much as it pains me, I'd have to put that first, too. But for him, it ranks below preserving his branch of Cyrist International, and there we part ways.

"But how did you *find* me? How did you know where to look?"

"No thanks to you, that's for sure, since you wouldn't leave me the coordinates. I was about to go back to Plan A—the jet packs—but that black hole isn't there anymore. It's smack dab in the middle of a wall or something. We were trying to figure out some way to work around that when Dunne showed up with the info. Where did he take the keys?"

"I don't know."

He curses and spits into the corner, which is ick and adds one more reason for me not to like him. "They're probably in Saul's hands already."

"If Kiernan was going to turn them over to Simon and Saul, why would he have given you the coordinates to find me? Once I'm out of here, he'll give me the keys, and Connor will destroy them."

"No. We have people to handle that. You bring the keys to the hotel, and we'll take it from there."

I don't answer. If Max takes my silence as agreement, then fine, but no way in hell will I put those keys into the hands of these unnamed *people* of his, none of whom I've met.

There's a noise in the distance. Max must hear it, too, because he pulls up the gun, pointing it toward the door. "When was the last time you tried the key?"

"Maybe five minutes ago?"

"Well, try again. The hotel first, five fifty. If that doesn't work, then this room, three nights back. I'll follow."

"Why not five thirty? I could keep you from—"

"We don't want the double memories. Just go!"

"Can you get back?"

"Yes." There's not a hint of hesitation, so either he's tested himself on a long jump like this or he's not someone I'd want to face at poker.

I balance the gun against my shoulder and stare menacingly at the two hostages as I yank out my CHRONOS key. This would be the perfect time to gang up and attack me, while I'm distracted. I can tell the security guard is thinking the same thing, even if she doesn't have a clue what I'm doing with the key. "Don't even think it. Move all the way back. Both of you. On your stomachs, hands behind your heads. Now!"

Yeah, it's straight out of *NCIS*. I guess Mom's crush on that Gibbs guy came in handy.

Just as they lie down, Max begins firing. I don't have time to check on his progress, so I pull up the stable point at the hotel and blink in.

∞

RESIDENCE INN
BURTONSVILLE, MARYLAND
September 12, 5:50 p.m.

I arrive at the center of a strange tableau. The first thing I see is Eve, on the sofa, still duct-taped. Still wearing her nasty little smile, too, but it fades fast when she sees me. Tilson sits to her right, his crutches against the wall. He's holding her wrist, and he doesn't look pleased about it, but I guess it was the only way to extend the protection of the CHRONOS field without the risk of returning her key.

Charlayne is in front of me, holding a rifle identical to the one in my hand, raised to shoulder height and pointed at Kiernan, who's sitting on the bed. He looks more bored than afraid.

Trey must have been behind me, because I feel his arms surrounding me as I step toward Charlayne.

"Put down the gun! Kiernan's not the enemy. Have you all gone crazy?"

Charlayne gives me a nervous look, but keeps the weapon up.

"God, Kate. You're okay."

I hear the question in Trey's voice as he pulls me toward him.

"I'm okay." I close my eyes for a second and lean into him.

"Kiernan told me," he whispers. "That it's not you in Rio."

He clutches me against his chest. A bit of the tension drains away, until the sensation of hot metal against my skin brings it rushing back.

It's the barrel of Max's gun brushing against my bare shoulder as he jumps in. Trey and I are mere inches from the stable point, and I guess Max didn't have time to scan forward. How many shots did he have to fire to get the barrel that hot? I just hope none of his targets were human.

And then Max is in Kiernan's face shouting about the keys, and I'm shouting for him to back off.

"Quiet!" Tilson bangs his crutch against the metal air-conditioning unit near the window for emphasis. "You're going to get us kicked out of here with this commotion. And I think you can lower the guns. He's not going anywhere as long as Charlayne has his key."

I give all of them an incredulous look. Obviously Kiernan's wearing his backup, since he's still here. But they didn't know that. None of them did.

"Were you people not listening earlier?" I yell. "It's possible none of us with the CHRONOS gene exists right now outside the range of a medallion. Who took his key?"

"That would be Max," Trey says, giving him a foul look. "I told them Kiernan was on our side and tried to stop them. I was worried he'd vanish like Katherine did, but let's just say I was outvoted. Or rather, *we* were outvoted," he adds with a glance at Tilson.

Charlayne looks uncomfortable, but she still doesn't lower the gun.

Ben puts his arm around her and says, "We were following orders, Kate."

"This isn't the freakin' military!"

"Maximilian," Tilson says, "tell them to stand down. And come deal with your fiancée."

"She's not my fiancée."

"Well, she sure as hell isn't *my* responsibility." Tilson pushes himself up with the crutches. Eve makes a panicked noise, grabbing his shoulder as she stands and nearly causing both of them to tumble. The instant she regains her balance, Eve pulls her arms over her head. I rush forward, thinking she's going to hit him. She does yank downward, hard, but straight down rather than toward Tilson, grinning triumphantly when the duct tape on her wrists splits straight up the middle.

Eve grabs for Tilson's pocket, where the blue glow of the CHRONOS key is shining through the fabric. Tilson dodges to the right, whacking her with a crutch as he stumbles backward into the chair.

Charlayne turns her rifle on Eve, but Max is already there, pulling her away from Tilson and the key. That's when Eve sees a closer option than the key in Tilson's pocket—Max's key, which is still in the open, hanging from the dark leather cord around his neck.

She grabs the cord and yanks. Max's body is blocking my view, so I can't tell whether the cord snaps or Eve manages to pull it over his head, but either way, it's in her hands.

Max clutches her arm and twists.

That's not a bad move for disarming your opponent. It's definitely a bad move, however, if you want to keep yourself in contact with the object in your opponent's hand.

Their faces don't even have a chance to register surprise as the medallion falls from Eve's hand and skids across the carpet and under a chair. It's less than a foot away when they both blink out of sight.

We just stare at the empty space for a moment, and then Charlayne looks at me and says in a strangled voice, "Go back. Go back and stop him. Tell him what happens."

"I don't think it will work, Charlayne."

But I try. I roll the key back, and, sure enough, they aren't there. It's like everyone in the room is viewing a blank spot on the carpet.

"It's possible," I say, "if we manage to fix the timeline, that they'll pop back in. When Katherine's key was yanked in the other timeline, it was because she'd been killed in the past. I stopped her from being killed, and it repaired the rift. But Max and Eve—they're gone because CHRONOS never exists in this timeline. Their parents, grandparents, whatever, were never born. Without the key, I'd disappear, too."

As I say that, I realize that, aside from Trey, the same is true for everyone I care about: Mom, Dad, Katherine, Connor, Kiernan. But it's also true for the Cyrists. Does Prudence know this? Do Simon and Saul?

"Maybe once we fix this, Max and Eve will be back like Katherine was. I mean, they weren't killed . . ." I press my palms into my eyes hard enough that it hurts, hoping it will distract me from the raging headache this is causing. "They were just erased. I don't know if you come back from that."

"So why didn't he vanish?" Charlayne nods toward Kiernan. "After Max took his key, he should have disappeared, right?"

"I would have," Kiernan says, "except someone was wise enough to give me a backup when I was eight. This isn't the first time it's saved me. And before you decide to go looking for my spare key, could we have a few moments of rational discussion? As Kate said, I'm not your enemy. And given that your Fifth Column is now down several members, I'm thinking you need all the allies you can get."

∞

BETHESDA, MARYLAND
September 12, 6:23 p.m.

Dad and Connor are in the kitchen drinking a beer when I jump in. I'm tempted to join them. I doubt either of them would lecture me about underage drinking after the day I've had. But I have no idea how it would mix with the tonic from the Juvapod. And truthfully, I'm already feeling a little buzzed. Whatever they put in that drink beats the hell out of Red Bull.

My original plan was to jump back to earlier in the afternoon, before Pru arrived, and warn Dad and Connor that they were about to have a guest. But Kiernan convinced me that would only be a good idea if Pru was actually a threat. A quick skim through the two hours between her arrival and the current time showed her crying, talking, drinking coffee, sitting on the floor to pet a very nervous Daphne, and at one point yelling at Dad and Connor. They both seemed confused and on edge, and something looks a little different about the area around the sofa. Tiny shreds of fabric are scattered in front, covering most of that side of the carpet. At no point, however, did I get the sense they were in danger.

About ten minutes ago, Pru collapsed on the couch, and I took that as my cue to enter. We need a few minutes without her in the conversation, so I hope she's really asleep, not just catnapping. On the other hand, the Culling bomb is ticking, and I'm really hoping Pru has some ideas on where the virus was kept. And that she's not only willing but also coherent enough to share them.

Neither Dad nor Connor mentioned, or even seemed to notice, that I'm now dressed in a toga. I think that fact is a pretty good indicator of exactly how bizarre our lives have become.

Connor lifts one finger to his lips, gesturing toward the living room, where Pru is on the couch. At some point recently, one of them pulled the comforter over her. Her face looks strangely peaceful.

I nod toward the patio, and they both follow me. Actually, all three, because Daphne rouses herself from her spot under the breakfast nook and limps after us. Connor pulls the picnic table a bit to the left so that we can still see Pru through the window as we talk. I'm not sure it matters, though. The key in her arm means she can leave anytime she wants, unless we restrain her.

"What's that stuff on the floor?" I ask.

"One of the sofa pillows," Dad says. "Your aunt ripped a hole in the side and then methodically pulled out the stuffing piece by piece. She got a little upset when I mentioned it."

Connor gives a short, nervous laugh. "A *little* upset? She threw a lamp at you."

I must have skimmed past that bit when watching on the key. That's why the area around the sofa looked different—no lamp.

"He ducked," Connor adds. "But Prudence is a real trip. Not always a pleasant one, either. Did you get the keys?"

"Yes. But I couldn't bring them here once I saw her. And I'm pretty sure Simon's watching the library, so we can't put them in the safe, either."

Dad looks a little uneasy. "You left them with those Fifth Column people?"

"Not exactly."

"Good, because Connor found something on the security camera. In the library."

"We have security cameras?"

"Yes," Connor says. "I told you we have two different systems guarding the house. Anyway, Simon didn't set that fire. It was Max."

"What? You're sure?"

A moment ago, I was feeling bad about him vanishing. Now I feel confused, but also strangely vindicated. A sixth sense told me from the very beginning that Max couldn't be trusted. Why would he torch the library?

"It was definitely him," Connor says. "I got a clear look. So I guess he's working with Simon."

"That doesn't make sense. Max . . . he's the one who rescued me in 2308."

I give them a quick summary, ending with Max and Eve's disappearance, but they both seem more interested in the fact that it's not me, or at least not *this* me, in Rio.

"So I was right," Connor says.

"How can there be two of you?" Dad asks.

"Because we're both under a key. Without a key, Other-Kate would disappear."

"Or maybe go back to her original timeline," Connor says.

"Maybe." My voice is hesitant, because I'm not really sure about that last part, although to be honest, I'm not sure about anything at this point.

"But . . ." Dad pauses for a moment, his expression troubled. "If that's the case, there should be two Prudences, too. Right? There wouldn't be duplicates of Deborah or Katherine because they weren't wearing keys. But Prudence must have been under a key when the shift happened. Where's the other Pru?"

That hadn't really occurred to me, but he's right. "Add that to the list of things to ask her when she wakes up."

"What about the rest of the Fifth Column?" Connor asks. "You mentioned before that this was just one cell, so . . ."

"Max gave Tilson and Ben the contact information he had before he vanished. Tilson was going to get in touch, let them know what's up. Before Max vanished he was insistent that I bring the keys to them, that they'd handle deactivating them."

"Because Pru's here?" Dad asks.

"No, I didn't exactly tell them about Prudence. I think it's more of a control thing, and . . ." I shake my head. "It doesn't feel right. Can you deactivate them the way you did the others, Connor? Although I'm not sure how you'd handle it with Simon watching the library."

"Not a problem unless he's also watching the shed." He nods toward the small building in the backyard where the lawnmower and assorted tools are stored. "I did the first one inside, but I had to heat the metal to a high temperature, and the chemicals gave off fumes. Katherine's already queasy from her medicines, so I moved the gear outside."

"That's good," I say. "I'll bring them to you there. I have to get back soon. I think they'd have tried to stop me from leaving the hotel if Kiernan and Trey weren't staying behind as . . . collateral, I guess? Especially Kiernan, since he knows where the keys are."

A squirrel is perched on the swinging bench, eating an acorn as the early evening sun dips behind the trees. Daphne would normally have chased it away by now, but she just watches from the edge of the patio, probably due to her injured leg. That's when I realize her key—the one we attached to her collar—is missing. Simon must have yanked it. I suddenly imagine her blinking out like Max and Eve, which is exactly what would happen if she took off after that squirrel.

"Daphne?" I click my tongue to call her, and she limps over, stretching out near my feet. "Do we have another spare?"

Connor turns a little pale when he realizes why I'm asking. "No. Trey and your mom have the last two—and then there's the spare you take when you jump. I'll just keep her close."

"Okay." I draw in a long, slightly shuddery breath. I feel wired. Maybe there are some caffeinelike side effects to that Juva-boost stuff. "I'm so glad I ignored Julia and went to London. If Mom hadn't been wearing a key when that last shift happened, she'd have vanished. Although I guess we can't be sure either she or Katherine still has it. Simon could easily have—"

"Shh." Dad puts his arm around me. "That's part of what had Prudence so wound up about an hour ago, before Connor gave her . . . What was it you gave her, Connor?"

"Some of Katherine's sleeping meds. Although she was back to acting like a little kid even before the stuff kicked in. Her moods turn on a dime. It's sad, but also kind of creepy." He glances through the window at where she's sleeping. "She kept talking about Simon grabbing Deborah and then a bunch of people we've never heard of, going on about how they're gone now. Not dead. Just gone. Kids, too. You'd think Saul would have made sure his people were under a CHRONOS field."

"Do you think they vanished because we have those medallions now?" Dad asks. "The ones that would have protected them?"

"I think a lot of those people were never under a key. Kiernan said most of them couldn't jump. Saul kept them around as workers, but I doubt he'd have cared whether they were protected by a

CHRONOS field. And even those who will eventually wear these keys . . . they wouldn't have them yet."

"But the keys are a constant," Dad says. "That's why you were able to find them, even though the timeline changed. So wouldn't they . . ." He shakes his head, unable to find a way to frame the question.

I sympathize. I think I know what he's trying to ask, however, so I take a stab at explaining.

"The keys are a constant. But they have their own chronometer, internal clock, or whatever. Tilson said one of the chips inside is a counter of some sort that ticks off the days since the key was created. Prudence grabbed them from CHRONOS on the same day I did . . . just not in the same timeline."

"Do you know when it was?" Connor asks. "I mean . . . for her. How old was she?"

"Maybe nineteen. She'd only had the one baby. The Cyrists may also have had a few offspring from the stranded historians who could use the equipment at that point, but they'd likely have come in with their own keys. From what Kiernan says, Pru's trip to grab the keys that were stored at CHRONOS was *before* she did the egg donor thing. So at the point she brought back the keys, Saul only had a few people who would have needed to be under a CHRONOS field, and most of them had their parent's or grandparent's key. So I'm guessing the medallions sit in a vault somewhere for at least a little while, until the surrogates start giving birth to all of the little Pru babies."

"Yeah," Dad agrees. "In fact, they probably weren't being used for years. If we're assuming the other Cyrists hadn't even been born yet, wouldn't they have had to wait until they were old enough to use the key?"

Connor shakes his head. "'Fraid not, Harry. If you have people giving birth to your offspring in 1905 or whenever, you wouldn't need much time at all. The kid would be an adult by 1925 and could jump forward a hundred years to join you in the future. Twenty years for the kid would seem instantaneous to you. The only thing they'd need is time to set up the whole thing with surrogates, or at least take care of the medical side of things. So if you're certain they hadn't already started—"

"I'm not certain of anything, but that's my best guess. And . . . does it matter? I mean, practically, in terms of what we have to do in the next—what? A day and a half, at most? Does it matter?"

"Well . . . no," Connor says. "Just thinking out loud, mostly. Trying to understand why Saul—or at least Simon—would encourage you to grab those keys and not make arrangements for his . . ."

Connor's voice trails off, and he glances at Pru again, still curled up on the couch. "But yeah. The whole question of whether it's due to the keys you grabbed or not is moot. I'd bet the Cyrists loyal to Saul and Simon are somewhere under a key, just on the off chance that this latest shift erased CHRONOS. Eve was on their side, right? And she had a key, at least until Max took it from her. The ones who have vanished were *Pru's* people. They didn't know when the time shift was coming, so it wiped them all out."

"Maybe a kinder end than having them wait around a few days and die of this virus," Dad says.

"Yikes. That reminds me." I turn away from the two of them so that I can pull out the tattoo stamp discreetly. Like the catsuit, there are no pockets in this toga. The stamp is stashed in the bodice, along with my phone and the spare pack of contacts.

Dad gives me an amused look. "You *are* your mother's daughter."

"Yeah, well, I don't design these outfits. Anyway, give me your hand." I stamp a blue lotus on the back of Dad's hand and then reach for Connor's.

"Come on, Connor. The ink is temporary. It'll fade in a few days."

"Maybe. But in the meantime, I'll have to look at that damned tattoo on my hand."

"Really? You'd rather get a deadly virus?"

For a moment, a cloud passes over his face, and Connor looks like he's considering the question . . . and as I think about his situation, maybe he is. If each shift has pushed our little time train one track over, how far are we from the reality where he existed outside of a CHRONOS field? Where his kids existed? That was a pre-Cyrist timeline, and I can't see a path for restoring it. And here, in this reality, or one of the neighboring realities that we might actually be able to achieve, Katherine's days are numbered.

But then he rolls his eyes and gives me a half smile. "Fine. But if you must give me the Mark of the Beast, at least put it where I don't have to see it constantly."

"Such as?"

"If we want to be in keeping with what I think of the damned symbol, I'll drop trou and you can stamp it on my ass. But in the interest of propriety . . ." He rolls up his left sleeve, and I stamp the inside of his arm.

"Wish I'd thought of that," Dad says, giving his hand a dubious glance.

"We can be twinsies," I say, and cringe inwardly when I remember that Pru said the same thing to Kiernan when she had the key embedded in his arm.

"What's the matter?" Connor asks, but my phone buzzes and saves me from explaining.

It's Trey. "Hey. Just checking in. Nothing much going on here. Just finished another game of Blip."

Translation: The blip has stopped. Mom's not on the move anymore.

We're pretty sure my phone is tapped, possibly his as well. And I'm guessing anyone listening who has even half a brain will realize that we're speaking in code, but hopefully they won't know *what* we're saying. I'm trying to think of a way to ask him where the blip stopped when he says, "High score, at least for me. Still *sixteenth* overall, but better than I've done in a *dog's* age."

Sixteenth. Dogs.

We're totally off-script now, so it takes me a moment, but I get it. They're at the Sixteenth Street Temple.

"Oh, wonderful," I say, even though I'm thinking the opposite. I really, really don't want a return trip to the Church of the Snarling Dobermans.

"Were you able to find what you needed?" Trey asks.

"No. The . . . librarian . . . is in the back room. I'm beginning to think she's gone to sleep."

Long pause on his end, and I'm about to try another stupid clue when he says, "Oh, okay." Another pause, and then, "I know you had that *smoothie thing* earlier but . . ."

What?

"Trey, hold on. This is stupid."

I pull out the key and set a stable point next to where Dad and Connor are sitting. "Be right back."

∞

RESIDENCE INN
BURTONSVILLE, MARYLAND
September 12, 6:37 p.m.

Kiernan is now stretched out with his back against the headboard of one of the beds, eyes closed. He seems pretty relaxed, maybe even asleep. While he's no longer actually at gunpoint, Charlayne is still holding the gun. I'd like to think she wouldn't use it, but . . . who knows? Trey is just behind me, still holding the phone. He gives me a lopsided grin. "Yeah. Makes more sense than superspy code. Did you get that I was saying they're at the temple?"

"I did. And did you get that Prudence is asleep? Connor gave her something. I'd rather not wake her—she strikes me as very likely to wake up on the wrong side of the bed if roused too soon. But we may not have a choice. I want to talk to her before we try any sort of rescue. She may have information that will help."

"Yeah. Tilson's on the computer in the next room. Secure channel. He's trying to get permission to go in—"

"Permission? Permission from whom?" My voice rises at the end. "Are you saying we can't act until we cut through a bunch of Fifth Column red tape? Because I never agreed to wait for—"

Charlayne mutters a curse. "You're not the only one in this, you know. I think it's perfectly reasonable for Tilson to get us some backup, if possible. Maybe turn this rescue mission over to professionals? It'd be much safer for everyone involved, especially those of us who can't just blink back to yesterday if we run into trouble."

I'm about to fire back an angry retort, but she's right. I may not like it, but yes, she's right.

"I'm sorry. It's just . . . that's my *mom*, Charlayne. My grandmother."

Her expression softens a little as she adds, "Everybody's mom, grandmom, dad, brother, second cousin, you name it. They're *all* in danger right now. Just keep that in mind."

"Please tell me you used that little stamp on your families before they left DC?"

"Yes. And no, Julia didn't authorize it." She shrugs, looking a little embarrassed. "The point still stands. If you think the only danger is the virus, you're wrong. Ben has this computer model, and he thinks many of the survivors won't even make it due to the chaos after the virus hits. Loss of medical services, rioting, and so forth."

"It's okay, Charlayne. You're right. If we can get backup, that's a very good thing." I turn to Trey. "On the phone. You were saying something about a smoothie, and I have no idea where that was going."

"Well, Kiernan and I . . ."

I follow his gaze over to Kiernan, who opens his eyes. "You're still tired," he says. "Yes. I know you had some futuristic superpotion, but who knows when that'll wear off. You need real, actual sleep. We can't risk you getting stranded somewhere else—"

"If you know a way to stop the Culling clock that's currently ticking, I'd agree, but we still need to get the vials."

"They don't mean sleeping here and now," Charlayne says.

"So . . . at the cabin."

Kiernan shakes his head. "I suggested that, but you'd be all alone"—he shoots Charlayne an annoyed look—"since the consensus seems to be that I remain here. And while I don't think the cabin is compromised if we choose our dates carefully, it's not worth the risk. I'd suggest my *old* place."

I shake my head, not following him. He sighs and glances at my key. "The one I mentioned when we were in 2308? It may smell a bit like tobacco, but it's clean, warm, and safe."

At the word *tobacco* it clicks. Jess's shop. That's where he's stashed the keys. But when?

"Give me your key," he says, "and I'll—"

Charlayne snaps the gun up, and I turn on her. "Will you put that thing down? He can't go anywhere as long as I'm holding the key. He's just entering in the date."

She relaxes slightly but doesn't lower the weapon. Just as Kiernan finishes, the door opens. Ben and Tilson don't seem happy, and they're not making eye contact with me.

"What?" I ask.

Tilson sits on the sofa, parking his crutches back in the spot they were before Max and Eve vanished. The same thought must occur to him, because he glances at Max's CHRONOS key, forgotten under the chair in the chaos of Max and Eve vanishing.

"I've just been speaking with . . . Max's main contact. The person Julia answered to. She was teleconferenced in to our meeting."

"Okay." He must mean the woman who was shocked that the conspiracy might have gone beyond a few rogue Cyrists. I sit down on the edge of the bed next to Trey and wait for Tilson to go on.

"What did she say?" Trey asks when Tilson remains silent. He's clearly expecting something bad, because he puts a protective arm around my shoulders, as if bracing me for the news.

"They've found Mom, haven't they? And Katherine." My voice is strained, because from the look on their faces, whatever they have to tell me isn't something I'm going to like.

"No! They haven't found them, Kate. It's just . . ." Tilson gives his thin shoulders a tiny shrug. "It seems Max explained the situation to her earlier, at least in part. She knows Simon is holding your mother and Katherine. I didn't give up the location, but I think it could easily be a place they'll suspect. And . . ." He pauses, looking pained. "Julia wasn't the only casualty. All three of the officials who were at the meeting—Ellicott, West, and Pearson—were found dead in their offices. Similar crime scene for each. No one saw or heard anything."

"That's . . . awful," I say, again remembering Julia's body slipping from her chair onto the blood-soaked floor.

"Yes, and it's one reason Julia's superior has decided we can't risk any sort of rescue attempt. She believes this cell, the destruction of the keys, and tracking down the virus need to be under her direct control. A car should arrive in twenty minutes or so. You're to retrieve the keys and bring them back here for her people to pick up. They'll store the keys in a safe location and then take you to meet with her so that you can discuss plans for retrieving the virus."

"And you can't tell me who this person is?"

"No."

I stare at him for a moment, speechless. "And you expect me to just do as this nameless, faceless Fifth Column person commands? When she's not even offering to protect my family?"

"No," Tilson repeats. "I expect you *won't*."

I'd fully anticipated a lecture about the importance of the chain of command, so this takes me a bit off guard.

"But," he continues, "five young people against one old man on crutches? Even if I was inclined to stop you, could I?"

Bensen shoves the two rifles that were on the bed into the bag at Charlayne's feet. "Can you pack up the rest, Char? I'll pull the van around to the back entrance." He hesitates for a second, maybe in response to her expression, which I can't see from this angle. "You can wait here with Tilson, if you want."

"Ri-i-ght," Charlayne says. "If you're going, I'm going, too."

"That's what I was hoping," Ben says, planting a quick kiss on her forehead. "I like our odds better if you're there, too."

"Why?" I ask them. "You were just holding a gun on Kiernan. Why help us now?"

Charlayne glances at Ben and then says, "Julia, Max, Tilson, you. I don't know anyone outside this cell, but I do know that's the chain we're supposed to follow—and if you're in trouble, we get you out. That's a cardinal rule that even those outside this cell should know. And if you go into this alone, you're *going to be* in trouble."

In a perfect world, she'd have said, *Of course, I'm helping you. I'm your best friend. Duh!*

But I'll take it.

I grab Max's CHRONOS key from under the chair and stash it in my pack. Tilson tosses me another one . . . Eve's, I guess.

"No," I say. "Keep it. If another shift happens, we need your memory intact. But hide it if you can, just in case this Fifth Column honcho doesn't agree."

Once Ben leaves to get the van, Charlayne pulls out Kiernan's key and tosses it to him, although I still get the sense that it's against her better judgment. "Exactly where are we going?" she asks.

Everyone looks at me for the answer, but all the places I can think of—their houses, Katherine's house, even Mom's townhouse—are probably being watched.

"Well, wherever it is, I don't need to know," Tilson says, enunciating each word carefully. He was pretty certain earlier that the room wasn't bugged, so I'm guessing he just doesn't want to have that information in case he's questioned. "The beds look quite comfortable. Perhaps one of you can pick me up in the morning once all of this insanity is over. Assuming they don't cart me off for obstruction of justice."

"Okay, let's take it outside," Trey says. "But, Dr. Tilson, are you sure you don't—"

"Positive. I'd slow you down. And maybe I can steer them off course a bit."

"Thank you," I say, slinging my backpack over my shoulder. "For everything." As we're heading out the door, I turn back. "Did you know that Max was the one who set fire to Katherine's library?"

"No," Tilson says. "But I'm not surprised. Julia . . . and others . . . saw those books as a threat."

"Max?" Trey says, closing the door behind us. "And here I was feeling a little sorry that Eve erased him."

The back lot is mercifully empty of people. Ben pulled the van right up to the sidewalk. Charlayne is already inside, and Kiernan is about to join her when Trey and I catch up with them.

"Why didn't you just use the—" I begin, and then say, "Oh. Tapped out?"

"I don't think so," Kiernan says. "Spent a few days at the cabin before I came here. But I'm not going to waste what I have left on a lateral jump when a car can get me there nearly as quickly."

I'm tempted to note that he hasn't dealt with DC-area traffic if he thinks a car can get him anywhere quickly, but he's probably right about conserving his jump juice.

"And you shouldn't risk it much further, either," he says in a lower tone. "Go to Jess's. Get some rest and then get the keys. Have you checked to see what time Pru wakes up? She'll be disoriented. I need to be there."

"About ten minutes before eight."

"Kiernan's right," Trey says. "You need rest. I'll drop him at the back hedge and then join Charlayne and Ben at your dad's place."

I'm not entirely sure how I feel about Trey and Kiernan in a car, talking, without me knowing what's being said. And yes, that's probably paranoid and self-important and a host of other things. It still makes me nervous.

"Okay," Charlayne says. "That settles who's riding with whom and where *he's* going. Now where are the rest of us going?"

Good question.

"What about the cottage?" Trey asks. "The one you and your dad lived in at Briar Hill? Do you still have the key?"

"Yes." I gesture toward my backpack. "Front pocket. Officially, Dad's still living there through the end of the semester. It gives him a place if he needs some time alone." Or, more accurately, some alone time with Sara, but I don't go into that. "But Briar Hill is Cyrist now . . . at least partly."

"True," Trey says. "Still, you could say the same about pretty much anywhere these days. And it's close to Katherine's."

"It could work," Ben says. "We all have school IDs, and there are activities most nights. If anyone gets nosy and spots the jet packs, I think I can explain them away as a science project. The weapons, though . . ."

"Give them to me," I say. "I have a local point set at the cottage. From when I was proving all of this time travel insanity to Dad. I'll drop them before I go to Jess's."

Kiernan hoists one of the bags and slips the strap over my shoulder. I grab the other one, and soon I'm loaded like a pack mule, lugging two bulky military duffels in addition to my backpack.

Trey leans down to give me a goodbye kiss, but his lips are quivering with barely suppressed laughter.

"What?"

"You should see yourself. The toga, the sandals, and now this. You look like a short Greek Rambo."

"Athena, Goddess of Modern War," Kiernan cracks as they get into the car. And now they're both laughing.

I pull up the stable point and blink out, now completely certain that the two of them riding in the same car was a very bad idea.

∞21∞

I'm awake a few minutes before my phone starts to vibrate. The air smells of tobacco, just as Kiernan said it would, and while the room itself was a bit nippy when I jumped in last night, the quilts on the cot kept me nice and warm. The pillow carries the faint scent of the soap Kiernan uses—Ivory, I think—and there's a copy of Sherlock Holmes stories on the crate next to the bed. It's *The Return of Sherlock Holmes*, and I'm pretty sure it's the same one I saw at his apartment in 1905. I get the feeling Kiernan has used this spot more than once in the past few years.

Two of the Sherlock stories kept me company last night while I was waiting for the tonic to wear off enough that I actually could sleep. I haven't sat in bed reading for months, and reading by the light of the CHRONOS key was almost like reading by flashlight under the covers when I was a kid. Between that brief escape and a solid eight hours of sleep, I'm more fully rested than I've been in weeks.

Time to get the keys and go home. The sooner Connor has them reduced to a pile of useless metal, the happier I'll be.

I tug down the sweatshirt I'm wearing—one of Dad's that was in the dryer downstairs. Ideally, I'd have grabbed the 1905 dress from my bedroom, but Simon has eyes in that room, and it didn't seem like a good idea to telegraph any clues about my destination. If male time travelers are okay in jeans, then I guess I'll be a tomboy this trip. And yes, Katherine would be appalled.

God, I hope they're still safe.

Lifting the hook-and-eye latch on the door, I peer cautiously into the store. It's a sunny morning, with light pouring in through the large windows, and it takes my eyes a few minutes to adjust after the dim light in the storeroom. There's a new sign on the wall—a little boy in a yellow raincoat advertising Uneeda Biscuits—and I think Jess moved the candy jars. Otherwise the store looks pretty much the same as when I was here with Kiernan seven years ago. Or a few weeks back, if you're using my calendar.

Jess is behind the counter talking to a customer. He must catch the movement of the storeroom door, however, because his manner shifts from friendly chatter to brisk and businesslike.

The little bell above the door rings. I'm about to peek out again, to see if it was this customer going or a new one entering, when Jess says, "Whoever you are, come on out, but keep your hands above your head. If I see a weapon or hands near your pockets, I'm gonna shoot."

I have the strong feeling I've stepped into a cheesy western movie, and I'm a little nervous about going in with him armed. Jess must be getting close to ninety, and the fact that he has severe arthritis makes me wonder exactly how steady his trigger finger can be.

"It's Kate!" I wait a moment, then push the door open slowly, hands raised.

Jess is still aiming the gun, but his grip seems fairly steady.

"What's the name of the drink you like? So I'll know it's you and not your aunt?"

Really?

I think back, but I can't remember the name. "Something . . . *Club*. Started with a C. The stuff is wicked strong. And . . . *Clicquot! Clicquot Club.*"

Now that he's convinced, he stashes the weapon under the counter and breaks into his usual smile, shuffling around the corner to greet me. "Miss Kate! It's been too long. Way too long! I thought it might be you, from what Kiernan said yesterday, but he also told me that precautions were in order."

He hugs me like he did last time, and my return hug is a bit less forced this time. When he pulls away, he says, "You're the younger Kate, aren't you? Not the one he married."

I nod, even though the label *younger Kate* gives me a chill. It's much too close for comfort to the *Younger Pru* and *Older Pru* we've been using to differentiate between Pru's different ages and levels of sanity.

"Thought so," Jess says.

I glance down at my odd clothes, and he laughs. "Well, partly because of that, yes. But you also seem a little shy. The Kate I know best would've already asked if the coast was clear."

"For . . . what?"

"For us to run off to Niagara Falls," he says with a cackle. "Leave Kiernan and Amelia to handle the store. She'd tease right along with me, though she didn't mean it any more'n I did. No way she could love anyone 'cept Kiernan. You could see it in her eyes the day he slipped that ring on her . . . finger."

Jess seems to realize this might be an awkward conversation for me, because his smile fades. He clears his throat and says, "Follow me, and we'll get what you've come for."

He disappears behind the counter, and I follow, standing at the edge as he crouches down and opens a large wooden chest. I can't see inside, but a tiny gust of cold air hits my ankles, so it must be an icebox. One by one, he pulls bottles out and arranges them on the shelf near his head until he finds the red-and-white container full of medallions near the bottom.

"They might be a tad cold. I had them down under the bottles. Figured if anyone did come around looking—" He stops as the bell over the door jingles.

A man is stepping inside, his body outlined by the sun streaming through the doorway. There's no doubt in my mind that it's Simon. I leave the keys in Jess's hands and lean a few feet over to grab the gun under his counter. The man takes two more steps toward us, and I freeze.

Not Simon.

He's the same height, about the same weight, but now that he's away from the glare of the windows, I see that he's at least thirty years older with an olive complexion and thinning black hair. And if he was a few feet closer, he'd be able to see that the gun I'm holding beneath the counter is aimed straight at his chest.

Jess chuckles softly when he sees my expression, but his eyes are a little worried. "Easy does it, girl." Then he says in a louder voice, "I'll be with you in just a moment, sir."

I take a few calming breaths and put the gun back. "Sorry, Jess," I whisper, bending down to retrieve the keys. "It's been a rough couple of weeks for me."

"I can see that. It's been a rough coupla years for Kiernan. You give him my best, okay? And . . . tell him I'm not expecting to see my Irene back, although if by some miracle it happens, I'd be mighty grateful. But I *am* expecting him to make those sons a bitches pay, you'll pardon my language."

"Yes, sir. I'll tell him."

∞

Connor is standing at the workbench, wearing gloves. One of those masks that cover your nose and mouth hangs around his neck, and there's a small torch and several bottles, along with an eyedropper, in front of him.

He casts a dubious eye at the container I'm holding and tugs the dust mask down. "I'd have thought they'd be in a flashy gold-plated urn or something."

"Nope. Nothing but a Ziploc logo on the bottom."

His eyebrows shoot up. "Really?"

"Gotcha."

"Ha. Funny. Now go. But leave the door open, okay? I need some ventilation."

"Can I help?"

"No you cannot. Go. Just . . . you and Harry keep an eye out, okay? I'll be a lot less nervous once I turn these things into cheap costume jewelry."

"Sure, but first . . ." I snag one of the keys from the bucket. "For Daphne."

Connor sighs, giving me a sad smile. "Okay, Kate. But . . . not for long. Once you stop the Culling, we destroy the rest of the keys. The timeline we get is the timeline we get. And it may not be one where Daphne's running around the backyard. If it's any consolation, I feel sure she'll be running around *somewhere*, but . . . we can't keep a key around in order to hold her here."

There's suddenly a lump in my throat, making it hard to breathe. It's not just the idea of losing Daphne, as bad as that would be. It's what Connor's *not* saying that has my eyes on the verge of spilling over. He means we can't keep a key back for him, either. And while I can easily imagine shoving this time train back onto a track where we have Daphne, I don't even remember the track where Connor existed without that key, the track where his children were alive.

"Connor, no—"

"Kate." His eyes hold mine for a long moment. "I need to focus on what I'm doing here, sweetie. Go outside and wait with Harry."

I don't move at first, just stare back at him, torn between the impulse to punch him and the impulse to hug him. "Okay," I say finally. "I'll go. But this discussion is *not* over, Connor. Not one bit."

Dad's on the bench outside the shed, the Colt sticking awkwardly from his belt. I can tell he heard everything we said. He pats the spot beside him and puts an arm around me. I'm glad he knows me well enough to keep quiet, because if we start talking about this, I'm going to lose it. So we just sit there silently and watch as Connor destroys another key.

There's still no sign of Kiernan. I pull out my phone and check the geo app, pressing my finger to the dot on Sixteenth Street.

"She's still at the temple. Unless it's just the phone," I add, because I know that it could be and assuming it's not seems like it's a jinx or something. If Simon or his henchgoons found out she was carrying it, this would be the perfect trap. Leave the phone there, take Mom and Katherine somewhere else, and just wait.

Dad shakes his head. "She's there, Katie. They might have taken a purse, which she never carries, or a backpack. They might even have checked her pockets. But this is your mom." He glances down at the phone in my hand, the one I just pulled out of my shirt. "Where was her phone?"

He's right. It's tucked under the left shoulder strap of her bra, in front and on top, where she can discreetly snag it without digging around too much. She's at least as bad about sticking her phone there as I am. There are some styles of bra that both of us refuse to buy simply because they don't provide adequate phone support. It's still no guarantee they didn't find it, but I push the thought away. The odds are good that she's still got it, and dwelling on the negative isn't going to get me through the next few hours.

Daphne begins to bark as blue light flickers briefly between the branches of the hedge at the back of Katherine's property. I reach over Dad to grab the gun, just in case it's not Kiernan.

But it is. I glance at the time and realize Daphne's intruder alarm is probably what woke Pru up when I watched her through the key earlier.

I squeeze Dad's hand. "Keep an eye on Connor. Kiernan and I are going to talk to Prudence. I just hope she has some idea when and where the virus was stored."

Pru is halfway to sitting, rubbing her eyes with the back of her hand, when Kiernan and I step into the kitchen. He pushes me toward the breakfast nook, pressing a finger to his lips. There's a dab of something that looks like taco sauce on the front of his shirt. "Coffee, love?" he calls out.

I think he's talking to me until Pru says, "Yes, please. I feel . . . funny. Fuzzy."

There's about an inch of coffee at the bottom of the pot. Kiernan snags a mug, which I'm pretty sure is used, from the sink. He adds the coffee and some milk before sticking it in the microwave.

"Where are we?" Pru asks.

"Just a temporary stop. I'll bring it to you. Wait there." He looks at me as he says the last two words, and I slide onto the bench.

When the timer rings, he starts hunting around for something. The sugar bowl is in front of me, so I tap twice on the table. He heaps three spoonfuls into the mug, sips it, and then adds one more before carrying it out to her.

I wait, annoyed that I can't see into the living room. Annoyed that they're not saying anything. But since he knows her better than I do—much, *much* better—I just wait.

"More coffee," Pru says finally. "And I need to pee."

"Um . . . that's the last. I can make another pot, if you'd like. And the bathroom is . . ."

He probably has no idea, since the only room he's been in prior to this is the kitchen.

"Actually, someone else is here," he says, a bit louder. "In the kitchen."

That's apparently my cue to enter. I do so hesitantly, peeking around the corner first. The conversation so far has given me little clue as to which Prudence we're dealing with. Is it the placid, child-like version, or the one who hurled a lamp at Dad's head?

"This is . . ." Prudence is looking around the room when I enter, like she's trying to get her bearings. Her right hand clutches the remnants of the pillow she destroyed. "I was talking to two men. They were going to help me . . . help me find Deborah. Simon has her . . . at least I think it's Simon . . ."

She stops, her eyes narrowing as she looks at the kitchen door where I'm standing. "You."

I'm not sure what I'm going to say until I'm already speaking. "I got them, Prudence. Like I promised. I got your key from Victoria Woodhull, and Tate and I kept you from giving the keys to Saul. Now we just have to stop them from killing everyone—and find . . . and find your sister."

Prudence just stares at me. It feels like we're teetering on the edge of a cliff. I'm scared to speak again, and Kiernan looks like he's holding his breath.

Then her chin comes up defiantly. "It will be better . . . after. You'll see. And it won't kill everyone."

"No. Not everyone," Kiernan says, "But close enough. Pru, you can't really . . ."

Even though he's still talking, I'm too intent on her eyes to follow what he's saying. Maybe there's a moral compass in there somewhere, but we don't have time to search. And maybe that's not the safest route to take.

"Simon is going to kill your sister, Pru. And CHRONOS will never exist. *Tate* will never exist if we don't stop the Culling."

I'm about to add that none of us will exist, at least outside of a key, but Prudence is twisting the shell of the ruined sofa cushion so tightly that it looks like her knuckles will slice through her skin.

"Give me the key. *My* key. The one you took from Woodhull. So I can see him."

I untie the cord from the belt loop of my jeans and hand the key to her. "You can see the coordinates. But you won't see Tate. He's not there anymore, Pru. Whatever Saul told you, the Culling won't fix anything. The keys still exist, but CHRONOS is never created in this timeline. So Tate is never born . . . at least, not the Tate you knew."

Prudence slides her fingers over the key, and for several minutes she browses through the local points, her expression growing more desperate with each one she tries. Finally she flings the key onto the carpet at her feet and grinds the heel of her boot into it. Pointless, and she probably knows that, but maybe it makes her feel better. There've certainly been times I wanted to do the same thing.

Kiernan waits a moment and then asks, "Will you help us fix this, Pru?"

She doesn't respond, just stares down at the still-intact medallion on the carpet. There's a stubborn set to her jaw as she flips her arm over to activate her embedded medallion.

Kiernan grabs her hand. I'm trying to think of something else to say, something to convince her, when I remember the promise I made Tate.

"Tate told me to give you a message when I saw you." She's still staring at the CHRONOS key on the inside of her arm, but her eyebrow flicks upward in a silent question, so I continue. "He said he's sorry. He doesn't blame you . . . for this mess with CHRONOS or for the baby. And he wishes he could make you another mix tape."

She's completely still, staring down at her medallion for so long that I start to worry she's gone catatonic. Then her eyes close, and I expect her to vanish, but she must have broken contact with the location at the last second. A solitary tear leaks from the corner of her eye and down her cheek. Otherwise her face stays blank.

"I don't know where they're keeping the virus," she says in a small voice. "And I don't know where to find Simon. But Saul can't jump. I can *find* him."

∞

MIAMI, FLORIDA
July 13, 2030, 9:50 a.m.

"I've been here before," Kiernan whispers. "The last meeting . . . they wiped the location from my key."

"Not mine," Pru says. "I left early. Shh. This is the door."

We listen, but I don't hear anything. Apparently neither does Prudence, because she inches the door open, looking around, and then shoves it inward.

It's a conference room, with a shiny black table at the far end. The wall to our left is glass, overlooking the ocean. It's stunning. And it's also empty.

"He was here!" she fumes. "I peeked through the door. I saw them in the mirror. Saul and two guards."

Kiernan spins around nervously, eyes flicking between the door we just entered and one at the other end of the room. "You forgot to mention the guards. *Kind of important*, Pru!"

"Why? You've got a gun. And Evie says your friend there is a baby ninja." She kicks one of the chairs aside. "Simon must have changed something. Damn . . . him . . . to—"

Prudence stops abruptly, bending down to pluck something from the carpet. She holds it up to the light streaming in through the window and grins.

Kiernan nods and pulls out his key.

I've no clue why. She's holding up a clump of straw.

∞

ESTERO, FLORIDA
July 13, 2030, 9:53 a.m.

I open my eyes to a larger, more modern version of the barn where Kiernan and I watched three people slit their own throats. We're on the ground floor this time. There are dozens of stalls, but I only see one horse, a palomino, housed a few doors down. There's a faint, oddly familiar smell—sweet, but not in a good way. Horse manure, maybe?

Pru walks over and holds out her hand for the animal to sniff. It immediately nuzzles her arm. She's cooing something when we catch up to her, rubbing the horse's neck as she reaches for the latch to open the stall.

Kiernan clears his throat, and Prudence looks at him, puzzled.

"You can ride later, Pru. We're here to locate Saul, remember?"

She shoots him a petulant look. "I haven't ridden Wildfire in ages—"

"But Simon has Deborah. Remember?"

"Deborah's right behind you," she says with a little smirk. "That's what she called herself in New York. Funny how you keep calling her Kate."

He's about to argue with her, but I just say, "Your *sister*. Simon has your sister." She still doesn't move, so I add, "Are you really going to let him erase Tate? He's counting on you to fix this. So . . . do you want to fix it or do you want to ride a horse?"

"Fix it," she huffs in a singsong voice. And yes, I feel a little guilty for manipulating a mentally ill woman, but I don't have much choice.

"Then come on." I relatch the gate and look behind me for Kiernan. There's a door a few feet to the right, but he's hurrying off in the opposite direction.

Something is wrong.

"Kiernan?" I run after him. The odor is stronger in this direction. It's not manure. It smells a little like the linen closet at H. H. Holmes's hotel.

When Kiernan rounds the corner at the end of the stalls, he steps back sharply, almost like someone has shoved him. One hand is over his mouth. He holds the other toward us, cautioning us to stop. I do, but Prudence pushes forward, so I follow.

An old-fashioned tub, exactly like the one I remember from the other barn, is shoved into the corner. It might even be the *same* tub. This time, however, there's no sheet of glass on top, and the glow of the CHRONOS key isn't coming from above the tub. It's coming from within it.

Saul's knees are bent and tilted toward the back of the tub, but his hands are folded serenely across his shirt. A CHRONOS key hangs from his neck on a leather cord, resting on top of his hands.

He's older than I remember, and although his face is nearly as pale as the tub, the collar and upper half of his white shirt are now the dark, reddish brown of drying blood, like the jagged slit across his neck. A large fly crawls up the side of his face, while several more circle around the tub.

I gasp and cover my nose and mouth, but Prudence shoves Kiernan aside so that she can get a better look. Her eyes are open wide as she stares into the tub. She lowers her head, hair falling forward over her face, and her shoulders begin to shake. Kiernan reaches out for her, but she shrugs him away.

She's not crying. The laughter bursts out of her in waves as she braces herself on the edge of the tub.

"Oh my God," she gasps. "It's perfect! No matter how much I hate the Rat Bastard, this is so, *so* perfect."

"What? You think it was *Simon*?" Kiernan says.

Pru wipes a tear from her eyes, still fighting back the laughter. A speck of Saul's blood must have been on her hand, because there's now a faint pink trail running across her cheek.

"Who else?" she says. "Wasn't me. Wish it had been, but—"

She looks up as the door behind us creaks open. Kiernan pushes me behind him, whipping the rifle up to his shoulder.

The woman jumps back when she sees the gun. Then her eyes shift to his face and she relaxes. "Kiernan. Put that thing away."

"June." He lowers the gun slightly, still looking past her.

She's somewhere between Mom's age and Katherine's. Her hair was probably a lot like mine when she was younger, but it's mostly gray now, and her nose is slightly hooked, like Eve's. And . . . the name is familiar. Kiernan's mentioned her. I glance down at her hands. She's wearing clear gloves like doctors wear.

Right. She's the doctor at the Farm, Nuevo Reino, or whatever they're calling this place in 2030.

June follows Kiernan's gaze, looking back into the garden behind her. "Unless someone else showed up in the past minute, I'm the only one around. Except for my patient. Almost every soul at Estero is gone . . . everyone who wasn't under a key, at any rate. And I'm thinking Simon made sure most of them weren't under a key."

Prudence laughs again, a single snort.

The look June gives her is sad and maybe a little protective—but there's a healthy dose of fear in that expression, too. Kind of how you might look at a pet rattlesnake that's escaped its terrarium.

"I was coming out to deal with the body," June says. "Or to jump back a few days and stop Simon from killing him. I hadn't quite decided which."

Pru reaches down into the tub and yanks her arm back, hard. The bit of Saul's knee that was visible above the rim vanishes and specks of blood fly into the air before evaporating.

"There. All taken care of." She shoves Saul's medallion into her back pocket and starts to wipe her hands on her pants, then apparently thinks better of it when she sees the blood spatter on her arms. "Yuck. I'm going to take a shower and change. Don't leave without me, okay, Kier?"

I step toward the tub, half expecting to see that Saul's knees simply slipped down and the body's still there. The surface is now white, with a few splotches of black where the enamel has chipped away. Not a single trace of Saul. All that remains of my grandfather is the blood on Pru's arms and clothes as she saunters out of the barn. And I'm guessing she'll have no trouble removing the bloodstains from her clothes—just toss them into a corner outside of a CHRONOS field and they'll be squeaky clean.

The three of us just stand there silently for a moment, staring as Pru walks away.

I have a hard time believing that Saul is dead. *And* gone. I'm relieved beyond measure that I won't be the one to kill him. I'm sure that I could do it, given the circumstances, but I'm not especially wild about the idea of killing anyone, even the monster that is—*was*—my grandfather. I don't feel a single shred of regret that he's gone.

What worries me most is the *why* question. What would push Simon to slit the throat of the man who more or less raised him—and to toss his body in a bathtub?

And then I remember that the same man is holding my mom and Katherine, and I have to push down my panic. I don't have time to think about that now, and I refuse to even imagine a scenario where we don't get them back.

Kiernan finds his voice first. "Any idea where Simon might be?"

"No," June says. She keeps looking at me, like I'm a puzzle she's trying to solve. "But he'll be coming back this afternoon. I told him to give it a full twenty-four hours, which would be around dark, but . . . you know Simon. He never listens. I'm guessing he'll be back by three or four at the latest. He'll probably have Patrick with him. And I doubt he's going to be happy to find you working with Pru, since he seems to think you're on his side in this whole schism mess. In fact . . ."

She glances over at the tub as her voice trails off. Whatever she's thinking, she decides not to say it.

"I'm not on anyone's side." Kiernan must notice that June's eyes keep drifting toward me, because he takes my arm and pulls me a step forward. "June, this is Kate."

"I already know her name, kiddo. I'm just trying to figure out why she's here . . . and how she's connected to the near carbon copy Simon has handcuffed to the bed in my clinic."

∞

I don't follow Kiernan into the room. I don't even go inside the building. This is private, between him and . . . her. It felt like a giant intrusion of Kiernan's privacy just witnessing the expression on his face when he realized what June meant. It's like his entire heart and soul were there in his eyes.

And, to be honest, I'm also out here because I'm a little worried about my continued existence. Kiernan said this isn't the same thing as the extra version of myself in the library. That was a splinter, two versions of me from the same timeline with the same key who crossed paths. The Kate inside the clinic—Kiernan's Kate—doesn't belong in this timeline at all. But on the off chance that she and I are carrying the same key, and on the off chance that Kiernan is wrong about any little part of this, I'm keeping my distance.

Because this time, *I'm* the later version. If either of us goes poof, I have a feeling it will be me.

There's a little garden about twenty yards from the clinic with two chairs and a wrought iron bench. I feel a bit more protected over here on the bench than I did on the clinic steps. Squat, barrel-shaped palms surround me on three sides, along with lush, tropical-looking bushes. Birds are chirping everywhere, and even though I can't see the water, I smell it on the occasional breeze—a faint, salty tang in the air. It would be pleasant if it wasn't already too hot and muggy for comfort. And if I wasn't sitting with a rifle across my lap, watching for Simon and Conwell.

The door of the clinic opens and June comes out, carrying two glasses of orange juice.

"Thought you could use a drink out here in the heat," she says. "In this same spot back in 1903, a July morning would have been maybe five degrees cooler on average. You'd still get the occasional scorcher, but nothing like what you see now. Hoped that might change with the last time shift, but Brother Cyrus says it takes a while for the earth to heal itself."

On closer inspection, it's not orange juice . . . it's slightly pinker and sweeter.

"Papaya," she says. "With a few other fruits thrown in. It's one of the few things your twin in there keeps down in the mornings."

"Is she okay?"

"More or less. Pregnancy doesn't suit her, although it might've been easier if she wasn't worried half to death and being forced to jump constantly. We've had two close calls with miscarriage already, so I told Simon she had to have a full day of rest between each jump from now on. That's why he'll be coming back this afternoon. Guess there's some other damned thing he needs her to do."

June sits down in the other chair and adds, "I also thought the two of them could use a moment alone, which I'm guessing is why you're out here, too. Kiernan explained things, more or less. And Kate—the Kate who is in there, that is—has already given me her version of what she thinks Saul and Simon . . . although I guess it's just Simon now . . . are up to. She's talked about pretty much nothing else for the past two weeks."

She doesn't seem to expect me to answer, and I really don't know what to say, so I just drink my juice and let her talk. I'm scared I'll make a misstep, and Kiernan clearly knows June far better than I do. They look at each other like they both want to apologize for something and don't know how.

"She seems to think everything we've been working for here at Estero is based on a lie. That Brother Cyrus's goal was never about bettering humanity in the long run. Never about restoring balance to the earth, like the people have been trying to do here on the Farm for well over a century. She says he's nothing but a murderer, a genocidal maniac."

"What do you think?"

June takes a sip from her own glass and stares at the clinic door for a long time before responding. "I've seen too many *accidents* here over my lifetime not to realize Brother Cyrus is more than willing to . . . sacrifice . . . for the greater good. Sometimes those sacrifices didn't make much sense to me."

She nods toward a large house a few buildings away from the clinic. "The woman in the big house over there scrubbing her father's blood off her body? Technically speaking, she's my mother, but I was ten years older than her when I met her, and I've probably got twenty years on her now, so . . . maybe our roles have gotten a little reversed. I watched the two of them—Brother Cyrus and, later, Simon—push that poor girl through time in so many directions it's a miracle she remembers her name. I brought her babies into this world through the bodies of thirteen different mothers—women who viewed it as the highest honor to help bring about a new world, a world where men and women live as equals, where the races live in harmony, and where we no longer pillage the earth we live on. Where there's no war. Kiernan's mother, Cliona, was one of those women, you know. She died believing that she'd served a higher purpose. I even let Saul convince me it was her time to go. I could have jumped forward. I could have gotten medicine to save her—there's a whole cabinet of out-of-timeline meds in that clinic. But Saul said he'd had a vision. That it was *forbidden*."

I note the sneer in the last sentence. I also note the fact that she called him Saul this time, not Brother Cyrus.

She tosses the last few drops of the juice onto the lawn. Her voice is tense when she continues. "I picked up the body of a nine-year-old boy whose neck had been snapped and repeated the lie that he fell from the second-floor railing. I repeated it, maybe even believed it a little, because I didn't want to accept that everything I'd practiced my entire life might be a lie. We all knew Saul was a little crazy, but that didn't mean he wasn't telling the truth. If you look back through history, most visionaries are one step away from madmen."

I give her a hesitant shrug. "I suppose. But Saul never wanted to help anyone. He didn't want to create a better world. He just wanted to win. To be proved right. And I think Simon might be the same."

"Anything Simon is, Saul made him," June snaps. "The fact that Saul's own cruelty came back around to bite him on the ass may be the closest thing I've ever seen to evidence that there's justice on this earth."

"But . . . you said you were thinking of going back to stop him?"

"Not for Saul's sake. For Simon's. I should never have told him Saul was here earlier this week. If he'd been forced to go looking for Saul, maybe he'd have had time to cool off. The boy has blood on his hands now, and it's partly my fault."

From what Kiernan has said, I suspect Simon's had blood on his hands for a very long time, but I don't correct her.

"'The earth belongs to those who follow The Way and glorify their *inner* power,'" she quotes. "'Those who falter cannot be blessed.'"

Despite the heat, I feel a tiny shiver. "From the *Book of Cyrus*?"

June nods, a defensive little wall going up behind her eyes. "Chapter eleven, verse thirteen."

"What does it mean?" She gives me an odd look, and I add, "I understand the *words*. I just wondered what they mean to you. How do you interpret them?"

"You have to find your peace from within. That's your inner power. Murder isn't part of The Way, and striking Saul down means Simon will never know peace."

It's an interesting interpretation, although it's not the first one that comes to mind for me. I can think of at least a dozen other verses from that little book that could be used to justify murder as the strong taking their rightful dominion over the weak. I wonder how June interprets those verses. Does she twist them into something she can accept? Or maybe her eyes just glide past them as she reads because they don't fit her personal interpretation of her faith?

I'm tempted to tell her what Tate said, that the *Book of Cyrus* was written as a joke when he and Saul were stoned out of their minds. But I'm not sure she'd take it well, nor am I sure it would serve any real purpose, so I shift to something concrete.

"Do you think Simon will know any peace if he's responsible for the murder of nearly a billion people? Because that's what happened with the last shift. The one you say erased most everyone here at Estero."

She considers it for a moment. "I don't think he'd see it as murder, so . . . I can't say. But he loved Saul at one point. Worshiped him, even. And there's some good in Simon. Otherwise Kiernan would be dead by now. Simon passed a test of loyalty—not to Saul, but to Kiernan—that I failed when I let Cliona die. I can't sit in judgment."

June looks up from her empty glass and adds, "I suspect Simon's also the only reason that another version of you is in that clinic with Kiernan now. How do you feel about that? Are you in love with Kiernan, too?"

"No."

I can tell by June's expression that she doesn't quite believe me, so I go on. "I could've been. It would have been really easy to fall in love with him. But there's already someone else, and . . . I guess my heart was spoken for. Good thing, right?"

And it *is* a good thing, because there's a part of me that is still a little possessive where Kiernan is concerned, still inclined to corner my Other-Self and tell her that she'd damned well better be good to him. That she'd better not ever break his heart again. Which is stupid on several levels. Leaving him wasn't exactly her choice. And if I feel that way about Kiernan when I'm in love with

Trey, how much more must she feel—married to him, carrying what I really, really hope is his child?

We both sit there, lost in our own thoughts, until Kiernan comes out, slamming the door behind him. "We're leaving, June. I need to find some tools to remove those cuffs and get her away before Simon arrives."

"That's not a smart plan, and you know it. If Simon shows up and she's not here, he'll just backtrack and stop you from leaving." She nods toward me. "While you both have guns, he'll be armed, too, with at least one other jumper tagging along, probably Patrick. And if something tips them off that you and Pru are here, this place will be crawling with a hired security team, so I really hope Simon jumps in without winding back to check the comings and goings today. Pru yanking Saul's medallion wasn't the smartest move, either. Simon will know I wouldn't have handled it that way."

I've no clue about the last part, since I really don't know her, but she's definitely right that Simon will have the upper hand if he realizes we've been here.

Kiernan curses softly and runs his hands through his hair. He stares at me for a moment and then grabs June by the shoulders. "Has he had her here the whole time, June? She said she told you who she was! Why in bloody hell didn't you try to find—"

Her hand comes up and smacks him smartly across the face. "And why should I? She's why you walked out on a dying mother—"

"Don't you bring my mum into this!" he snaps, but he takes a step back, releasing her.

June steps forward again so that she's right back in his face. "You walk away from her, from me, from everyone who ever loved you, from everything you believed—"

"Because the Cyrists were built upon a bloody lie! And you know it, June. I think you've known it for years, so don't lay a guilt trip on me."

Her eyes are blazing, which strikes me as odd since she basically admitted the same thing to me only a few moments ago. Not that the faith was a lie, but certainly that it was built by a deeply flawed leader.

But she doesn't back down. "Did your mother think it was a lie? No, she didn't. If it gave Cliona's life purpose, then to me, it doesn't matter if it was a lie. And tell me, how was I supposed to find you? I looked for you when she was dying . . . jumped all over the damned place. Even asked Simon and Pru, and I'm guessing they could have found you. And even after you knew, after you knew she died wanting to see your face one last time, you didn't even have the decency to jump back and grant her that."

Tears stream down Kiernan's face. "Because she'd have asked me again, asked me if I believed in the truth of Brother-Bloody-Cyrus's message, and she would have known, no matter what I told her, that I don't. That I hate everything she found holy. This way at least she died thinking there's a chance I'll be among the Blessed, that I'll find mercy, even if you and Saul couldn't find the mercy to cure her."

June winces, almost as though Kiernan struck her. A flicker of regret crosses his face and he softens his voice a bit, but there's no questioning his resolve as he speaks.

"My loyalty right now lies with the woman in your clinic and the child she carries. Cliona's grandchild. If you ever loved my mum, you'll help me end this so I can get them to safety."

They start to argue again. I step between them. "We don't have time for this, Kiernan. Did . . . she . . . have any information about when and where we could intercept the virus?"

He shoots me an annoyed look, obviously aware that I'm trying to get him back to our original objective when every instinct is telling him to get his wife and child out of danger.

"She never saw all of the vials together. They delivered them to five of the regional temples, but not to North America yet." He turns to look at June. "She said you never had the vials here at Estero? It seems like the clinic would have been a natural spot—"

"No, I had the vials," June says, her voice still a bit shaky. "I ordered them years ago from the medical supply company—four hundred units. But I refused to help Saul with the virus when he came here to pick them up. The oath I took said 'first, do no harm.' No matter how necessary this Culling might have been in the grand scheme of things, I told him I wouldn't have any role in taking lives, no more than a medic would in wartime. That's not my path along The Way. If he wanted to parcel out whatever he had in that cryo kit of his to fill those vials, he'd have to do it on his own."

"And Saul was okay with that?" Kiernan seems skeptical.

"Yeah," she says. "It surprised me, too. I half expected refusing him to be the last thing I'd ever do. Maybe he just didn't want to get rid of his only doctor who can use the key, but I think it's more that he was kind of glad to do it himself."

"And then Simon got the vials from Saul in Miami?"

"I guess, Kiernan. What has me puzzled is why you don't know all this from Simon. He's been trying to convince all of us for the past six months that you're back in the fold, the Prodigal Son returned at last. Trying to convince your Kate, too. Said he had you keeping Pru out of Saul's hair—keeping her occupied, out of trouble, helping her make contact with her sister."

My mouth falls open. *Helping her make contact with her sister?*

Kiernan avoids my gaze, but his eyes flick nervously toward the rifle in my hands. "Let's just say Simon's been . . . judicious . . . with what he reveals to me, and he's had a great deal of *leverage* over my actions for some time now. Once I found out he was holding her . . . yes, I did everything I could to make him think I'm on his side. Keeping Pru out of their way was my idea. You know as well as I do that Saul would have liked nothing better than to snap her neck. Even Simon thinks Pru's more trouble than she's worth, and I'll admit there are times . . ." He shakes his head. "Simon swears he's kept Kate hidden for the past few months—only it's six and a half *years* for me and, what, four years maybe for him?—because he was trying to hide her from Saul. That he did it for me. That he was supposed to erase her, but he . . ."

Kiernan's eyes slide toward the barn where we found Saul's body. Whatever he was going to say, he doesn't finish it.

"Maybe Saul forced him to choose?" June says in a softer voice. "And Simon's never been the type you want to back into a corner. Saul should have known that."

The sound of a slamming door in the distance reminds me that I probably don't have much time before Prudence joins us. "Could we just back up a bit? Back to the part where you helped Prudence find my *mom*? Because I'm having a hard time getting past that."

Kiernan sighs. "Prudence has debated contacting her sister every single day I've known her. All I did was say it might not be a bad idea."

"Which intentionally put Mom in harm's way!"

"Your mother is safe, Kate. So is Katherine."

This is the second or third time he's told me this. "I get that you're trying to be reassuring, but it really isn't helping since there's no way you can know that."

"Yes. I can. They're both at the Sixteenth Street Temple. They're both okay." He pulls the CHRONOS key out of his shirt and scans for a stable point. "Do you want to see them?"

I clench my teeth, angry tears springing to my eyes. "You know damned well I do."

I snatch his key toward me. Once I stabilize the view, I see Katherine and Mom in a dimly lit room. The time stamp is 8:45, right after Kiernan and I left Katherine's house with Prudence. Mom and Katherine are seated facing each other across a metal bench-style table. It looks familiar, kind of like a gym or . . .

It's the room where Trey and I attended the Cyrist youth meeting. Mom and Katherine are eating doughnuts. Neither of them seems too enthusiastic about it, but their hands aren't tied. They look much more comfortable than either of them did when Simon let me see them earlier.

Two men are seated at the next table, talking. I don't recognize either of them. There are guns on the table in front of them. Two Dobermans, quite possibly the two that I fought in the other timeline, rest nearby.

There's a flash of blue light as one of the doors along the wall opens. Another man enters, and I do recognize him. It's Kiernan.

I break eye contact with the medallion and stare up at him. "How?"

"Come on, Kate, you *know* how."

"Fine then. *Why? When?*"

"Because we need someone on the inside. We're walking a bloody tightrope, and we need every advantage we can get. I'm the reason the phone is still on your mom. I made sure I was the one who searched her. I even slipped Katherine some pain medicine around five, and while I don't think it's what she usually takes, she's doing okay. They're both okay. And when? On and off between all of my other jumps. This was . . . between leaving you in 2308 and giving Max your coordinates."

"How long are you there?"

"Until around nine-ten. Then I went back to my time. Rested up a few days, then jumped to the location you gave me at the hotel."

I understand a little better how Connor and the others feel now, because I'm ticked off that he left me waiting there in a Juvapod in 2308 while he made all of these side trips. And that's stupid. I waited exactly the same amount of time either way, but it still feels inconsiderate.

"But why didn't you just *tell* me? I've been worried sick—"

"And so have I!" he yells. "I've been worried for the past six years! Hiding away for weeks on end so I'd be able to use the key to spend a day with Pru and get information to feed Simon. A few more weeks at the cabin, or at Jess's, so that I could spend a day feeding Simon that info and then doing whatever the hell he wanted, because it almost always included two or three jumps— another bloody Yankees game, popping up in the middle of some battlefield, planting ourselves into the crowd scene in some film. Do you know how many movies have me and Simon in them now? At least a dozen, including that one with the DeLorean."

He stops for a second, clearly trying to rein in his temper. "So . . . I get that you're angry, love, but don't talk to me about being worried for a few hours, okay? No offense, but you're not the best actress, and you're being watched when you're there. You needed to look scared. You needed to look worried. And don't blame me for lying to you about any of this. Not when you know bloody well you'd have lied to me every hour of every day if someone was holding Trey."

I have every reason to still be angry, no matter what Kiernan has just said, but it's hard to ignore the anguish in his voice. And while I'm not comfortable with some of the choices he's made, he's dead on with that last statement about Trey. I know it, and he *knows* I know it, so we might as well just move on.

"We don't have time for this discussion," I say, struggling to keep my voice calm.

"I agree. But I need you to trust me . . ." He pauses, probably because I squeeze my eyes shut in frustration at those two words. "I need you to trust me if we're going to get through the rest of this. Anything I've done has been to keep you—*both versions of you*—and everyone else safe."

Another door bangs shut, closer this time. I jump to my feet, turning toward the sound. It seems to have come from the direction of the barn. A moment later, Prudence barrels down the path between the buildings, her body leaning forward, her face pressed close to the horse's white mane.

Kiernan mutters a curse. "June, can you follow her in the jeep? Maybe it's best that she has something to occupy her for a bit, but we do need to keep her in sight." June nods, and he adds, "Oh, and is that key you've got in the field expander the one my Kate was wearing?"

"Yes. Why?"

"Because I need to run a test before Kate meets Kate."

∞22∞

ESTERO, FLORIDA
July 13, 2030, 10:47 a.m.

It's not the same as being in the room with the other Other-Me, the one at Katherine's during the fire. No feedback loop this time, and this Kate is so thin and so obviously pregnant that even though I was in an almost identical toga not so long ago, I don't feel like I'm looking in the mirror. But it's the nonphysical similarities that are the most eerie. We've jinxed each other three times in the past five minutes. It's to the point where we both hesitate momentarily before speaking, certain we're about to make the exact same observation.

Her right hand, the one with knuckles chafed like my own, grips Kiernan's arm fiercely, almost as though she's scared he'll vanish if she lets go. Two pairs of black cuffs secure her to the bed—one around her left wrist and the other around her right ankle. Her upper arms are marked with small circular bruises where some-one—Conwell, probably—grabbed her.

The good news? We don't carry the same key. I sat outside, under the protection of my spare, for ten minutes while Kiernan was inside this CHRONOS field with the other one. And then he tested my spare key, too. All of the keys are still here. It was more a case of double-checking, anyway, since Other-Kate says the key in this field-extender gizmo of Simon's is Katherine's original key—the one Katherine wore at CHRONOS, the first key I ever held, the one I'm pretty sure Katherine is wearing today.

The field extender, wedged into a corner of the examination room near the sink, is an odd contraption. It looks kind of steampunk to me. The only similarity to Connor's gadget is that it extends the range of the key. It's shaped a bit like a hand mirror, with the CHRONOS key embedded in a wire brace at the top, and has a long handle that branches off into two separate grips. Dozens of booster cells are attached to the clinic walls. They look more like stick-up air fresheners than the tiny booster cells Connor uses to extend the range of the key to clothing or other items.

"No," she says, tapping the sheet of paper where Kiernan is making a note. "Sydney was before Brussels. Patrick would hand over the tray, I'd say a few words to bless it before giving it to the Templar to distribute. And then we'd leave. And I think most of the district leaders—whoever those forty people were who got the vials—believed they were something that would *save* the faithful, not the thing that's going to kill them."

"But the regional Templars know?" I ask.

"I think so. Rio was the last jump, the only one where there was a public appearance. Simon and Conwell argued about it. Conwell wanted it, Simon didn't, since he was worried Saul might see, might notice differences between me and Younger Pru. And Simon was livid that I made a scene. He said my screaming out like that could ruin everything. Big fight between him and Conwell. Simon wanted to go back and change it so I never gave the speech, but Conwell wasn't down with that. When we came back here, Simon was raging about how Saul would figure out he'd saved me, and now he'd probably have to kill all of us—me, Mom, Katherine, even Pru—just to shut Saul up. He didn't mention killing you, Kiernan, so I guess you're still his golden boy."

There's a teasing note to her voice, and she smiles as Kiernan strings together several choice words about Simon.

"But," Kiernan says, "we'd better hope I'm still in his good graces. Otherwise getting your mum and Katherine out of the temple is going to be complicated."

He's looking at her when he says it, and I really want to scream that it's *my* mother and *my* Katherine in danger. I squash it down because it's unfair, unkind, and unimportant—and because it hurts to even think about the fact that Mom and Katherine, not to mention Dad and Connor, don't exist in her timeline. Or do they just exist without her?

"*Did* Saul figure out that Simon didn't erase you?" I ask.

"I don't know. The last I saw of Simon was when he dropped me here at the clinic. I fainted back in Rio. Just after I threw up on Conwell's shoes."

"Why did Simon bring you here? Or rather, *now*?"

"I guess because he knew June would be here. And probably Saul. June took care of me when I nearly miscarried a few months ago. It was . . . earlier . . . an earlier time period, though, maybe 1960s? The medical equipment in here doesn't change much, but . . ." She nods toward the screen on the wall. "That was a small square box with rabbit ears when I was here before. Black and white. I spent about a week watching *Gilligan's Island* and a bunch of other old shows, but they weren't reruns. This time when we arrived, I didn't find out we were in the same time as Saul until June found the body. Simon wanted me to leave when he did, but June told him I needed at least a day to rest before I jump again. It's partly the pregnancy, but mostly it's that thing." She gives the field extender a hateful look.

"I get that it extends the CHRONOS field, but why does it make you sick?"

"It makes everybody sick," Kiernan says. "It was designed by one of the guys who joined the Koreshans back in my time. He came down with Edison one summer and stayed. I think he worked with Tesla before that. Kind of an oddball. I talked to him occasionally. Saul sent back some plans, and the guy spent a couple of years working on the bloody thing. I think the principle is the same as the device Connor put together, except it allows two people with the gene to jump using a single key. It's fine for the person actually holding the key, but hell on the hitchhiker, especially for really long jumps. I tried it a few times, since Simon thought it might be a solution to my difficulties jumping, a way that I could bounce around time with him even when I was tapped out."

"He keeps going, and going, and going," Other-Kate says softly, and a smile sneaks across her face. Kiernan rolls his eyes and returns the smile, but neither of them bothers to explain what's so amusing.

How cute. They have a shared joke.

And although that really shouldn't annoy me, it kind of does, so I direct their attention back to the device. "But why would Saul need it? Didn't you say they had at least as many keys as jumpers?"

"Yes," Kiernan says, reluctantly pulling his eyes away from Other-Kate. "I think the original idea was to maximize the number of people with the gene who could travel under a single key before Pru got the ones from CHRONOS. But it was probably a control thing, too. Anyone with a key had a lot of autonomy. They could change things Saul didn't want changed, and maybe he was a bit jealous that Pru and the rest of us had the freedom to go place to place when he was stuck here. For that matter, more freedom than Saul had at CHRONOS. Eventually people stopped using the gadget. They'd wait until someone—Saul, Simon, or Pru—gave them access to a key rather than feeling disoriented, or worse, puking your guts out after tagging along with that thing."

"So that's how Conwell's taken you along to pose as Sister Pru?" I ask Other-Kate. "And how Simon took you on the trips to watch Kiernan's show at Norumbega?" She nods, and I add, "But . . . if it made you sick . . . why go? I mean, those trips to see Kiernan were—"

"My idea, yes," she says, ripping the words out of my mouth. "It was stupid. I just kept thinking he'd look out and see me in the crowd. That he would put it all together . . . the stars on the ceiling . . . and somehow he'd know I was—" She catches Kiernan's expression out of the corner of her eye. "No! It's not your fault. You had no way of knowing. Of course, Simon knew the whole damned time that *she* was around, that you'd never even realized . . ."

The word *she* sounds a bit accusatory. I guess Other-Kate realizes it, too, because she quickly apologizes. "I'm sorry. I'm not blaming you, either. It's just . . . all of this is new to me. I'm trying to get a handle on things. I didn't know about you until Kiernan told me just now and . . . Simon took advantage of that. Hmph. Of course, he took advantage. He's freakin' Simon."

"It's okay . . . Kate." I force myself to use the name. It's as much hers as it is mine. "Could we just get back to the vials?"

I'm pretty sure the look on her face is the same one I wear when I'm annoyed and don't want to admit it. I doubt she likes being chided for straying off task any more than I do, especially when I'm the one who keeps asking questions.

"Fine." She looks back at Kiernan. "If you activate the key, I'll walk you through the jumps—although we went into an adjoining room for two of them. The date coordinates are easy. September 11th, 8:45 a.m., Eastern Standard. Just adjust the time zone for each temple."

"That's when—" I begin.

She nods, finishing the sentence. "When the first plane hit the twin towers on 9/11. Yeah. Guess they couldn't resist. But it makes it easier in a way—since they're all hit at the same moment, they won't have time to contact the other temples to warn them."

Kiernan runs his hand across the front of the device that holds the key, and I discover another difference. Usually when you pull up a stable point, only the person holding the key can see the location. Even if there are others in the room with the gene, it's a one-person show. This time, however, I can see small beams of light projecting from the key. I guess that would be necessary if two people were blinking in—

"What if two people are supposed to jump but only one blinks?" I ask. "Or only one holds the handle?"

"If the person holding the device has firm contact with the second jumper, she still travels," Other-Kate says, her eyes flicking down toward the bruises on her arm. "But the side effects are magnified in that case. I guess the brain has less chance to . . . acclimate to the location, since it doesn't have the visual. It's disorienting. No one does that twice, believe me."

"Pull that chair over here so you can see," Kiernan says, nodding toward the space just to his right. "Or . . . um . . ." He glances at me, then back to his Kate. "Maybe the other side of the bed there would work better."

It wouldn't. Other-Kate only has one free hand, so he'll have to lean across her in order for all three of us to see. But he's clearly feeling awkward about being too close to me in her presence. I flash back to the memory of the two of us outside his cabin the day he was shot in Copenhagen, my hands in his hair, my legs wrapped around his waist. A hot flush rises to my cheeks, and I tug the chair around to the other side of the hospital bed without comment.

Kiernan pulls up the first location, and I see a small auditorium. I instinctively flick my eyes sharply to the left in order to pan, but the view shifts down to these specks of colored light glimmering on the wooden floor and then up again to the right. That's when I realize it's not responding to me but to Kiernan, since he's the one holding the device.

A flash of white comes into view. It's Other-Kate's dress . . . the one she's wearing now or else a carbon copy.

"How long ago was this for you?"

"Three days. I think. It's hard to keep track when . . ." She chuckles softly. "Never mind. You know that as well as I do. Anyway, this first jump is in Sydney."

In the display, she and Conwell walk toward a middle-aged woman wearing a gray dress and a long gold brocade clerical scarf like the one I remember seeing Conwell himself wear at the temple. He's not wearing it now, so I guess it's something reserved for the six regional Templars.

"That's Jeanine," Kiernan says. "Regional Templar for East Asia."

She's pretty, with dark hair and pale skin. In fact, she looks like Saul and . . . someone else, but I can't quite make the connection. Her smile is nervous as she leads the two of them toward a doorway.

"The other Templars were waiting in the main chapel," Other-Kate says. "There were about forty of them. Conwell said a few words, supposedly on behalf of Brother Cyrus, and then I led them all in the Creed. Afterward, I blessed the vials—they're in this round holder that I'm pretty sure is a communion tray. Anyway, I say a line from the *Book of Prophecy*. 'We cleanse the Earth that we may find mercy.' And then we leave."

She talks us through the other four jumps. We also take a peek at the one she hasn't taken yet—to the Sixteenth Street Temple—just long enough to see Conwell and Other-Kate arrive in the large atrium near the bookstore. Apparently our finding her wasn't enough to change things, and she's still on course to make that jump with Conwell. That's unnerving. We quickly move on to the next jump.

The stable point for the temple in Addis Ababa is in the sanctuary itself. The Templar is a tall woman with ebony skin and closely cropped hair. Her outfit is slightly different from the other Templar, and her CHRONOS key hangs from a wide gold chain around her neck. The chain is nearly invisible against the gold of her clerical scarf, making it look like the key floats on her chest.

"That's Edna," Other-Kate says. "She may be trouble, not just because she wears a key, but also because I suspect she's one hundred percent okay with the Culling."

"Not surprised," Kiernan says. "Pru convinced seven of the historians' offspring to come here and meet with Saul. Four of them rejected him as crazy right out of the box—and my da eventually joined them once he realized the strings attached. Edna and Patrick are the two that Saul won over on ideological grounds."

"Whose daughter—" I begin.

"Esther," Other-Kate says. "Studied some group in Africa. I think—"

"She was friendly with Saul," I say, ignoring her annoyance at my interruption. "Tate mentioned her, said she was with Saul before he began dating Katherine."

"Well, for whatever reason, I never remember Edna or Patrick questioning Saul. And Edna's definitely loyal to Simon. You'll need backup. She's not going to believe anything you say."

"Then I won't try to persuade her. In fact, I don't think we have time for persuasion with any of these people if Simon could be back soon. I'll jump in with the gun and tell them to hand over the vials or I shoot."

"Wow," Other-Kate says, sliding closer to Kiernan. "You didn't tell me Other-Kate was so trigger-happy."

I can even hear the caps and the hyphen when she uses the name. I want to scream, *No! You're Other-Kate, not me.*

But I restrain myself. "Not trigger-happy. Just a realist."

"And if they don't hand the things over?" Kiernan asks. "After you threaten them?"

"Then . . . well, then I shoot." I don't sound all that confident, and he does this annoying little exhale, like he doesn't believe me. "No, Kiernan. I don't like it. I'll probably hesitate. But I'll do it. You know I will. What choice do I have?"

"So then you just jump out of the temple, while keeping the gun aimed at them and holding this tray, which doesn't have a lid, by the way, so you're going to have to hold it level, and somehow *still* have both hands free to use the key?" He shakes his head. "We'll need two people."

"How many jumps can you still make today, Kier?" Other-Kate asks the question just as I'm opening my mouth to ask it, although I wouldn't have tacked *Kier* onto the end.

"These aren't especially long jumps," he says, "but . . . two. Maybe."

"Then I'll have to take a few of them," she says, shaking her head when Kiernan starts to protest. "You have a better idea? Find some way to get me out of these cuffs."

"No," June says from the doorway. "I don't have anything that'll cut through those cuffs or the bed, and I can't even imagine what would happen if you tried to pull something that large with you. And you need to be here in case Simon or Conwell shows up."

"I thought you were keeping an eye on Pru," Kiernan says.

"She's putting Wildfire up. I'll go with Kate on the jumps. Jeanine will give me the vials. I think she'd give them to pretty much anyone just to wash her hands of the affair. I can probably convince Josef, the Templar in Rio, and Bernard, too—and they don't have keys. But Edna and Martin will fight, and they'll have guards."

Other-Kate nods. "Edna, definitely. Addis Ababa was the only temple where I saw armed security. Martin was New Delhi, and I didn't see anyone who was armed, but they could have been hiding."

"But even on the jumps without guards there will be people watching," Kiernan says. "The other Templars."

June shrugs. "They won't be armed. And the rank and file are in awe of anyone who can blink in and out with a key, so we'll have a few seconds."

I shoot Kiernan a very worried look. He's asking tactical questions when the much more important issue to me is why on earth we should trust June.

"What changed your mind?" he asks.

"I never said I approved of Saul's methods. And . . . even if I had, there's no Brother Cyrus now. I've stayed clear of this silly feud between Simon and Prudence, but apparently fence-sitting is no longer an option. Pru's with you, and I'm with her." She draws in a deep breath and then says in a softer voice, "And you were right. About Cliona. About this baby. I failed your mother once. I won't do it again."

This idea of including June bothers me. It really, really does, but I'm not sure we have much choice, so . . .

Twenty minutes later, we've decided on a jump order—Sydney, Brussels, and Rio are first, since June thinks they'll be easier. Then New Delhi, with the guy who might resist and might have guards but who doesn't have a key. Edna in Addis Ababa, who has both a key and armed guards, is last. Kiernan will be watching through his medallion, and he'll jump in as backup there if we need him.

We'll jump in ahead of time at each location and set a stable point in the . . . I don't know what you call them in a church, but if this was theater, it would be the wings. Then we'll skip ahead to when Conwell and Other-Kate arrive, wait for them to do their bit, and leave. June will try to get the Templar's attention and pull her or him aside, then we'll snatch the tray and blink out.

Prudence came into the clinic at some point. She's leaning against the wall when I look up, her face red and puffy. I think back to Katherine's comment about the Shaw women not crying pretty. Even though I didn't get the sense that Saul's death saddened her, he was her father, so maybe there's something under the surface. She must not like me looking at her, however. Her lips press into a firm line, and she turns to go back into the waiting room.

"I think this can work," Kiernan says, pulling my attention back to the discussion. "But, while I really hate to add a wrinkle . . . I think we're going to feel a time shift as soon as those vials aren't handed out. It could even hit when we're in the middle of all this. And you all know how that works—doesn't matter when we are, anyone with the gene, or at least with the active version, is going to feel that impact on the timeline at the same instant. That includes Conwell and Simon."

My stomach sinks. "And Simon's still got Mom and Katherine."

"And the last set of vials. If the shift hits before you're done, I'll blink back into the gym where he's holding them and do my damnedest to get them out. But either way, we need to have Charlayne and the others ready to come in as soon as I give the signal. Someone needs to go back and get them organized. You okay to add in an extra jump?"

Now that the shoe is on the other foot, I get why that question bugged Kiernan so much. "Yes. It was the going three centuries forward, three centuries back, over and over, that tapped me out. And I hadn't had much sleep. These are short hops in comparison—and I can just go from Katherine's house and meet June in Sydney, so that I don't have to come back here. Then from Sydney to Brussels and so forth, bam, bam, bam. Those are so recent, they're barely even time jumps for me, just geographic. I'll be fine."

He nods and looks through the doorway to where Prudence is sitting in an armchair, browsing on some sort of tablet. "And what about her?" he says in a lower voice to his Kate. "At some point, it's probably going to be just the two of you here. Are you . . . comfortable . . . with that?"

"I've spent the last five months mostly with Simon, aside from these lovely recent interludes with that snake, Conwell. Pru's an upgrade." Other-Kate looks at me. "Three things. First, that rifle might be necessary at Addis Ababa, but I think something a little more . . . subtle . . . would be better for the first four jumps. Second, you need this key so you can transfer the coordinates to June. Leave me your spare key and take this one. It has all of the coordinates you'll need."

"Except for Dad's cottage, but I can transfer that." I toss her my spare, which Kiernan snaps into the field extender, and then I reach over to take the other medallion. Other-Kate's hand jumps back from the key at the same instant mine does, and the key falls to the bed. It wasn't much . . . not even what I'd call a real shock. More like a tiny power surge or static electricity.

I reach one finger out and touch the edge of the key, then pick it up and hold it in my palm. Nothing.

"Hand it back to me," she says.

When I do, it's the same abrupt, slightly painful tingle. She hands it to Kiernan, who hands it back to me, but the only time it happens is when the two of us—the two Kates—touch the key simultaneously.

"Maybe it's confused?" Kiernan says. "Two very similar, nearly identical genetic signatures. It's trying to decide whether it's being handed off to someone new or if it's still with the same person."

"I guess." I turn back to Other-Kate. "You said three things?"

"Oh, right. You need my dress. Can you unhook the back, Kiernan?"

"Don't bother. There are six just like it in my closet." Pru is leaning inside the doorway again. She looks at Other-Kate with narrowed eyes for a moment, then back to whatever she's viewing on the tablet. "Although I suspect it's only five right now, because I'm pretty sure the Rat Bastard stole the one you're wearing."

"I don't need it," I say. "Strangely enough, I have a toga back at my place. Custom tailored."

Pru gives me a *suit yourself* shrug, still swiping through what she's viewing. "Does it have pockets? Mine do. With Velcro. They won't hold an M-16, but they're probably the right size for your Colt."

I'm about to ask how she knows about the Colt, but Pru continues, "How many people do you have?"

"For . . . what?"

She sighs, a world-weary gesture that suggests she's surrounded by idiots. "Your rescue team? Kiernan said you were going back to alert them. How. Many. People?"

"Dad, Connor, Trey, Charlayne, and Bensen. So five, plus me and Kiernan."

Pru curses, snapping the cover of the tablet shut. "Do you have any idea how I hate it when idiots prove Saul right? 'We don't need to worry about this Fifth Column,' he said. 'A bunch of navel-gazing idealists playing spy.' You have *five* people? How are you planning to get into the temple with five people? What happened to Max? Julia? To all of the so-called New Cyrists?"

"Simon went on a bit of a shooting spree," I explain. "He killed Julia and several others who were in key positions in the government. There *are* other cells, but they won't help me rescue Mom and Katherine, at least not until all of the vials are destroyed. They don't seem to get that when the other side can time travel you kind

n/a

of need to do everything at once. So we have five—and me—and, like I said, Kiernan's there, too. On the inside."

Prudence closes her eyes for several seconds like she's praying for patience. "June, take her to my suite and get her into a dress. We need to hurry, and I need to think."

I follow June outside. "Okay . . . what just happened?"

June shakes her head. "Hmph. You just entered into an alliance with a crazy woman. Don't imagine for a moment that she's stable, and you should avoid crossing her. But Pru knows Cyrist International . . . and Simon . . . as well as anyone. If she doesn't run off on a horse ride or decide she needs a manicure or a trip to Fiji, she might actually be an asset. Maybe."

∞

BETHESDA, MARYLAND
September 12, 7:55 p.m.

It's strange to see Charlayne and Bensen sitting on Dad's sofa, the one I used to sleep on three or four nights a week not so long ago. Trey is in the armchair in the corner. An industrial-sized Taco Bell bag sits on the coffee table, with empty wrappers wadded up into a ball beside it.

Charlayne doesn't even startle when I jump in. She's finally getting acclimated to her role as time travel support ops, I guess.

"Another toga?" Trey inquires when I give him a hello kiss.

"Yes. Do you like?"

"I like *this* part," he says, running his hands over my bare arms and shoulders. "But it's hard not to associate flowing white robes with Sister Pru and the Cyrists."

"I know, but I'm jumping straight from here to Sydney, so . . . What's in the bag?"

"Burritos, tacos, nachos. They're probably still a little warm. Take your pick."

"All of the above. I can't remember when I ate last."

He laughs. "I kind of forgot drinks, but I found bottled water in the fridge. And I bought a bunch of extra food because Kiernan said Connor and your dad would probably be here later."

"Calling them now." That explains the taco sauce I noticed on Kiernan's shirt back at Katherine's. The least he could have done was bring me a burrito while they were still hot.

I grab my phone from the counter and dial, rummaging around in the bag for a bean burrito as it rings.

"Is he finished?" I ask when Dad answers.

"Um . . . he's on the last one. Where are you?"

"At the . . ." I almost say it, then remember to be cryptic on the off chance anyone is listening in. "At the place where we ate that really good jambalaya. As soon as he's done, I need you and Connor to come straight here."

"What?"

I huff because I thought Dad would get that. I've said many times that his jambalaya is the best, hands down.

"I'm at—"

"No, no," he says, "I got that part. It's just . . . I looked inside, and you're still in the living room. That's kind of disorienting."

"Oh, yeah. I'll be there another ten minutes or so. But we need to get moving. There's a lot going on. Bring Daphne, too. I don't want her there alone . . . not after today."

"Sure. See you in a few."

I sit down on the arm of Trey's chair and sink my teeth into the barely warm burrito. The fact that it still tastes amazing to me is a pretty good indicator that I'm starving.

"So what happened?" Ben asks. "Did you get the vials?"

"Not yet. That's . . . next." I start to launch into the details of the trip to Estero, but my mouth is full of the last bite of burrito, and I really want a second one.

"Can we hold off on that question for about five minutes? Otherwise I'll have to do it all over again when Dad and Connor get here."

"You need one of those recap sequences," Trey says. "Like, 'Hi, I'm Kate. Here are a few things you might need to know.'"

Charlayne smiles. "Previously on *The Vampire Diaries.*"

"Or," Ben says, "'The Timeline So Far,' like on *Supernatural.*"

Trey gives my knee a gentle squeeze. "I put one of those recaps together for myself once upon a time. It came in handy."

We share a smile. Of course Ben and Charlayne have no clue what he's talking about. And having just sat through Other-Kate and Kiernan trading their little lovers' "in-jokes," I pull the discussion back to TV shows and grab that second burrito. We're doing fake recaps for other shows—with Trey clearly taking first prize for his version of Cartman doing "previously on *South Park*"—when Dad and Connor arrive. Connor holds up the plastic container, now open and not glowing in the slightest. They both seem a little surprised that we're laughing, but hey—it was a nice brain break while it lasted.

Charlayne takes a moment to coo over Daphne, who, despite being a little nervous about the new location, laps up the attention. Dad and Connor pull up chairs from the tiny kitchen table and grab some food from the bag.

"Okay, so previously on *The Cyrist Hunters* . . ."

After I've finished the recap, Connor asks, "So what's Kiernan's signal going to be? For us to get into position?"

"Mom's phone goes silent. You won't see the blip."

"Um . . . that could happen anyway," Dad says. "How long has it been since she charged it?"

"I mentioned that, but he wasn't sure of any other way to get word to you outside the temple. But hold on. There's another way to check."

I grab my phone and go into Dad's room so they don't have to watch me blinking in and out. Then I tug out my key—or rather, Other-Kate's key—and jump forward to 9:25 p.m., which is about fifteen minutes after Kiernan says he used the excuse of a bathroom break to blink out of the temple, and five minutes before our tentative go-time for the rescue mission. I pull up the geo app, and sure enough, it's still active, so Mom's battery must be fine.

When I'm navigating to the stable point to go back to my current time, one of the locations on Other-Kate's key catches my eye. It's outdoors, so it's brighter than the most recent, indoor jumps to the various temples. I think the vivid gold strip at the bottom is the main reason it stands out.

Expanding the view, I see that the gold is a field of wheat beneath a blue, almost cloudless sky. The time stamp is July 21, 1848. Even though I've never been there, the scene is instantly familiar. I'm certain it's the field I saw the very first time I touched the key in Katherine's kitchen. The only thing that's different is that I don't see Kiernan—it's just the field, with stalks of wheat blowing gently in the wind.

Scrolling through the rest of her stable points, I see several other familiar spots—Kiernan's room in Boston 1905 and the stage at Norumbega. There's also one I'm pretty sure is the Chicago World's Fair, based on the date—1893—and the architectural style. July 10th isn't the day I was there, however, and I don't remember seeing that building. It still seems vaguely familiar. Maybe I saw it in a photograph when I researched the Expo. Or . . .

It could be the building I saw that first time I held the key. After the wheat field and before the dark cavelike place.

I file this away as something to ask Other-Kate, assuming we ever have a second when lives aren't on the line. Then I jump back to the present and join the other intrepid Cyrist Hunters in the living room.

"Mom's phone is still going at nine twenty-five. Around nine thirty Kiernan will grab her phone and—" Smash it? Turn it off? He never said which. "And he'll disable it. Somehow. At that point, you need to be ready to come in the side door. Trey, it's the one we ran through when the Dobermans—"

He gives me a wry smile and shakes his head. "Wasn't there."

"Oh. Right. Could someone pull up the temple on Google maps?"

"That reminds me," Connor says as Trey takes the tablet out of my backpack. "Charlayne and Bensen, you need some new jewelry."

He pulls two medallions from the pocket of his jeans and tosses one to each of them. They catch the keys and stare down at them as though they're holding tarantulas.

"Yeah, I know," Connor says. "I don't like the damned things, either. But we don't have any idea when the next shift will occur. We could be in the middle of this rescue attempt, and suddenly the two of you . . . well, I don't know. It depends on how many tracks the time train jumped."

Charlayne and Ben give him a blank look, and I say, "Connor means that you might still be here, still be holding the rifle or whatever. Or you might not. We don't know. Katherine was worried about Trey initially—worried that wearing the key during a shift could harm him since he doesn't have the gene, but he's been okay. So has Jess, the friend of Kiernan's who hid the keys for us."

"But . . ." Charlayne glances over at Ben and then says, "There's a duplicate of you now, right, Kate? Because she was under the key when there was a time shift. Wouldn't we be creating . . . duplicate usses? Which isn't a word, but . . ."

"There's no duplicate me," Trey says, still looking down at the tablet. "I've been under the key during two time shifts."

"He's right. Unless Simon or someone goes back and changes the path of your grandmother, or parents, or something, and I think even then they'd have to be time travelers." I stop and think about it. "Or maybe not . . ."

"No, no, no," Trey says as he puts the tablet into my hands. "Do not follow that rabbit down the hole, Kate. It. Doesn't. Matter. There won't be duplicate Bens or Charlaynes because there are no duplicate Treys. No extra me at my house or in Peru or anywhere else. I checked, okay?"

"Yeah. No extra Connors, or Harrys, either," Ben says, putting the medallion into his pocket. "We'll be fine, Char."

She nods and stashes the medallion in the zip-pocket of her shirt, but she still looks nervous about it. And I don't blame her at all.

"Okay," I say, leaning forward to show them the map that Trey pulled up. "If you're facing the front entrance, it's the road on your left."

"That's Lotus Lane," Charlayne says. "Don't even get me started on their street names—the road on the other side is Cyrist Way. Get it? Ha, ha."

"You seem pretty familiar with the area," Trey says. "Maybe we don't need the map."

"This is my dad's church. Until a few years back, I was there every other Sunday and sometimes during the week, too. Seventeenth Street runs along the back. The playground is over there," she says, tapping one spot on the screen, "along with the basketball court. We used to go out and shoot hoops while we'd wait for Dad to finish sucking up to the other elders. Lotus Lane runs between the parking garage and the temple itself."

"Then the door is the second-to-last entrance on Lotus," I say. "Two of you will need to enter from there—the door will already be unlocked."

"By Kiernan?" Dad asks.

"No. Probably by me. Kiernan will be getting Mom and Katherine out of the gym and into that hallway for you to pick them up. Someone needs to have the van running as close as possible to that entrance . . . but there are security cameras on the grounds, so try not to be too conspicuous."

Pulling the sheet of paper from my pocket—as Pru promised, it has a nice Velcro seal—I show them Kiernan's rough sketch of the grounds, which, unlike the map, has the buildings labeled. "This side over here with the entrance along Cyrist Way is the employee parking lot. That's the day care center and kids' playground Charlayne mentioned. There aren't any activities going on tonight, but the café and bookstore are open until eight, so there could still be people around. And there will be security cameras and at least two guards on duty even after the others leave—and that's not counting the two guys in the gym watching Mom and Katherine. We need to be subtle."

I turn toward Charlayne. "How good are you with that jet pack thing?"

"I'm okay, I guess. But if you're thinking we should use those, it's not a good idea."

"Why not?"

"They're loud. Really loud. It sounds like about a million cans of whipped cream being emptied at once."

Ben nods. "Over a hundred decibels. Definitely not an option if you're going for subtle."

"Okay," I sigh. "That complicates things."

"But . . ." she says, with a familiar, devilish twinkle in her eye, "that could make them an excellent *diversion* if we need one."

"So why did you need the jet packs?" Trey asks.

"To come in from the back, go over this narrow building, and drop down into the courtyard"—I tap the space in the middle—"right here. That's just outside Conwell's office—or what used to be his office. I guess it belongs to the other Templar now. There's a large fountain in the middle and a door along this glass wall. The goal was to have two of you come in that way as backup support for getting Mom and Katherine into the hallway. I was in that office once. It looked like this was a private courtyard, and I didn't see another entrance. I would have asked Prudence, but . . . she sort of took a little vacation while we were discussing that part."

Charlayne's brow creases. "I think there *is* another way in. I remember a walkway—kind of an alley—between the two buildings here, leading out to the employee parking area. I think it's gated, but that shouldn't be a problem. If Ben and I make it into the courtyard, will the office door be open?"

"Um . . . it'll either be open or there'll be someone there to meet you. But you and Ben are the only two who have really trained with those rifles, so I think we need to split you up—one at the side door on Lotus and one coming in from this way."

Charlayne clearly doesn't like it, but she nods and then asks again, "So you'll be the one meeting me at the office door?"

"Possibly me. And . . . possibly Prudence."

There's a collective exhale and a wide array of emotions, mostly negative, on the faces in front of me, and they're all talking at once. Dad says something that ends in "nutcase," and Connor clearly agrees.

Charlayne is the only one who seems remotely pleased. "See, Ben? I told you Prudence wasn't behind all of this—"

As much as I hate to burst her bubble . . .

"I don't really know on that count, Charlayne. All I know is that she's angry Simon has her sister. Kind of angry that Simon . . . breathes. No love lost between the two of them. She still seems kind of torn on the whole Culling thing, half believing it's a necessary evil and half not. I think maybe she's been in it so deep and so long that it's hard to see things clearly. And Dad's right. She's crazy. Totally unstable. But she knows that building better than any of us do. She also knows the Cyrist organization."

"What about the last set of vials?" Connor asks. "Even if you get the other five, you said Simon still has the last one—the one intended for North America."

"Yeah. Forty or so church officials from the U.S. and Canada meet—or met?—at the Sixteenth Street Temple on the 9/11 anniversary, at eight forty-five Eastern Standard. But Conwell and Other-Kate haven't done that one yet." Their expressions are a mix of pained and slightly confused. "Yes, I know it's September 12th, which means it already happened. But Conwell has a key, so it hasn't happened for him or for Other-Kate yet, even though it's already . . . happened. I don't know why."

"Okay," Trey says. "That's headache inducing. So does that mean it wasn't part of the whole shift that you felt earlier? That we're going to get another one? Or . . . what?"

"I don't know. We're in Schroedinger's cat territory, I think—it's both happened and not happened. And since our goal is to make none of those events happen . . ."

I'm even confusing myself at this point, so I just shut up.

Dad has been kind of quiet. He has that look on his face he always gets when he's trying to figure something out. I assume it's just the temporal confusion everyone else is trying to sort through, but then he says, "How are they going to distribute the virus? I mean, I know it's spread from person-to-person contact after the first round of infection, but *initially*. We assume they're putting it into the water supply, but I remember reading a few years back about Homeland Security beefing up their protection at reservoirs, treatment centers, etc. In some of these less developed regions, it might be just a matter of dropping it into the local river or whatever, but here, and in Europe, and in the more urban areas elsewhere . . . they'll have security."

"It's true," Bensen says. "One of the men at the meeting at Langley—the one with the bow tie—was some DHS bigwig. He told us that there was no way. But the Cyrists have members in every agency, probably with direct contact. There could be sleeper agents. And they might even think they're protecting people rather than—"

Ben stops midsentence, as though he's just had an epiphany. He points straight at me, or more specifically, at my hand, which is holding a bottle of water. "Or they could take the commercial route. How many people drink a few of *those* every day? Hit one of the main distributors and . . . you've easily infected enough people in an urban area to reach maximum spread for the virus."

I recap the bottle and put it down. For some reason, I'm not very thirsty anymore.

∞23∞

ADDIS ABABA
September 11, 8:45 a.m.

The gigantic cathedral here in Addis Ababa is probably twenty times the size of the tiny chapel at Six Bridges. There are no dead bodies in the pews, just forty middle-aged clerics settling in and chatting with their neighbors. Still, the nervous feeling in the pit of my stomach, the intense dread I'm feeling as June and I wait for Conwell and Other-Kate to appear, stirs up a strange sense of déjà vu. I'll breathe much easier when these vials are with the others inside the bleach-filled tub in the bathroom at June's clinic.

Things went incredibly, unbelievably well at the first three temples. Jeanine, the Templar in Sydney, looked positively relieved when she saw June in the wings standing next to me. June whispered something in her ear, and I handed her our substitute—an identical communion tray with vials of plain saline. I don't think any of the Templars in the audience even knew we made the exchange. The same thing happened in Rio. The Templar there was the same man who translated at the "Sister Pru" press conference we saw on the Cyrist news. He looked a little confused, especially when he glanced at me, but he nodded vigorously and said, *"Obrigado!"*

Brussels was different, simply because there was nowhere to hide. The temple is a large theater-in-the-round type, with an open stage. All eyes were upon me when I blinked in alone holding the duplicate tray of harmless vials.

I just said, "Sorry. I gave you the ones for Africa—there won't be enough!" Which was total bullshit because all of the trays have exactly forty openings, all filled.

The men and women in the pews laughed good-naturedly, apparently amused that even a demigod or prophet or whatever they think Prudence is can make a stupid mistake.

The Templar smiled, too, although I could tell from her eyes that she didn't believe a word of it. Her fingers tightened on the edge of the tray. Kiernan and June were watching through the key, and I was about to give the hand signal indicating that I needed backup. I tried a simple appeal to the woman's humanity instead. "I think you mean well," I whisper. "But this isn't the way."

I hadn't really planned what I was going to say in advance, and I believe she may have interpreted my *the way* as *The Way.* Whatever. It worked. She took the substitute I was holding, and I blinked out before she could change her mind.

Even New Delhi, where June and Kiernan were both pretty sure we wouldn't be welcomed, went much better than we'd feared. The Templar, Martin Something-or-Other, wasn't important enough that he'd been issued a key, but June said he sucks up to Simon and Saul so much that the other Templars call him Hoover behind his back. She didn't think there was any way he'd hand over the vials without a threat. I followed the same plan that I did in Brussels, except this time June had a rifle pointed at Martin from behind the curtain. At the first sign of resistance, she'd shoot and I'd grab the tray. If for some reason that failed, the Colt was in my pocket, and as a last resort, Kiernan was watching, ready to jump in.

All I had to do, as it turned out, was utter the magic words—*Simon says*. As in, "Simon says I gave you the wrong tray—that's the one for Brussels!" Martin didn't even look uncertain until a couple of seconds later, when his eyes strayed down to my no-longer-pregnant abdomen as I blinked out. But by then, it was too late.

This, however, is Addis Ababa, the African regional headquarters for Cyrist International. The head Templar, Edna Sowah, wears a key, has three armed guards in this room, and by all accounts won't be handing over the vials or her key without a fight. June says Simon recruited Edna, rescuing her from a thirteenth-century African village when she was a girl. June confirmed our suspicion that Edna's mother may even have had an idea that Saul was planning to destroy CHRONOS when they made that last jump. While neither Kiernan nor June know the exact circumstances of Edna joining the Cyrists, they're positive that her loyalty lies with Simon.

If Prudence has any information on that point, she didn't share it. She was off in her own little world during that part of our conversation, stacking some sort of small containers from the clinic cupboards as high as she could until they tumbled down. She played there in the corner for a good ten minutes and then rejoined the conversation as if she'd never gone on temporary sanity leave. The memory of her playing with those cups, saying "Oh, no!" each time the tower collapsed, has me at least as nervous as anything we're likely to face here in Addis Ababa.

We're pressed against the wall here in the wings, so I can't really see the pulpit, just June's mass of gray curls in front of me. So I watch through the key, which probably makes more sense anyway, given that I'll need to jump into the spot Other-Kate is currently occupying only a few seconds after she leaves. The Colt is in my pocket, but I doubt I'll have a chance to reach it, since the hand not holding my key is brandishing a large pair of garden shears.

The plan: Cut the gold chain. Catch the communion tray when Edna vanishes. Snag her key. Blink out.

Edna is speaking now, something about the great honor, a rare appearance from the "mother of our faith," a title that probably wouldn't go over well with Prudence from what Kiernan has said. And then I hear Conwell's voice, with the same message from Brother Cyrus he's given on the other four jumps. The day of reckoning is nigh, but the faithful may know mercy. Yada yada yada.

The Creed follows, led by Other-Kate, whose voice is reedy and hesitant until the Templars join her. Then she blesses the vials. "We cleanse the Earth that we may find mercy."

Immediately after, Patrick grabs Other-Kate's arm, and they're gone. That's my cue. I draw a deep breath and blink in.

I start raising the shears toward the key on Edna's chest as I open my eyes, hoping to benefit from the element of surprise. Edna startles, moving her arm in front of the shears. The edge scrapes against her forearm, but the blades snip easily through the gold chain holding the key.

The medallion clatters to the floor. I drop the shears as well, freeing my hands to catch the tray of vials when Edna disappears.

Except, she doesn't disappear. And when I bend down to grab the key, her knee connects hard with my shoulder.

She's wearing a spare. I was afraid of this. I'm wearing a spare, Kiernan's wearing a spare, so why wouldn't at least *some* of the Cyrists have a spare?

Edna lets out a staccato scream. A fine mist of blood sprays from her head, and the tray falls from her hand as she slumps to the floor. I catch the tray one-handed and, unfortunately, at an angle. Two of the vials tumble out and roll away, one toward the Templars in the audience and the other toward June. She drops the rifle from her shoulder as she stares at Edna. Her face is ashen. I say a silent prayer that she doesn't pass out.

Shouts arise from the audience. The two men in suits at the back of the auditorium come rushing forward just as a flash of blue lights up the space underneath the second pew. Three Templars spring up from their seats as if they've seen a snake. I catch a fleeting glimpse of a man's hand scooping up the second vial, hopefully still intact, as I dive behind the pulpit. Someone yells for everyone to get down, and a few of them comply.

When I peek around the edge, the blue light has vanished.

Two shots ring out. I can't wait any longer. I should have blinked out as soon as I had the tray and the key—something Kiernan stressed several times when we were planning—but I'm worried about the last vial and about the look on June's face. I give one last glance her way before pulling up my stable point. The little bottle is maybe two yards from June, and she's diving toward it when I blink out.

∞

ESTERO, FLORIDA
July 13, 2030, 3:47 p.m.

The bleach fumes hit my nose before my eyes open, and I sense Kiernan nearby. He yanks me aside. June appears about three feet behind us, the last vial in her hand. Blood pours from her right arm, a few inches above the elbow.

"Flesh wound," she says between gritted teeth. "Entry and exit points, thank Cy . . ." She stops and grimaces, then continues, "Thank God." The two of them stick the vials they retrieved into the empty spaces in the tray, and Kiernan pulls on the long rubber gloves and stacks it on top of the other four already in the tub filled with bleach. Each of the vials in the other trays has already been punctured using the large ice pick on the floor by the tub, allowing the bleach to seep inside and destroy the virus.

"Did you get Edna's key?" Kiernan asks, glancing up at the clock near the doorway. It's 3:27, still several hours before June told Simon to arrive, but less than a half hour from her estimate for his actual arrival. And that was her estimate *before* we started mucking around with the vials. We still haven't felt any countershift, anything pushing us back to a previous timeline, but what if Simon gets—or got?—a call from Addis Ababa?

"Yes," I tell him, "I got this key. But she must have had a spare. Are we sure she's dead?"

"She's dead," June says, glancing toward Kiernan. "How on earth did you get that other vial, kiddo?"

Kiernan starts rummaging through the cabinets. June nods toward the one on the right. Once he has the gauze open, he answers her question. "When I saw we were in trouble, I jumped back to last night and set a stable point under the pews. Knocked the bloody hell out of my head trying to reach the vial. There's a Templar who may have a broken toe, too." He shoves the gauze and antiseptic into my hands. "Can you take over here? I need to see about—"

I nod, and he leaves to check on Other-Kate. Luckily June knows what I need to do, and she talks me through it. By the time I have her sleeve cut away, the wounds disinfected and packed with gauze, and the entire thing wrapped and in a sling, she's looking about as faint as I feel. I'm sure she's seen plenty of blood before, so she's probably woozy from the blood loss and maybe a bit shaky from having taken a life. My reaction is from the sheer amount of blood, which has my mind skipping back to the floor of Julia's office, the car seat beneath the guy's head inside the blue van, Saul's body in the tub, and the spray of blood that filled the air moments ago in the chapel at Addis Ababa. I've seen far more blood in the past few days than in all my previous seventeen years, and hopefully more than I'll see in the next seventy.

Kiernan sticks his head back in, motioning to me. "We need to go. June, can you finish off this last tray with just the one arm?"

"I think so. Good thing I'm a lefty. Don't know if I'll still be able to handle that rifle, though."

"You don't need to. Kate, can you go forward—no, I mean *back*—and set a stable point in Bensen's van when it's parked outside the temple?"

"Uh . . . yeah, I guess. But I don't have the location."

"I have one set near the parking garage and another on the other side at the Cyrist Way entrance. Near the playground. I transferred them to your key." I glance down at the key around my neck, confused, and he shakes his head. "No. That's *her* key. *Your* key is still in the field extender. Swap out so that you'll have all of your local stable points. Once you find the van, come back and get June and Kate out of here."

"No," June says. "I'll stay. In case Simon comes back."

"That's why you need to *go*," Kiernan says. "If he sees these vials—"

"When have you known Simon to hang around the clinic? He'll pop into the room where your Kate is, and all he'll see is me, wounded. I tried to stop you, and you shot me."

"Unless he's already spoken to someone in Addis Ababa," he counters.

"It's possible. But it's damned hard to find a time traveler. Simon might have a message waiting for him somewhere, but it's not like Edna's people can phone him directly."

Kiernan's still shaking his head, and she finally says, "Leave me the stable point. If I need to escape, I will."

I'm about to remind the two of them that his Kate is still attached to a hospital bed when I see her in the hallway. She's dragging a rather large piece of plastic from her ankle. There's a cuff attached to her wrist as well, but she's mobile.

"How did—" I begin.

Other-Kate raises her eyebrows. "That would be Prudence."

"She was at it when I went in, just before we jumped to New Delhi," June says. "Three versions of Prudence, actually. At the same time with the same wrench."

"I ended up closing my eyes because it hurt my head to watch," Other-Kate says. "She kept talking to herself—herselves, I guess—the entire time. One of them blinked out just before they were done. The splinter thing you talked about, I think," she says to Kiernan.

"Where is she now?" I ask.

"Gone. One of . . . her . . . said she'd see us later and jumped out. The other one picked up the tablet she'd been reading and waited in the chair for a few minutes until she finally disappeared. And . . ." She looks from Kiernan to me and back again. "I told Kier a minute ago, but you need to see this, too, because we don't know what it means."

She runs her fingers across the medallion and opens up the view in the field extender. It's the Sixteenth Street Temple stable point we viewed earlier, the jump to get the final set of vials. The jump that Other-Kate and Conwell haven't made yet.

I wait for a moment, expecting to see her jump in with Conwell like the last time we watched. They jump in, walk down the hallway, and enter a door. But nothing happens.

"Can you pull up the time stamp?" I ask.

"It's the same time we watched before. Something's changed."

∞

OUTSIDE THE SIXTEENTH STREET TEMPLE
WASHINGTON, DC
September 12, 9:12 p.m.

As soon as Bensen's van passes the Lotus Lane entrance, I blink into the little niche outside the parking garage. They pass the entrance, pulling up to the curb maybe four or five car lengths from Seventeenth Street. I'm about to cross the street when I see Dad's Subaru coming toward me. Connor is on the passenger side in the front. I give him a little wave from the bushes, and he rolls down the window.

Dad looks over, too, and they both ask, "What happened?" almost in unison. Connor nods at the skirt of the toga, which I've forgotten is a bit on the gory side.

"The blood isn't mine," I say for the second time in recent memory. "June, the doctor at Estero, was hit. Or it could be from the Templar in Addis Ababa. That jump . . . didn't go so well. Dad, can you circle around Seventeenth to Cyrist Way . . . inconspicuously, if possible . . . and look for the walkway Charlayne was talking about? Then head back here. I need to check in with the others."

As I approach Ben's van, I see that the rear seats have been yanked out. Trey and Charlayne are sitting on the floorboard, backs propped against the other side.

"Are you two aware that it's illegal to ride in the District of Columbia without a seat belt?"

Charlayne snorts and nudges the duffel with her foot. "Least of our problems if we get stopped, believe me."

Just behind her are two contraptions with air tanks and a harness, strapped to what looks like a gigantic set of handlebars with a few extra bends along the way. Two motorcycle-style grips are attached to the ends, with silver levers extending parallel to each of the grips that look a little like hand brakes. I say a silent prayer of thanks that I never had to strap myself into that contraption, especially not while in the middle of a time jump.

Trey tugs at the edge of my toga, one eyebrow raised. "You okay?"

"Yes, it's not mine. I'll explain later."

"And you got the vials?" Ben asks from the driver's seat.

"The five sets that they've delivered, yes. Grabbed them and destroyed them. We still have no clue what's up with the ones planned for North America. Simon must have them with him." I set a stable point in the back of the van. "Can you two scooch over a bit? I need to bring someone else in."

I blink out, and when I return, I'm dressed in my jeans and Dad's sweatshirt again, another toga stuffed under my arm, in case I need it.

Other-Kate blinked into the van just before me. In retrospect, I probably should have warned Trey as to exactly who I was bringing in.

"I thought she was you for a moment—"

"Until he saw the baby bump," she says, lowering herself awkwardly into a sitting position against the other wall.

"Well, to be fair," Trey says, "the handcuffs and the . . . is that a bed rail? Those were also clues."

Her eyes give Trey a quick appraisal. "So is this who you chose over Kiernan?" The tone of voice isn't quite dismissive, more curious, really. But there's a hint of something in there that suggests she doesn't believe she'd have made the same choice.

"Yes, he is," I respond, moving a little closer to him as I shoot her an annoyed look. "Trey, meet *Other*-Kate. This is Charlayne, and the driver is Bensen. Fifth Column."

Other-Kate isn't looking at them, however. I don't think she even hears them say hello. She's staring out the passenger side window where Dad and Connor are approaching. Tears are already pooling up in her eyes. Although I want to keep this other me at arm's distance emotionally, my heart goes out to her, because I know exactly what she's feeling right now, and I know how much it hurts. It hasn't been that long ago that I sat across a picnic table looking at the dad-who-wasn't-my-dad in another timeline, who had two little boys instead of me. Does it make it any less painful for her to know that he's *my* dad and I'm *almost* her? Somehow I doubt it.

I should have warned Dad and Connor, too, because they both look like they've taken a blow when they see her.

"Sorry," I say. "I had to get her out of Estero. And she can help. She'll be doing surveillance, watching some different locations to keep an eye out for Simon, and also monitoring the three stable points we have here—one inside the gym, one outside the parking garage, and the other over near the playground and employee lot. But once we get Katherine out here, someone needs to keep her and Kate apart. I think they've got the same key, and it *might* not be an issue, but . . ."

"It's not an issue," Other-Kate says. "Different person, probably a different time stamp for the key."

"Fine. But is it worth risking it?"

She shrugs. "I'll jump to the stable point near the garage when I see them coming and hide in the Gray Ghost."

Dad nods, and there's an odd expression on his face when she uses the car's nickname. He shakes it off visibly, eyes moving from Other-Kate back to me. "We checked the employee lot. The walkway is there. Gated, but not guarded, about seven feet high. I think I could climb it. I'm certain Charlayne or Trey could. But it looks like there are surveillance cameras on that side."

"Yeah, but the parking lot is open to the street," Connor says. "Five cars still there, and the cameras aren't pointing at the gate. Security could just think it's someone leaving late."

"So we try stealth first, but if security heads that way . . ." I look over at Charlayne. "Maybe create the diversion you mentioned back at the cottage?"

"We have it ready," Charlayne says as Ben pops the rear gate of the van. "That's why he parked so far down. The playground is shared between the temple and the day care center. It backs to Seventeenth. We'll go over the fence and strap these puppies to two of the trees. I also have a few M-80s."

"M-80s?" I ask.

Charlayne grins. "Cherry bombs. Hella loud."

Bensen is at the back of the van now, pulling a black ski mask over his face. "Those are just to draw attention. I have a timer to start the motors—it's the gadget Tilson and I were working on when we thought Kate might have to use these things to jump into CHRONOS. So you'll have an explosion, and then the jet packs will stir up every speck of pine straw, leaves, dirt, you name it, within a ten-foot radius. It'll look like a dust tornado has swooped down on the parking lot. Security will be focused on *that* side of the grounds at least for a few minutes."

"Okay," Trey says. "Sounds like a good backup plan if we can't sneak in. I'll go with Charlayne, and Ben can take this door with . . ." He looks from Dad to Connor.

"With me," Connor says. "Harry's the driver. We drew straws back at the house. Do you have another face mask, Ben?"

Dad's expression is fleeting, just a subtle tightening of his mouth, but I know instantly they didn't draw straws, flip a coin, or even discuss this matter earlier. And Connor seems to know I know, because he gives me that same look he gave me back at Katherine's when he was destroying the keys.

"Okay," Ben says, handing Dad something that looks like a remote control wrapped in electrical tape. "Charlayne and Trey will set up the jet packs in case the diversion is needed, and then they'll head back around the preschool building. If they don't get in—or if you see security moving toward them—start the motors and fire off a few M-80s to draw attention in that direction."

"We have a stable point at the front entrance," I tell them. "One that Kiernan set. Other-Kate can watch it, and that should give you a few seconds' notice that they're coming."

"More than that," she says. "I'll watch a minute or so ahead. Someone just needs to leave me a cell phone so I can call him."

Trey tosses her his phone. "His number is under recent calls."

"Okay," Dad says. "So once they're in, I circle back around and watch for the rest of you on this side?"

"Yes." Connor straps one of the rifles over his shoulder. "And then we all get the hell out of here before the cops arrive. Because I really don't think it will take very long, especially if you do have to set off that diversion."

They start discussing the exact timing, and Ben shows Dad his gadget to start the engines. I'm paying attention, but only with half of my brain. The other half is cycling through the many different ways that this could go horribly, horribly wrong.

For the first time, I get—I *really* get—how stressed Dad is when I'm about to go on a jump. Watching people you love walk into danger is a hundred times harder than walking into it yourself. I catch a glimpse of Other-Kate from the corner of my eye, and she's watching them, too. She gives me a shaky half smile, her eyes as worried as I feel. Even though she doesn't know Trey, Charlayne, or Ben, I guess this dad and this Connor are as close as she'll ever get to her own versions. She hasn't seen them for months, maybe never thought she'd see them again, and here they are preparing to go all Rambo.

And what pisses me off most is that none of them should have to be here, or at the very least we shouldn't be in this alone. The Fifth Column—or rather the rest of the Fifth Column—should be supporting us. And in a sane world, a world where the Cyrists weren't running things, we wouldn't be worried about whether the authorities will catch us. If, by some crazy set of circumstances, my mother and grandmother had been kidnapped by a madman, the authorities—the ones who are actually trained for this—would be the ones running the show.

∞24∞

OUTSIDE THE SIXTEENTH STREET TEMPLE
WASHINGTON, DC
September 12, 9:23 p.m.

I don't like this hallway.

I'm almost afraid to open my eyes, scared that I'll see Eve in the doorway up ahead, her face bleeding from being whacked with that office chair. I can almost hear the Dobermans barking even though I know they're at the far end of the corridor right now, in the gym with Kiernan, Mom, Katherine, and the security guards. The dogs are already snoozing, and one of the guards is nearly there, thanks to a little something extra in the filling of the jelly doughnuts they wolfed down. The other one told Kiernan he's eating Paleo (which I had to explain), but I think he sneaked a doughnut when nobody was watching, because he's looking a little groggy now, too.

What I don't know is where—or when—Simon is. Or Conwell. Or Prudence, for that matter, and she's supposed to be here. This was *her* stable point, the closest one she had to the Templar's office, and she should have been here when I blinked in.

I press my back against the wall of the dark hallway and pull up the stable point in the gym. Katherine's head is on the table, like she's napping, even though Kiernan says their doughnuts were just glazed, without the knock-out meds. Mom is upright and alert, her eyes scanning the room. I don't know if Kiernan gave her a heads-up or if it's just her Spidey sense, but she knows something. Kiernan is casually leaning against the edge of the table, talking to the guards. One of them glances up at the clock and—

"Psst!" The voice is little more than a whisper, but it startles me. I jerk back, banging my elbow against the wall.

Prudence's head pokes out from the doorway, almost exactly where Eve stood before. She motions for me to follow.

"Why weren't you paying attention?" she hisses.

"Why weren't you on time?" I hiss back, remembering a second later that I probably should avoid getting her angry.

But she's ignoring me anyway. There's an access badge in her hand like the one Eve carried last time I was here. Pru waves it in front of the sensor, then walks quickly down the hall toward the office on the left.

"You're sure the side door is unlocked?" I ask.

"Yes. I unlocked it." She waves the badge and steps aside. "And the office is empty. I checked."

Pushing the door open, I see the room, a large library and office combo, lit only by moonlight from the courtyard and the glow of our CHRONOS keys.

She shoves the badge into my hand. "In case you need it. And you should hurry. They could come back any minute."

"Who could come—" I begin, but I'm talking to empty space before I can finish the question.

Mom's right. That's really annoying.

I draw the Colt and hunch down to keep a low profile, moving quickly toward the stone fireplace that juts out a few feet into the room, dividing the two halves of the glass wall. Pressing my back against the stone, I look out into the courtyard. I was never on this side of the room last time, and I can now see the small alleyway between the buildings that Charlayne mentioned. Unfortunately, I can't see to the end of the alley from this vantage point, so I unlock the door and step out, hoping to see whether she and Trey have made it to the gate.

The second I step into the courtyard, the entire place lights up. My heart hammers in my chest. I jerk my head upward where motion sensor floodlights point down from all four corners. I haven't even had time to catch my breath from that shock when I hear a clanking noise off to the right. Someone drops from the gate, which is about seven feet high, into the alley.

Trey and Charlayne sprint toward me. And as happy as I am that they got in, they both look so very *wrong* with the rifles in their hands.

If this goes as planned, neither of them will ever have to use them, I remind myself, pushing away that nagging little part of me that's sure everything that can go wrong will go wrong.

We enter the office now almost fully lit by the floodlights from the courtyard.

There are two wooden doors inside the office, one on each side of the massive desk. Charlayne turns toward the first one, which is partially open. "No! I think that's a closet. The other one is the exit!"

I push the two of them in that direction and start to follow, but something on one of the bookshelves near the other door catches my eye. The floodlights reflect off the polished silver curves. It looks very familiar.

"Kate?"

Trey stands frozen in the doorway, a question in his eyes. Beyond him, shouts and footsteps echo in the hallway. One of the voices is Kiernan's. Two shots are fired in rapid succession.

"Go!" I tell Trey. "Back up Charlayne! I'll be right behind you."

He hesitates for a moment, then nods and takes off running.

I hurry back to the shelf. It's a communion tray, filled with the same small injection vials as the other five I've handled today. If not for the floodlights I was cursing a moment ago—or if it had been made of wood, like the ones at Grandma Keller's church—I'd have walked right past it again.

The fact that the communion tray is silver is also why I see the tiny blip of blue and know someone else has blinked into the room. If the stable point had been facing me, I'd have been screwed, but the jumper comes in facing the fireplace, and I have a fraction of a second to slip through the open door on the left.

But, unfortunately, not enough time to grab the vials. It can't be Pru or Kiernan—if they'd had a stable point in here, Pru wouldn't have had to meet me in the hallway. So it's either the other Templar—and I doubt he's a jumper—or Conwell. Or Simon.

I lean back against the wall of the small, dark room. It's a bit large to be a closet. There's a couch against one wall, and I see a sink and toilet through an open door at the back of the room. I slide my key back into the leather holder to hide the light, hoping whoever it is leaves quickly so I can grab the vials and blink out. And also hoping Trey and Charlayne don't backtrack to check on me.

"What in hell?" It's Conwell.

Has he seen Trey or Charlayne? Or maybe he noticed the light from the key before I could hide it.

I'm about to spring out with the pistol when he mutters, "Why am I the only one who can remember to turn off the damned floodlights?"

He stalks toward this side of the room, and my heart leaps into my throat when he approaches the door. A hand reaches inside the frame, and I hold my breath, pointing the gun in front of me.

But he's only looking for the light switch. His fingers flick the switch closest to him downward and the one next to it upward, turning on the lights in the main room. At least now that the light is on, Trey or Charlayne or anyone else who comes looking will know someone else is in here.

"So where is she?" he says.

I don't even have time to wonder who he's talking to before I hear Simon say, "Shut up, Patrick." His voice is tired.

"No. Like I told you earlier, you need to stop putzing around—"

"I said shut up. Just shut up and give me the vials."

"Yeah. As if." I press one hand to my mouth to hold in a fit of nervous laughter. Did Conwell get that stupid phrase from his daughter? I can almost picture her tossing her blond hair over her shoulder. "Saul told *me* to handle that side of things. Apparently he didn't think you had the—"

Conwell breaks off. The room is totally silent. When he speaks again, his voice is shaky at first, but then he gets it under control. "Is that a gun of some sort? Put it down, Simon. Be serious. You want to run Cyrist International on your own? That would cut into your playtime a bit, wouldn't it? We have an agreement. I run the business, and you play time tourist. Just leave me the girl and the keys."

It's not until Conwell says the word *keys* that I remember I could just jump back to a moment before Pru and I entered the library, before I let Trey and Charlayne in the door, and grab the tray of vials. It would be risky to make a jump right now, since Simon and Conwell would almost certainly see the glow of the key if I pull it out in this dark room, but I could probably jump out before they reached me.

Probably.

But . . . if I do that, wouldn't Simon just jump back to before I took the vials and put them somewhere else? And even if jumping back gets the vials, it won't get me *answers*. I need those, along with the keys around Conwell's and Simon's necks, if we're really going to end this. Unless Saul brought a large amount of the virus with him when he sabotaged CHRONOS, which seems unlikely, then someone had to jump forward to 2070 and steal it. The two most probable candidates are in that room. What's to stop them from jumping forward and grabbing more of it once they discover we've destroyed the last batch? Or jumping back to kill us at some previous point in time?

We can't stop this without information, and I'll never have a better chance than now to get it—and hopefully the vials, too. So I shove the key pouch back into my shirt and listen, something that's not as easy as it might seem. My heart is pounding so loudly that I can barely hear anything else.

Breathe, Kate. Calm down, and breathe.

Simon is saying something about renegotiation when I tune back in. ". . . have your Sister Prudence. This one's even younger than the other one. She's not pregnant, but that can be remedied easily enough if you really think the whole Madonna Pru bit makes a difference to the sheeple. And the keys aren't a problem. Pru's people don't have keys anymore—hell, most of them don't even *exist* anymore. Kiernan helped me get the keys from CHRONOS, and almost all have been deactivated now. Like I told you and Saul before, when you play things smart, when you use your head, you can get other people to do your work for you."

I grit my teeth at that last bit, thinking how very much I like Prudence's name for Simon. Rat Bastard pretty much nails it.

"Aside from this bit about the girl," Patrick replies, "that's the deal we had before. So why are you waving a weapon?"

"Like I said. I need that last tray. We're not going to distribute those vials."

"What?"

Conwell echoes my thoughts exactly. My mind starts reeling through the possibilities. Has Simon changed his mind about the Culling? Is that why he killed Saul? Does he know we've destroyed the other vials? Was that more work he was waiting for me to do?

"Think about it, Patrick. We don't need to distribute the last set. What was Saul's goal? Wipe out the weak. The parasites. Reshape history. Fix the future. You dropped your little viral bomb on the other five regions. Within the next few days, they start dropping like flies. But here on this continent . . . we're not the weak. We're the doers. The idea people. There are exceptions, of course, but we've got the strongest military, the strongest economy. With that virus wiping out most everyone in the other five regions—everyone except those already loyal to us—we'll have rolled the clock back on pretty much every environmental problem there is within the next quarter century. The ones left out there around the world will be *our* people, Patrick. Handpicked. No religious wars. No sectarian conflicts. A perfect little paradise, just like Saul wanted."

"I'll admit you have some valid points, Simon."

I want to scream, *No, he doesn't!* All he has is a callous disregard for the rest of the world, a flawed assumption that might makes right, that we can solve all global problems simply by eliminating those who are different. Dead bodies are okay elsewhere, but not here. Not in his playground.

"But," Conwell continues, "there would be spillover. Our borders are porous. A deadly virus in Europe, Latin America? It'll reach us, too."

"So Patterson steps up border security. I'll go back a bit, give her the vaccine, let the CDC start producing it. And yes, we'll lose some people, but not as many as overseas. We come out on top."

The phone rings as Conwell says, "I'm willing to take it to Saul. If you can convince him, we do it your way."

It rings a second time, and Simon says, "Answer it! On speaker. And careful what you say."

"Hello."

The woman on the phone sounds a little hesitant. "Templar Morton?"

"No, this is Templar Conwell. I've taken over for Morton effective immediately. Permanent reassignment."

"Well, that explains why she asked to speak to you. Video call. On the secure channel. It's Sister Patterson, sir."

"Give him two minutes," Simon tells her. "Then patch Patterson through, okay?"

"Oh, is that you, Mr. Rand? You . . . you want to make the president *wait*?"

"Can't help it, Mitzi. The computer has to boot up, so—" Simon breaks off suddenly as a loud whooshing noise fills the air, followed by several loud bangs. A second later, the security alarm sounds.

What the . . .

Oh. The jet pack diversion. Which almost certainly means they're sending someone in after me. Or does it mean they still haven't gotten Mom and Katherine out?

Mitzi's voice cuts through the sound of the alarm. "Sir, the security cameras are picking up a disturbance near the employee parking lot. Not sure what it is, but you might want to follow the standard protocol."

"Send someone out to check," Simon tells her. "Have the other guy check the surveillance cam in the Acolyte Rec Room. And turn off that damned alarm until we're done talking to Patterson."

That settles it. I'll have to risk using the key. I inch my way along the wall toward the nearest corner, banging my toe on a coat rack and very nearly toppling it.

"What did you mean about the rec room?" Conwell asks. "And what are we going to tell Patters—" There's an odd noise—*thwommp*—and then something crashes into the bookshelves, shaking the wall I'm leaning against. Something or, more likely, some*one*.

Once I reach the corner, I turn inward to shield the light of the key as much as possible. Then I set my current location as a stable point and blink back two minutes.

∞

OUTSIDE THE SIXTEENTH STREET TEMPLE
WASHINGTON, DC
September 12, 9:34 p.m.

Ben is again in the driver's seat of the van. I don't see the Subaru, so Dad must be the one over on Seventeenth, getting ready to set off the diversion.

I push my way out of the bushes, and as I round the front of the vehicle, Mom grabs me into a hug. "Thank God, Kate!"

I give her a quick return hug—much quicker than I want—and then pull her into the van. Charlayne is in the back with Katherine, and she's now the one with Trey's phone. "Charlayne, no. Don't call my dad!"

Charlayne stops dialing, and everyone gives me a questioning look. "I was just going to tell him you're out. We may not need—"

"This is two minutes earlier for me. Simon will have a double memory if anything changes, so Dad still needs to set off the diversion and I need to jump back in. The vials are on a shelf in the library. I saw them, but couldn't grab them before Conwell and Simon arrived."

"So jump back earlier," Ben says. "Grab them before you let Trey and Charlayne—"

"That may not work," Katherine says as I reach forward to squeeze her hand. She looks drained, and I can tell her head is hurting. "Or at least it won't work if Kate goes back alone. If Simon doesn't see the vials, he'll know something changed. Maybe you could set a trap?"

"Maybe. But I'll need Kiernan for backup. Where's everyone else?"

Mom pushes into the van. "Your dad and the other . . . you . . . left to set off the diversion. Trey, Kiernan, and Connor haven't come out yet. I don't know if they're trying to get to you or—"

No, no, no, no, no. I bite my upper lip hard, pushing down the panic so I can focus on what needs to be done now, right this second.

"Ben, once I'm gone, get out of here. An alarm goes off as soon as they hear the noise from the jet packs. We'll rendezvous at the cottage."

"I'm coming in with you," Charlayne says.

"No. I'd appreciate the company, but I can use the key. You can't."

"Do you want a rifle?" She starts to hand me hers.

"I'll stick with the Colt. Once you're down the road, wait about thirty seconds and call Dad to update him, okay?"

Katherine and Mom are both trying to talk to me, and I hear Prudence's name, but I can't wait. "Please," I say to Charlayne. "Just get them out of here. Keep them safe."

INSIDE THE SIXTEENTH STREET TEMPLE
WASHINGTON, DC
September 12, 9:34 p.m.

Something is being dragged. The sound is moving closer, so I shove my key back into the holder, then down into my shirt, and crouch in the dark corner. I pull the Colt from my pocket and hold my breath, waiting.

Simon crosses in front of the door, hunched forward, dragging Conwell by the feet. There's a thump, and then he returns to the desk.

A few seconds later I hear Simon saying, "Sister Patterson! So good to see you!"

"Where is Conwell?" Her voice is familiar. And yes, I may have heard her on television, but she was only vice president in my timeline. I don't think I'd remember her voice. And the memory feels more recent.

"Conwell is otherwise occupied. I'm the one you need to be talking to anyway."

A very long pause, and then she says, "My understanding was—"

"Conwell worked for me. Not your Fifth Column. He was feeding us information all along. If you want to minimize the damage to the country, Madame President, I'm the only one who can help you. See that silver tray on the shelf behind me? The contents will determine whether you come out of this next week on an equal playing field with other nations, or whether you come out as the leader not just of the *free* world but of the whole damned globe. Would you like me to explain?"

"Please do." Patterson's voice is calm, measured, and I've placed it now. She was the woman teleconferenced in at the meeting with the Fifth Column. The one Tilson said Julia answered to.

Simon launches into a full-blown speech, one I suspect he's practiced in his head for a very long time. And this speech, while Simon's all wrapped up in the wonderful sound of his own words, may be my best chance to get those vials.

"At exactly eight forty-five on the morning of September 11th, Sister Prudence and Conwell distributed a virus to five regional temples. The vials will be introduced into the water supply on each continent. It's fast moving and lethal, and it mutates quickly. It will be airborne within about a day. I watched it happen in 2070, and it is a masterpiece of efficiency."

I move slowly until I reach the doorway and then slip across the opening to the opposite side. I can see Simon's reflection in the glass walls, staring at the monitor in front of him, giving his sales pitch. The vials are on a midlevel shelf, one row over. If I have two clear seconds, it's an easy grab.

Unfortunately, the fact that I can see Simon's reflection means that he'll also be able to see me if he glances this way. Possibly even in the reflection of the monitor. I'd gladly trade the CHRONOS key for a cloak of invisibility right now if that were an option. Because even if Simon doesn't look back, as soon as I pivot around those shelves, the webcam will probably pick me up. Will Patterson react? Will she tell him?

"The good news is that it doesn't have to be that way here," he says. "You have time to lock down the borders. I have the vaccine. If you're feeling magnanimous, you could even share it . . . maybe save a few allies."

I cautiously step over Conwell's feet and press my back against the bookshelves, watching Simon's reflection. There's never going to be a perfect time, so I wait until he's in midsentence and step out holding the Colt in front of me.

Shoot him. Just shoot him.

It shouldn't be a problem after everything he's done. I shouldn't even hesitate. But I can't. Patterson is watching. Still, even if she wasn't, even if the president of United States wouldn't be a witness to the act, I don't think I could shoot someone in the back.

And Patterson *does* see me. I'm banking absolutely everything on the note of shock, of disgust, that I heard in her voice at the Fifth Column meeting when she learned how deep the conspiracy went. If her compassion was an act, I am so far beyond screwed.

I take two steps and carefully pull the tray toward me, holding my breath, trying not to make even the tiniest sound. It slides silently off the shelf, not even a whisper, but it doesn't matter.

Maybe Simon caught movement in his peripheral vision or saw Patterson looking beyond him. Or maybe it was just that odd sixth sense that tells you someone is behind you. Whatever the reason, his chair starts to spin in my direction.

"So let me get this straight," Patterson says, in a much louder voice. "You're saying we could come out of this ahead? That the Culling doesn't happen here?"

Simon halts, turning back to the screen. I reverse course, hoping to duck back around the shelves.

But I don't make it. The room begins to spin, and it's all I can do to keep the tray upright as I drop to the floor a few feet from Conwell's body.

Grabbing those vials must be what finally triggers the time shift. It's as massive as the last one, and Connor's analogy of a train being shoved from the tracks seems dead on.

Simon lets out a roar and swipes the monitor off the desk. It crashes to the floor. He stands and staggers in my direction, but he only makes it a few steps before he drops to his knees.

There's no time to grab my CHRONOS key. I point the Colt at Simon, and he points his weapon right back at me.

It's a strange gun, nothing like the Colt or the rifle I carried earlier. Neither of us says anything. He's probably struggling to keep down his last meal, just like I am. Conwell's cologne—an acrid scent that burns my nose—isn't making things any easier.

My head begins to clear. I push myself up to a half-lotus position, gripping the tray of vials between my thighs, and move my hand slowly toward my key.

That's when Simon finds his voice. "I'll shoot before I let you jump out with the vials."

"And I'll shoot before I'll let you have them."

You should have shot him, Kate. Right square in the back. He'd be dead, dead, dead, and you'd be out of here.

That thought must be written on my face because Simon laughs. "You have to be willing to fight dirty to win. And if you were willing to fight dirty, I'd be dead already. And yes, I *do* see you back there." Simon is glancing beyond me at the glass doors. "Connor Dunne, isn't it? Pretty sure I know your great-grandpa."

I can't see Connor from this angle without turning around, and I don't dare take my eyes off Simon. He has the clear advantage, because he can see both me and Connor's reflection at the same time.

"Whoever's back there behind you in the hallway? If I see any movement at all, I *will* shoot her. And just so you're aware, mine isn't the only weapon aimed in her direction."

"He's lying!"

"No, he's not." The voice behind me is weak, but unmistakably Patrick Conwell. He snakes one arm around my waist and jabs something against my back, hard enough that I wince. "Although I haven't quite decided who I'd rather kill," he adds in a softer voice clearly meant for Simon.

Connor says, "I'm not armed, Simon. Just here to make a trade."

"Really?" Simon says brightly. "Whatcha got?"

"Kate for the keys. They're all here."

"Bullshit." Simon keeps the tone friendly as he adds, "We both know there are others out there, including the one in your pocket."

Connor moves a bit farther into the room, and I can now see him over Simon's shoulder. He holds the red-and-white container in one hand. Pulling the key out of his pocket, he shows it to Simon. "Not a problem. You'll get those, too. In fact, I'll toss mine into the pot the second I know she's safe."

"No, Connor!"

"Kate," Simon chides. "Stay out of this, darlin'. The men are doing business."

His grin fades a bit when he sees my expression. Or maybe it's my twitchy trigger finger that does it, because part of me wants to pull the trigger right this second, regardless of the consequences.

"Conwell, the whole idea of holding her at gunpoint is to make her *lower* the damned weapon." Conwell digs his barrel in a little deeper, and once I comply, Simon goes on. "Before we do any sort of negotiation, however, Kate needs to slide that tray in her lap toward me."

"No," Conwell says. "I think I'll keep it closer to me until we talk to Brother Cyrus."

Playing these two off each other seems like our only hope at this point. "He's dead," I say. "Simon killed him. Slit his throat and dumped him in a bathtub at Estero."

"True enough," Simon admits. "He wouldn't listen to reason. Saul's way and only Saul's way. You've seen that, Patrick. I seem to remember him making you give up something—someone—once upon a time, just to show your loyalty."

Conwell is already on a pretty tight spring, but I feel him tense up even more.

Simon gives Conwell a sympathetic smile. "But you and me, man, we're on the same side now. We both need those vials because I'm pretty sure that jolt we felt just now means Dora the Explorer there erased everything you accomplished on your recent trips abroad."

"What jolt? The only jolt I felt was from your PEP gun."

Then I see a flash of blue a few inches from Connor. I let out the breath I've been holding . . . and then I tense right back up. It's Prudence.

She hates Simon, but she's about as reliable as a tissue paper bridge. I can't imagine any scenario where her being in this room improves the situation. She's not even armed. Connor's expression tells me he's thinking the exact same thing.

Prudence glances from Connor to Simon, then over to where I'm wedged up against Conwell, then back across the room. And then she bursts out laughing, holding one hand up to her face. "Oh my God! Lover boy's over there in the doorway, too. He looks like a Ken doll playing GI Joe."

She clearly cracks herself up, because it's a good ten seconds before she catches her breath long enough to speak. When she finally sobers, she looks at Conwell and shakes her head sadly. "You're picking the wrong team, Patrick. Your father would be sad."

"Get the hell out, Pru." Simon glares in her direction. "Go back to the Farm, and I'll leave you be. Go ride your stupid horse. Listen to your crappy mix tape, and leave the business to the people who still have brains enough to manage it."

Pru takes two menacing steps toward Simon, and then everything happens at once. Simon whips the strange gun toward her. Behind me, I feel something move quickly across the back of my hair. Conwell makes a gurgling sound, and something warm and wet gushes against my back. Then someone yanks me up and over Conwell's body.

I hear the *thwommp* sound I heard earlier, but it's louder this time. Longer.

The bloody knife clatters from Kiernan's hand, and he whips his rifle upward, pointing it toward the library, where Simon is still sitting on the floor.

Beyond Simon, Connor and Prudence are sprawled on the ground, so Simon's PEP gun must have hit both of them. The container of keys was open, and deactivated medallions are scattered across the carpet.

Connor's fingers rest on the very edge of the only bright blue key. I try to push through, but Kiernan blocks the doorway.

"Kiernan, I have to—"

"Not yet, Kate."

"Maybe they're just stunned, like Conwell was?"

"I don't know," he says. "The weapon has different settings."

"You're helping her?" Simon stares at Kiernan, mouth open, eyes wounded. "But why?"

Simon still has the gun, or whatever the thing is, pointed in our general direction, although I'm not sure he's even aware he's holding it. "I kept her safe for you, man! Just like I promised."

"Drop the weapon, Simon."

"She's with June at the Farm. The baby's fine, too. I'll give you the coordinates. I'll show you."

Kiernan's jaw is clenched tight. "She'd never have been in any danger in the first place if it wasn't for you and Saul and this whole Cyrist insanity." Kiernan turns slightly toward me and whispers. "Go, Kate. Get the vials to Estero."

But I'm rooted to the spot, staring at the scene in the other room, looking for any sign that Connor is still alive. And yes,

Prudence, too. I'm never going to feel all warm and fuzzy about my aunt, but I don't want her dead.

Simon keeps talking, shaking his head slowly as he looks at Kiernan. "You saw the same things I did, Kier. People don't stop. Saul was wrong about a lot, but he was right about that. The world needs a fresh start. A guiding hand, not a haphazard, half-assed evolution."

"A guiding hand with that much blood on it isn't a fresh start, Simon. I told you that years ago."

"Yeah, but then you . . . Christ! I thought you'd *finally* grown up. Gotten a clue how the world really works. But . . ." Simon's voice is strained, almost like he's on the brink of tears. "It's her, isn't it? What is it with you? I saved *your* Kate. The one you claim to love. So what are you doing with the spare? She wouldn't even exist if Pru had—"

I didn't realize Kiernan's hand had relaxed on the rifle, but it must have, because now he yanks it back up. "She's not a bloody *spare*, Simon! There are . . . no . . . spares! People aren't expendable."

Simon is silent for a moment and then says, "You sure about that? Because the way you've got that gun pointed at me, I'm feeling a little expendable." Simon laughs softly and pulls the CHRONOS key from his pocket. "You must've thought Patrick was. The man wasn't even armed, just poking a keychain flashlight into her back, and you slit his throat."

I glance down at Conwell's body. Simon's right. Kiernan's mouth tightens, but he doesn't look down to confirm what Simon said, so I'm guessing he realized it when he pulled me into the room.

"Same thing you did to Saul," Kiernan says. "And how many other people? I can think of five off the top of my head. Patrick killed more than a few himself and was on his way to killing a whole bunch more, so . . ."

"Saul got what he deserved," Simon says as he looks down at his key, preparing to jump. I wait for Kiernan to say something. To do something. But his hands are shaking on the rifle.

A slight movement pulls Simon's eyes away from the display, toward the single bright blue CHRONOS key.

I see it too. Connor's hand flexes, grabbing toward the key. Any hesitation I felt about shooting vanishes instantly.

I lean through the doorway with the Colt and do what I should have done earlier. I do what Kiernan can't.

My bullet hits Simon in the back of the neck, but my gun isn't the only one firing. I hear shots from the hallway, and Kiernan's gun fires, too, a moment later. Trey calls out my name, and behind him in the hallway I hear shouting. "Federal agents! Drop the weapons and come out with your hands over your head."

I fire again, and Simon crumples forward as the last bullet hits him, his head inches from Prudence and Connor. His body twitches a few times, and then he's still.

But not before he pulls that last active key toward him.

Not before Connor vanishes.

∞25∞

ESTERO, FLORIDA
July 13, 2030, 12:54 p.m.

"Easy, love. The idea is to destroy the nasty stuff in the vials, not send them crashing to the floor."

Kiernan's right. While the bleach in the tub is industrial strength, there's no point in taking chances. I should stop letting anger and frustration rule me. This is the last tray. June managed to disinfect the vials we brought back from Addis Ababa, even with her wounded arm in the sling. She's in the other room now, on what's left of the bed Pru dismantled.

I drive the pick into the next vial with a little less force, but I still move quickly. I want this over. I want it done.

Not because I'm worried there's anyone to jump in and prevent me from finishing the task. Anyone who can both use the CHRONOS key and who thought the Culling was necessary, or even a necessary evil, is dead. Except maybe Prudence. I don't know what she thinks. I'm not even sure she knows.

I hurry because I want to get back. I want to find a way to fix this.

At the very same time, I know I can't. If Connor was dead, then yes, I could change things. I could empty every single bullet in that gun into Simon before Connor ever walked into the room and prevent his death.

But I can't prevent Connor from not existing in this timeline. The CHRONOS field was the only thing that held him here. To anyone not under a key in this reality, Connor Dunne never existed. It won't matter if they'd interacted with him daily. Even the Valenzia's Pizza guy wouldn't remember him.

I wonder if the company's profits are down, and that stray thought has me somewhere between laughing and crying. And I don't want to do either of those things. I just want this over. I want it *done*.

"So . . . June's going with you?" I ask, mostly to get my mind on something else.

"Yes. Kate's worried Katherine is going to argue against us keeping the keys at all. Having all three of them in the past, so that we can get them to you immediately in your present, is the safest option."

I nod, pretending that makes sense. And maybe it would if my brain wasn't still replaying the scene in Conwell's office.

"You'll be in Georgia, then?" I ask.

"We might go there occasionally, but I kind of lost track of what days I've been in Georgia over the past few years, and I need to minimize interaction with Martha since I have no idea how that might affect the future. I bought a little place up in New York."

"Let me guess. You've been gambling again."

He gives me a half grin. "As I've said before, it's not gambling if you know you'll win. It's just a little house on the Finger Lakes, near Skaneateles."

The way he pronounces it, it's almost a rhyme for Minneapolis, but it seems familiar. "Was that . . . ?"

"Yeah. It was on the note I told you to give to the driver of the surveillance van. Kate and I spent some time up there once. It's beautiful."

"I think I've seen it. Through Katherine's key, the first time I touched it."

Kiernan looks a little confused, but then he says, "I'll leave you the coordinates when we go. If the keys don't arrive, whatever plans I made for getting them to you fell through, and you'll need to let me know."

"Are you sure June won't use the key?"

He thinks about it for a moment. "I can't promise she won't use it. But she won't use it in a bad way, not to change anything. And she can't stay here. Have you looked outside?"

"No. Why?"

"The Farm looks like no one has been here in years. I think the Cyrists are on a very different trajectory now."

"I'd be happier if there was *no* trajectory. I'd like to go back and erase those vile little books from existence." And with that thought, I turn back to jabbing the stupid vials as hard as I was before.

"And maybe erase yourself along with them, Kate? I wouldn't want to test how that little conundrum played out."

"It might not change anything. Connor was working against Saul before I even came into the picture, and nothing happened when Simon erased him."

My voice breaks at the end. Kiernan steps forward and puts his hands on my shoulders. That one touch is enough to start the tears I've been holding back. Even though he's behind me and can't see my face, he knows. He always knows.

"Why don't you let me finish these?"

"No," I say, pulling away from his hands. "There are only a few more, and I need to stab something. I'm okay."

Kiernan sighs and goes back to leaning against the wall, probably thinking that *I need to stab something* and *I'm okay* don't really belong in the same sentence.

Blinking back the tears, I manage to drive the pick through the last few seals. I'm scrubbing my arms at the sink when Kiernan speaks again.

"I am so sorry, Kate. For all of it. If I'd fired the gun earlier, Connor would still . . ." He's on the brink of crying as well. "I'm sorry."

Part of me wants to agree. An angry voice is yelling, *You're damned right! Why didn't you just shoot him?*

But that same voice is yelling the very same thing at me. *Why didn't YOU kill him?*

"I had the chance to shoot Simon when he was talking to Patterson, Kiernan . . . and I couldn't. Even though he was willing to kill billions of people, would have killed them if we hadn't changed things, and would have gone *back* to kill them again if he'd gotten away—I still couldn't fire the gun until I saw him grabbing for Connor's key. So if it's anyone's fault, it's mine."

I don't mention the other question in my mind, the one I'm pretty sure is going to haunt me. Was I able to shoot at that moment because Simon now posed a direct and immediate physical threat to someone concrete, someone right there in front of me, rather than the faceless, nameless multitude who would die in the Culling? Or was I able to shoot only because he now posed a direct threat to someone I loved?

"That's not the only thing I have to apologize for, Kate. What Simon said . . . about you being a spare? I never thought that, but my actions? They put you at risk. They . . . made it seem that I valued your life less than hers. And that's never been true. You're as much her as she is, at least to me. I never, ever thought of you as expendable."

He takes my face in his hands and presses his lips to mine. I think he meant it to be brief, almost platonic, but that doesn't seem possible for either of us. And although I know I should fight it, I don't. Because this will be the last time I kiss Kiernan. Even if I see him again before they leave, this will be our last moment alone before he goes back to his time, his Kate, his wife. And I can't stop my mind from wondering about that other life, my own road not taken. I love Trey, I'm *in love* with Trey, but whatever the future holds for us, part of me will always wonder.

When I pull away, he says, "What I told you in Georgia? That I've only ever loved one girl? It's still true, and I count myself lucky beyond belief that she is alive and waiting for me. That our child . . ." He laughs softly and shakes his head. "I still can't even wrap my head around that."

I hold back the question of whether he's certain the child is his, remembering what he said before. Whatever happened during the time his Kate was missing is between the two of them, and I don't want to dim the smile on his face when he mentions the baby.

"What I'm trying to say is, *you* are my Kate, too. My first Kate. The girl with the funny painted toes, whose eyes were still young and who could laugh in a way my Kate had lost by the time we met. I'm just glad I have the chance now to set that right. And one day, if I see your smile on her face, maybe that'll keep me from feeling I've left a piece of my heart behind."

∞

Outside the Sixteenth Street Temple
Washington, DC
September 12, 9:39 p.m.

The Gray Ghost is parked half a block down. I wave to get Dad's attention, and a few seconds later, he pulls up next to me. Other-Kate is riding with him. As soon as the window is down, she asks, "Where's Kiernan? Is he okay?"

"Yes. He'll meet us at Katherine's at midnight." I look back at Dad. "Trey will run out that door in less than a minute. If he doesn't show, wait ten more seconds and then go. Get back to Briar Hill. The police will be here really soon."

"What about you?"

"I have to get Prudence. Simon and Conwell are dead. Connor—" I shake my head because I can't say it. I can't. But they both know. Dad gulps and squeezes my hand.

"Awww, Kate, no . . ."

"I'm going back to pull Conwell and Simon's keys. Hopefully their bodies will vanish like Saul's did. It will make explanations a lot easier."

Other-Kate looks doubtful. "I don't think that will work. They all vanished because there was no CHRONOS in that timeline. But when you stopped the Culling, we shifted again. CHRONOS might still happen in this timeline. And June said Simon and Conwell's dad was one of the historians."

"They're *brothers*?"

"Well, half brothers. Conwell isn't Pru's son. He's one of the offspring Simon or Edna convinced to join. If CHRONOS exists in this timeline and Pru is under a key . . . then Simon probably still exists."

I fight the urge to kick the tire. So much for a quick and easy cleanup.

"Go," I tell Dad. "I love you. I'll be at the cottage when you get there."

I roll the key back one minute and jump into the hallway where I met Prudence earlier. Letting myself through the door with the access badge she gave me, I turn down the smaller corridor. Trey is in the doorway with his rifle pointed into the library. I know this will give him a wicked double memory. Still, it's better than him being caught in the hallway with an assault weapon.

Simon's voice comes through the doorway, ". . . kept her safe for you, man! Just like I promised."

Sneaking up on Trey in this situation seems like a horrible idea. We're in a hurry, though. I just hope he's not as jumpy as Charlayne when she's holding a gun.

I whisper Trey's name, and he does startle, but his finger doesn't pull the trigger.

"Oh, God. Kate. Something's wrong. Connor—"

"Shh. I know. Give me the rifle and go, okay? I'm . . . I'm safe, I swear. The police are coming. Dad's at the entrance waiting for you."

He starts to hand me the gun. "Um . . . fingerprints."

I glance down. He's wearing the same kind of dark gloves that Charlayne and Ben were wearing earlier.

While I seriously doubt that it matters at this point, I pull the sleeve of Dad's shirt over my hand and grab the barrel.

"You're sure you'll be okay?"

"Yes. Just run!"

"Love you." He presses a kiss to the top of my head and takes off.

From inside the office, I hear Kiernan saying, ". . . told you that years ago."

I should just blink out. I need to get both of these guns out of the building before I do anything else. And the expression on Trey's face as he said Connor's name gave me my answer.

But I can't leave without checking. I move two steps forward to where Trey was standing and lean to the side so I can see. Simon is there. Prudence is there, sprawled out with her hair fanned over her face. Deactivated CHRONOS medallions cover that patch of carpet, along with one that remains bright blue.

No Connor.

I drop Trey's rifle and my Colt off at Estero, and then I roll the key back to 9:39 again. As soon as I see Earlier-Me and Kiernan disappear with the vials, I blink into the darkened room near Conwell's office. Kiernan wanted to come back with me, but police will be crawling all over this place at any moment. It will be hard enough explaining the situation if Prudence and I are still here when they arrive, and that's doubly true if Other-Kate's right and we're stuck in the room with two dead bodies. Adding Kiernan to the mix will just complicate matters.

Conwell's key is attached to him by a long gold chain tucked inside his shirt. I slip my fingers under the chain at the back of his neck and quickly work it around until I can unfasten the blood-slicked clasp. The key comes away from his body dripping. I fight back a wave of nausea, hoping the blood will vanish along with his body.

But Other-Me was right. Conwell's corpse is right where it was a moment ago, and I now have even more of his blood on me. I guess it's possible he's hiding a spare somewhere on his body, but I don't have time to check.

Prudence moves slightly as I approach the spot where she and Simon are sprawled on the floor. I lift Simon's hand to grab the medallion underneath. It's still warm and slightly damp from his grip. And just like Conwell, Simon's still there when I pull the key, still bleeding all over the carpet.

Connor's key is a few inches away. It's lying at an odd angle, not flat like the others. A small black rectangle is taped to the back. It looks like . . . a thumb drive?

There's noise in the outer hallway. I'm pretty sure that the same federal agents who yelled at Trey are now in the building. They don't call out the warning this time, probably because there's no longer an armed man outside this door.

Prudence moans, pulling herself up onto one elbow.

"Can you use the key?" I ask her. "We need to get out of here."

"No," she replies. "I can hardly see. Just . . . shapes. My head hurts . . ." She puts one hand up to her forehead, which now sports an angry red circle that looks like a burn. "Can't believe the Rat Bastard *shot* me."

"Yeah, well, he's dead. Conwell, too. I grabbed both of their keys, but they didn't disappear like Saul did earlier. Do you know if they're wearing backup keys?"

She thinks for a second, and then she smiles. Her lips are twitching, however, and it almost looks like she's going to cry. "Simon, maybe. But Patrick didn't have a spare. They wouldn't have allowed it. That means Tate is safe. CHRONOS exists in this timeline."

Although I have some very mixed feelings about CHRONOS existing, I'm glad for Tate. Now I need to get Simon's spare and find some way to get us out of here.

I've tried not to look at Simon too closely, but now there's no choice. I have no idea where he stashes his spare key, and I really don't want to have to do a physical search. One of my bullets entered the back of his neck. Either my other bullet or Kiernan's must have hit his torso, because there's a separate pool of blood near his stomach. His body is sprawled in a slightly different position than before, closer to Pru's foot than her arm, so at least one of the bullets Trey fired from the hallway—or rather, would have fired if I hadn't just intercepted him—must have hit him, too.

"Pru, if Simon has a spare, where would it be?"

"Sock, maybe? Or in his boxers?"

Ick. Double ick. Definitely trying the socks first.

"Where's Deborah . . ." Pru begins as I tug off one of Simon's boots.

"Deborah's on her way home."

No key in that sock, so I lift the other boot.

Still no key. But we do have voices in the outer hallway again.

Flipping Simon's body over, I grab for his belt and am about to unbuckle it when I notice an odd square shape outlined by his blood-soaked shirt. I rip it open to reveal a bandage about three inches below the bullet wound. The edge of the adhesive is slick with blood.

I wipe away the blood with my sleeve and finally pry one edge up. Something brushes against my shoulder. Before I can react, Simon's hand is wrapped in my hair, yanking me downward.

I bite back a scream as my head hits the floor.

Trey's bullet must be the one that actually killed Simon. Even though the carpet is soaked with his blood, Simon has still got one hell of a grip on my hair.

And I no longer have a gun. Pivoting my body around, I plant a kick into Simon's wounded side. He grunts but doesn't let go.

"Kate? What's going on?" Pru yells.

A door slams in the hallway.

"He's alive." I kick again, connecting with his leg this time.

"Federal agents!" a voice yells from the hallway. "Come out with your hands up."

A third kick doesn't connect at all, but Simon's fingers slip through my hair to the floor. As I sit up, I see Pru holding a CHRONOS key in one hand and a bloody bandage in the other. Beyond her are two very confused men in SWAT gear pointing their guns directly at the two of us.

I nod toward the glass door. "We were attacked! Two men." I press the bandage that was holding Simon's spare medallion against his bullet wound.

"Are you wounded?" one of them asks, glancing at my shirt, which is covered not just with fresh blood but with darker splotches of dried blood. Neither of them moves toward the door.

"No, I'm trying to stop his bleeding, but it's not working. And Sister Prudence is hurt."

"I can't see," Prudence says. "Call 911!"

A third man and a woman, also in SWAT gear, are now in the room. "We've already called," the woman says.

"Isn't anyone going after them?" Pru screams, and the first two men finally take off into the courtyard.

The woman kneels down next to Simon. "He's still breathing."

Prudence's expression is odd, like she can't decide whether to be relieved or disappointed. When the two officers move on to check Conwell, she tosses Simon's spare key into my lap.

As I shove it into the side of my bra with the other two, it occurs to me that Prudence has remarkably good aim for someone who can't see.

The medical team arrives a few minutes later. Simon is on a portable gurney and out the door first. Then one of them comes over to us, stopping first at me, no doubt due to the blood.

"My niece is fine," Pru says. "They used some sort of weapon that caught me in the face. I can barely see."

He takes her pulse, examines the odd wound on her head, and uses something to look into her eyes. "Get another gurney," he tells one of the others. "You're showing symptoms of shock, okay? I'm going to roll up your sleeve to take your blood pressure."

When he sees the key embedded in her arm, his jaw falls open. "What's . . . what's that?"

"It's my key," Prudence says matter-of-factly. "I didn't want to lose another one. Are we going to ride in an ambulance?"

After Simon and Prudence are gone, I'm the only one left to question. I repeat the story about two men breaking in, but I can tell the federal officers are suspicious. There's a flurry of activity near Conwell's body, and I see them dropping the knife into an evidence bag. I really should have remembered to cart that out along with the guns. Kiernan's prints are on it, although even if they happen to be in some database, which I doubt, they'd have a hard time pinning the crime on someone born in 1885.

The female officer comes back over. "Are you carrying any weapons, Miss Keller?"

I could kick Prudence for giving them our actual names. I have no ID on me. I could have just blinked out. But no. They ask for names, and she gives them. She even referred to herself as Prudence Pierce, complete with a driver's license that showed Katherine's address.

"No," I tell the officer. "I don't have any weapons."

"I'm sorry, but I need to verify that," she says.

It's not a thorough search, although I suspect one may be coming soon. They won't find any weapons, but they'll find the other medallions I'm carrying—Connor's with the thumb drive attached, another one covered with Conwell's blood, and two covered with Simon's. They'll probably find gunpowder traces on my clothing and skin as well.

And since Prudence gave them Katherine's address, that's not all they'll find. When the woman goes off to some other task, I pull out my key and check the stable point in the foyer. It's dark, but I roll forward a few minutes at a time, and sure enough, three men in dark uniforms, similar to the ones in this room, are in the house about twenty minutes from now. Which means they'll probably find the body in the van. And my fingerprints on the door handle.

"What is that thing?"

I pull my eyes away from the key to see one of the younger agents who has been left to watch me. He nods down at the medallion.

"Religious medal. I've just seen two men die, and my aunt is injured."

"I don't think that other guy is dead," he remarks, still watching me.

"Maybe. But I thought he was." I wait a moment and then say, "It's hard to pray with you staring at me."

That does the trick. When he turns away, I check the stable point in my room. It's dark and empty now, but the bathroom door is closed, and I don't think I closed it. If they conducted any sort of search, they found the clothes covered with blood, Julia's blood, in my bedroom.

I switch to the stable point in the library. The room is no longer filled with blue light.

None of the officers who were in the house could have seen the light from the medallions. The only way they'd know the keys in Connor's device were more than just odd jewelry in a display case is if someone told them to look for them.

Prudence? I don't think so, although her giving the address makes me wonder.

Or maybe Paula Patterson?

I can't erase any evidence they may find in the house, but I *can* keep them from getting those keys.

I tuck the medallion back into my shirt. "I need to go to the bathroom."

The man looks over his shoulder, annoyed. "You can wait."

"No. I can't. I've *been* waiting. The bathroom is right in there." I nod toward the small room where I hid earlier. "If you don't want this crime scene contaminated with additional bodily fluids . . ."

He huffs and escorts me past the officers, including the sole woman in the bunch, who are currently zipping Conwell's body into a bag. For a moment I think he's going to call her over to accompany me, but he glances inside. It's just a toilet and a sink, so he steps aside for me to enter.

As soon as the door is closed, I yank out the key and roll the time back one hour. The library is dark . . . still no keys.

I roll it back another half hour. Still dark.

I roll it back to 8 p.m., when Dad and Connor left to come to the cottage. Still dark.

Then I scan back slowly, stopping at 7:52, which is the last time the room is lit. I pan toward the device and see Connor. He gives one last, sad look at the bookshelves and the computers, then pulls the keys that project the CHRONOS field around the house. And with that one simple act, all of the works that existed in a pre-Cyrist world—history, literature, art, even a few science and technology volumes—are now gone.

It's the exact same thing I was about to go back and do, but I still want to scream.

A tap on the door reminds me that I've got other problems to address. I wait a moment, then flush the toilet and run the sink.

When we're back in the main room, the older agent comes over. The look in his eyes tells me he's decided my story does not compute. "When did you say you arrived at the temple, Miss Keller?"

"Around nine thirty," I repeat. "I came in with Sister Prudence. My aunt."

"Which entrance?"

I'm tempted, so very tempted to answer his question by using the key around my neck to take the same route out that I took in. But I just tell him what I told the others. "The back."

"And why were—" There's a buzzing sound from his jacket. He answers, gives me one quick glance as he listens, and then puts the phone away. "She's clear. Take her home." There are a few raised eyebrows until he adds, "POTUS orders."

The female officer drops me at Katherine's just before eleven. I have to feel around the underside of the porch swing for the extra house key Connor taped there, because Charlayne has my keys. And then I listen to the woman lecture me on why it's a bad idea to hide a key outside and grumble about having to leave a minor alone when the house is dark and empty. If not for the fact that the president herself just vouched for me, Mom and Dad would probably be getting a visit from Child Protective Services bright and early tomorrow morning.

∞

BETHESDA, MARYLAND
September 11, 10:21 p.m.

Daphne's not a fan of activated CHRONOS keys, so she steers clear when I first blink back to Dad's cottage. But she waits only a moment before coming over. She must have been nervous here in this strange place all alone.

Bensen's van, with Mom and Katherine, will be here in about ten minutes. Dad will pull up with Trey and Other-Kate about five minutes after that, and this tiny room is going to be very crowded until after eleven, when the coast should be clear for us to move to Katherine's. I jumped in early because I need a few minutes to just *be.* I don't even turn on the lights, just sit on the floor with my back against the sofa and sink my face into Daphne's fur.

The cottage smells like stale Taco Bell. And even though I showered and changed at Katherine's, I must still smell like blood, because Daphne keeps sniffing me, and every now and then she gives a sad little whimper.

Or maybe she *knows*. She's going to miss Connor so much. And as happy as I am to be able to tell Katherine that it's over, that Saul is dead, and the Culling did not—will not—happen, I dread telling her that Connor is gone.

When the van pulls into the parking area, Charlayne gets out first, hurrying to the door with her hand tucked inside her black windbreaker. I guess she's on point or whatever they call it.

I'd planned to open the door for her, but I just back up, one hand raised and one on Daphne, and let Charlayne use the keys I gave her. I've seen enough bullet wounds for one day.

When she sees me, she waves for the others. Then she drops the gun onto the couch and rushes over to pull me into a hug.

"Oh, thank God, Kate! Your dad called and said you went back in. We were all so worried."

I hug her back. Hard. No, she's not *my* Charlayne. It's not the same history, and my memories of the other Charlayne will always be just that—memories. But this version is close enough. She's my friend. Maybe not my BFF, but it's something to build on.

"Max is alive," she says. "Tilson called Ben. Said he popped back in around nine thirty. One second he wasn't there, and the next he was."

"But no Eve?"

"No. Tilson said she must not exist in this—"

The rest of what she's saying is drowned out by Daphne's excited bark when she sees Katherine come through the door. I

502   *Time's Divide*

grab her collar, worried that she'll knock Katherine down because her tail is wagging and her entire body is shaking.

Mom is right behind her and she's moving toward me, but Katherine gets there first. She pulls me into a fierce hug, and I know immediately that Dad told them about Connor.

"I'm so sorry, Katherine. So sorry. He was still alive, but I couldn't . . . I can't . . ."

I break down into tears, and Katherine holds me. She doesn't cry, just rocks me back and forth. "It's okay, Kate. It's okay. Listen to me. Every day, every single day, Connor thought about pulling that key. About testing whether he'd end up back in the other timeline. Back with his kids. And maybe he did end up there. We can't know, but . . . maybe he did. He told me he wasn't going to let you keep a key back for him. This is what he wanted, Kate."

Maybe. But I can't help picturing his hand, grabbing for the key as he blinked out. I'll never tell Katherine that, never, never. But that image starts my tears again.

After a few moments, I pull myself together and see Mom standing back against the wall, near the kitchen table. Her eyes are sad. Maybe she's a bit hurt that she's not the one comforting me, maybe a little angry at Katherine for pushing her aside. Even though she didn't know Connor, I can see that she's hurting, too, probably because she can see how very much this hurts me. I mouth a silent *I love you*, and she gives me a tiny smile and the little I-love-you-too hand sign that we've shared since I was a toddler.

And then Katherine's shoulders begin to shake, and it's my turn to hold her.

∞

BETHESDA, MARYLAND
September 11, 11:43 p.m.

"It's canned, but it's the best we can do." Dad ladles more tomato soup into my bowl and slides one of the grilled cheese sandwiches next to it.

Because this is what Dad does when anyone around him is hurt. Or sad. Or angry. He cooks. And you don't want to disappoint him, so you eat.

Other-Kate sits across from me, next to Mom, in the breakfast nook at Katherine's house. She's wearing a pair of my yoga pants and one of my oversized sweatshirts. It's still too tight around the middle, but she must have been happy to ditch the toga, which I found stuffed into the trash can in my bathroom.

The question of whether we'd have some sort of temporal disaster if Other-Kate's key, which is also Katherine's key, were in the same room together was answered back at the cottage when we realized they *were* in the same room and nothing happened. It may be the same key, but Katherine says it's locked onto a different genetic signature. And it's not the same key at the same time, at least not from the key's perspective. Whatever the hell that means.

"Are you sure they took Prudence to Walter Reed?" Mom asks. "I thought that was a military hospital."

"That's what they told me, Mom. Maybe they've decided she's a national security threat." She looks at me like I'm joking, but I'm really not. Simon's there, too. "I don't know if they'll let you in to see her."

"Well, I have to try. I can just take a cab, though."

"No need for that," Dad says. "I'm happy to drop you."

Charlayne and Ben drove Trey back to retrieve his car from the cottage and then to the hotel to take Tilson home. Katherine is in the shower. I think it's partly an excuse for some time alone. Or *almost* alone. I wouldn't be surprised if Daphne climbed into the shower with her. She refuses to let Katherine out of her sight.

Dad slides into the breakfast nook with his own plate and tells me, "There are six more sandwiches in the oven on warm, and you can heat up more soup if I'm not back when the others get here."

"I swear, Harry was a Jewish grandmother in a past life," Mom says as she swallows a bite from her sandwich.

"Food heals, bubala," Dad replies.

Mom rolls her eyes. "Is he like this in your timeline?"

My alter-self gives her an awkward smile. "More or less." The smile becomes fixed and, after a moment, fades away completely. "You're both pretty much the same as they are. Or should I say *were?*"

"Maybe they still exist," Mom says softly. "Like Katherine was saying about Connor?"

"Maybe," Other-Kate says, and goes back to eating her soup.

Dad catches Mom's eye across the table and gives her a look that clearly means she shouldn't go there. He's obviously thinking the same thing I am, and I'm pretty sure the same thing my other-self was thinking. Now Mom realizes it as well. Two Kates here means that if their other-selves do exist, they're missing a daughter.

Awkward silence follows, and there are equally awkward goodbyes when Mom and Dad head to the car. Kiernan should be here shortly, and Other-Kate is adamant that they'll be leaving right away. Both Mom and Dad sneak looks at her belly as they leave, one last glance at the almost-grandchild they'll never see grow up.

Once they're gone and it's just the two of us, she says, "Kiernan said they're divorced. How long?"

"Since I was nine. Why? Are they together in your . . . reality?"

"Yeah. It was touch-and-go for a few years, but they came to some sort of mutual agreement to stay together because it was better for me." She wrinkles her nose.

"Not better, I take it?"

"Definitely not. I lied earlier. They're different. Even with all of this insanity, your parents look happier than mine did last time I saw them. I love them both, but they're really good at making each other miserable. And if that timeline does still exist, they wasted a decade on a daughter who's not even around anymore. When they could have been finding other things to live for."

"They probably don't think of it that way. As wasted, I mean. But some things apparently don't change. Mom and Dad get along much better when they're not in the same house."

Kiernan blinks in halfway through that sentence. Other-Kate breathes a visible sigh of relief. She pushes herself up from the table—not exactly a graceful exit, since these benches aren't really designed for pregnant women. Kiernan pulls her close to him, and she grips the front of his shirt so hard that the raw patches on her knuckles look like they're going to split open. It's only then that I realize how difficult this evening must have been on her. I'm sure she's unbelievably happy to be back with Kiernan and glad the past few months of hell are over, but seeing this version of Mom, Dad, and Katherine when she's about to give them up forever can't be easy. And there was a Connor in her timeline, too. Were they close?

"Have you said your goodbyes, love?"

She nods, and he pulls the chain holding her medallion out of the sweatshirt, pressing it against his key to share a stable point.

"You haven't said goodbye to me." Katherine stands in the doorway, her hair still damp from the shower. Her eyes are puffy, and she's in her red robe, the one that she wore that first day I met

Kiernan on the Metro, the day that everything began. It looks different, but I can't place why.

"And I haven't had a chance to say thank you," she adds. "To both of you."

"Kiernan, maybe," Other-Kate says. "I failed. *She's* the one who fixed it." There's a note of resentment in her voice as she nods her head in my direction. While I don't think I really deserve it, I guess I understand. How would I feel if the situation were reversed?

Kiernan is about to object, but Katherine beats him to it. "I'm sorry. That's a total crock. Kate had your videos and your research to work from. You also spent the last six months keeping yourself and my great-grandchild alive under rather perilous circumstances, so have the good grace to accept my thanks before you blink out of here."

Other-Kate's mouth twitches. I almost think she's going to cry, but then she bursts out laughing. "Okay," she says to me, "what I told you about Mom and Dad? It doesn't apply to Katherine. This one . . . she's the exact same."

I look over at Kiernan. "While we're confessing failures, Simon was still alive when they took him away. Trey's gun must be what finished him off, and when I got Trey out of there early . . . that changed. He's at Walter Reed with Prudence."

"Damn it, Kate! I should have come in with you."

"If you had, they'd probably have you in custody right now, because they found the knife. You might have been able to escape using the key, but . . . is it worth it? Simon's in bad shape, so he may not make it anyway. And I did get his keys, both of them. The president knows he's a threat, so maybe . . ."

"She'll see to it he doesn't make it." Other-Kate finishes the sentence, sounding much more certain than I am.

Because they'll take samples of his DNA. And run other tests. CHRONOS still exists in the future. We know time travel didn't start until around 2150, but when did the research start? What if Simon's DNA is what starts the CHRONOS ball rolling?

The worried look Kiernan gives me suggests that at least some of this is running through his mind, too.

"They have Prudence, too," Katherine says. "Along with her key. And from what you told me, Kate, they carted enough evidence away from this house to indict you on at least one murder. But they still let you go. So even though it's contrary to my nature, we may have to simply trust that Patterson will do the right thing." She gives Other-Kate a smile and walks over to where she's standing. "Do you mind?" she asks, holding her hand a few inches from Other-Kate's stomach.

"No. But I don't think he's awake."

"It's a boy, then?" I ask.

Kiernan shakes his head. "We don't know. June does, and I think she's itching to tell us, but Kate said no."

"No other woman in 1912 will know the sex of her child ahead of time. Neither will I. It will be a surprise. But . . . yes. I kind of think it's a boy."

"And I kind of think it's a girl," he says.

Katherine steps away and looks up at Kiernan. "You'll be able to find her a decent doctor in 1912?"

"We're bringing one with us. June still has her key, and she'll stay until the baby is born."

When he says *key*, I realize what's different about Katherine's robe. Before, the blue glow of the CHRONOS medallion made the top half look sort of purple. But now it's a solid red.

"Your key, Katherine. Where is it?"

"In the safe along with Daphne's and the ones you gave Deborah and Harry, waiting for Harry to go out to Connor's workshop and deactivate them."

I narrow my eyes. "But you knew the house wasn't protected anymore. Dad told me Connor was following your orders when he removed them. How could you risk taking the key off? You could have disappeared."

"My passport was still in my desk, even now that this house is unprotected. Still stamped. I have an active checking account and a doctor's appointment next week. Pretty strong evidence that I still exist. And we all know the keys have to be destroyed." She gives Kiernan a meaningful look at the end.

He nods. "Agreed. We'll get the keys back to you when we're done with them, so . . . pretty much instantly from your perspective. And Kate, your Kate, will know where to find us if something goes wrong."

Kiernan's eyes meet mine when he says *your Kate*. He gives me one last long look, and then they're gone.

∞26∞

SIXTEENTH STREET TEMPLE
WASHINGTON, DC
September 14, 2:55 p.m.

It feels wrong, so very wrong, for Julia's memorial to be held in this temple. She spent her entire life working to protect people from the atrocities planned by the man they still view as their prophet. And even though we prevented the larger Culling, almost every branch of her family tree was culled in the process.

But Julia was officially a member of this temple, and she was adamant that there was good in this religion, too. That we shouldn't, as she put it, throw out the baby with the bathwater.

The media rolled into full national emergency mode, with 24/7 coverage of a preempted bioterrorist attack that government officials claim would have wiped out thousands, possibly tens of thousands, around the world.

If they only knew . . .

The basic story is that a small group of Cyrist extremists executed moderate church leaders here and abroad, along with three Cyrists within the US government. The leaders of the ring were killed in a raid on the Sixteenth Street Temple, where they had been holding hostages, including Sister Prudence and her niece. Some pictures leaked showing a much older Sister Prudence, leading to speculations about the exact nature of her role in Cyrist International, and even questions about my role, since I look a lot closer to the young woman recently seen speaking as Sister Prudence in Rio. That, in turn, led to news vans outside the house for the past two days. So, yes, it's over . . . but not over.

The coffin at the front is closed, which doesn't surprise me. I suspect it's empty, unless they removed Julia's key after our time train landed back on the track where CHRONOS exists and the Culling never happens. According to the *Post*, separate services are scheduled for Patrick Conwell, Senator Ellicott, Pearson, and West.

No memorial for Eve, who doesn't exist in this timeline. Since Patrick didn't vanish, I guess the fragile link in Eve's chain of existence was her mother.

No memorial for Simon. No mention of Simon, for that matter.

No memorial for Saul, either, but then his likeness is in every Cyrist temple in the world. Last time, my eyes were drawn to the panels representing Prudence, but today I can't tear my eyes away from the ones showing Saul as he heals the sick and feeds the hungry. I want to yell out to everyone in these pews that their Brother Cyrus is a fake. That he didn't bless children, he killed them.

There's movement in the pew behind us, and someone taps my shoulder. "Glad to see two more heathens here," Tilson whispers. "I was worried I would be the only one attending. Do you know if Max has arrived?"

"We haven't seen him," Trey says.

Truthfully, I'm not looking forward to talking to Max. On the one hand, I owe him a debt of gratitude for getting me out of 2308. On the other hand, he's a sneaky, lying arsonist.

If your faith is so shaky that it can be undermined by books that challenge it, then something is rotten at the core.

And it hurts to know that Max got a pass and Connor didn't. I know it's because Max exists in this timeline and we're still two or three tracks removed from a timeline where there's a Connor. I get that. But it still seems unfair.

Trey's parents move into the pew next to Tilson. While Trey was trying to convince his dad to take Estella and get out of DC, his mother was worried enough to request personal leave to fly back home. I've seen Trey maybe an hour over the past three days. Mr. Coleman's eyes drop down to his son's arm around my shoulders, and then he looks back up and gives me a smile. It's not quite the warm and friendly version that I received the first time I met him, but it's a start. And it's a lot warmer than the look Trey's mom gives me. I have a long way to go to get into her good graces.

Charlayne and Ben are seated a few rows over near their families. I was introduced to all of them when we arrived. Mrs. Singleton pulled me into a warm hug that kind of surprised me, and said thank you. So did Ben's mother, gushing about how many lives I'd helped to save. It was a little unexpected, and a little undeserved. If not for me, neither of their kids would have been in harm's way. But I guess being on the inside gave them some time to adjust to this strangeness, unlike Trey's parents, who had it dropped on their heads all at once.

Prudence sits in the front row, next to Mom. A man wearing the clerical scarf of a Templar is on Pru's right, whispering something in her ear. She nods occasionally, looking a little bored. Her dark glasses clash with the white dress—basically a toga with long sleeves to cover the key in her arm. But I can still see it glowing through the thin white fabric.

I shiver, and Trey slips his arm around me. "You okay?"

"Not really. I kind of wish we'd stayed home with Katherine and Dad. But . . . I guess I owe Julia this much. And I'm curious to see how Pru's announcement plays out."

"Yeah, me, too." He's in the dark blue shirt I like, and every time I look at him I think how very, very lucky I am. I have my family back. I have Trey, and he loves me. It's everything I wanted, everything I hoped for.

Except for Connor. He should be here, too. At the very least, there should be a memorial for him, because we could never have stopped the Culling without everything he did behind the scenes. There should be something. Some way of showing he was here. That he mattered.

The lights dim slightly as the Templar steps onto the stage. I don't think he's one of Pru's offspring. Just an average, ordinary, run-of-the-mill Cyrist, I guess.

The plasma screen behind him lights up as he talks about Julia, her years of public service, her dedication to Cyrist International. How she would want to be remembered for the way she lived, not the tragic way she died.

On that point, we agree. Julia annoyed the hell out of me pretty much from the moment we met, but she deserved better.

Max plays a very pretty violin solo. I wouldn't have pegged him as a violinist. Of course, I didn't peg him as an arsonist, either. The Templar then launches into a sermon about how extremism can mar the soul of any religion and how sad it is when anyone dies, especially at the hands of those who claim to be fellow believers. There's actually a lot of truth in his words, and he picks a few of the least offensive passages of the *Book of Cyrus* to support them.

When the Templar finishes speaking, Mom leads Prudence to the stage and then returns to her seat. This speech, part of which was leaked to the press last night, is the reason the news cameras are here and, most likely, why most of the pews are full. Prudence grips the podium with one hand and reaches out with the other, groping around until her fingers find the microphone.

I'm all but certain that Prudence could see when she left the temple the other night. But Mom swears she's blind now, completely. According to the doctors, the weapon damaged Prudence's visual cortex, which Dad says is toward the back of the head.

That doesn't make sense to me. I saw where she was hit, and it was in the front. Still, I don't think Pru has the mental capacity to fake anything this thoroughly. The past few days have been hell on Mom, because each time Pru wakes up, she realizes all over again that she can't see and freaks out.

I think this speech is a bad idea. So does Mom. But no one asked us.

"Children of Cyrus," Pru begins. "We are here today to mourn a great loss to our faith, to our nation, and to the world. But our losses could have been far greater. As President Patterson has noted in recent press conferences, the terror cell was deep within our organization. If they had not been stopped, global fatalities would have been . . . immense."

Pru's voice is almost monotone. The speech was sent to her rehab center via messenger. Mom spent hours helping her to memorize it.

"So as we mourn this loss, we must also ask what seed within our faith allowed this viper to grow in our midst. In the coming months, Cyrist International will hold a global synod to examine our tenets of faith, our Creed, and our governing policies.

"At the conclusion of that synod, I will step down as head of Cyrist International and a successor will be chos . . . en . . ."

Pru's jaw takes on a determined set, and she clutches the edges of the podium. When she speaks again, the monotone is gone and she speaks quickly.

"Brother Cyrus was a foul toad of a man named Saul. He loved no one but himself. He never blessed a single child, but he killed plenty of them. And he killed—"

She's rushed from the stage and out of the chapel. Mom throws a glance at me over her shoulder and follows.

I can't tell for certain, since her microphone was cut, but it looked to me like the last word Prudence said was *puppies*.

∞

Trey and I are almost through the door when the Secret Service—the same woman who took me home the other night—pulls me aside.

"The president would like to have a word with you in the executive conference room. If you could follow me? I'm sorry, sir, you'll need to wait here."

Trey isn't happy about that. He pulls his phone out, probably planning to call Dad. Or a lawyer, though I doubt it would do me much good.

I'm not happy, either, but I clearly don't have a choice. I put my hand on his arm. "Wait on the call, okay? Grab something to drink. If I'm not back in twenty minutes or so, then call the cavalry."

I leave him in the Cyrist Café and follow the guard down a long hallway.

Paula Patterson is alone when I enter. That kind of surprises me, but one wall is mirrored, so I'm guessing there's at least one guard watching our every move. Probably recording us, too.

Patterson always looks perfect on television. Today, there are dark circles under her blue eyes, and her auburn hair, which is usually impeccably styled, looks like it could use a touch-up. I suspect the past few days have taken a toll on her, too, because her voice is tired when she greets me.

"Hello, Kate—and thank you for meeting me here. Please, have a seat." I do, and she continues, "I believe you have something for me?"

I open my purse and pull out seven deactivated CHRONOS keys in a plastic baggie.

"And this is all of them?"

"No," I say. "We're waiting on three more."

"Waiting? On whom?"

"You'll get them." Honestly, I'm starting to worry a bit. It's been two days, and if the keys that Kiernan, Kate, and June took with them aren't back soon, I'll have to go looking.

"And once I have those three, that's the last of them?"

"It's possible that there's one in Addis Ababa that might not have been destroyed," I admit. "And there could be others. We never got a precise number. Then, of course, there's Prudence's key, and Julia's, which must be the one you're wearing." I nod toward the left side of her blazer.

Patterson glances down at her chest, surprised. "Is the glow really bright enough for you that you see it through my jacket? I can barely even see it outside the fabric."

There's also the key I'm wearing. I don't mention it, but she probably knows anyway. What she might not know is that it has company inside the little leather pouch—the flash drive that was taped to Connor's key, filled with the works that she very likely ordered Max to destroy. Katherine says about 70 percent of the library had been digitized. I've only skimmed the first few pages of the table of contents, but there's a story called "The Lottery," by Shirley Jackson, that for whatever reason never saw the light of day in this timeline. Two Shakespearean plays in their original form, before Cyrist censors changed them. Sonnets and sonatas, paintings, and history. The records of lives that never happened.

Mom says I should erase it. That this present is our reality and everything on this little drive is fiction.

She may be right. But there's plenty of truth in fiction.

"I was probably the only person in the auditorium who could see your key," I tell her. "Assuming Prudence—"

"No. She can't see anything. The doctors assured me of that."

The words are innocent enough, and there's even a note of regret, but something in her tone is chilling. Or maybe it's just because I'm all but certain Prudence *could* see when she tossed Simon's spare key into my lap.

I don't like thinking that the woman across from me would have authorized doctors to take her sight. Still . . . how else would you control Prudence? Remove the key from her arm and she'd no longer exist. Give her a chance to use it, and who knows what she'd do.

"You shouldn't worry," Patterson says. "Sister Prudence will be given excellent care. And I think she'll be . . . happy. Your mother seems determined to take personal responsibility for her, and that's admirable, but the attorneys will be talking to her over the next week or so to be sure she realizes all of Prudence's wealth will revert to Cyrist International after her death."

I'm trying really hard to be respectful. This is the president of the United States, duly elected, and I am well aware of the power differential here. Even though I know she could squash me and everyone I love with one official flick of her finger, her implication makes me angry. I'm already worried that Mom got more than she bargained for, that caring for Prudence will become a huge burden, and here she is implying that Mom is in it for the cash.

"Mom doesn't want Pru's money. She only wanted her sister back."

"I'm sure."

"You should be. Feel free to have your lawyers draw up any papers they like. As long as they don't interfere with her access to her sister, I'm quite certain Mom will sign them."

"Oh, they aren't *my* attorneys," she says. "I have no official connection to Cyrist International. It's simply my religion, and obviously I have an interest in the national security implications of recent . . . events. And your role in those events. Just to put your mind at ease, all of the items taken from your residence and your actions during this entire affair have been sealed and classified for reasons of national security. The same goes for your friends and family. But please understand that this could change in an instant. If you start making statements to the press, or if there's any indication you've withheld information, or, most importantly, if there are any changes whatsoever to the timeline, I will have to reassess that decision. As would those who follow me in office."

"I understand." She's silent for a moment, and I wonder if she's waiting for me to thank her. Perhaps I should. She could have taken a very different track here, one that would ruin my life and the lives of everyone I care about. But I can't quite muster up a thank-you when she's also the person who could have sent backup to the temple instead of putting the people I love in danger. Connor might even . . .

"What are your plans for the future?" she asks.

That came out of left field. "Umm . . . school? I've got a bit of catching up to do. And then college."

"Have you considered joining the Cyrists? You'd make a wonderful Sister Prudence."

I laugh, but apparently it isn't a joke.

"They could make it worth your while . . . and I do think there will be some major changes in Cyrist International in the coming years. You'd be in a position to do a great deal of good, even if you're not a believer."

"No thanks." Although I'm ready to get out of here, there's still one thing I need to know. "What about Simon?"

"Oh. I thought you knew. DOA at Walter Reed." I try to read her face, but I've no clue if she's lying. "I thought it strange that he didn't have a key. Conwell, either."

I nod toward the baggie of dead keys. "They're in the bag. What about the one you're wearing? Do you plan to have it deactivated, too?"

Her eyes narrow the tiniest bit. "No, Kate. I don't. If reality changes around me, I want to know. I'm sure you'd feel the same . . . I mean, if you were in my position."

In one sense, she's wrong. I've wanted to take this key off since Katherine gave it to me. Yeah, life-threatening aspects aside, this has been an incredible adventure. I'll probably look back years from now and wish I could relive the not-awful parts of the past few months. But I'll take that bit of nostalgia in exchange for security—for knowing my family is safe and that the people around me might actually know who I am from day to day.

That the important things in my life happen in order.

But, on the other side of the scale, Pru's key is still active. Patterson's key is still active. One is unstable and the other . . . is a Cyrist in a position of power. Who might be lying when she says Simon is dead. Who has the resources to search for others out there who might have the gene or, for all I know, to create them.

So, yes, she's right. I'm not sure what I could do about it, but if reality changes around me, I want to know.

∞

BETHESDA, MARYLAND
September 14, 6:57 p.m.

Katherine's contribution is a picture of a hotel in Naples, where the two of them spent Connor's fiftieth birthday. The edges curl and brown when it hits the flames.

Dad's next. He adds a handful of coffee beans to the fire pit, along with a pretzel rod, which he says is from Daphne.

Now it's my turn. I toss in a piece of cardboard torn from the top of a Valenzia's Pizza box.

We watch as it burns away. A tiny white flake of charred paper catches the breeze and takes flight. I watch for a moment, but decide I don't want to see when it catches on a leaf or drifts to the ground. I want to believe the wind will take our burnt offerings to Connor somewhere in an alter-reality, where he's sitting on his back porch eating pizza with Andi and Christopher.

I want to believe. And stranger things have happened.

When our private memorial is over, the others arrive, the ones who knew Connor, but not as well. Trey. Charlayne and Bensen. Sara, who didn't actually know Connor at all, but who stops by anyway, because she's barely seen Dad in the past few weeks. Not Mom and not Prudence. There are tentative plans for a dinner—me, Katherine, Mom, and Pru—next week. Maybe. Depending on how Prudence and Katherine are both feeling. And while I can tell Katherine wishes for more, it would be a step forward. I just hope they all stop being stubborn and actually take at least that one tiny step while Katherine is still alive.

It's annoying that everyone has to park one street over and squeeze through the hedge, but there are still two cars out front with reporters wanting an update on Sister Pru. We trade Connor stories around the fire pit, which fittingly smells a bit like burned coffee.

When the doorbell rings a little before eight, Dad and Daphne go inside to answer, hoping that it's the pizza delivery and not the paparazzi. I peek through the kitchen a minute later and see him in the foyer paying the driver, so Trey and I head inside to help him with the boxes.

But someone else is walking into the kitchen. It's a young woman, tall and pretty—and at first I think Dad let a reporter in. Then I notice that she has a toddler perched on her hip who seems determined to get down. His eyes are fixed on Daphne, who's sniffing curiously at his wiggling feet.

The woman looks surprised when she sees my face.

I smile politely and sigh. Because this is getting old.

Trey catches my expression and laughs. "We need to get you a sign that says *Not Sister Prudence*."

"Sister . . .?" she begins. "Oh, that one with the Cyrists. Is that what's going on with the news truck outside?"

"Yes. I'm her niece, but we're not . . . close."

She looks a bit confused. "Okay. But that's not what . . . stop wiggling, sweetie, and let Mommy get something."

The woman puts the little boy on the barstool so that she can take an envelope out of the oversized bag she's carrying. The kid wastes no time—he's down before she even gets her hand into her purse. I kneel and grab for Daphne's collar, thinking she might jump on him, but she just sniffs the boy and gives his outstretched hand a gentle lick.

"Your father said she's friendly?"

"Oh, yes. Just a little too enthusiastic sometimes. But she seems to be reining it in around this little guy."

Dad and Trey come through with the pizza boxes, casting a curious glance at us on the way to the patio.

"I was actually thinking you look more like *her*." The woman hands me a small photograph album. A sealed envelope sticks up out of the pages, and there's a family photo on the cover—a tall, dark-haired man with a very familiar grin holding a little boy. He's standing behind a young woman who does indeed look quite a bit like me. She holds a baby in her lap, and an older girl of maybe seven or eight stands next to her.

"The woman who's seated is my great-great-grandmother. She's a little older here, but there's a photo inside taken a few years after they were married, and . . . you could be her double." She sticks out her hand. "I'm Jennifer Meeks. And this little guy is Connor Dunne Meeks."

Oh, wow.

I look away from the album. The boy's coloring is dark like his mother's. He looks nothing like Connor. But his inquisitive brown eyes do remind me a bit of a somewhat older boy I met at the 1893 World's Fair.

"Hi, Connor."

He grins when I say his name, but then Daphne licks his cheek, and he's too busy giggling to pay attention to anything other than her.

"This is technically Connor's job," Jennifer says, "since the will decreed that the youngest Connor Dunne in the family deliver *this* envelope to Katherine Shaw at *this* address. We were supposed to be here two days ago, but Connor had this tummy thing, and we had to cancel the flight."

Katherine closes the patio door behind her. "Hello? I'm Katherine Shaw. Harry said you're looking for me."

"Yes. I'm Jennifer Meeks. As I was telling this young lady, you're the reason we flew in from Ohio this afternoon. I believe you knew my ancestors back in the 1950s, when you were a little girl. Kiernan and Kate Dunne?"

Katherine smiles. "Why, yes. I do remember them."

"Well, apparently you made a very strong impression, because you're part of a rather strange provision in their will. They named their oldest son Connor. That's the one Kiernan is holding in the picture. And they asked that the tradition be passed down in each generation. But . . . no boys in my family. My dad—Connor Dunne the Third—passed away unexpectedly six years ago, and we thought my older sister would be the one to deliver this to you, but then this little guy was born two years ago, and . . . well . . . here we are."

She hands Katherine the manila envelope. "There's an odd diary of some sort in there, written in Gaelic, as best we can tell. I'm supposed to leave you that and a copy of the photograph album they handed down to my grandfather, which I gave to . . ."

"Kate," I say, glancing down at the envelope sticking out of the photo album. It has my initials, PKP-K, written on the front.

Jennifer laughs, shaking her head. "I swear, you must have been reincarnated. That was her name, too. Oh, and the other . . . I don't know if you'll even remember these things, Katherine, but you must have liked them as a kid." She looks over to see if Connor is occupied. He is, with his tiny palms pressed against the glass patio door, looking out at the others sitting at the picnic table. She lifts a chain that holds three CHRONOS keys. Then she quickly drops them back inside. "*Don't* let Connor see what's in this envelope because he'll pitch a fit about me giving them away. I don't know why, but he's fascinated by those pendants. I'll be honest—I think they're ugly. But Connor would rather play with them than with my phone."

She closes the envelope and hands it to Katherine, then scoops Connor up into her arms.

"Have you had dinner?" Katherine asks. "We'd love to have you join us. There's plenty of pizza."

"Pee-dah." Connor looks out at the patio, then back up at his mother.

"Oh, dear." Jennifer laughs. "I'm afraid you've said the magic word. You'll never get rid of him now."

Katherine opens the door, but I hold back. "I'll be out in a moment, Katherine."

I duck into the living room and open the envelope. The letter inside is just a single page in my own handwriting, although it lacks some of the little flourishes I like to use.

March 2, 1969

> *If you're holding this, it worked. We've revised our plan every few years . . . first leaving the keys with our attorney, and then later, after the children and grandchildren came along, we decided to keep this in the family. We've also rewritten this letter every few years, adding bits and pieces and dropping others. It seems to get a little shorter each time, because in the end, the photographs in the album tell our story.*
>
> *This is the first time I've written this note without Kiernan. He's still alive, but his memory goes a bit more each day. He knows me, knows the children, but he gets confused, especially when he first wakes up. He touched my face today, smiled, and said, "The scar is finally gone," so I know he was thinking of you.*
>
> *Kiernan thought about you a lot for the first few years. I'll admit I was a bit jealous at first, until he told me that I'm a better kisser.*

She adds a winky face at the end—I'll bet she was a pioneer with emoticons.

I know that no time has passed for you. You're still young, with your life ahead of you. I only hope it's as happy as mine has been, and that one day, you'll hold a book of memories like this one in your hands—although I guess you may click through the pictures. That's one of the things I still miss. We've made it to the radio and finally to TV, but we'll never make it to the iPad.

Kiernan sends his love—and I guess I'm okay with that. Give mine to Mom, Dad, and Katherine.

Kate

My fingers flip through the small photo album that chronicles over fifty years of the family Dunne. Birthdays, weddings, graduations. A picture of Other-Kate in a cap and gown outside of a university. But the one that I look at longest is near the end. The date stamp on the margin reads 1962, and someone has scrawled "World Series Champs" beneath it. He would have been nearly eighty. He's at a stadium, wearing a Yankees cap, with a bunch of kids around him.

Kiernan's grin is as wide and happy as the one on the face of the little girl he holds in his lap. Does she know that Grandpa (Great-Grandpa?) has already seen that game? Probably more than once, in fact.

I stare at that picture for several minutes. Mostly at Kiernan's eyes, which, despite the wrinkles around the edges, are still the same. Then I stick the letter and the book back into the manila envelope on the counter and join the others on the patio.

Little Connor is a friendly guy, full of energy. He chatters and climbs in and out of laps while we eat. He has a blast throwing the Frisbee for Daphne, and she's pretty good-natured about the fact that it only goes a few feet. One sight makes me a little teary-eyed, however. I pull out my phone and snap a picture. Katherine holding her great-great-great-great-great-grandson has to be one for the history books.

∞

I shove the last pizza box into a trash bag, and Trey walks out back with me to drop the bags into the bin. Jennifer and Connor left around nine, when Katherine went to bed, because they have an early return flight to Columbus. There were promises to keep in touch, but I don't know if she will—I think we may have struck her as a bit too friendly and definitely too emotional. Jennifer kept giving me the oddest looks, like maybe she was really wondering about that whole reincarnation thing. Ben and Charlayne exited shortly after they did, followed by Dad and Sara—all of them probably seeking a few minutes alone.

This is also the first moment that Trey and I have been alone, totally alone, since our drive to Tilson's the day Julia was killed. And here we are carrying trash bags. How romantic.

That doesn't seem to bother Trey. The garbage can lid is barely down before his arms are around me, and his mouth is on mine.

"I've needed to do that for . . . I guess it's only a few days, but it feels like a year."

"Shh." I reach up to kiss him again, and he lifts me so that my face is level with his. I wrap my legs around him, and we enter that other reality—the one where there's nothing else except for his body and mine, his lips and mine. I could keep my time train on that track for all eternity.

He presses my back against the wall of the garage and pulls away from the kiss so that he can look at me. "I missed you. And I'm sorry I haven't been here for you. Mom's still a little freaked out, saying I took too many risks, and—"

"It's okay, Trey. Just give her time. I understand how she feels." And I do. I never wanted Trey in the middle of all this, and if he'd been hurt . . . I can't even think about it without shuddering.

But if I hadn't pulled him in, if I'd waited to hand him that envelope, we'd still be strangers. And what if we never reached this point? What if one of the necessary ingredients for rebuilding *us* was that touch of danger, that risk of losing love at its very start?

"The only reason I'm here tonight is because I gave her an ultimatum," he says. "I'm eighteen, and—"

"You are not moving out."

"Well, no. She backed down, and Dad took my side. Estella, too. She'll come around."

Trey kisses me again. When we come up for air, I run my finger across his lips. "So . . . I'm okay at this? At kissing?"

He laughs. "No. You totally suck at it. That's why I keep coming back for more. What's with the fishing for compliments?"

"Nothing. I just . . . wondered."

"You know, if anyone should be insecure right now, it's me. Kiernan was kind of intense on the ride over here that night."

"Oh God, I knew that was a bad idea. What did he say to you?"

"Um . . . he said he knew times had changed and that an eighteen-year-old guy might not be thinking in terms of forever, but that he'd be long dead by this time, and he would haunt my ass for all eternity if I hurt you."

I cringe, covering my face. "I'm *so* sorry."

"It's okay. I told him that was fine by me, because I don't ever want to hurt you. In his place, I'd have said the same. But later, seeing the other you . . . with him. That ring on her finger. It made me wonder if things had been different, if she wasn't still here, whether you'd have . . ."

"No." I hold his face between my hands so that he can see the truth in my eyes. "You're not my second choice, Trey. You never have been. I love you, I'm in love with you, and I want—"

I never finish the last words, because he knows what I want, and it's what he wants. He presses me so tightly against the wall that I can barely breathe, but oxygen isn't at the top of my priorities right now.

And then his foot hits the recycling bin and we come crashing back down to earth.

"Whoa," Trey says. "No. Our first time will not be in your grandmother's garage, five feet from the trash cans."

I pull his face back to mine and whisper against his lips, "I wouldn't mind."

He lets out a shuddery sigh, and we're kissing again. Then, "No. Not here. Not now."

And I smile. Because now we *can* take things slow.

Well, maybe not *too* slow, but there's no mad rush. No risk that reality will shift and yank him away from me.

We have all the time in the world.

∞Epilogue∞

Hon. Tegan J. Michel
Chair
Senate Select Committee on Temporal Mechanics
313 Franken Senate Office Building
Washington, EC 20510-3003-02
Date: April 1, 2141
Subject: Progress Report Q2/41
Attached please find the full quarterly progress update for AJG Temporal Studies.
Summary of activities:

1. Confirmed that the device is designed for viewing and traveling to set coordinates.
2. Access is limited to those with the specific genetic pattern that we isolated, as reported in Q1/41.
3. Seven tests subjects have successfully viewed events in the past for several seconds.
4. One test subject has completed a round-trip "jump" to one of the preset locations on the device.
5. Request extended funding for FY2143, so that the test group may expand to 200 subjects.

∞Acknowledgments∞

With my first two books, it never felt like the end until I started writing acknowledgments. The same is true this time, except now, it's the *END* end. Gulp. Kate and the rest of the crew have been hanging out in my head for nearly a decade now. They showed up when my two youngest boys, both now in middle school, were still in Elmo slippers. It feels a bit like Kate, Kiernan, and Trey are my other kids and I've just packed them off to college. Hopefully they'll stop by and visit on occasion. Or drop me an email.

I have a ton of people to thank for helping me get this far. But first, the history bits . . .

- I don't know whether Houdini had a CHRONOS key, but the vast majority of information in this book about the life and death of Houdini is based on the various biographies and information online about the master escape artist and his wife, Bess. The announcement of the challenge and Houdini's response are verbatim from an Eastbourne newspaper in April 1905.
- Houdini was friends with Arthur Conan Doyle, the author of the Sherlock Holmes series and also an avid proponent of spiritualism. The two did indeed part ways after

Houdini made a disparaging remark about spiritualists and a lady friend of Doyle's who was a practicing medium. That said, Houdini consulted mediums himself when he was younger, around the time that he appeared at the 1893 Chicago World's Fair.

- William and Ira Davenport were active in the spiritualist movement and also practicing magicians. Their paths crossed the lives of both Houdini and Victoria Woodhull, who—in addition to running for president in 1872—was also a leader in the spiritualist movement.

- Victoria Woodhull and her sister, Tennessee Claflin, were, as Connor notes, not angels, but they were also not the devils they were painted to be by the press of the 1870s. The sisters ran a newspaper, operated the first female stock brokerage firm, and ran Victoria's campaign for president under the Equal Rights Party long before women could vote. There are several excellent biographies out there for those who'd like to learn more about Woodhull and her sister. Barbara Goldsmith's *Other Powers* and Mary Gabriel's *Notorious Victoria* are good places to start.

- The Beecher-Tilton trial is a fascinating bit of history, both for the part that Woodhull played in the affair and the rampant hypocrisy of the era when it came to women's roles in society. This "Trial of the Century" is a wonderful reminder that even in this era, which clung to Victorian morality, people were still people with very human urges and foibles.

- The equine flu of 1872 resulted in the widespread illness and death of horses. Any visitor to New York City in November of that year would have seen, as Kate did, an unusual number of oxen pulling carts throughout the city.

- Anthony Comstock, Special Agent of the YMCA and later a federal postal agent, spent most of his life waging war on anything he believed to be immoral—tobacco, alcohol, birth control, and any mention of sex or the female anatomy. Comstock boasted that he drove at least fifteen different people to suicide in his efforts to keep America clean and chaste.

Finally, those who would like to learn more about Mr. Grumbine's treatise on auras that Bess Houdini mentions can probably find a copy online at Google Books, as I did. I'm still not convinced that's why some people see the CHRONOS keys as one color while some see it as another, but it's an interesting theory.

Now . . . back to the thank-yous.

A multitude of thanks to my wonderful team at Skyscape and Amazon Publishing. Courtney Miller has been there from the very start, and her help and wise counsel at each step of the journey is deeply appreciated. Andrew Keyser and Tyler Stoops, thanks for patiently dealing with questions on the business and marketing side. Timoney Korbar and Erick Pullen, although you've moved on to other realms in the APub universe, you started this ride with me. Thanks for all your work launching this series—you are missed!

Marianna Baer, my wonderful developmental editor, deserves an award for patiently enduring conundrums, confusion, and multiple time travel headaches. This series would be a tangled mass of wet spaghetti without you, and your efforts are truly appreciated. There would be a multitude of typos, missing words, and other glitches if not for the eagle-eyed efforts of my excellent copy editor, Renee Johnson. Scott Barrie and Cyanotype Design— thanks for creating gorgeous, colorful covers that grab the eye of prospective readers. Kate Rudd has my endless gratitude for being the "voice" of the CHRONOS Files and bringing my characters and stories to life.

As much as I chide myself about spending too much time on social media, the readers and writers I interact with every day on Facebook, Twitter, and Goodreads keep me motivated, informed, and amused. My fellow Skyscape and sci-fi authors can always be counted on to lend support, answer questions, and spread the word. And I need to give a very special shout-out to the members of JUGs, who allow me to vent in a safe space and provide me with a wide array of distractions.

The CHRONOS Files World launched in Kindle Worlds back in November, and an intrepid group of authors—David Estes, E. B. Brown, J. L. Johnson, and Patrice Fitzgerald—have already ventured into the timey-wimey, twisty chaos, with more still to come. Even as I wrap up this series, I'm happy to know that there are more CHRONOS stories coming, including stories that will be new to me. I love seeing where other writers' imaginations will take my characters and ideas.

Beta readers and book pushers, you are authors' angels. My Beta Bunch fearlessly braved the typos, unfinished sentences, and other insanity that comes with reading my early drafts, and instead of cursing me for messing with their brains, they actually thanked me and gave me wonderful, indispensable feedback. Other readers have tirelessly plugged my books to friends, book clubs, Facebook, and the entire Twitterverse. Since there is a lot of overlap between these groups, virtual hugs, margaritas, chocolate, and undying gratitude go out (in alphabetical order) to: Alexandria Ang, Ariana Ascherl, Mary Anna Ascherl, Karen Benson, Vanessa Bernard, Bill Brooks, E. B. Brown, Allison Clowers, Kristi and Marshall Clowers, James Cobalt, Lorca Damon, Susan Allison Dean, Elizabeth Evans, Patrice Fitzgerald, Rebecca Ford, Joe Frazier,

Mary Freeman and Maddy Freeman-McFarland, Jen Gonzales, Bonnie Harrison (thanks, Mama!), Donna Harrison Green, Mike and Lana Harrison, Matthew Izen, Stephanie Johns-Bragg, Joy Joo, Theresa Kay, Dana Kolbfleisch, Jeff Kolbfleisch (who also takes wonderful author photos!), Richard Lawrence, Mary Frances Lebamoff, Oleg Lysyj, Jenny MacRunnel, Cale Madewell, Nooce Miller, Tasha Patton-Smith, Lesa Ruckman, Simon Rudd, Sarah Short, John Scafidi, Lydia Smith, Gareth Sparks, Karen Stansbury, Teri Suzuki, Janet B. Taylor, Billy Thomas, Antigone Trowbridge, Ian Walniuk, Ryan Walniuk, Libby Wells-Pritchett (you too, Jebb!), Jen Wesner, Dan Wilson, Jessica Wolfsohn, and my multitude of nieces and nephews. There are undoubtedly a dozen or so other people whose names will pop into my brain the second I see this in print—apologies in advance!

To Ryan, Donna, and all of the others who argued so fervently that this book should be *Time's End*, I give you permission to call it by that title. I'll even make you a crappy fake cover. ☺

Many of Daphne's quirks and attributes are courtesy of my canine companions during this series—Lucy, our current office mate, and Mocha, the wonderful, stubborn, and loving beagle-and-who-knows-what-else mix, who was around when Kate's story began but didn't make it to the end.

Thanks again to the extended family who encouraged me, pushed books into my hands as a kid, and gave me your love and support.

To my kids—none of whom are exactly "kids" anymore. Thanks to all three of you for making your mom laugh and making your mom proud. To the two youngest, thanks for reminding me to feed you when my brain is in the Writing Cave, and thanks for putting your dishes in the dishwasher. (Okay, the last one is wishful thinking.) To Eleanor, thanks for the My Little Pony drawings and all of the other ways you remind me about the power of imagination and creativity.

This last book in the series is dedicated to Pete, but I want to elaborate a bit here at the end. He has managed to coexist in the same house with me for longer than anyone else on earth and even shares an office most days—that takes a special brand of patience, especially when I'm on deadline. Thanks for taking up the slack when I'm in the Writing Cave and for being my tech support, science consultant, idea sounding board, 3-D design guy, and very best friend.

And finally, the biggest thanks are reserved for you, the reader who actually made it to the end with me. Storytelling requires two minds. The writer draws the basic outlines and adds some detail. It's never complete, however, until the reader fills in that outline with the colors and experiences of his or her own life. Thanks for helping to tell my stories—and I hope you'll be part of my next storytelling team, wherever that journey may take us.

∞About the Author∞

RYSA WALKER is the author of runaway hit *Timebound*, winner of the grand prize in the 2013 Amazon Breakthrough Novel Award contest, and *Time's Echo*, the linked novella.

Walker grew up on a cattle ranch in the South, where her entertainment options included talking to cows and reading books. On the rare occasion that she gained control of the television, she watched *Star Trek* and imagined living in the future, on distant planets, or at least in a town big enough to have a stoplight.

She now lives in North Carolina, where she shares an office with her husband and their golden retriever, Lucy. She still doesn't get control of the TV very often, thanks to two sports-obsessed kids.

cl